DON'T YA KNOW

a novel

Suzanne McLain Rosenwasser

Manhasset Times Media Group, LLC. 2015

Always, with profound love for Michael and our spirit story

"The faces are
distant reminders
of all that was
at a time when
all that is
was beyond tomorrow."
          - M.A.R.

PROLOGUE

1928

Corycian Island, New York

The blazingly hot summer of 1928 inspired different patterns of nudity among the inhabitants of Corycian Island - some humorous, others horrific.

Twirly Wesley was cited with indecent exposure when she staged her topless bathing rebellion on the beach by the ramp to the Westside Ferry. Twirly always chose to picket when the ferry was packed with gaping tourists.

Also, reports came into the police about a man walking naked through yards in the center of the island. Each caller described the perpetrator as wearing only a cowboy hat and smoking a cigar. The locals who read these accounts in *The Corycian Island Reader's* police blotter had become accustomed to Twirly's nude protests, and they knew the naked cowboy to be George Stoli. George had been walking the streets of Corycian for decades, most of those years in clothes and carrying a brown paper sack. Though George had remained indoors for all of 1927, the summer heat of 1928 brought him out into the open again, adding new dimensions to his walkabouts: nudity, a hat, and a cigar. More people would have recognized him if he still carried, as he always had, the paper sack.

However, neither of these reports compared with the most startling event involving Inri Remie who, clutching his blood-spurting crotch and wolf-howling, streaked through the night-dark, school yard in the wee hours of July 15th.

A crowd gathered in their night clothes, standing on the playground to watch two island police officers chase Remie around the baseball field. One of the volunteer firemen said Inri had cut off his "don't ya know" with a hedge clipper. Finally Inri collapsed, and the Chief of Police asked male neighbors to help search the woods near the school so they could locate the severed appendage before any children arrived to play on the swings.

A man found the bloodied clippers before dawn, but it wasn't until mid-afternoon when Mrs. Peevy's chocolate lab, Reverb, came home gritting Inri's penis between his teeth that the actual evidence appeared. To the people who lived in the big houses on the periphery of the island, this event was realized only in the context of their favorite newspaper column, *The Corycian Island Reader's* "Blotter," which on this occasion reported benignly:

> "Inri Remie of Sanders Street was transported by ambulance to an off-Island medical facility Friday night after surviving an incident which brought police to the scene."

But every local who sat at the counter in Marmie's coffee shop knew the detailed facts and speculated knowingly about Remie's animosity toward his genitals.

Corycian Island: Ke'was End - 1928

A speculation of a different sort took place on the east point of the island at Ke'was End the last day of July that year.

Nuna Chepi Shellfoot sat in a rocking chair on the back porch of her white clapboard home facing the Long Island Sound. She spoke to a man whose appearance was Nuna's direct opposite, since he was clearly not of Native American descent.

He was a young, blonde, blue-eyed lawyer in the employ of land developers. He asked Nuna about 1882, the year the government enacted the Native American Land Grants, when Nuna was a wee child. Specifically, the lawyer asked about the Shellfoots' acquisition of four acres on Corycian Island.

Nuna answered him in her strange, rhythmic speech: "My faduh got tole like his faduh got tole. My faduh say dis place be called Kewasowok Eye-land a'fore de Dutchmens comes and calls it Cor-seen. Kewasowok mean 'Eye-land of de Gods' in A'gonquin talk, don't ya know."

"What were you told about how your family came to Corycian Island, Miss Shellfoot?" the man asked.

Nuna's small frame settled into memory. She tucked a stray, gray hair into her crown of dark braids, rocked with her graceful hands folded in her lap, and turned her caramel-colored face toward the sun: "De way my faduh tole it, de ancient peoples follows de river from up west a de mainland and comes down to de place 'Yapam Kewasowok' - de ocean Gods place. Den de Dutchmens comes a time afta and say dis place gonna be Corseen Eye-land."

The man referred to his notebook: "Uh, I see here that you are from the Poosepatuck band, is that so, Miss Shellfoot?"

"Summa me be. Summa me be elsewise," Nuna answered. "And lotsa me be Bims. Lissen and you hears de Bims good." Nuna smiled softly, deliberately luring the lawyer with her soft brown face to look directly into her black eyes.

Abruptly the young man cast his gaze away and cleared his throat: "Excuse me, Ma'am...Bims? What are Bims?"

"Bims be Barbados peoples - de ones dat comes wit' de Dutchmens ta works de land."

"Slaves?" the lawyer asked, looking up and and trying his best to hold Nuna's stare with the strength of his question. "Do you mean the slaves brought over to work on the Bakker homestead in the seventeenth century?"

"Dey be slaves whens dey workin' over at de Bakkers, but not whens dey runs here ta be free. My faduh got tole de people down here on de eas' side keeps dem Bims covered so good, no one finds dem. He say de Kewasowok - de spirit Gods - help de Dutchmens see de tru-way and soon de Dutchmens be helpin' de Quakers runnin' ta here from de mainland, too."

Nuna noticed the young man sitting across from her was stuck in a blank stare. He held his pencil aloft with that quizzical look on his flushed face. So Nuna tried her best to explain through her Bim-laced English: "Soon de Dutchmens, de Bims, de Quakers, and de people be one and de same. Dey be all-a-wanna so long, dat dey be alla-same by and by."

Nuna looked into the distance while her interrogator scribbled his version of her tale. So many years had passed since her father's death, Nuna thought, but she still heard him talking with the mixed rhythms of his origins about a belief so ancient it coursed through their veins. He taught her that the people of this place were "all-a-wanna" - all together, one with the Runapewak, the true people. They were all the people. Though, after her father died, only a few indigenous islanders believed or even knew this about themselves any more. Nuna was one who believed and her world was small enough to make it possible.

She said to the young lawyer: "Dat who we be here - all-a-wanna. Not bazodees, no way, don't ya know?"

"Bazodees?" the man asked, with his brows nearly touching his hairline.

"Duncies!" Nuna replied, feeling the presence of one in her midst. "Bazodees. De ones dat don't see de Makiaweesug - de spirit peoples." Then she caught the lawyer's eyes: "But now dey's more and more a dem damn Bazodees here."

"Ah," the man replied, pausing to regroup from the dizzying experience of trying to understand the woman and coming late to the realization she was including him.

"So...ah... once again, from which tribe do you claim your heritage, Miss Shellfoot?"

Nuna tried to contain her exasperation. She knew this lawyer represented thieves who believed only written history made a tribe exist and she tried to school him patiently: "My faduh say we be Runapewak. My faduh say our spirit story be ta watch dis place wit' de Makiaweesug - de spirit peoples. He say de Runapewak be de pure ones. We be spirit-tellers, all-a-wanna, don't ya know?"

"Actually, Miss Shellfoot, I don't know. I'm having a hard time following you. Is your daughter home or is there someone else who could help me understand you better?"

"You needs ta lissen, be why. You canst understand what you canst hear. We be de Runapewak, de tru-ones. We tells through spirit all-a-wanna!"

"But Miss Shellfoot, Runapewak is not a recognized tribe; that is, the United States Government doesn't list it among its bands of indigenous peoples."

"I be a Runapewak, Mr. Man. '*We* de peoples,' my faduh say. De true peoples, he say, de ones dat comes to'geder, all-a-wanna, ta tell 'bout spirit."

The lawyer spoke sternly: "To keep your land, Miss Shellfoot, we must prove you are from a recognized Long Island tribe with some kind of documentation kept by that tribe and certified by a Long Island tribal council."

"I tole you and I tole you dis land don't belong ta no one a us. Dis land be sacred. Runapewak don't own sacred. Dis be Maduh Eart'. We be here ta watch ovah dis place."

"Nonetheless, Miss Shellfoot, if you want your heirs to keep watching over this place, you're going to have to prove you are a Native American Indian with U.S. government-recognized, Long Island tribal roots."

"Dis man who say I ain't been doin' dat ever-day since I be born, who dat bougeley man again?"

"Well, it's a corporation, Miss Shellfoot, not a man per se," the lawyer said, shuffling through his papers. "But it is a business run by a group of men who believe you are residing on land illegally acquired under the false pretense of being a recognized tribe." He looked up from his stack of onion skin papers and spoke to Nuna very slowly: "Again for your benefit, I represent Long Island Resorts, Incorporated, a group pursuing an investigation of the Shellfoot Land Claim made in 1882 to four acres at Ke'was End under the United States Land Grant Act."

Nuna saw sweat break out on the furrowed brow of the blonde-haired, blue-eyed man who spoke as if he was impaired. Nuna asked: "1882?"

"Yes, Miss Shellfoot."

"Dat year de guv'ment say my faduh a indian, but dis year he disn't be no more?"

The lawyer gave her an irritated sigh. Nuna squared her shoulders and waited for the bougley man's reluctant eyes to look at hers. She said: "My faduh names me Nuna. *New-nah*. Dat be 'land' in A'gonquin. My faduh names me Nuna for Maduh Eart' and Chepi - for spirit. Dat, Mr. Man, be how my family be Runapewak - in land and spirit, all-a-wanna."

The white man fiddled with his briefcase. Nuna held the silence. The lawyer began to pack his files, speaking much more quickly: "The Court will look into your heritage more closely, Miss Shellfoot."

"And jus' how it goin' ta do dat?"

"I'm not sure. Perhaps your Makeewee...uh, your spirit people will help us find a way."

Nuna thought the man's use of the sacred was profane. She watched him walk to his automobile and then stood, folding her arms into herself and straightening her shoulders. She walked down the steps on to the yard and felt her feet sink into the soft soil. Her grandfather's voice spoke within her: "We stands between Maduh Eart' and Faduh Sky. We de keepers, all-a-wanna, Nuna Chepi. Dat be de Runapewak spirit-story."

Nuna looked out at a path worn through a meadow by her ancestors and softly at peace with its flora and fauna. Lines of thick trees formed a buffer between the meadow and a beach below. There, glacial deposits of large boulders formed a long tail of granite bones stretching into the waters swirling back and forth to the Atlantic Ocean. The sea cut a deep and narrow path between the mainland and the east end of the island. On maps, the area appears as: "Ke'was End," derived from Corycian's indian name.

A colony of three houses stood at the side of a dirt road layered with crushed oyster shells. The road led out to a hard-surfaced, main artery of Corycian Island which was Old Post Road, a two-lane, high-crowned thoroughfare. It curved along for six miles to a terminal at the Westside Ferry, a family run operation that had been taking islanders, visitors, and all sorts of vehicles to and from the mainland for more than one hundred years.

Nuna could hear the lawyer's car bumping and crunching through the potholes on his way out along the shell road. It was dusk and a flaming glow from the sun painted a still life of trees against a pink-scorched sky. "Faduh Sky," Nuna said aloud, "dem golliwogs be tryin' ta take dis land."

Nuna followed the path into the forest buffer while talking aloud in hopes the Makiaweesug might hear. Standing before a large rise of dirt, firs, and stones, Nuna looked up and saw streaks of spirit dash across an opening in the trees.

Nuna knew, but she didn't tell. She saw, but she didn't judge. Runapewak are spirit-tellers, her father told her.

Corycian Island: History

The most beautiful piece of land on this barrier island is at its westernmost tip where the glacial remains deposited themselves closest to the mainland at a wide-mouthed spot of the Long Island Sound. The natives found the site calm enough to traverse in canoes and had done so for hundreds of years.

The island was then known as Kewasowok, the "Eye-land of the Gods." It was a sheltered place to which nomad families of splintered Algonquin bands migrated. Mother Earth and Father Sky bequeathed the natives rich fruits of the sea and a nurturing womb of loamy soil blessed by "Kitci Manitou," the Great Spirit.

The dwellers became "Runapewak," the tru-people made up of many, but still only a few. The earliest natives had straight brown hair and copper-tinged complexions. A small band occupied the east end of the Eye-land of Gods as early as the fourteenth century.

Captain Johann B. Bakker was the first white man to come ashore in 1655. He was a Dutch sugar merchant who transported cane from Barbados to New York for processing. When he saw an island just a few miles in from the Atlantic Ocean's fury, he found a protected harbor for his ships beneath the cliffs of an astounding piece of land.

Captain Bakker was awed by the solid granite foundation exposed from its height above the level of the sea. He came ashore and claimed 200 acres as his own, trading them for sugar and rum with the welcoming natives.

Of course, the natives had no concept of land ownership. They thought the white man was offering to help them in their sacred stewardship of the earth and they were gratified.

Consequently, they watched in wonder as Bakker returned with scores of men whose skin was nearly black as pitch. The men cleared trees, planted crops, and crafted lumber while working from sunup till well into the night. There were also women of the same dark color who prepared meals, harvested crops, and butchered livestock. It was a phenomenal process the natives admired, so they watched it take shape each day.

That was until Jeremiah Remie arrived. The frizzy-haired and freckled-faced, white man was introduced to the natives as an "overseer," a word that sounded mystical to them. One native said the word had something to do with Remie's prominent forehead, a comment which brought natives from all over the island to see "the owl man with the bone-brow."

Remie was hired to manage the workers, which Captain Bakker observed the overseer doing with a sense of gentle command, a management style Bakker preferred. However when Bakker was on trade runs, the Runapewak watched in horror as Remie lashed and beat the black people with the fury of a wild animal in his red face.

The Runapewak retreated to their east side home and walked the earth to hear a solution from the Makiaweesug to the evil their own misunderstanding had wrought.

The spirit people answered by sending runaway "Bims," as the Barbadians called themselves, to share in the protection of Mother Earth and Father Sky at Ke'was End.

Remie lied to Captain Bakker about losing these black men and women to the far reaches of the island, saying they'd died from disease. Jeremiah Remie was just too lazy to look for those who made it across the six miles of thick forest separating Ke'was End from the Dutchman's house.

Hence the Bims and the natives became a community, soon to be joined by a few Quakers who had run from New England persecutors and had found themselves amidst the escaped Bims and natives on the east end. All-a-wanna. In time, Mother Earth and Father Sky answered the prayers of the tru-people. Captain Bakker retired from the sugar trade, an act spurred on by the burgeoning terrorism of slaves against the Dutch in Barbados. He left the Caribbean and settled on Kewasowak, converting the plantation into a thriving farm by 1690.

Johann Bakker lived to see it all. His four sons learned to grow wheat, corn and beans from the Runapewak. The Bims taught them how to manure a field of sugar cane, and the Quakers passed on the skills of tending livestock. "Bakker's Farm" made a name for itself, exporting fine grades of tallow, candles, molasses, flax, and cured meats to the expanding markets in Boston, Newport, and New York.

Jeremiah Remie moved into the thick woods on the island's north side, built a still, and sold his product to islanders and mainlanders alike. His descendants inherited his red hair and the recipe for Remie's Moonshine Whiskey, a brand that never tasted the same from one batch to the next.

By the eighteenth century, the Bakkers, the Runapewak, the Remies, and the Bims succeeded in populating all corners of the island. The Bakkers were the largest landholders, those who changed the bulky indian name of Kewasowak to "Corycian (*Core'seen*) Island."

Travel guides, in modern times, identify the place as: "Corycian Island, named for the most beautiful nymph gracing the sacred grotto of Mount Parnassus, the home of the Gods."

PART ONE (1900-1910)

1900

Ke'was End
"Lissen ta dat Oonuh talkin' in you."

Eula Morely sat in her kitchen preparing to read to her neighbor, Nuna Shellfoot, from a copy of *The Corycian Island Reader,* Vol. 7, No. 35, Thursday, August 30, 1900.

The two were a study of beauty in the afternoon light of the white tiled room. Eula was 24 to Nuna's 26 and she was taller than her lifelong friend. Eula's skin was pale white to Nuna's rosy brown. Eula had sun-bleached, blonde hair pinned-up in a knot while Nuna had tightly curled, brown hair gathered in a leather strap at her neck.

Eula snapped the broadsheet open to read the copy. It annoyed her that Nuna only put value in the stories of spirit-tellers. In turn, Nuna bristled at Eula's insistence on reading newspaper stories written by people who weren't even witnesses to the events. Also, if something needed to be read, Nuna would do it herself. The Morelys were always reading things to people, Nuna thought, remembering Eula's grandfather holding forth on a passage from some book or another.

"We be de story, Eula," Nuna said, knowing her stubborn friend was about to read the newspaper to her anyway.

Eula's family had lived across the road from the Shellfoots since the Morelys came to Ke'was End as Quaker refugees in the 1700s.

It was Eula's grandfather, a greatly respected Corycian shipwright named Ephraim, who built the farmhouse in which the friends now sat. The gracious homestead was surrounded by ten acres with a barn and a few outbuildings, all sturdily constructed by Captain Ephraim.

The Morelys and the Shellfoots shared in the upkeep of the oyster shell road, and the families had passed through generations side by side while working, loving, and caring for their rugged land - from crops, catches, concerns, and conditions to beliefs, griefs, chores, and wonders.

Nuna and Eula knew all there was to know about each other, and to this point, their lives had followed similar paths.

Each had lost her parents young, Nuna's to disease and Eula's to a horse and buggy accident that occurred on the mainland.

Each was raised by an elderly, now deceased, grandfather.

Each was the sole heir to her ancestors' property.

Each had married an island fisherman before the age of 20 and kept her own surname in the Corycian tradition, a practical matter which dispensed with all the guessing about lineage in a small island community.

Each had borne a child: Judah Morely was 7 years old; Bay Shellfoot was 5.

Each had become a widow when her husband drowned at sea in the same fishing boat during a ferocious storm off Montauk Point, July 15, 1900.

Eula crossed her long legs and leaned over. She tucked an escaped strand of hair behind her ear and tried to interest Nuna in the newspaper story:

"The *Reader* has a report about what happened to the fishing boat, if you want to hear about it," Eula said, ignoring the furrow in Nuna's brow. "They say pieces of it washed up on the beach at Pipers' Cove last week. Must have capsized in the storm, they say."

"Dat paper disn't change no'ting, Eula. Dey dead as dey goin' ta be."

"Doesn't knowing help, though, Nuna? Knowing what probably happened and all?"

"Humph!" Nuna said, without expressing her recent doubt that knowing is ever possible. Why didn't Nuna know that Ahane was about to die when he left at midnight with a shining moon, fresh from the warmth of their lovemaking? Was the story in their sweet goodbye, Nuna wondered?

"We be de story now, Eula, dat's de story we gots ta know."

"You know I hate it when you won't let me share the stories I need to hear. I listen to yours," Eula said, pausing to stop the direction of her words. "Look, Nuna, we're both angry and hurt, but we have to move on. We have to figure some way to survive. And right now, I feel like you're putting it all on me. If Grandfather Ephraim's spirit was here, I'd know it. He's not telling me any stories, Nuna. So, right now, the *Reader* is all we've got."

Nuna cast a wan smile at Eula, touched her friend's forearm, and said: "Bay and me's goin' ta walk a bit." Nuna took little Bay by the hand and walked out the screen door to the meadow, toward an ancient oak tree.

Nuna thought about how the "telling" left her when Ahane died. She no longer heard the osprey or the sandpipers though they were all around. The silence made Nuna deaf. Where once the sound of lapping waves washed Nuna's heart with joy, now she barely sensed the sea at all.

When Bay ran ahead to dance in the reeds, Nuna cried "Ahane! Ahane!" into the soft breeze, but no sound came back to her, not even her own voice.

Ahane had seen Nuna. His eyes gave her self form. Nuna hadn't possessed that as a child; her parents hadn't lived long enough to outline her image, and her grandfather was too old to know how to teach a girl about women.

Nuna had picked up a sense of who she was from the stories of spirit told around her, in the changes of the seasons, and the changes of her friend, Eula, growing along side her. But Nuna never had a complete idea of herself until Ahane saw her.

"What does the wind tell you today, sweet Nuna?" young Ahane asked one day when he passed her on the road. Nuna heard herself reply: "It be blowin' gentle, now."

Ahane nodded and began to walk with Nuna every day. With each step, Nuna marveled at her voice, wondered at her vision, responded to her emotions. She tasted and smelled her world as if for the first time.

With Ahane gone, Nuna was having trouble finding the self he had given her. Her "Oonuh." That's what the spirit-tellers called it. The you in you only known to you.

Ahane had gifted Nuna with her Onnuh and now she'd lost its essence.

Eula Morely watched her friend from the window, remembering with a stab, again, that she didn't love her man the way Nuna loved Ahane.

Eula remembered how her own husband changed so much when their courtship ended. He never wooed Eula again once they were married, and he seemed to be disgusted more than pleased if she enjoyed their sexual relationship. When she was six months pregnant, he told her to stop walking into town: "It's not right that people should know what we do," he snarled.

Eula didn't tell her husband that this was sick thinking, she just showed him and continued to walk to town while their baby kicked at her ribs. Eventually, her husband stopped talking to her, much less touching her.

This spousal rejection only drew Eula closer to Nuna and Ahane, who cherished Eula's son, Judah, from the day he was born with the affection the child's father couldn't seem to muster.

"You're the one who said he's a Morley when they put his name down in the records," the child's father said, referring to the Corycian way of insuring land inheritance. "You take him. He's all yours."

With that, Eula's husband moved into the barn. It was easier to drink there and to rustle himself before dawn to catch up with Ahane and head out with a fishing fleet.

Nuna gave birth to Bay two years after Judah was born. Bay was a sweet and engaging baby who charmed them all, except for Judah's father who left the barn only to go to work. He was as good as dead long before he and Ahane drowned.

After that, the people of Corycian Island mourned both of the deaths, but Nuna and Eula cried only for the loss of Ahane. They knew life without Ahane's laugh, without his care, and without his physical support would be a much more difficult one.

The early days of October were unusually warm in 1900. Eula Morely sat on the back stoop of her grandfather's house in the golden light of a waning sun. It reminded Eula of the afternoon her grandfather died, right in front of her, sitting just across the kitchen table.

Seconds before a brain aneurysm killed him, old Captain Ephraim looked at Eula and said: "Care for the house. I'll be staying close."

That hadn't been the case, as Eula told Nuna, but Nuna said Captain Ephraim was still in the house. "I disn't be hearin' t'ings too good since Ahane goes, but de Captain be waitin' on you, dat I know." Eula scoffed. Nuna reminded her that the Shellfoots were spirit-tellers. "We brings de news from spirit," Nuna said. "I be sayin' dat ovah and ovah. De Captain be talkin' dis I knows."

But Eula couldn't hear her Grandfather Ephraim. She had walked all over the house seeking the essence Nuna assured her was there.

"Lissen ta dat Oonuh in you," Nuna said. "De one you knows, but I disn't. Oonuh's got to be in you doin' right and you gots ta hear it. Oonuh goin' ta bring dat spirit, and spirit be tellin' good t'ings ta come, don't ya know."

While Eula's son slept soundly, she roamed the rambling house, hoping to find an answer to the question that kept her awake: "How do we go on?"

When Eula told Nuna about her evening wanderings, Nuna said: "Spirit say de Captain's 'round you. Lissen ta your Oonuh, Eula. Lissen ta your Oonuh. You gots ta."

Eula marveled at Nuna's strength and faith, even with the burden of her sorrow. It seemed natural and founded in prayer. Eula had overheard Nuna's plea to Ahane one night when each had sought the solace of Father Sky and neither knew the other was close by.

Eula listened in wonder to Nuna's private prayer: "Dis child be growin' and I feels tired, Ahane. She be a woman soon enough. I feels tired and I needs you here. Eula and Judah needs you too. Brings spirit ta help. We needs ta hear de story for us, Ahane."

Eula could hear Nuna's quiet tears, knowing they flowed steadily down her friend's upturned face.

Was this how to pray, Eula wondered? Would Ahane appeal to the Gods of the Bims? Of the old Algonquins? Of the Ke'was for whom these acres were named? Was this God not the Christ-God?

Eula prayed to no one and struggled with unbelief.

"The Morelys," Eula's erudite grandfather told the island preachers who occasionally showed up at their door, "are not a religious people. Never have been. Oh, we were Quakers once, but that's just a matter of history."

The Captain preferred to read "the wisdom of nature," as Eula recalled him saying. "The Shellfoots taught me that. Search yourself to find God, Eula. Find God in the world that bore you into existence."

So Eula wandered the nooks and crannies of "The Captain's House," as it was known locally, a masterpiece of architecture designed by a shipbuilder who fit it as tightly within and out as any of his finest sea crafts.

Interior, wood-paneled walls slid into phantom pockets to create one large room from two. Three flights of stairs held flip hatches above some steps and drawers beneath others. Panels hid storage behind the walls, in the ceilings, and in the third staircase leading to the finished, cedar-paneled attic.

Stepping into the Morely's center hall, luminous scallop and jingle shell mosaics offered indigenous details to a two-story, stained glass window which cast a stream of light on the hand-hewn, hardwood floors.

Captain Ephraim's house was a solid frame of natural beauty, bestowing an aura of serenity on all who entered. Once, standing in the light of the center hall, Nuna said: "Dis be spirit. Right here dis minute. Spirit be here."

Nuna said the house, like the cottages on her land, were as sacred as the ground on which they stood because they all had been built with only what the earth beneath them had to offer. "Spirit be all in dis house," Nuna said.

Under and outside these homesteads, the land stretched out in a glacial composition of earth and granite to the sea.

Some days, calm salt water swirled gently into the cove at the narrows of Ke'was End. On those days cool green waters lapped on the beach and the granite jetty seemed harmless; but on stormy days, a furious black sea rushed over the sharp rocks and thundered in huge waves that churned up the shores.

Calliope Point
"If we could only get a few more beautiful women here."

As a young man J. Burston Bakker V was the sole heir to a large fortune, much of it earned from investments made in the manufacture of French and American automobiles and the production of Coca-wine, an effervescent beverage unintentionally laced with addictive opiates.

The Bakker's Farm had ceased operation decades ago. Now it was a graceful home overlooking Calliope Point, where on a fall evening in 1900, Burston, as he was called, lounged aboard the anchored *Barna-call*, a finely crafted catboat owned by his neighbor, Tommy Lawson.

In the sunset's wash, Bakker and Lawson relaxed after a rousing cruise around the island, navigating the narrows at Ke'was End, sluicing through the current, and making a full circle back to Union Harbor where they tied up to Lawson's buoy.

The light of sunset lit Bakker's features. He bore the thick neck of his Dutch forefathers. He had their broad shoulders and large bones, the same coarse blonde hair and icy blue eyes. On this night, the collar of Bakker's pea coat was turned up to block the chilly winds blowing into shore.

An awkward silence hung between the two young men now that the demands of a hearty sail weren't filling up the gap so many years apart from each other had created.

Burston Bakker had left Corycian to attend posh East Coast schools after grammar school. The few times he returned, he made it clear to Tommy that Corycian Island was beneath both of them. In their late teens, the two friends came to blows over the topic and never went out of their way to get together on Burston's visits after that.

But Burston was back now, had been for awhile and knew why Tommy had arranged this night on the boat. It was an olive branch and Burston knew he owed Tommy an explanation, as well as an apology.

Tommy fixed them each a glass of whiskey. He raised the cat-boat's table, expertly balanced the crystal, and poured the liquor with out spilling a drop.

Sitting in teak deck chairs, the young men sipped their drinks and felt the rhythm of the sea rock beneath them. Lawson's long legs stretched from his lanky body to rest on a coil of rope. Tommy's windblown hair matched the soft brown of his eyes and the golden tan of his skin. He wore an Aran jumper, an oiled wool sweater knit by his, now deceased, Irish mother.

Tommy thought about the matter of his contention with Burston. Tommy had never wanted any home that wasn't on the land his family had owned and farmed for more than a century. In fact, after Burston left, Tommy swore a greater allegiance to Corycian Island. It had only waned when the living got tougher every year.

Tommy's invitation to Burston for a sail around the island came spontaneously. Tommy knew salt water healed wounds, and it was time.

He was the first to break the silence and begin the words they needed to fill the gulf between them. He pointed to the marvel of electric lights shining out from the newly built homes dotting the bluffs.

"If our fathers came back from the dead, they wouldn't recognize this shoreline anymore," Tommy said. "Used to be, all you could see from the Westside Ferry was your place and ours. Now look at it."

It was an impressive panorama and they took it in together. The Strand Hotel sprawled across the land above the harbor. To its left at Calliope Point, sloping hills led to the graceful pastures and Shaker shingled homes of family farms like Lawson's and Bakker's. Farther along the expanse, Edison's lights lit Victorian summer cottages newly built by the wealthy and occupied only June through August. The glimmer of lantern lights could be seen from the few remaining shacks where baymen lived. Burston said: "I remember riding the ferry across when I came home from college, the air smelled putrid from the fish oil factories and the bluff looked desolate, nothing but those horrible shacks everywhere with the Scalers in them multiplying like rabbits."

Tommy bristled at the way Burston spat out the name indigenous baymen used with pride to identify themselves: Scalers or fish-scrapers. Tommy replied, defensively: "The Strand and those prissy little houses took a bite out of the Scaler culture on this island, Burston. Don't get me wrong, the Strand saved plenty of us, but the change cost all of us, too."

"Oh so you're telling me you miss the smell of the fish oil wafting through the air," Burston scoffed. "Listen, I know the boom on this place saved me too, Tommy. I swore I wouldn't live here, but once the Strand opened, I began to reconsider, and now I can't leave. Unlike you who swore you were incapable of leaving the island until the economy got so bad here. Then you feared you couldn't stay. We're all here because the fish factories closed, the rich people arrived, and life is good again."

"I'm not denying any of that," Tommy said, "but at your father's funeral you told me you'd never come back now that your parents were dead. Imagine my surprise when I realized you had returned to stay." Anger welled between them. Tommy swirled the whiskey in his glass to bear the discomfort.

Burston quelled it. He spoke softly: "It's not Corycian Island I can't give up. It's the newspaper. I was going to get myself a real journalism job in Boston and show my father what a hick, weekly paper he ran. I only came back here to close *The Corycian Island Reader* down when the old man croaked."

Burston paused coming as close as he ever had to a eulogy for his father: "I thought the old coot would live forever. When I came back to close it all up, the island had blossomed. The Strand was opened; the Believers' Camp was under construction; the town had a civic center and a constable; the Presbyterians finally got the bell tower on top of their church. I felt the life of the place.

Then I found out my grumpy old man was loved and admired by his staff at the *Reader*, and the paper isn't a rag, and Corycian Island isn't stuck in another century."

"I hear you, Bakker, and I'm glad you're back." Tommy raised his glass and Burston tapped it with his. "Me getting the manager's job at the Strand was the best thing that's happened to a Lawson for a long time. We were going down. We had a bad five years with both of my parents being so sick. My sisters don't want to come back here any more. They just get too sad."

"I'm sorry about your father, Tommy." Burston said.

"Once Mother went, we knew he wouldn't last. I've been buying my sisters out. The job at the Strand's given me that."

Tommy reached into the coil of rope and pulled out the whiskey bottle. Refilling their glasses, a nod passed between them. It was a slight gesture, but it finished the conversation in a way words could not.

In acknowledgement, Tommy changed the topic: "Now if we could only get a few more beautiful women over here."

"What happened to all those cute girls we used to chase around the beach?" Burston asked.

"Most of them got caught and pregnant," Tommy laughed, adding:

"I don't know. I keep thinking someone will show up at the hotel. Single women started booking rooms with friends towards the end of July when those steamers you see in the harbor began running round trips from Wall Street. If that keeps up, I'll need to call on you to be an escort at the hotel. You know, to dance and chat with the ladies."

"Well, I'm your man for that," Burston said. Then he stood and pulled an oily, creased paper from his pocket: "Listen, Tommy, I got a strange letter at the *Reader* the other day. I have it here with me, if you'd take a look at it. Try to muddle through the spelling and tell me what you think."

Burston handed the note to Lawson and watched him read it:

To the newspaper, Any eyes can see that your
trying to take this lyland over and run it. Well to

*do it rite there no way you can less you get rid
of those ones at Kewas End. They comes here as
slaves and now they owning land that others who
comes here as white peeple dont have. you think
I cant read but I went to scool some and I can and
I read this newspaper and you selling land here
to white peeple, not slaves so why they getting to
keep land, huh? Why? And who said Gary Buckers
piece of crap sand spit of land is worth all that
money. I saw what you put it was for sale for.
Those coloreds at Ke'was End dint pay a red cent
and they sitting on the prettiest beach around.
Never you mind what you watching, because
I watching you. Someone whose been on this
lyland since before when.*

Tommy refolded the letter and handed it back:

"Geez that could be any of a dozen Scalers, Burston. Some of those baymen have hated the natives at Ke'was since the government land grants. Those are good people down there, you know that. Somehow the Scalers have it all backwards and think they were the first humans on this island."

"Remind me of that tradition of theirs. I've forgotten the details. The one about being born here?" Burston asked.

"Scalers must be born on the island and baptized with Corycian soil within minutes. Being born on the mainland negates the Scaler title."

"Is that why the Merkel woman died in her kitchen this week?"

"Yes," Tommy answered. "I hear she refused to get on the ferry. The Scaler legacy is even more important now that there aren't as many baymen here. When the factories shut down, so did the market for moss bunker."

"Assuming a Scaler wrote the letter, Tommy, why is he going after other people who were born here? People who are indigenous to the island like the Shellfoots?"

"That goes way back. I'm not sure anyone knows the reason any more, but Scalers have always steered clear of the folks at Ke'was End."

Pipers' Cove
"I was born here same as you was."

The threat was written by Josiah Remie, a descendant of the Bakkers' slave overseer and someone who had an inbred disregard for people of color. In addition to a distaste for all but white people, Josiah inherited his ancestors' wiry-red hair, freckled body, lemony-pale eyes, bony unibrow, and stinky still. The main difference in Josiah's development as a Remie was his status as a Believer, a religious sect which defined its members as "Muscular Christians marching through hell with the Lord." Josiah attended their mainland church every Sunday, taking an early ferry to be sure he wasn't late.

"I has my reasons to go," Remie told his only Corycian Island friend, Hector Wesley, who challenged Josiah about his devotions.

"Yeah, your reasons to go is you're a drunk afraid a hell if he don't go and repent every week," Hector said

They sat on the cool October ground of the woods by Pipers' Cove where the Remie's century old still put forth one of the finest, moonshine brews on the island. Through the trees, they could see the huge barn and community center that was to be the central focus of the Believers' Camp.

"They's givin' me a job, Hector."

"Who givin' you a job?"

"The Believers, that's who. They needs a camp director and I'm it," Josiah said, slugging back a big gulp of whiskey.

Hector Wesley thought for a full ten seconds, then said: "So we don't gotta move the still?"

"No, Nancy. You is such a girl, Hector. Them campers'll be walkin' all through these woods, prayin' and such. We're movin' the still to your place like we planned, shack and all. No one ever goes over to that side of the cove."

"You think you can pull this off, Josiah?" Hector whined. "I mean, they givin' you a paycheck and all. I do not think them Believers like alcohol, and that still and all the drinkin' could get you in trouble. And besides, I got women livin' at my place and they talk, don't ya know. They talk 'bout every damn thing."

"I have a plan, Hector. I have a plan to use my job in the Believers to lead all the sinners off Corycian Island and bring the truth of Muscular Christians marching through hell into the promised land to everyone left, in Jesus Lord's name we pray."

"Yeah, whatever you say, Josiah. I'm a *dis*believer and all." Then Hector thought of something else: "You know for them Catholics, it's okay to drink, even during Mass."

"What the hell's that got to do with this, Hector?"

"I don't know, Josiah. I just thought 'bout it and said it, like I do. But, anyways, it's the *still* that's worryin' me, no matter in whose name you prayin'. Town's got police now. Anyone sees that still and I'm cooked right along with you."

"Well, we Scalers is brothers, right?" Remie said.

"I tole you before," Hector said, "you ain't a Scaler cause first off, you ain't a fisherman. When'd you ever go fishin'?"

"I was born here same as you was," Josiah said. "And don't bring that dirt-baptizin' up again. I don't wanna hear it. This here's the thing: Jesus Christ was a wine drinker. I'm bein' the way and the shepherd. I'm gonna 'rip and tear and smite,' like the song says. I'm gonna 'let the gentle Jesus bless my dynamite.' We're soldiers, dont' ya know, like the song says. You wait and see Hector. I'm concealin' myself, but I am the way and the light, right like it s'posed to be."

"You is nothin' but a devil with a still."

"Well, close my still and see what kinda heebie-jeebies you get when you ain't drinkin' up my moonshine till you're soaked, Hector Wesley. Let's hear a little appreciatin' from you, if you don't mind."

Hector stood up to find a tree. Under his breath while he peed, he said:

"A shepherd, my ass. More like the black sheep, is what you is."

1901

Ke'Was End
"Spirit be tellin' dis story."

On an April night in 1901 Eula Morely finally heard from her grandfather's spirit.

Eula stood on the second story porch at the rear of the Captain's house. The wind roared off the mainland, picking up strength over the narrows, and blowing against Eula's face, whipping at her hair and burning her ears. The wool blanket she'd grabbed on the way out did little to keep the cold away. She was out there in the desperation of her endless wanderings, having walked in circles seeking a voice she didn't know how to hear.

Eula keened into the night: "We can't do this alone....." startling herself with the physicality of the prayer. She grasped onto the porch railing. The slap of a screen door thrown back in the wind made her jump.

"What don't I understand?" Eula asked the wind, feeling her shoulders fall in defeat. A sharp, icy rain hit Eula's face, mixing with her tears and sending her back into the house. She put the wool blanket over a chair, looked in on Judah, and went to her bedroom, climbing under the covers without washing the salt stains from her face.

When Eula's head sank into the down of her pillow, she felt the tremor in her body subside. She dozed into a peaceful relief and heard her grandfather, Captain Ephraim. His spirit came in a sound that had soothed Eula to sleep as a child, the soft shush-shush of his night-slippered feet along the worn wood floors below. She'd heard it every evening when the Captain walked about as he did aboard ships, checking this nook or that cranny, this window or that hinge.

25

Afloat in some nether place of sleep and dreams, Eula heard her grandfather making his rounds and knew what the message in his soft patter was. Of course it would be in what he loved best. Eula sat up straight in bed at 5:00 a.m. She hadn't changed clothes the night before, so she merely checked that Judah was asleep, left a note for him under a kitchen light, and headed over to Nuna's. She laughed when she saw a light come on in Nuna's kitchen window. Eula opened the door gently so as not to awaken Bay. Nuna was at the stove brewing coffee.

"How long have you been up?" Eula asked.

"Long enough to scare dem bazodees from my head," Nuna said, looking at Eula and seeing the clarity of her eyes. Turning the coffee down to a simmer, she said:

"I be seein' dat you be hearin' good t'ings. Disn't dat be so?" Nuna poured them each a tin mug of coffee and took a shawl from the pegs by the door. The two women walked out to a screened porch.

Last night's rain was dripping from tree limbs onto the meadow beyond and a blue swath of sky was dotted with fading stars. They sat and Eula said:

"We can do this, Nuna. We'll turn the Captain's house into a guest house, but more. We'll use the farm to attract people from the city, you know, cement-weary-people who don't see enough trees or who miss the old ways of their childhood farms."

Nuna listened with her whole self, absorbing the strength of spirit from Eula's story.

"They can take the Long Island Railroad almost right to the mainland ferry slip. We'll figure out how to get them over here, in a wagon-taxi, don't you think?" Eula was talking fast. "We can lease your other two cottages and, maybe even the one behind the Captain's, and rooms in the big house as well, of course. The Captain's house will be the center of things.

"The Strand and that holy camp at Pipers' Cove have brought a whole new group of people to Corycian, Nuna. They've discovered vacations within a few hours journey. I'll bet they want to get out of that tight-collared clothing as much as they do the stuffy city. You don't get around enough to see the people coming out here these days, Nuna. I was over by the Westside Market and I couldn't believe the fancy people getting off the ferry. People all buttoned up and sewn into themselves. People who need to feel the earth between their toes again."

It was true that Nuna Shellfoot had never been on the ferry, much less off the island, but she bristled inwardly at Eula's suggestion that she was unfamiliar with what went past her very eyes. Nuna had been all over Corycian Island, had helped all sorts of people, and had seen plenty in her time; but she pushed the ire away, and turned her attention to Eula, who was rattling on:

"Here's my idea or the Captain's idea....uh, I'm not sure how to credit that and I don't want to sow any bad seeds," Eula smiled. "Anyway, we'll attract some of those tired-looking city people over here. There have to be people who yearn for their youth or the pastoral lives they've heard about; you know, the old days on the farm, eating the food planted outside the door, nurturing its growth, and harvesting it for their daily bread.

"We'll make a little village of our own, Nuna, the exact opposite of that straight-laced Calliope Point. Here everyone can afford to be who they are, to go back to nature, to get away from the city noise. I think we should turn your third cottage over there into a fish and produce store. There's nothing like that on this side of the island. Maybe your cousin Henry would move over here from his sister's place. Last time I saw him in town, he told me he needed to find a new place to live. Henry could help us with the heavy chores and sell his fish and our produce there, and even your herbal teas. Henry could live upstairs."

Eula paused to collect her thoughts. She feared the vision would stop putting words in her mouth. She closed her eyes and took a deep breath. Nuna waited.

"I think they'd even like to help prepare the meals, the guests, I mean. You know, family style meals - nothing fancy, just hearty, farm food. They could even feed the animals. They'd think it was fun to throw corn at the chickens and to hand-feed the goats or to ride one of our old, slow horses along the beach...uhh, let's see, what else....."

Nuna sat in the dark, rocking in a chair Ahane had made. She sat upon land her ancestors had blessed, on a porch her father had built. She was wrapped in a shawl her mother had woven. She closed her eyes and soothed herself in the story.

The women talked about a plan all day while going from one chore to the next, with Bay and Judah helping them as they went along. The friends agreed they'd go about readying the place, put the word out, and see what came of it. They would have to save to buy a newspaper ad that was larger than the one the Believers' Camp published in the *Reader* each week.

That night, after Bay was asleep, Nuna spoke to Ahane:

"Spirit be tellin' dis story. I hears you in Eula's words, Ahane. We be great-filled in our hearts, in de work we do, and alla-round." Nuna looked up at the treetops swaying above her: "I feels rooted, Ahane. Dis be spirit right here pullin' at my soles to keep me firm."

***

THE CORYCIAN ISLAND READER
Advertisements May 23, 1901
SHOUT! Believers, SHOUT!
Join renowned Believers' Preacher
Abram Oberhoff of Manhattan
at a
PRAISE MEETING
THE BELIEVERS' CAMPGROUNDS
Pipers' Cove, Corycian Island
Sunday June 2, 1901 Sunrise to Dusk

The response to the advertisement posted in the *Reader* by the Believers' board was immediate. On Sunday, June 2nd the camp was crowded with mainland Believers who took the ferry over to discover its wonders

Thanks to the heavenly beauty of Corycian Island, and to the energy of Preacher Oberhoff, The Believers' Campgrounds at Pipers' Cove opened to crowds of families who sought peace, pardon, and comfort in an alcohol-free community set in the arms of the Lord.

Josiah Remie felt truly inspired, so he hid behind a tree to suck on a hidden bladder flask. He had never anticipated such success on opening day.

So with his heart swelling and his mind fogging, he walked into the audience and stepped in front of Preacher Oberhoff to lead the Believers in a well-loved tradition.

Preacher Oberhoff sputtered in shock:

"What do you think you're doing?"

But Josiah just kept walking among the congregants, shaking their hands, and singing along with them:

"Calling now for thee; Oh weary prodigal come..."

A stunned Oberhoff filed in behind, but there was no way his singing voice could drown out the deep-throated song of the little red-haired man who marched before him.

Josiah rose to inebriated heights of self-adoration with each hand he shook. He overwhelmed himself, and later, in the silence of a vacant campground, he dreamed drunken ideas about the glory he was going to arouse in these chosen people. His goals were so grandiose, they brought him to tears over his selflessness.

It only took Josiah a few shots of moonshine to become filled with the light of the shepherd he imagined himself to be. Within a few weeks he had devised a plan to save the Believers' board money by assuming the role of Christ's host himself, not claiming to be a preacher, but acting like one. The board members thought Josiah's plan was worth a try.

Soon, Josiah directed riotous frenzies of singing clapping, jumping, and jerking - allowing the Lord to flow through the assemblage with huge expenditures of energy, in accordance with the Believers' creed.

"We're Muscular Christians marching through hell with the Lord."

Josiah, bony man that he was, possessed a powerful singing voice. He moved through the group grasping outstretched hands, as an emissary of the Lord himself. Josiah sang:

"...Like a mighty army moves the Church of God;

Brothers, we are tread-ing Where the saints have trod!"

Early on during that season, a Believer on the other end of Josiah's handshake said: "The Lord has put the power in you, good man. Use it wisely."

A few days later, Josiah held a letter in his hand that reminded him what the man had said: "The Lord has put the power in you."

The letter was from Alvin Mannet. He was a well-known, shouting preacher scheduled the year before for a big fundraiser. Josiah had heard him over at the mainland church. Mannet offered daylong sermons, punctuated with calls for money in the style of an auctioneer. This produced a very competitive and cash productive atmosphere.

Mannet's letter said:

Dear Mr. Remie and Believers's Board members:

I am sorry to say I will not be able to honor my commitment to raise funds at the Pipers' Cove camp this coming weekend as I've been taken with the flu and am indisposed.

I apologize for the late notice, but there is little one can do. I am in the Lord's hands, as are we all.

Sincerely,
A. Mannet

Josiah read the letter and didn't bat an eye. "I can do this," he said aloud. "It's time to show that board it don't need no Alvin Mannet's for big money. They got Josiah Remie right here." He squeezed a shot from his flask.

That Saturday, Josiah called the campers into a "Convocation of the Blessed." He strode to the podium with square shoulders in his best white shirt and freshly washed, black pants. His red hair fell below his ears in an oil-slicked sheen. Josiah looked over the crowd and bellowed his first command into their silence:

"God told Abraham that His house on earth needed help from the people who came to it." [*Hallelujahs! from the audience*]

"This is God's house and your Almighty God needs your help." [*Amen!!*]

Josiah moved from the podium and jumped up and down on the platform.

"Can God hear you? Does God hear you? Let Him hear you! $10!$20!" [*Glory! Glory! Glory! the audience proclaimed*] "Shout to God's Glory! Celebrate God's love! Show him $30, $40, $45. More?"

Josiah appointed helpers to collect the bills and coins being passed down the aisles in religious ecstasy.

1902

Calliope Point
The first week of June

Sissy McElroy and her older sister, Pammy, found themselves on a steamer from Manhattan with plans to spend two weeks at The Strand Hotel on Corycian Island beginning June 4, 1902. The women made a vow to each other. They would return to New York City at the end of the fortnight with promises from men who wanted to marry them.

The sisters McElroy had rarely been apart in their youth. They looked alike, with the same shiny brown hair, but Pammy was three inches taller than Sissy, the only edge in the constant competition between the two other than clothes. They never shopped for clothing together, and rarely chose similar styles and colors. On the trip to Corycian Island, Sissy the younger chose a soft olive velvet cape tied at her neck with black grosgrain. Pammy, however, looked more suited for a voyage in her herringbone wool cape secured with substantial buttons.

As children, the sisters had made a pact to live close by in marriage. As adults, from what they'd heard of marriage, it was nothing a sister should go through alone. They promised one another to marry men who were brothers or close friends. During the search, their parents hounded them about getting it over with:

"For God's sake you're both pushing about in your 20s," their mother said in a recent argument. "You'll be spinsters soon. You should have entered the convent. At least you'd be wearing a ring."

But the women had no intentions of becoming "Brides of Christ," and it was time to find husbands. They heard about The Strand Hotel and reasoned that male friends or brothers who travelled together may want to live near each other in their married lives, as well. Once aboard the steamer departing Wall Street, Pammy and Sissy sized up every male passenger. "We can just blink once on the sly at each other," Pammy, the elder, said. "That will mean, 'this one's mine,' ok?"

Sissy thought Pammy had been blinking since she'd come up with the idea, so Sissy had lost track of her sister's claims.

At the hotel, when Pammy saw Tommy Lawson working behind the Strand's registration desk, she blinked before Sissy had a chance. So Sissy double-winked at Pammy, who laughed, and then tried to trump with a triple, until they both realized Tommy Lawson was speaking to, and staring at, them. The sisters composed themselves.

"I'm terribly sorry, ladies. Are you discomforted?" Lawson asked. "The Bradford Pears are blooming and the pollen causes some distress until you get used to it."

Sissy burst out laughing, followed by Pammy who spurted apologies to the hotel manager in staccato: "Gosh...So sorry... long day....long ride. We're fine...really."

Pammy signed the register and waited for the hotelier to escort them. Lawson was momentarily stunned. The smaller sister had reached her gloved hand forward in introduction and gently shook his hand. It was so unexpected and so, well, warm.

Coming to, Lawson scooted around the desk to escort them to their suite. He considered carrying their luggage, but on second glance, saw it was way too much for him to handle. He rang for the bellhop and told the clerk at the desk the McElroys' room number. While escorting the ladies to the elevator Lawson said.: "I think you'll find your stay at The Strand most enjoyable." The women nodded politely.

"Ahh, yes," Lawson continued. "We have lovely socials...with appropriate chaperones, of course, as I told your father when he called. Some are in the evening, others are in the afternoon, and we provide many entertainments on the grounds, like golf and tennis." The sisters nodded again. "Our shoreline is exquisite. Oh and we have an orchestra on Thursday and Saturday nights. Well, not an orchestra exactly, a group I guess, but they're good and..." Lawson felt foolish for some reason "....and you'll...we, that is...and, uh, everybody anyway...likes them."

The elevator arrived. Lawson nodded to the attendant as the scrolled brass doors opened. Then the hotelier turned to the women and said: "Ladies first."

They rode up to the top floor and walked out of the elevator into a rounded alcove. With a great flourish, Lawson opened double doors to a lush suite. Its focus was a full scope of the blue harbor, dotted with the white sails of yachts and schooners. The Westside Ferry churned a white wake toward the mainland, and a flock of seabirds flew southward over several huge boulders reaching from the water.

Pammy stepped onto the verandah and inhaled the salt air. She saw a gentleman on a knoll of grass far below her. He was dressed in a fine shirt and waist coat, smoking a cigar and standing on a verdant hill rising above a stretch of graceful, lacy cottages.

"What's that over there?" Pammy asked Lawson, pointing to the village and not the man.

"It's Calliope Point, a small village of Corycian Island." the hotel manager said. "There are some lovely houses - you might enjoy a walk through there. I can arrange it. Actually, the fellow standing on the hill lives close by. In the large clapboard house, see? Just on that point along the curve above the harbor."

Pammy stared at the man below her. Something about him drew her to think she could see him perfectly.

Sissy came up behind her sister and asked: "What do you see?"

Wordlessly, Pammy drew her sister's eyes to the man below, and blinked, slowly, once.

Ke'was End
The first week of June

The Captain's Guest House booked its first guests through Rosie Griffin, the island's switchboard operator. Rosie directed an inquiry about inns their way as a favor to Eula Morely, who had mentioned the possibility in passing.

Two spinster friends, who only required admiration for their easy-going and caring demeanors, were delighted to find such convenient accommodations. They were religious women from Brooklyn, on a mission to trace the journey of the Quaker's founder, George Fox. This great man of solace, upon touring the colonies in 1672, was said to have held a silent meeting in the Corycian Island Founders' Cemetery which was on the other side of the shell road past the Shellfoots' property.

The pair arrived at Ke'was End by way of a horse and buggy taxi. Addressing her friend with the accustomed titles of their Quaker sect one woman exclaimed: "Oh my goodness, Sister Arletta!"

The other replied: "Oh my goodness is right, Sister Beth. Our Brother Fox felt spirit here, indeed."

The women were thrilled to find the tranquil setting of the Captain's place, having made many stops at Quaker Meeting Houses on Long Island.

The first morning at Ke'was End they prepared breakfast before sunrise, leaving behind lovely scones they'd baked and jams they'd been gifted, then heading out to tend the graves in the Founders' Cemetery.

"It doesn't look too bad from over here, Sister Beth," Arletta called over her shoulder when they stopped, putting their baskets of tools on the ground. "It's larger than we thought, isn't it?" Beth said.

The cemetery stood in a field off the turn-around where the shell road ended, not far from the Shellfoots' land and a good stretch from Scylla's Cove below. An expansive wrought-iron fence surrounded a motley outcropping of gravestones. Some of the island's earliest dwellers were laid to rest there; two graves, with faded names, dated back to the 1730s, several slates stood like tiny teeth among them. They were markers for small children.

Arletta pointed toward a tall obelisk rising from the center of graves:

"Well, look at that fine memorial! I believe it's one of the most grand we've seen on this graveyard trip, don't you Sister Beth?"

"Indeed, Sister Arletta. It is clearly a piece of the same rock we saw on the cliffs and in the harbor on the way over. Glacial, but that's not unusual. It's how this piece has been - well what do I say? Worked? Chiseled? As if it formed right in this spot."

"And polished, too, from the looks of how it shines with the sun," Arletta said.

They picked up their baskets and entered the elaborately scrolled iron gates, admiring the details and remarking on the craftsmanship.

"Notice how none of the gravestones is significant, Sister," Beth said looking around. "No angels or such, just natural rocks and simple names and dates. Seems like the same names. Morely, Shellfoot. That one says Griffin. There's two fresh-looking ones over there, see?"

Arletta was examining the obelisk which she judged to be eight feet tall. "I don't see any name on it," Arletta said. "Do you think that's been polished? I mean by a human or just by age?"

Beth came over and looked more intently. "It reminds me of that one at the Whalers' Cemetery. Where was that again? Something-tuck? Oh wait a sec, Sister Arletta. Oh my, take a look at this. What do you suppose that is?"

"Mercy me, Sister," Arletta said, bending down to see what appeared to be stick figures carved into the very base of the obelisk. "Hmmm. I have no idea."

Mid-morning, Eula and Nuna joined the sisters out at the cemetery. Judah and Bay frolicked among the stones as they often did, while Eula poured the adults hot cider from a thermos.

"It's wonderful that you honor your belief with service," Eula said, handing a cup to Arletta.

"We are on a mission to pay respects to our ancestors, as Brother George Fox did, by caring for their graves," Arletta said. "The Quakers who came to this island were especially brave as I'm sure you know. Can you imagine facing persecution in

America from the neighbors who had run from your intolerant motherland with you?"

Looking at Nuna, Beth feared there might be misunderstanding. She quickly added, with a nod of respect, "Our work is to honor all people who have dealt with intolerance, those who came before us and those who stand before us."

Nuna smiled. "We be all-a-wanna down here at Ke'was End."

"All together," Eula explained and the sisters nodded back.

The four women sat under an old American Plane tree that rose above the obelisk, directly in front of them. Remembering the group of stick men chiseled into the monument, Sister Beth asked:

"What is the hieroglyph at the base of the tall stone? Do you know?"

"Dat be Runapewak words dat means all to-geder." Nuna got up and pointed at the extended arms of the stick figures. "See how dey be holdin' on ta each one? Hand ta hand? Dat's de story dey tells."

"Oh yes, I see and each looks different from the other, am I right about that? This one has shaded skin and this has an oval face. This one a different talent. I see. All-a-wanna!"

"How long has this cemetery been here?" Beth asked.

"That's hard to say," Eula answered. "Those who lived down on this end in the beginning are buried here, and that's many different people. Bims - those from Barbados - and the Quakers and the natives; but those strains weren't pure within a generation, so all-a-wanna. Our husbands' graves are the new ones."

Eula got quiet for a moment. "But that center rock's been here close to forever, according to those who know such things. No human placed it there. Similar glacial deposits exist all over the island, but this one appears to be a shard of larger rocks farther down on the beach. See them down there past the big trees? Like a tail stretching out into the water? On maps they call it Scylla's Neck."

"Are the Shellfoots the last of the native people?"

"I be de last grandchild of de sachem here on de eye'land. Henry gots all sorts in him," Nuna said, pointing to and waving at her dark-skinned cousin who was making his way up to the house from his boat, toting a basket of freshly caught flounder.

"Henry?" Beth said.

"He be my auntie's boy from de whalers - Runapewaks, too - Bims and Quakers and Montauks all mixed up. See?" Nuna pointed to the hieroglyph again. "All-a-wanna."

At dusk, fresh from their baths, the children walked ahead of the adults toward the worn path leading to the woods.

The children plopped into the pine cozy at their favorite spot.

Then Beth pointed in the distance toward a tall hillock ringed with scallop and oyster shells at its border

"What is that?" she asked as she stared at the high rise of moss, vines, shells, and dirt surrounded by feathery cedars.

"Our faduhs say de fields at Ke'was be all fulla Runapewak in de ol' times. Many peoples, all-a-wanna. Den de fever come and kills dem dead. So many, our faduhs say, dat alla dem put like dat back inside Mudah Eart' risin' wit' Faduh Sky."

Eula added: "There are a few Quakers in there. It was small-pox. It took half the island population - on this end, anyway - a hundred years ago. Too many bodies to bury separately and the soil down here is rocky so this is the way they buried the dead when mass graves were in order. Our grandfathers always told us to stay away, but that just made us drawn to the spot."

"So it's another gravesite?' Arletta asked.

"Only for those who pay it any mind, I guess," Eula answered.

"It's so strange how the light comes in and flits about like that over there," Sister Arletta said.

"Dem lights be Makiaweesug," Nuna replied.

Pipers' Cove
The first week of June

"Stand! Stand in complete stillness, feeling the awe of your faith without moving a muscle." This was Josiah's favorite new command to the flocks of Believers who came to the camp-grounds to feel the energy of their Lord.

SUZANNE MCLAIN ROSENWASSER

The faithful stood above Pipers'Cove for lengthy and gruel-
ing periods of time. It was an event to which Josiah turned when
his liquor sodden, throbbing head couldn't take anymore shouting and jumping. Josiah got them all lulled into standing stillness
and then retreated to some distant spot where he administered
whiskey to himself sparingly, just enough to calm his jangled
system.

Remie reappeared after a very long time, stood above the still
congregants, and called out with his arms outstretched:

"Release yourselves from your pain, in the name of the Lord."

The expressions of joy came in what the Believers called a
"shout song," a deafening "pray down" during which their calls
for "Glory!" their jumps for "Joy!" and their dances for the Lord
were performed "to shout Old Satan's kingdom down."

Josiah catered to the religious fervor. He planned outdoor
picnics during which the families pretended they lived in Jesus'
time, eating the "food of Jesus and speaking His words." For
most of the campers this meant saying "thou" and "thee," while
quoting Psalms, eating hard bread and even harder cheese.

However, Remie's most classic production debuted the first
week of June. Having noticed a distinct drop in attendance at
his "Muscular Sing-a-Longs," Josiah came up with his own version of Jesus' Sermon on the Mount, casting himself in the lead
role. He fashioned a choir robe into a Jesus outfit by tying a gold
drapery cord around his waist, which had a tendency to slip below his pouchy belly, getting lost in the folds of the robe. Josiah
fashioned a pair of sandals with a knife from an old pair of boots.
In this glory, Josiah presided over the self-dubbed "Saturday
Sermon on the Mount Spectacle" held on a slight promontory
just above the beach.

Saturday mornings Josiah's Jesus preached about "turning
the other cheek" and adoring "the light of the world" or being
"the salt of the earth." Josiah's Jesus belabored the issue of suc-
cumbing to false prophets, pointedly identified as "darker spirits
promising a link to eternity," a phrase Josiah had picked up from
Abraham Oberhoff's shouting sermon.

Remie rose to the occasion of condemnation with the terror of fire and brimstone, backing up his claims by shouting the word of Deuteronomy 13 in his deepest voice with perfect biblical dialect:

"If a prophet, or one who foretells by dreams, appears among you and announces to you a miraculous sign or wonder...and says: 'Let us follow other Gods and let us worship them,' you must not listen....That prophet or dreamer must be put to death because he preached rebellion against the Lord, your God.... You must purge this evil from among you."

The faithful spoke to Josiah in whispers, as if he was Jesus:

"May thy blessings fall upon me, dear Lord," or "May thy mercy be great, Holy One" and once, "I feel thy power, Master."

Josiah's faith in himself continued to grow.

Saturday evenings Josiah allowed the crowd to gather and mill about for awhile to create tension in his audience. Hiding behind a cluster of trees on a slight rise, Josiah watched them and sipped from a hidden flask. A murmuring restlessness developed. When Josiah felt its crescendo, he emerged from the midst of the enormous glacial rocks rising above the cove, lit by the sun's rays. Josiah-Jesus raised his arms and the Believers below hushed.

"Blessed are you," Josiah-Jesus proclaimed, as his brain filled with alcohol and he tried to remember the beatitudes, which he'd practiced in the woods for days. But the words of love didn't fall from his lips with the ease of Deuteronomy's wrath. Josiah fumbled, and mumbled:

"Blessed are the meek in spirit, for they shall get all the keys to heaven.

Blessed are the poor for they shall ...uh possess the....uh... possess the land.

Blessed are they who mourn, for theirs is the...their thirst shall be filled.

Blessed are the suffering peacemakers for they shall get...uh, their thirst will get, uh, better. Yes it will."

Josiah, a distant relative of the son of God, finished his sermon and descended from the mount. He walked among his followers, a loving sentinel for his Lord. Josiah touched hands, shoulders, and the heads of children. Followers behind him distributed small baked rolls with an invitation for the guests to join the Lord for fried flounder and cabbage slaw in the community center.

That week Josiah met a young woman who came to the Believers' Camp with her aged parents. Ruth Corcoran was plain and quiet. She lived to serve God first, and then her father and mother, who were blessed with their only child in their late 40s.

At the Believers' Camp, Ruth saw Josiah Remie as her savior, while he looked upon her as a solution. When Josiah asked the elderly Mr. Corcoran for permission to marry Ruth, the father didn't hesitate to give it.

The Corcorans winterized their small, summer cottage on the periphery of the Believers' Camp. They had a carpenter add two rooms for the newlyweds as a wedding gift when the couple married. From that day on, Josiah wished Ruth's parents an early death.

Early on Ruth knew the marriage was a terrible mistake.

Primarily Ruth cared for her demanding parents who were housebound. This gave her an excuse to miss Josiah's convocations. Time had changed her view. Where she once had thought Josiah was Jesus incarnate, she now thought him lower than "a cussed fool."

Ruth avoided the Sermon on the Mount because she knew that attending Josiah's performance presented her with "an occasion of sin."

Instead, sitting on a bench far from the huge glacial rocks where Josiah-Jesus appeared, Ruth prayed aloud:

"God, take away my sin of...well, my sin of...is hate too strong or not strong enough, God? I felt love for Josiah when I saw him as Jesus, but now, he's a man, more likely and, excuse my sin again God, a son of a bitch than a son of God. Forgive me for that, dear Jesus....what happened? This sin. It's the greatest of sins to feel for my husband."

As Ruth prayed she thought how easy it must be for Catholics to confess a sin and then get on with it.

Burston sat in his evening suit in the lobby of the Strand hoping Tommy Lawson would appear before the ladies arrived. Burston's starched collar itched. When he turned his head to adjust it, he saw two women at the top of the stairs and thought: "Tommy said sisters, didn't he?"

Sissy and Pammy paused at the balustrade overlooking the lobby. Sissy felt her sister find Burston Bakker, just as he noticed them. Sissy noted Burston's broad shoulders and his thick stand of blonde hair, but those blue eyes were icy. Her assessment was a quick one: "Good-looking in his staid way, but not my type." She looked over at Pammy and saw her sister and Bakker exchanging eye contact. Pammy was batting her eyelashes and trying to look coy without much success.

"For heaven's sake, Pamela, calm down." Sissy whispered. "He'll be thinking you suffer fits."

The two sisters started to laugh, big laughs they tried to contain at first, but couldn't hold in any longer. Having been through these nervous responses before, they backed away from the bannister to an alcove out of sight. They laughed as quietly as possible, with tears rolling down their cheeks, so they heaved in breaths to stop the flow. But bursts of giggles came in waves, only to catch the curl of another roll of laughs. They waited until some kind of appropriate decorum was sustainable.

When Bakker lost sight of them, he scanned the upper floor and then walked toward the staircase. As if from nowhere, the women reappeared, walking gracefully down the wide steps. The taller sister wore a soft blue linen skirt. An embroidered blouse, fitted at her narrow waist, bloomed at her shoulders in the mutton chop style with a high collar at her neck. Falling tendrils of brown hair framed her oval face. Had she been winking at him? Burston cleared his throat and adjusted his waistcoat.

Tommy Lawson came from a door beneath the stairs just as the ladies took the last step into the lobby. Tommy bowed in greeting: "Good evening..." he said, keeping his eyes on the younger Miss McElroy, who wore yards of expertly crafted voile in a fitted and feminine summer frock. Sissy McElroy's pale skin had already caught a kiss from a week in the sun and a band of freckles crossed her nose from cheek to cheek. The women returned Lawson's gesture with a slight curtsy, and then Pammy walked boldly over to Burston Bakker. She stretched out her hand.

"Mr. Bakker. I'm Pamela McElroy. It's a pleasure to meet you. Mr. Lawson has told us you're an intriguing man."

Burston took Pammy's fingers and bowed his head: "Miss McElroy, the pleasure is all mine, and might I say, you're quite intriguing as well."

Lawson had Sissy McElroy's hand tucked into the crook of his arm: "I thought we'd start with champagne cocktails. I've had the Maitre'd set up a beautiful spot for us out on the Grand Verandah. We can enjoy a sunset. It's fine entertainment."

Tommy opened the tall doors and his guests stepped out to a private belvedere, supported by Grecian columns, and open to the Long Island Sound. A uniformed waiter was there with a tray of champagne flutes. They all raised their glasses as Tommy led them in a toast:

"Welcome to the Eye-land of the Gods: Kewasowak..."

Burston cut Lawson off: "Nonsense, that's the past. Welcome to Corycian Island named for the most beautiful nymphs on Mount Parnassus."

They all laughed and sipped their drinks. Tommy pointed to different boats in the harbor: "Of course you recognize the *Menantic*, the ferry you took over here, and that huge yacht bobbing out there belongs to a friend of John Philip Sousa's. Sousa was here last year. We have a staff versus guest softball game occasionally. Sousa happened to be a guest and he pitched, poorly."

"Seriously? "Sissy said. "Oh, tell us more stories about famous people. Who does that fine looking sailboat belong to? The one moored closest to the end of the cove..."

Lawson realized Sissy was pointing to the *Barna-Call*. "Oh..." Tommy laughed. "Me, actually. That's an old catboat, kept bright and primed by yours truly. She's named for my mother's birth place, Barna on Galway Bay. An island boatwright crafted her, Ephraim Morely was his name. His people still live here on Ke'was End. You've got an eye to notice the catboat. She's the best looking one for miles around. I'll have to show her off while you're here." Lawson turned away from the balustrade: "Oh, the oysters have arrived! I've ordered us a real treat. We're known for our oysters, of course. So I thought you'd like to sample some of our best oyster fare - just a bite or so of each because I've ordered us a wonderful entree, as well."

The servers set platters on a table adorned with wildflowers in various heights of vases. The plates held oysters on the half shell sitting in shaved ice; broiled, fried, and roasted oysters spread on toast; ramekins of oysters au gratin, oyster stew, and a platter of oyster fritters with a lemon-dill sauce.

Sissy caught Pammy's eye when Tommy was reeling off the assortment. "I wish I hadn't worn this damn corset," she said. "I'm starved."

"Well, you're all flushed," Pammy whispered. "Stop drinking so fast and eat something."

"I'm all flushed? You should see your scarlet cheeks..." Sissy countered.

After they tasted at least one bite of every oyster dish, Lawson announced their entree:

"Again I've ordered servings of our best. Chauteaubriand Parisienne; a Vol-au-Vent of sweetbreads, roasted Long Island rabbit tartare, and broiled sea bass, Meuniere. There will be several potato dishes and vegetables, like lima beans and tomatoes, picked and canned right here on Corycian Island."

Pammy had drunk two champagne cocktails, not anticipating the wine "produced from the Strand's grapes," as Lawson said - but sipping it throughout the meal, fighting the stab of each stay in her corset.

When they finished eating, Lawson placed his napkin on the table saying: "So it sounds to me like you two might enjoy a golf lesson while you're here."

Pammy said: "Just one? You think we can master the game that quickly. I understand it's quite difficult."

"I'm told, like so much in life, it's all in the stroke, " a tipsy Sissy said, before taking a sip of wine.

Missing whatever had made Lawson blush, Burston plundered ahead: "Well, from my experience, one can't master the game, so why take more than one or two lessons?"

All of them laughed and Pammy felt herself grow warm when Burston smiled at her.

"I'll get us tee times for tomorrow," Tommy said. "You can play while you learn. It's a magnificent course, just nine holes but all along the coast. I'll see that we have clubs and caddies. For now, however, I suggest we take a walk and help ourselves digest this meal."

Murmurs of agreement followed as Tommy led them to the boardwalk outside the hotel. "We have some lovely private pavilions on the beach. I'll have coffee, sherry, and desserts sent out after our walk."

Each couple headed in a different direction. It was a calm, moonlit night. The bay rippled against the shore.

"Have you lived here all your life, Tommy?" Sissy asked.

"Yes. I was born in that house I pointed out to you above Calliope Cove."

"Has Burston?"

"Yes, he was born here. But Burston went to boarding school and college in Boston, so he was gone for ten years or so."

"He's different from you. You feel like this place, he doesn't."

"I'm not sure that's a compliment," Tommy laughed. "I didn't go to college, but I had some great teachers here. When I got my first job at the hotel, people just took me under their wings. That's worked out very well."

"Is it hard to live here? It seems so calm and beautiful now - like a fairy land. But I know the winters have to be long and cold."

Tommy stopped Sissy and turned her towards him.

"What's got you talking like you'll be spending winters here," he teased.

"Would winters be warmer with me here?" she asked.

Tommy was afraid his knees might buckle, a woman had never spoken to him so provocatively. They continued along in silence for awhile and Tommy took Sissy's hand. When they turned to head back, Sissy paused. She was just close enough for Tommy to smell her hair. She leaned into him and her brown curls brushed his cheek. Tommy felt dizzy. Then Sissy boldly grazed her lips across his. Just as quickly, she pulled away, leading him by the hand toward a candle lit canopy. In a clear voice she said: "Oh, is this the pavilion you mentioned?" Sissy could see the linen-clothed tables and wicker chairs inside the tethered tents that bloomed on decks built off the boarded walks.

"Yes, " Tommy said, still gathering himself. "I'll light those torches there and the servers will bring us the desserts I've arranged."

Tommy walked toward the torches and dug around in his pockets for a box of matches. Sissy climbed the steps to the pavilion and looked up when she heard a short gasp just above her. Sissy saw Pammy and Burston, sitting on a wicker couch. Burston was kissing Pammy's arched neck. Her left leg was resting atop Burston's whose right hand was under Pammy's skirt.

1903

Pipers' Cove
"With this soil I baptize you a Scaler."

Josiah Remie performed the marriage act with Ruth routinely, and within two months, Ruth was pregnant. When she told Josiah she was "expecting," he spent the next months arguing about who would deliver the baby. Ruth wanted to go to the hospital on the mainland, but her husband wouldn't hear of it. Josiah wanted his child to be born on the island, as any Scaler would - plain and simple - but their options were limited. The island doctor insisted that mothers near term required hospitalization on the mainland, and there were only two midwives anyone knew about. They were both "them indians and those kinda people," Josiah said, which Ruth knew closed the discussion.

"Your mother can do it," Josiah declared in a tone of finality during Ruth's eighth month. "She's always talking about her nursing days, so she can do it."

"Nursing days?" Ruth replied with a guttural tone. "Nursing days?" she shouted, finding her voice. "She sat with sick people and read to them!"

"Enough of this. God wills it," Josiah used his trembling son of God voice and left the house with a slam of the door. Josiah had begun to believe something about himself that made his wife fear him.

When Ruth's time came, the birth was tortuous. Josiah left at the first inclination the process had begun, and in her horror, Ruth realized where he went. On many nights after she had endured the marriage act with Josiah reeking of alcohol, Ruth heard the screen door creak open, then close. On a few occasions, she crept toward the window to watch as Josiah unlocked the shed where she knew he kept whiskey. When he came out, he was wearing his Jesus robe. He took a jug with him and ran stealthily away.

In the extremities of Ruth's labor, while her mother administered the soft shushes that were the extent of her medical training, Ruth thought of god-damned Josiah out there running around scaring people as the devil-ghost he was. The fury she felt at the sins he was committing, and the ones he was forcing her to commit, made Ruth push at the contractions with the strength of a Titan. Their son rushed into the world on thoughts of profound hate.

When Josiah showed up to see the boy, he reached down to the bed and took the baby out of Ruth's arms. His mother-in-law protested, but Josiah turned toward her and said: "The boy needs to be named. That's my job."

Josiah took the whaling baby out by the place where he performed the Sermon on the Mount. He crouched down, scooped a small handful of black earth from the ground, and dribbled it on his son's skull, saying:

"With this soil I baptize you a Scaler, and I name you with the word of our Lord. I name you: Inri. Inri Remie."

Where did Josiah get this name, his wife and mother-in-law asked again and again.

Josiah just smirked and said: "You can find out if you read the Bible."

This was an insult to Mrs. Corcoran whose distaste for her son-in-law had grown acrid. She told her deaf, and increasingly dense, husband that she knew of no one in her extensive biblical readings named Inri.

Well, Josiah, who couldn't read or write very well, happened to have been paging through the New Testament before his son's birth when he came upon the sign that Caesar had placed above Jesus' cross which said INRI.

Josiah mistakenly believed he was naming their child with the Latin word for Jesus. Had he been a scholar of any depth, he would have known the letters INRI were indeed placed above the crucified head of Jesus; however, the letters were an acronym for a taunting name: "Iesus Nazarenvs Rex Ivdaeorvm" or "Jesus of Nazareth, King of the Jews."

The Captains' Guest House
"Go Fishin'"

At Ke'was End, Nuna Shellfoot and Eula Morely possessed a shared interest in survival that kept them focused on Eula's vision for The Captain's Guest House.

They chose the larger of two vacant cottages on Nuna's property to house "Henry's Produce and Fish Store" and readied the smaller one in the event an opportunity came to lease it. They moved Eula and Judah to rooms on the first floor of the Captain's house and readied the upper levels to accommodate guests in two large suites on the second floor or three smaller rooms on the third.

Eula devised amenities that included placing sheets of old newsprint and pairs of shears on a table off the pantry. Near them stood a large folded card bearing Eula's lovely script in a large scrawl that read:

"For those who choose to head to the wildflower meadow. Empty vases are in the front closet of each room."

On an idle counter in the kitchen, Eula set out pre-measured ingredients with the required spatulas and bowls. This note read:

"Go ahead and bake a few cookies to share."

Bait, hooks, and bamboo poles sat on the back porch with another note: "Go Fishin'!"

The first guests of the 1903 season came in the end of May. They were a brother and sister who booked two rooms. Henry Shellfoot met the guests at the Westside Ferry with an old buggy restored for the purpose, drawn by an older horse who was surprised to be back in service.

The woman booked the reservations by telephone, having heard of the inn from Eula and Nuna's first guests, the Quaker sisters. The caller said her only desire was to gather eggs and feed hay to the livestock, feats she had accomplished on her family's farm as a youngster. She added that her older - quite old, in fact

- brother wanted to milk cows, though in their absence he would accept the farm's she-goats. Each desired to groom a horse.

One hour after their arrival, the guests were working at their chosen chores. The two could be heard across the meadow as their laughter rang out from behind the barn.

Eula and Nuna watched them from the garden. Each of the siblings wore men's trousers and flannel shirts. Their jewelry, and both arrived wearing plenty from watch fobs to rings, had been left in their rooms. The woman's hair was unpinned and tied loosely with a scarf; the man wore a bandana in place of his felt fedora. Their expensive riding boots were already muddied, and they'd worked up sweats that would be inappropriate for either of them to sport among their elite, Manhattan friends.

Eula heard her grandfather's voice in the revelry coming from the barn, at the same moment, Nuna said aloud: "See? We help dem, don't ya know?"

That night at dusk with Bay safe in bed, Nuna set off on a walk to find the Makiaweesug and hear "what be what." As she strolled, she stopped at the oak tree spreading out from the field's center. Nuna focused on the forms in front of her and saw the siblings from the guest house standing there. The sister spoke:

"The Quaker sisters told us about the Algonquin Makiaweesug and we hoped to find them here, Miss Shellfoot," she said without any sort of greeting. "Can you lead us to them?"

Nuna hesitated, thinking: "Dem ladies jabber plenty much for bein' Quakers." Then Nuna drew in a deep breath and told the first spirit story that occurred to her:

"You gots ta find dem on your own, but I takes you where mine be."

***

Many of the early guests at the Captain's house were Quakers, people who were accepting of others by their very credence, so most of the guests were amenable and polite; however, issues did arise from other visitors who weren't as tolerant. A married couple took umbrage at being co-hosted by Nuna Shellfoot because of her color and her strange accent. The offended marched up to Eula Morely, and the husband spoke:

"You should have mentioned your leanings on the phone, Mrs. Morely. We are not the kind of people who take up with coloreds."

Eula looked the man square in the eye and responded:

"We don't do that way on Ke'was End"

Then, while handing over a refund and a ferry schedule, Eula added with a forced smile: "I'll get you a cup of mint tea to soothe you down while you wait for your transport."

Not wanting to get Henry involved, Eula called the island taxi. The haughty guest started spewing venom about how he would ruin Eula's business. Eula ignored him, though she could hear him giving the taxi driver, Hector Wesley, an earful on his way out.

Nuna walked into the front foyer just after the couple left and asked about the row, Eula replied:

"We've each had more than our share of ugly, Nuna. I'll not have it sleeping in our beds."

That night Eula and Henry accompanied Nuna on her walk to hear from the spirit-tellers. They all sat on the forest floor, looking at the hummock heights casting a dark triangle against the blue-black sky. The sea was still and no wind stirred the hardwood and fir trees. They sat in the peace of darkness except for the lacey lights that glistened and spread across the large gravesite.

"Dat be spirit," Nuna said.

"How do you feel about these other people looking for spirit here, Nuna?" Eula asked.

"Dat de story spirit be tellin' now," Nuna said.

CALLIOPE POINT
THE CORYCIAN ISLAND READER
Vol. 10, No. 24 Thursday, June 18, 1903
DOUBLE WEDDING CEREMONY FOR
PUBLISHER AND HOTELIER

Mr. Burston Bakker, publisher and editor of this newspaper, was wed to Miss Pamela McElroy, alongside Mr. Thomas Lawson, manager of The Strand Hotel who took Cicely McElroy as his avowed wife. Mr. Conor McElroy, Vice President of the Chemical Corn Exchange Bank in Manhattan and uncle of the brides, gave his nieces away in marriage last Saturday. Constable Hansen Ratliss presided over the civil ceremony and joined in the dinner reception at The Strand Hotel. The McElroy sisters wore distinctly different gowns styled from antique lace made by prominent New York seamstress, Mae Curtin. The brides carried Corycian Island wildflower bouquets, including.... *(cont'd 9)*

What the newspaper didn't report was:

The brides, raised as Catholics, gave little regard to those religious traditions, refusing to partake in the sacrament of marriage officiated by a Catholic priest. Consequently, relations with the senior, staunchly Catholic, McElroys are on shaky grounds. This explains the absence of the brides' parents at the wedding.

Sirens' Beach
Màthair

A convent of nuns came to occupy a large property on the north side of Corycian Island in 1903. The Catholic Church had inherited an unoccupied stone mansion built in the Tudor Elizabethan style by a wealthy "utilities man" who kept it up, but never lived in it. The large parcel on which the manse sat overlooked another of Corycian's harbors known locally as Sirens' Beach. Constructed of multi-colored bricks with a limestone trim, the roof boasted 18 chimneys and three high-rising towers. The porte-cochere was guarded by sculptures of male and female saints. It covered the entrance that led to elaborately carved, double doors. The floors throughout were Jacobean wood and the ceilings were replicas of those in Buckingham Palace. Oreo windows and French doors looked out onto garden paths designed by Olmstead and Associates.

The house contained 42 rooms and a chapel which was built in Europe, brought to Corycian Island and, piece by piece, reconstructed. Stained glass windows and wood carvings depicted the stations of the cross on three interior walls. The back of the altar was a clear window looking out above Sirens' Beach. The focus was on a large statue of the Blessed Virgin Mary - "Our Lady of the Seas" - with her head bowed and her arms reaching out at her waist, palms open. The statue faced the chapel from its place high on the berm above the beach.

The house was built because a rich Italian importer told the rich Irish utilities man that the Cardinal of the Archdiocese of New York needed an appropriate retreat for Pope Pius X, who was contemplating a visit to the U.S. - the first ever by a Pope. The wealthy utilities man sought history by building a palatial, Papal retreat house on Corycian Island and naming it: "Màthair," Gaelic for "Mother," a word carved into the limestone above the port -cochere.

Neither the Pope nor the owner ever occupied the house. Pius X chose not to come to the U.S., the rich man died unexpectedly in 1901, and the property was left to the Catholic Church.

The serene spot became home to the Sisters of Saint Anthony, a nursing order which treated convalescing priests and nuns. The arrival of the good sisters to Màthair in 1903 passed by quietly for most islanders, other than the smattering of Catholics who were delighted that mass would be offered in St. Anthony's small chapel on Sundays when a priest was available.

The only people who cared about the new residents were Josiah Remie and his friend, Hector Wesley, the Scaler who subbed as a taxi driver when the fishing fleets weren't calling for crews. The two of them, relatively respectable citizens by day, became disrespectful malcontents at night, meeting at Josiah's shack in the woods and often drinking moonshine from the still until they passed out.

SUZANNE MCLAIN ROSENWASSER

However in between the first drink and the last, they always found something about Corycian Island to hate. In the fall of 1903, Hector Wesley defined his hatred for the entire Roman Catholic Church which he directed at the Sisters of St. Anthony who had invaded their island home. Hector leaned against some rocks by the still which was now in the woods behind his house. Josiah sat close by. A jug of whiskey stood between them. The ground was cold and the night smelled dank from the fallen leaves rotting around them.

"My daddy always said them Catholics answer to that Pope a theirs first, even before the USA, he said." Hector looked at Josiah for a reaction that didn't come, so he went on. "My daddy said if the President and the Pope knocked on a Catholic door at the same time, the President would have to wait out on the stoop and come in second. That's why they have their own schools and such, don't ya know."

He heard Josiah fart and scooted away. Being down wind from Josiah's body odor was acrid enough without adding intestinal fumes. But Josiah saw Hector move, so he redirected his hips, lifted his cheek, and let one go full force at Hector.

"Ugh. You could get yourself clean more than on Saturdays, don't ya know," Hector said. "And that what you did there is babyish, is what it is. Kids do that. You're just a baby kid sometimes, Josiah."

"Shut up and tell me some more 'bout them Catholics. I was just tryin' to show you I been concentratin' " Josiah replied, too drunk to care if he was babyish.

"Well..." Hector rubbed his forehead and tried to get back to where his mind had been. "Let's see. Oh, I know. They'se the only ones who can get into heaven the Pope says."

"The only ones?" Josiah slurred. "That don't seem right." He was trying to listen so he wouldn't pass out.

"Yessirree," Hector said, encouraged by Josiah's assessment. "That's why it's a cult and the nuns is the whores, my daddy always said. What we need to do is scare the bejesus outta them, Josiah. I drive them priests over to that place at Sirens' Beach when they get off the boat. I'm tellin' ya, mosta them priests smell like they been in bars for weeks. I drops 'em off like they's about dead, picks 'em up a few weeks later and they is fresh as daisies. Carnal acts is being committed there. Carnal acts, don't ya know."

Hector heard Josiah snore. He shook Josiah's shoulder and the drunkard's head bobbled. Then his eyes rolled open and through a slack jaw Josiah said: "The priests are sots, Hector. I told you that a hundred times," and with that, he was out again, head leaning back on the granite and mouth agape.

The truth was, Josiah knew what he was talking about. He'd sold whiskey to a few priests who'd found out about him somehow. One told him the priests got sent to Sirens' Beach for the nuns to dry them out.

Hector curled his lip at Josiah's final statement. So what if Josiah had talked to one priest. Hector talked to all of them on the ride and some of them were down right chirpy. Who's chirpy about drying out? Hector drank and thought about this point until Josiah awoke from the constant movement of the jug being lifted and set back down between them. Seeing Josiah's open eyes, Hector moved close and said:

"So what would you say if I told you I took one of them priests there and back more'n four times?" Hector sat back, scratched his crotch, and reached for a victory sip from the jug.

Josiah sat up, grabbed the whiskey away, and, two inches from Hectors's face, belched full force. Josiah said:"I'd tell ya he couldn't dry out, ya dumb shit."

Hector had all he could do not to smack Josiah in the head, but Hector was much bigger and twice as strong.

"It's time to shut the hell up," Josiah said morosely.

"Oh, yeah, 'cause what time is that, huh? What time is that, Josiah?"

Hector was assessing where to make Josiah black and blue. But Josiah surprised Hector and said with a drunken grin:

"Let's go ahead and scare the bejesus outta them whorin' nuns!"

Corycian Island Town Center
"This time it's chicken guts."

1903 was the year Corycian Island took shape. The thriving center of the town now had a public library, a brick schoolhouse, a stately Town Hall, a soda shop, funeral home, police station, and all-volunteer fire department with a horse-drawn, water truck.

Communities of homes appeared all around the center along with houses of worship, adding a sturdy Methodist Church of solid brick, a simple Baptist Church in a renovated house, and a small Dutch Reformed Church built into a lush grove at Calliope Point.

Hansen Ratliss, the Constable, was a mainlander, an off-islander who came to Corycian Island to fill a position every islander wanted filled, but no islander wanted to take. Policing one's relatives led to a highway of disaster, according to local thinking.

Ratliss was a spit-polished, dark-haired man with a naturally fit physique and a kind smile that added a dimple to the edge of his trimmed mustache. He added stature to the single-breasted, uniform jacket the Town Board had ordered for the position. He wore the badge on its inside pocket.

No one could deny the Town Board was right to hire Hansen Ratliss. The drunken tourists, and the undisciplined teenagers they brought with them, created havoc all summer. So most of the island locals supported Ratliss, until one of them ended up in his sights.

After his first week on the job, Ratliss saw that the moonshine problem alone was enough to keep him busy; add some hot-shot, visiting drunks to the mix and all hell broke loose.

When Ratliss agreed to the low-paying job, which came with an apartment over the station, he had no idea what he was in for and had less than a broad idea of law enforcement. He used the "Constable's Manual" as a guide to what he thought was the application of common sense. Ratliss was a kind and fair man who thought every decent human had a right to live in peace and quiet. But within weeks on the job Ratliss had learned how many "decent" people lived lives of chaos and disharmony. The summer started with a phone call from the Mother Superior at St. Anthony's Retreat House whose anger came through the earpiece clearly:

"Constable, this is the Mother Superior of St. Anthony's speaking from Màthair. Another incident has taken place and I want you to see that this ends immediately."

Shortly after the nuns' arrival, piles of manure began to appear on the entry steps to the manse. Once it was a paper bag of dog shit. The perpetrator rang the front doorbell and listened for the nun's shoes to echo along the stone hall while walking toward the entrance.

At that precise moment, the prankster set the paper bag afire. The unsuspecting sister opened the door, saw the fire, and stamped it out with her brogans.

Josiah and Hector watched it all from their hiding place. Hector had a moment of regret when he saw the beautiful face of the young woman who answered his ring. But Josiah was laughing so hard at that point, Hector knew he'd better join in or Josiah would start whaling on him.

Ratliss became aware of Josiah Remie and Hector Wesley when he overheard Remie bragging about their antics in the Westside Market, almost taunting Ratliss while standing in line behind him at the cash register:

"Has you urges to eat some nice fresh, chicken innards, Hector?" Remie said to his friend.

Wesley, not one to catch a hint, said: "That's all I do eat if I ain't been out fishin' Josiah."

"Aint it bad when all ya gots left to eat is the guts." Josiah snickered.

It was a conversation intended for Ratliss because the Constable had just spoken by phone to the Mother Superior again:

"This time it's chicken guts, Constable Ratliss. The fools threw chicken guts all over the entrances to the manse. I want you to find these waste-products and hold them accountable. Do you hear me Constable Ratliss?"

Ratliss gave assurances to the nun, but he knew he couldn't be everywhere at once. Remie and Wesley operated in the woods in the dark. Selling whiskey offered them protection, too, otherwise the night watchman hired by the nuns would have caught them.

1904

Ke' Was End
"Come find your spirit again."

Muscular Christians, lovelorn secretaries, breathless bachelors, wealth seekers, disgraced priests, and naive nuns disembarked from the Westside Ferry with regularity by 1904. They were slowly joined by others, shoreless refugees seeking a connection beyond themselves to an ether sifting through the universe. Word spread that Ke'was End was the place to find it. People said spirit seeds were sown there, where the water baptized the land in cleansing laps and spirit brought peace to those who sought it.

Nuna's personal evening walks began to draw the Captain's guests who always appeared under the oak tree, awaiting her. Nuna nodded and indicated they could follow her in silence. Nuna would stop at the woody copse near the rise and, if the awe of spirit appeared, Nuna waited for someone else to mention it. Only then did she acknowledge the connection. She said to Eula one day: "Summa dem don't see no'ting. Dey just wants to be de one who see, so dey say so." Nuna shook her head: "Too much dem in dem, don't ya know? No Oonuh, just dem." The attraction of their guests to the Makiaweesug annoyed Nuna, but she tried to keep it to herself.

Then Adelaide Coeur arrived.

Miss Coeur was an upstate New York Quaker from a radical sect devoted to the rise of spiritualism sweeping across America. The success of New York colonies, like Lily Dale, had paved the way for Miss Coeur to bring her vibrations to Ke'was End. There, she intended to rattle the bones of spirit and make a little cash. She booked a week at The Captain's Guest House.

Adelaide Coeur and a wagon full of registered guests crossed to Ke'was End in Hector Wesley's taxi on a breezy June day. When

Wesley halted his horse at the farm's gate, Miss Coeur stood her ample self up, threw her hands into the air, and shouted, much to everyone's surprise:

"Exalt, one and all. Bare your souls to this hallowed land."

Following her bellowing exclamation, Miss Coeur promptly sat down on the wagon's bench, brushed back strands of her auburn hair, and, in the shocked judgement of her fellow passengers, removed her shoes. Then, scandalously exposing her ankles, Miss Coeur pulled her stockings off with a flourish that produced a gasp from her fellow riders and a whinny from the wagon's horse. (Due to the later proceedings, the rapt attention of the horse was cited by island gossips as evidence that matters of the occult had taken place). Meanwhile, with shoes and stockings in hand, Adelaide turned to the other passengers and explained with a trill:

"My soles will not impede my soul from receiving the energy beneath my feet."

With that, Miss Coeur squared her broad shoulders, refused Hector's offer to help, struggled down the wagon steps, and planted one large foot after the other on the Morely's land. She said to all: "Prepare yourselves to step on holy ground."

Eula and Nuna had become accustomed to the eccentricities of their mainland visitors, and watching from the front stoop of the Captain's house, they knew a load of adventure had just arrived. Adelaide strode toward them exclaiming that her spirit had found its home. "Its roots are tickling my feet!" she warbled, turning to entice the others along. But no one followed her. The rest of the guests had yet to move from Hector Wesley's taxi.

Eula snapped to attention, fearing the others weren't going to get off the wagon, but Nuna had already summoned help from Henry, and the three of them hurried past Adelaide Coeur with polite nods.

***

Later that day, while Nuna prepared dinner with a few female guests, Eula walked the grounds with a more sedate, and now shod, Adelaide Coeur. Eula listened to Coeur's stories of her life as a spiritualist, talking of mediums, crystal balls, spirit cabinets, vibration photography, and séances. As they approached the Founders' Cemetery, Adelaide grabbed Eula's arm and said:

"You live with spirits? Why didn't you tell me this? Do you take care of them?"

"Yes," Eula replied, and then, turning to point in the opposite direction, she said: "And them. Come, I'll show you." Eula led Adelaide into the copse beyond the cemetery. "See?" Eula said pointing to the ring of shells that encircled the high rise of rocks, soil, and moss surrounded by cedar trees, shielding its size until one passed beyond the wooded entrance.

Adelaide was astonished. She judged the flat-topped land mass to be more than five feet tall. It took her awhile to gather herself:

"Why this is a burial mound, but....mound builders? Mound builders this far east?" Adelaide asked, breathlessly.

"Well," Eula replied, unsure of the intensity of Adelaide's question, "I don't know anything about that. This is a grave for victims of the smallpox and such. They were buried 'all-a- wanna' as Nuna would say, that means all together. They were buried all together to keep the illness of their spirit seeds in one place. The graves have been here for at least 100 years, maybe longer. We used to play on the hill as kids, but we protect it now."

Adelaide stood still, transformed. She became legitimately reverent before she spoke:

"Mound builders are not indigenous to this area, Mrs. Morely."

"Excuse me," Eula said, "what does that mean, Miss Coeur?"

"Mound builders are pre-Columbian, at least that's what I think." Adelaide saw the confusion in Eula's expression. "I'm a student of the ages, Mrs. Morely, a graduate of Vassar. There are all sorts of beliefs about the mounds, generally that they begin in south Georgia and travel up through the mid-section of the continent. There have been hoaxes, of course...but... well....never mind those. Thomas Jefferson personally excavated a mound in Virginia and concluded from the burial practices that the remains were directly related to the of the indians of his time." Adelaide was rambling and walking back and forth as she continued: "Joseph Smith's *Book of Mormon* attributes the mounds to the Ten Lost Tribes of Israel - the Jews - but I've also seen many credible references about mounds being pre-historic." Adelaide spoke her next words pointedly: "You've got something here, Mrs. Morely. The mounds are mystical; they house ancient spirits who have lain undisturbed since their souls blended with the earth centuries ago. These vibrations are valued above all by the true spiritualist."

Eula could see the evangelist rising in Adelaide Coeur. The woman's demeanor changed and her voice sang as she spoke: "These virginal, undisturbed, innocent spirits long to be part of the human plan. We can tap into their souls, Mrs. Morely."

Adelaide paused, then looked Eula in the eye and said: "You've got a gold mine here. An absolute gold mine, Mrs. Morely. Don't you see? The Ten Lost Tribes? That's a very popular theory, which means we'll attract the Jews, and maybe a few Mormons, too. I repeat, you've got a gold mine here. And on top of it all, I sense spirit. I have a gift, Mrs. Morely; much like Mrs. Shellfoot has, but I use mine to earn my living. Trust me. I was sent here to help you. That's what spirit told me and this mound here is a draw."

Eula noticed that Adelaide had a way of absorbing the air around her and leaving it empty when she finished speaking. And if Adelaide Coeur was here to exploit them, Eula would have none of it.

"Miss Coeur," Eula said, aware that she had to break through some vacuum: "Miss Coeur, I know you're an educated, academic scholar with credits and all, and I don't want to be contrary; but diseased corpses were buried to keep them in one spot. No one wanted the disease getting into the farm soil. That's why they're all back here away from the fields. That's all there is to it."

Adelaide hadn't moved. She held her chin with her hand as she tightened her gaze on the mound: "Mrs. Morely, how many people know that for sure? And what aren't you telling me? There is something very impenetrable out there, and we can use it to our mutual advantage."

Adelaide took hold of Eula's wrists and spoke directly to her eyes. "I have been sent here to help you, Mrs. Morely. Surely you can see that. It's what you've asked for."

Eula told Nuna about her exchange with Adelaide Coeur and, with Nuna's reluctant agreement, they invited Adelaide to speak to the other guests about what Eula was now calling, "The Mound."

When Nuna frowned at the usage, Eula said: "Well, we never have known what to call it."

"Dat be since no one ever be talkin' 'bout it no more."

Nuna felt caught. Adelaide Coeur saw something when she arrived. Nuna saw the bougley woman see it and in the house Nuna felt a rhythm with Adelaide that emanated familiarity. Nuna didn't like it, but she couldn't deny it.

Eula asked:"Is she one of those you say only pretend to see?"

Nuna felt like sulking, but she had to tell Eula the truth. "Dey be some t'ing 'bout her."

"Adelaide says she heard spirit who told her to help us."

Nuna frowned again, but coincidence was not a sign she ignored. She nodded her approval.

"Ok," Eula said, "and I'm sure all the guests want to know what's going on with her. We'll let her talk in the parlor during afternoon tea. I'll ask her to keep her energy at a more acceptable level."

***

Two couples, the hosts, and Miss Coeur assembled in the parlor for an afternoon respite, enjoying Nuna's homemade elderberry wine.

The guests fell into sedate bits of conversation with each other, accepting a small plate and napkin from sweetly-skirted Bay while Judah, dressed in knickers with a starched shirt and tie, offered a tray of goat cheese wrapped in basil leaves and cucumber sandwiches topped with dill. Eula followed, pouring more wine into proffered glasses.

The focus seemed to turn naturally to Adelaide Coeur who soon held the group in rapt attention as she poured forth her knowledge about the mysteries of burial mounds. After her second glass of wine, Adelaide enhanced the facts of the day by acknowledging a *presence*, as she called it, who continued to interrupt her.

"We came upon a sight few mortals are blessed to see today, my friends. Excuse me. I'm sorry. Did you hear that?"

The guests in the parlor looked about, hearing nothing. Adelaide continued. "Your forgiveness, please. That was an entity I attracted at the sacred mound today. She's a spirit child and quite ill-mannered. As I was saying..."

Eula scanned the other faces while the spiritualist spoke. She fixed her gaze on a New York banker, Autler Goldsmith, who was there with his wife for a second visit. His look caught Eula up short, especially the banker's reaction to the part about Adelaide's visitation from a spirit at the mound. Adelaide said:

"The spirit child appeared when I visited the mound today. She said her tribe had been lost from nine other tribes who were wandering endlessly, seeking the families from whom they were parted," Adelaide added, asking a plaintive question:

"The spirit child asked Mrs. Morely for help. Didn't she, Mrs. Morely?"

Of course, Eula hadn't expected the question and her reaction was close to cardiac arrest. She looked back at the penetrating eyes of the others in the room. Eula stammered through her stupor and before she could refute Adelaide, the savvy spiritualist spoke:

"Well, it was quite a shock, as you can see!" Adelaide went on as if Eula's oblivion was an affirmative. "The spirit was very small, so her essence was hard to read, but her vocal message was clearly for someone here. I couldn't get the name."

The spiritualist held her audience. Eula saw one woman was stuck in a bug-eyed stare; her husband held her hand in a clenched grasp while they hung on Adelaide's words:

"The message is about a stick that appeared before me. It is a hollowed branch with a name carved on it. At the sacred mound, the spirit said: 'Seek the scroll.'" Adelaide allowed a few practiced beats to pass before adding a smiling disclaimer: "Now let me say this dear friends: I don't know what it means, I'm just the messenger. If the message is for you, it mightn't make sense now, but it will later."

Autler Goldsmith, who had been shifting in his seat throughout Miss Coeur's talk, cleared his throat with great authority. Adjusting his weskit he stood, looked at Adelaide Coeur, and said:

"I believe that your message, Miss Coeur, is delivered to provoke and it has worked since I take great offense at your use of sacred Talmudic beliefs to perpetrate the fraud of spiritualism. I am a Jew and I find your reference to the Lost Tribes of Israel inappropriate."

Adelaide took the reprimand in stride: "Personally, good sir, I mean nothing offensive. My lips are given voice by forces stronger than each of us. Again, no offense meant. I am the messenger, the conduit if you will."

Goldsmith contained his anger before speaking: "Miss Coeur, I'll have you know that I come here to visit my brother who lives in a small cottage on a property down the lane from this one. He is a scholar of the Talmud who studies here in relative seclusion. I visit Ke'was End on a path of faith to honor him. I do not come here to be bamboozled by false prophets and do not care to hear any more of your preposterous notions."

The banker then addressed Eula: "Mrs. Morely, this is not a reflection on your hospitality. You and Mrs. Shellfoot hosted a fine mix of open-minded countrymen on our last visit, and that's why my wife and I felt comfortable to stay here again. Tonight, however, this false prophet has been allowed to spin unfounded ghost stories. It is important for me to add that I do not abide by all that Jews believe; however, I know this to be true: The Lost Tribes do not communicate through gentile spiritualists. Your perpetration here is a crime against the Lord himself. You are a fraud! You will not prey upon me and my family."

Mr. Goldsmith herded his flustered wife out the door, muttering about packing up and leaving on the next ferry. Eula ran after them, imploring Goldsmith to reconsider.

The remaining guests turned back to Adelaide who asked in a chirpy voice:

"Who'd like to take a sunset walk to tour the mound?" Hands slowly rose all around the parlor.

Realizing Eula was attending to the Goldsmiths, Nuna accompanied the group, reluctantly. When they came to the gravesite, Adelaide stopped and held them all in silence as they took in the glory the sun cast as it set. Just as the orb's light drew a natural aura around Adelaide, she whispered:

"Spirit is here. Can you hear her gentle call?"

Each person leaned slightly toward the indian mound seeking the sound of spirit beckoning softly.

"Who hears?" Adelaide asked.

The light threw a hazy dusk over the hillock as the cedars waved their feathery arms. Adelaide Coeur turned toward the group and, with her eyes closed and her strong hands reaching toward the sky, she asked again:

"Who hears?"

As the sun sank, the purple sky pulsed into night. Adelaide opened her eyes and looked straight into Nuna's:

"Who are you?" she said. "What is the name of the one spirit calls?"

Nuna Shellfoot held Adelaide's gaze, but Nuna didn't speak. This was not her story to tell, but there was a story among those here. Nuna could hear it stirring in the air, though spirit hadn't told it to her yet.

"Bring wisdom to those who've come to suck peace from the sea," Adelaide chortled.

A whispered plea echoed through the trees and rustled on falling leaves:

"Help them. Help them, Help them. Help them."

Nuna saw that Adelaide heard it. None of the others did. Just she and Adelaide.

***

70

As it turned out, the Goldsmiths could not leave the Captain's house that night for three reasons: Autler Goldsmith's brother could not accommodate them in his small cottage; Hector Wesley's taxi was not available immediately; and the ferry stopped running at 7 p.m.

Consequently, the Goldsmiths were doomed to await the morning ferry and remained at the Captain's house, requesting that dinner be sent to their suite.

Autler Goldsmith imbibed himself into an early bedtime which gave his wife, Leah, the opportunity to come down to the parlor for a séance, which another guest told Leah about upon meeting in the hall.

"A séance?" Leah whispered.

"Yes," the female guest replied as if she was out of breath. "We heard voices at the mound and Miss Coeur said at dinner that this old house is a prime place for a séance. We all agreed to give one a try. It's at 9 p.m. Maybe you could find a way downstairs?"

Autler was snoring in a deep sleep by 8:30. Leah saw her opportunity and took it.

Leah Goldsmith hoped to contact the spirit of her recently deceased mother. She followed the other guests into a dark room and sat at a round table covered in a heavy damask fabric. A low light glowed from gas lamps nearby. Leah saw Adelaide on her left and Nuna Shellfoot on her right. She felt a strange fear and heard whispers, one voice and then another.

"Lay your wrist on the open palm of your neighbor to the right and so on around the table," Adelaide said softly. She straightened her spine dramatically as if aligning every vertebrae while the circle joined hands as instructed. After inhaling three deep breaths, Adelaide opened her eyes and made contact with each person before she spoke:

"Being a medium for spirit is waring, and the ancients I transported here from the sacred indian mound are powerful and urgent souls. In fact, this transport has been especially exhausting, and quite honestly I have never been in the company of so many porous humans. Each of you has an aura that makes me quiver at the strange forces which brought us together to chan-

---

nel spirit this evening." Again, she closed her eyes and aligned her spine, speaking with a mix of chants, tongues, and loaded silences.

Ten minutes into this, the group turned its attention to Leah Goldsmith who had started mumbling like a person talking in a dream. They could make out one word that Leah said repeatedly: "Mother." Leah's fixed eyes streamed with tears.

Then the group heard Nuna telling Leah a spirit story. "Your mama say she lovin' you still, Missus and sum'ting 'bout a bebe ring, she say: 'De bebe's ring for her bebe.' Indeed she sayin' dat a bebe comes ta help you rest."

Leah Goldsmith heard what she came to hear. Not just her mother's voice, but the assurance that a child was coming. Leah looked at Nuna and saw truth in the brown woman's black eyes.

Mrs. Goldsmith quietly nodded to the others at the table. She stood, straightened her dress, and climbed the stairs. She opened the door to her husband's bedroom while unbuttoning her blouse and closed the door while discarding her skirts. She saw her husband awaken. Leah sensuously removed her linen underclothing, sidled up to Autler's prone body, and straddled the erection he had produced at the site of her bare skin.

When Leah Goldsmith first stood up to leave the séance, Adelaide Coeur had no trouble reading the look of complete faith on the woman's face.

The other guests stared at Nuna who bowed her head graciously and said: "I be turnin' in now," and excused herself from the table.

The guests looked to Eula and Adelaide and asked:

"Is it over?"

"What'd she go upstairs for?"

"Is Mrs. Shellfoot allowed to do that?"

"Was that it?"

Adelaide answered them: "We all can be conduits of spirit's message. Tonight, Mrs. Shellfoot spoke for the mother of Mrs. Goldsmith. These are wonders we behold, but can't explain. I hope to be scheduling many more séances and, perhaps other practitioners of the art of spiritualism at the Captain's Guest

House. A matter I will discuss further with our hosts. For now, goodnight."

***

The next afternoon, after Hector Wesley taxied the Goldsmiths to the ferry, Eula asked Henry Shellfoot to take her up to the west side office of *The Corycian Island Reader*. Eula put on her best dress, stashed the cash she had on loan from Adelaide Coeur in her purse, and climbed in to the wagon next to Henry.

"You sure looks pretty, Miss Eula," Henry said. "My Neeley was pretty your way. I do miss her since she gone. I never sleep wit' out her for 20 years till she die on me." He waited for Eula to settle in. "This horse be slow, so there be plenty of time for tellin' all 'bout that lady. When Nuna say someone a bazodee-head, there's a story comin' for sure."

They rode along while Eula framed her words.

"Well, Henry, that crazy lady, Adelaide, saw spirit."

"No way she did no how!" Henry replied. "Who she anyways?" They bounced along the shell road. Eula held on to her hat with one hand and the bench handle with the other, trying to survive the rickety ride. She looked over at Henry. White hair framed his dark, chocolate skin in a cloud of curls. Eula was thankful for his imposing height, his barrel chest, and his broad shoulders - all of which made Nuna and she feel less vulnerable living alone by the sea. If the women asked Henry why they glanced him from a window, roaming about at any hour of the night, he said: "I hears things when I goes to the mainland. This place ain't so safe in this day and time. All the peoples aren't so good likes you two."

Guiding the horse along Old Post Road, Henry asked: "So, is that Adelaide lady a gypsy or some such thing?"

"No, she's a Quaker, but also a spiritualist whose friends are all spiritualists too, as I understand it."

"You mean spirit-tellers?" Henry asked.

"Well, sort of, but the white man kind. Adelaide Coeur believes spirits contact the living, but to do it, she has people hold hands around a table while she goes into a trance. It's a little strange. She told me she talks to an 'infinite intelligence.' She called it discarnal or something like that. It all sounds the same with different words used for what Nuna says, but Nuna *is* spirit and this woman, well..."

"Hmmm," Henry said, "so how else it different from spirit-telling ?"

"Adelaide Coeur makes money doing it," Eula said.

Henry didn't reply at first. He gripped the horse's reins and steered the wagon on to Midway Road.

"That don't sound right, Miss Eula. What Nuna say about it?"

"Well..we... we need money to keep all the houses going, Henry. I'm just as surprised as you are, but Nuna seemed to go along. There's so much upkeep in our two places...you know that better than anyone. Anyway, we agreed this is the thing to do. So I'm going to buy newspaper advertisements to make it work. We're going to draw on the patronage of people interested in spiritualism."

"So we all be runnin' the guest house and such while the Coeur lady gets people to read palms and such?"

"Well, yes, but spiritualists known to Miss Coeur as decent people. We don't want to trick people. We'll run the guest house as we have been doing. We'll lease space to recommended practitioners and also earn part of their income. Nuna thinks Adelaide Coeur really did see spirit and some strange things happened at the séance last night."

"If you two says so," Henry said.

It felt surreal for Eula to be walking up the steps into the *Readers'* office in the "Heights," a hilly area of the island just up from the ferry slip. Eula knew the woman who sold the advertising and had already spoken to her on the telephone. She showed Eula the ad she had typeset, saying it would run in the Corycian paper as well as three other newspapers on the mainland after the *Reader* mailed them copy. It was one rate, an astounding cost Eula thought, but Adelaide Coeur had assured her that advertising was worth it.

Eula studied the bold-faced type on the proof copy:

***

Buston Bakker walked around the production boards reading the ads for errors as he did every Tuesday afternoon. The ad boxes were laid out first to determine the space available for copy. The summer issues held the best percentages of ads to text. This paper would be 36 pages in a five column broadsheet. There wasn't much new: The fish store that opened up in some Scaler's house every spring and closed in the fall and an ad for someone selling a chifforobe. There was one for Hector Wesley's irregular taxi service (flagged with a collection notice), Marcia Owen's produce stand, and Henry Shellfoot's store down at Ke'was End. The Westside Marina and the ferry, the Strand, and the Believers. had ads. Nothing new there. Then Burston saw the 4x4 ad for "The Captain's Guest House" and stopped abruptly.

"Clarence?" Burston called out to the front office, checking the time on his pocket watch. "Clarence?" his voice boomed. "Come in here a minute will you?"

Clarence McCarey was the managing editor of the *Reader*. He assigned stories, went to meetings, wrote copy, edited other's copy, fought with Bakker about copy, and laid out copy every week. He walked into the production room.

"Did you *see* this ad, Clarence?" Burston asked in a condescending tone, turning from the boards and looking down at Clarence McCarey.

"I did Mr. Bakker," Clarence said returning his boss's glare. "You weren't here when the ad came in, and I accepted it because you have said repeatedly that the *Reader* is here to bolster the Corycian Island economy."

"And don't I also say we're here to promote the island's self-image?" Burston deepened his voice to a low roar. "Now we're going to have the wackiest group you can find on this rock- and that's saying something - inviting people to 'eat the fruits of Mother Earth's glory'? What in God's name are they doing over there? Call that Morely woman up and give her the money back."

"Of course, Mr. Bakker, but you might want to know: Mrs. Morely bought a full season of 4x4 ads with the LI newspaper promotion."

"Hmmmmm. I see," the businessman said with an uptick in his mood. His barrel chest puffed out a bit while he waited for Clarence to say more, but Clarence rarely contributed much beyond the facts to any conversation. So Bakker complimented himself. "I knew that promotion had great potential. Didn't I say that when you argued with me, McCarey? I knew that it would work, didn't I now! Give people an inch and they'll want to buy a yard. That's what I said, at the time, and I was right!"

Burston was beaming, patting the Morely's ad, smoothing its glued sides more securely onto the board with a small roller. "And that's a good spot for it. Page three. Maybe I'm not giving these Ke'was people enough credit. This spiritualism wave is all the rage, I hear. Hell, we're in the news' business, McCarey. Go with it!"

Calliope Point and Ke'Was End
"We'd like our babies born here."

Pammy Bakker and Sissy Lawson, the inseparable McElroy sisters, planned simultaneous conceptions (of sons) to occur almost immediately after their nuptials. When neither of them conceived in a timely fashion, Sissy came up with a plan.

Pammy wasn't entirely enthusiastic about her younger sister's idea, mostly because it involved Nuna Shellfoot and Burston had a lot to say about "the Ke'was craziness."

"I don't care what you hear at the hotel, Sissy," Pammy said in response to her sister's suggestion. "Burston says they are frauds. Clarence McCarey went to some kind of mind reader down there. You know, to investigate for the newspaper. He said she must have been asking other people about him before she came in because he sat in a dark room for awhile all alone. He said that's how she got things right about his dead father."

"Nuna Shellfoot isn't a medium, Pammy. I told you that. She's a spirit-teller, they say. She doesn't take clients and only sells her herbs after you've tried them for free."

"I think it's just as strange to go to a - what'd you say she was again?"

Sissy was unpinning stiff cotton shirts from the clothesline out back. The fresh smell of the sea wafted from the woven fabric as she folded each item and placed it in the wicker basket on the grass. She paused mid-fold to answer Pammy:

"Well, the Scalers say she's a spirit-teller; she tells you what your spirit already knows and helps you hear it yourself. At least that's the way I understand it. She's one of the indigenous people of the island. Her skills go way back, Pammy. It's not like she only started doing this. She listens to spirit tell what's going on with you if you tell her what to ask. And she makes these herbal potions that the girls at the hotel say help get babies made."

Pammy Bakker frowned: "Spirits? Since when is Miss-who needs-religion talking about spirits? Are you out of your mind, Sissy?"

"No, Pammy, and it's not about religion. Besides, I'm not fool enough to think that allowing nature to take its course will produce boys. This woman is really supposed to have talents."

Pammy was so much more practical than Sissy, but she needed to be pregnant sooner than later. She was closer to 30 than she liked to admit.

"Ok, Sissy," Pammy said. "I'll go over to the Shellfoot place with you, but I'm not making any promises."

"It will be a delightful outing," Sissy said. "I'll make sure Tommy leaves the Rambler for me. There's a wonderful old cemetery on the east side and the Shellfoots sell fish and produce that Tommy's chef buys for the hotel kitchen."

The sisters pulled up to Nuna's cottage off the shell road. Nuna was tending her herb garden with her daughter at her side. Bay stood straight up at the sound of the car's wheels crunching the oyster shells and bouncing in the pot holes.

When Pammy saw the girl stand, she asked Sissy:

"Who is that child?"

"That's Nuna's daughter. Her name is Bay. The one on the right is Nuna. They're beautiful, aren't they?"

"Why she's not an old lady at all! I just imagined a crone, you know? My word, Sissy they're remarkable."

Bay looked back at them, shielding her eyes from the sun. She was 9 years old; lithe with brown hair, streaked from the sun and tied with string at the nape of her neck. Bay's scrawny, sun-bronzed arms and legs stuck out from a pinafore worn over a long gingham dress.

Nuna had a floral bandana wrapped around her hair and twisted securely at the crown of her head. Her face glistened with sweat that she mopped with a handkerchief pulled from the puffy sleeves of a simple, blue shirtwaist. Nuna leaned on the hoe she was using and asked Bay:

"Who be dem?"

Wet curls had sprung from Bay's head and circled her face.

"Two ladies. That car is from the Strand. Mr. Lawson comes in it when he picks up fish at Henry's."

"Not summa folk?"

"No that's the Strand's car for sure," Bay said. "I never have seen a lady driving a car before, have you Mama?"

"Bay, I only be gettin' used ta autos, at-all, at-all," Nuna laughed, hugging her daughter into her. "Let's see who d'ese ladies be."

Sissy, who wore an a-line riding skirt, got out of the car with ease while her sister struggled with the many folds of her voluminous skirts. Squaring her shoulders, Sissy waved, and walked forward. Upon reaching Nuna, she extended her hand:

"Sissy Lawson here from over at the Point. That's my sister Pammy Bakker coming up behind me. I've heard a good deal about you, Miss Shellfoot."

"What dat you hear'd?" Nuna said, with one eyebrow raised while accepting Sissy's fingertips and squeezing them in greeting.

"Well, I'm interested in herbal medicines and treatments, especially for women. My husband Tommy Lawson manages The

Strand Hotel and some of the people who work there marvel at your skills and I - we - have come on their recommendations."

Nuna waited to hear more. Sissy continued, nervously.

"Uh, well, let's see, there's uh, a young telephone operator whose menstrual cramps you helped and a maid who said she was having trouble conceiving before...uh...you...uh... and another maid at the hotel told me your herbs gave her a girl after she had four boys."

Sissy feared another exchange with the dark eyes of Nuna, so she looked back at Pammy who was standing stock-still 20 feet away. Sissy motioned sternly for her sister to move.

"Dey be Scaler ladies," Nuna said, indifferently.

Sensing Sissy's discomfort, Bay said:

"Mama still talks in the old Bim way."

"Yes, well, she can understand me, right?" Sissy asked, noting a disdainful frown on Nuna's brow, but plowing ahead without thinking, and appearing to talk to Bay:

"As you may know Mr. Bakker and my husband, Mr. Lawson, were born on the island," Sissy replied, and then regaining her focus, she nodded and said to Nuna "... and we'd like our babies born here, too." Sissy smiled, but Nuna said nothing.

Awkwardly, Sissy added: "You know Miss Shellfoot, my sister and I are great admirers of women. We are suffragists, dear friends of Carrie Catt." Sissy realized Nuna was looking at Pammy. "I..well...I'm talking too much. Could we do this inside or in the shade? My sister doesn't care for the sun."

Nuna led them to handmade twig chairs sitting under the arms of a gnarly old tree. Pammy chose to sit on a swing five feet away, as if merely attending her sister's mission and not participating in its delicate nature.

Bay and Nuna sat on a stone bench. Sissy cleared her throat into the silence and said:

"It's lovely here. A lovely spot."

Nuna replied:

"How you do sex with your man?"

Sissy snapped her head from Nuna to Bay who had no reaction whatsoever. Sissy looked back at Nuna who waited for her answer:

"Uh...we...how do I..I...," Sissy stuttered. "Well, we're still enjoying each other frequently....uh..let's say two or three times a week."

"How?" Nuna persisted, which made Sissy blush.

"Well...we...I'm not sure I understand your question, Miss Shellfoot?"

"Who be on top?" Nuna asked without the slightest hint of embarrassment.

"Uh...Mr. Lawson is, of course. That's how it's done...uh... right?"

Sissy looked over at Pammy who was leaning forward on the swing to make sure she heard every word.

Nuna said: "Dey's lotsa ways. And you wants boys? You sure 'bout dat? Boys be gone soon from mamas don't ya know," Nuna cautioned.

"Our men want boys," Sissy said. "Boys first, then we can work on all the girls to be had," Sissy laughed.

Nuna shrugged: "Ok. Let's see what's what. You stay here, Miss Suff'rage," Nuna laughed. " Weed wit' Bay. She shows you how." Nuna smiled good-naturedly and looked over at Pammy who stood as soon as their eyes met. "And you comes mix up summa my herbs wit' me," Nuna ordered.

Pammy followed Nuna through the white front door into a small parlor with a wood stove at its center and open to the kitchen beyond. The house smelled like baked apples. There were two bedrooms adjacent to the parlor with what Nuna called her "keeping room" beyond them, off the kitchen.

When Nuna opened the door to the keeping room, Pammy's senses were overwhelmed by the herbal bouquet wafting from its core. Lavender, rosemary, and citrus peels were drying by sunfilled windows.

Nuna halted Pammy with her hand and motioned for her to breathe in deeply:

"Slow, Mrs. Take a deep breat'," Nuna said, touching Pammy's shoulder softly and sending a charge through her with each breath they inhaled together. When Pammy's breathing became even and relaxed, Nuna took her by the hand and walked her through a door that led to a screened porch behind the house.

The fresh air hit Pammy smack in the face. She started to laugh, but tears were rolling from her eyes.

"I don't know what happened to me back there when you were talking to Sissy, Miss Shellfoot...I feel so idiotic..."

"Let it be. We on de right side now. I sees you knows dey be ways to do sex when mens don't gets on top."

The two women laughed and Pammy paused again to note this wise woman was about her age, maybe a bit older, her mid-30s or so. Pammy said:

"Yes, that's right. Mr. Bakker and I really enjoy our times of intercourse; but I worry it's keeping me from having babies. You know, it's not all about procreation, it's..well..it feels so good!"

With that admission, Pammy burst into sobs.

"Now, now," Nuna pressed Pammy's shoulder again. "Dat be helpin' more den any'ting, don't ya know. De tears just be washin' de clouds away. Sh, now. Shhhh, now. Shhhhh.

"Dat be lovin' you doin. Dat why it be feelin' good. When you be happy, spirit be happy, too. You sits here and t'ink about dat. I goin' to mix up sum'tings."

When Nuna returned, she was holding several muslin bags. She sat across from Pammy and handed each over with instructions.

"Dis one be pep'mint and dis be red clovah," she said. "Mix dem to get mens jac up. Den when teasin' goes by and by, summa dis red clovah goes on his don't ya know. Just sprinkles it from a shaker."

Pammy accepted each parcel, listening intently to what Nuna said:

"Ok, den. So afta jac-jac..." Nuna stopped to make sure Pammy understood. "Jac-jac?" Pammy nodded and Nuna smiled. "After jac-jac, send bebe seeds to spirit." Nuna went on to tell Pammy that it was necessary for the women to put their feet up against the wall and raise their hips to spirit. "Get on it after, right soon," Nuna said, adding that if the women could get the men to assume the same position up against the wall, it may afford the opportunity for more spirit seeds to be sown.

Pammy emerged from the front door. She and Nuna were laughing. Sissy and Bay, hearing them, turned from their places, sitting on the grass next to a long row of herbs. They were pulling weeds and laughing as well.

Bay jumped up and said:

"Mama, Miss Sissy knows Mrs. Stoli, the school principal's wife. You know, the lady who works in the school office? They're friends! Isn't that so keen?

Sissy stood, brushed off her skirt, and said: "Keen is it? Well, in spite of your slang, young lady, and your mama's 'Bim,' I believe I understand how to weed." Sissy looked over at a smiling Pammy who had linked arms with Nuna Shellfoot.

"What just happened in there?" Sissy whispered to her new friend, Bay.

"Mama happened," Bay replied. "Mama's a spirit-teller."

As the sisters walked toward Sissy's car, Nuna called after them: "Comes ta see us some new time, but wait tills you carries de bebe seeds in you."

"I'll say hello to Mrs. Stoli for you," Bay hollered, as Sissy navigated the car back on to the shell road. "They sure are pretty, those two," Bay said to her mother as the car drove away. "I know that pretty is everywhere if we look for it, Mama. Grandpa's sayings have made their way to me," Bay laughed, putting her arm through Nuna's with a hug. "But those ladies are pretty in a modern way, you know? Like they were pretty to start out with and then they dressed themselves in more prettiness. Oh, I don't know. It's just different. That's all. There are mothers at school who look like them, not many, but a few."

"Dat Missus Stoli a pretty one, too, like dem. I knows. She come to Henry's store all time. She pretty just like dey is. You like dem braids summa dem girls gots? Let's do summa dem braids like dat for you."

While Bay sat on a stone beneath a hickory tree, Nuna braided her curly hair, combing it through her fingers and twisting it into long spirals. Nuna thought of Bay's father, so long gone yet at the tip of her very fingers. Ahane's hair was Bay's hair, too.

"You still miss Papa, don't you Mama?" Bay asked, feeling the longing in her mother's touch.

"I disn't get tole a story about how to stop missin' someone," Nuna said, pausing. "But the tellin' be here. You faduh be in you, little one. He love us two so good, it be everywhere in us. Down deep."

Nuna felt the clench in her heart that came with the sense of Ahane's spirit. It was a pleasant pain, gone before she could wrap herself in the joy of it.

1905

Calliope Point
"Find out what's going on in your personal paradise."

Pammy Bakker may have been shy about the public acknowledgement of her sex life, but like any naughty Victorian, she knew her way around a bedroom. Burston was delighted with the cannabis tea and was startled, to say the least, by its arousing effects which his lovely wife enhanced with God-knows-what she had in her hands. He followed Pammy to the wall and raised his hips as she did after he came, they laughed till they cried and fell into each other's arms again and again.

"Spirit bebe seeds and then some!" Pammy thought as she gazed at the ceiling after Burston had rolled over into a sublime sleep.

Nonetheless, it was Sissy's belly that bloomed with a child who kicked, turned, and beat his fists within it, while Pammy's womb remained uninhabited.

Pammy returned to Nuna's by herself without even telling Sissy. Nuna dispensed different herbs and Pammy made love to Burston with more ardency than she ever had, but her bebe seeds wouldn't grow and a hard stone started to stick in her chest whenever she saw Sissy who was flowering in pregnancy.

Sissy felt her sister's emptiness and sought a way to fill it. She told Pammy about a plan she had to provide a mother's care center at the Strand. Sissy said:

"So many of the women who work at the hotel are new mothers. Sometimes I think Tommy understands when I tell him about the value of these children getting their mother's milk and comfort in the first year of life. Offering them a place at the hotel so the children can thrive will allow their mothers to work even more industriously at their jobs. Most of these babies spend the day with people ill-equipped to care for them, like other children or elderly relatives. Constable Ratliss told me terrible accidents happen - you know, burns and broken bones. One toddler was playing with a fish hook. Oh God, I can't even imagine it, Pammy. The Constable told me the baby was being cared for by a seven-year-old all day."

Sissy let these images sink in. "You could help me get the Strand center open, Pammy. It's a place to start. Then we can go to the churches and other places, using the Strand as the model. If Burston backed it - well, maybe even put some money behind the idea - Tommy would be more likely to give in."

Pammy laughed. "Burston is the first one to say these Scaler woman drop babies like rabbits, only they expect everyone else to take care of them. You've heard him. He's not exactly a do-gooder."

After Pammy left Sissy's, the picture of a baby playing with a fish hook wouldn't leave her mind. When she mentioned the care center to Burston however, his reaction was typical:

"The men who fathered these children need to work a bit harder so their mothers can stay home with them. That's what's wrong with this idea, Pamela. We're making it too easy for the fathers to be lazy...make that: too easy for them to be lazier."

Pammy said: "You don't know anything about how hard some of these families work to feed themselves and keep warm, Burston Bakker. Get off your high-perch in that newsroom and find out what's going on in your personal paradise. Children come to the island school with lice, rickets, and wracking coughs. They're hungry, tired, and lonely. We could do something to ward that off early on. The Strand's center is just a starting place, Burston. Sissy and I hope to take this kind of care further for the children who will grow up beside our children."

"Humph," Burston said, with an air of superiority that made Pammy's spine crawl. "So this is what you're going to do if you don't get your own baby, Pammy. This is how you're going to take control of it?"

They exchanged a look that hadn't passed between them before. Burston averted first, saying gruffly: "I've spoken the last word on it, Pamela."

Pammy left the house and walked down the grass hill above the harbor to Sissy's. Moored below her, the Lawson's catboat glistened with class next to sleeker boats, all belonging to the male residents of Calliope Point. For some reason the sight infuriated Pammy even more. It emphasized Burston's sense of male entitlement. She said aloud:

"We've got our own money, Mr. I-Control-Everything! The hell with your last word on it."

By the time Pammy arrived at Sissy's door, she was on a crusade.

She walked into Sissy's kitchen talking:

"Here's what we can do, Sissy. We'll lease one of the conference rooms near the back of the hotel. You've got to pick one that has windows and good light. We can call for a reservation and fake the name of a company that's using it. The maids can sneak us a few of the cribs you provide guests. Didn't you say there were still a bunch in storage..."

Sissy derailed her sister's excitement:

"Hold on, there. Tommy knows everything that's going on in his hotel, Pammy."

"Then...uh...well, then..we'll tell him. We'll lease the space in the name of Women for the Mothers of Corycian Island, a group you and I are going to form and fund with Grandma's inheritance. Agreed?"

"Absolutely! What a great idea." Sissy gleamed with pride. "You know if there's one woman who would appreciate this it's Grandma O'Neill." Sissy raised an imaginary glass: " To Maureen O'Neill!"

"And to Nuna Shellfoot," Pammy said, surprising Sissy, who waited for her to explain.

"I'm going to ask her to come to the first meeting we have with the mothers," Pammy said. "I've gotten to know Nuna Shellfoot. She's a good woman, Sissy. She's so caring and has a way about her that will bridge the gap between us and some of the mothers." Pammy stopped when she saw Sissy looking at her. "Well, I've gone over there myself a few times. We're, that is, Burston and I are quite fond of Miss Nuna's teas," she smiled sheepishly.

"Go on," Sissy said.

"I've gotten to know her, that's all and I've talked to other women around the island. They trust the people at Ke'was End. I'm not sure their husbands do, but we don't care about them. I think it's a good time to nurture a new generation. Mothers never have trouble helping each other and Nuna's poultices and herbal teas can help with their minor ailments. Too many babies die on this island from easily corrected problems...." Pammy's voice caught and tears rolled down her cheeks: "Burston says I'm doing this because I can't have my own babies."

Sissy reached out and drew her sister as close as Sissy's big belly would allow, holding on until she knew Pammy could feel all three hearts beating in rhythm:

"We're going to have *this* baby first, Pammy. We'll learn how to be mothers together, and then we'll be perfect at it when your baby comes."

Sissy gently pushed her sister away and smiled into her eyes: "Hope you're busy planting 'dem bebe seeds'."

Sirens' Beach and the Town Center
The Keyclose Clan

Hector Wesley asserted himself with Josiah Remie by coming up with a plan to really scare the "whores at Sirens'Beach," as Hector insisted on referring to the nuns at Màthair.

It was one of those moonlit nights when Ruth Remie saw Josiah sneak out of the house. She had gotten up because their baby, Inri, was fussy. While trying to comfort him, Ruth looked out the window. She saw Josiah slink away into the woods wearing his Jesus-robe and carrying his jug.

"What is that man up to," Ruth wondered, with chills tingling in her spine.

She couldn't have imagined.

When Josiah met up with Hector Wesley he said: "Let's stop here for a refresher." There was a goat pasture off the road to the right. Hector agreed: "We still got another half mile before we get to the whore house, and I wanna hear 'bout that Wer-ster man again."

"Woo-ster," Josiah corrected. "He was from a Massachusetts place called that. Ok, we'll sit just for a minute. I could use me a sip."

Josiah took a long swallow and handed the jug to Hector, who was glad to unload the paint and the mallet he brought along for the mission. Hector drank while Josiah talked:

"Yeah, so this Woo-ster man comes with a whole group and they stays at the camp for two weeks. Never had a group stay that long, but they comes across from the mainland over to here because they been to the Believers' place up around there on that Cape and heard about us," Josiah accepted the moonshine back from Hector and continued: "So this guy tells me about a group called the Keyclose Clan. They go around and scare people in Wooster who don't abide by the code, don't ya know, like the.... uh...well...the guy said...code...uh..."

Josiah struggled to identify exactly what that was when Hector Wesley broke in: "You mean like those women over there living like whores together? Bullcrappy they'se nuns," Hector said. "I mean, who asked the Cath'licks to come here with all their mumbo jumbo anyways. That's breakin' a code, and that's why we're goin' for the statue they put up out by the water. I have this plan here."

Hector tried to show Josiah his home-drawn map. Josiah snatched the paper with a move so swift, it startled a nearby goat whose loud bleat made Josiah jump. Collecting himself, Josiah said: "Well, it's my plan now, ya hear? We're goin' for the statue, but we're doin' it the way I say."

***

Mother Superior Augustus called the police station just after sunrise to report the damage done to the Blessed Virgin of the Seas.

Ratliss ran downstairs from his apartment and picked up the telephone in the police station on the tenth ring.

"The Virgin of the Seas has been decapitated and defiled," Mother Augustus stated firmly into the Constable's ear.

Ratliss got to the scene within 30 minutes. The statue had been knocked hard enough to have its support rod bent sideways at an angle to the pedestal. Another blast had sent her head to the ground below, and, the...well, Mother Augustus couldn't say it, but Ratliss wrote it in his report:

"The breast area was painted with red nipples. At a point where the statue's legs supposedly meet, black lines of an inappropriate and sexual nature appear to have been painted in a triangle. The letters 'hoer' appear on the out-stretched left hand of the statue."

As Ratliss took notes, Mother Augustus stood ramrod straight with her arms tucked into the sleeves of her brown serge habit and her jowls spilling over her taught linen collar.

"Have you any idea who is responsible for this desecration, Constable Ratliss?" the nun inquired. "One might assume it's the same oafs who play with manure?"

"That sounds about right, Sister," Ratliss replied.

"Mother," the nun corrected, tersely.

"Oh, yes, excuse me, Mother....errr...excuse me Mother Superior Augustus."

"Just 'Mother' will suffice."

Ratliss was happy to be driving away from the convent. He did not like calling that woman "Mother." The whole mother, brother, sister, father thing with the Catholics annoyed him. What amazed Ratliss was the attitude of expectancy for one who was not Catholic to call someone else "Mother" or "Father." He'd never had to address a nun or priest before the Catholics bought the property at Sirens' Beach. Now it irked him personally, but he knew a law had been broken and Hansen Ratliss served the island population without bias.

When the constable returned to his office he found Burston Bakker waiting for him with his reporter pad in hand.

"I heard about the desecration at the convent from the caretaker, Hansen. He works over at my place, too. So what's the story?" the newspaper man asked.

"Here are the notes for the files," Ratliss said, handing over the pages on which he'd jotted down the facts.

The *Reader* was the town-designated newspaper, an official sanction which allowed Bakker access, by law, to police records. "You won't report all those details, of course. People would think we have a maniac in our midst." Ratliss waited for Bakker to read the report, then said: "What do you make of it?"

"Honestly? I don't know what to think. The things these fellows do are so childish. They have to be locals because the incidents happen well after the ferry's down. You know as well as I do there's a bunch of ne'er-do-wells in this town. How do you want to handle it?" Bakker asked.

"Could you bury it until I have a better bead drawn on the guys I'm watching?"

THE CORYCIAN ISLAND READER
Thursday April 13, 1905
The Police Blotter
(cont'd from page 7)

Residents of Sirens' Beach reported a disturbance early Tuesday morning. Constable Ratliss discovered damaged property, upon responding to the call. A full investigation is underway. A Pipers' Cove man ran his car aground while driving in the rain last Monday. Good samaritans helped set the car and driver back on their way along Old Post Road.

An eight-point buck frightened a local woman enough to prompt a call to the police. The woman, who was attempting to scare a raccoon from her trash can, came face to rack with the buck."It was the ugliest creature I ever saw," the woman said. There has been no comment from the buck.

The Strand Hotel
"A spiritual connection with the earth."

Tommy Lawson agreed to lease Pammy and Sissy a large room with windows that was off the Strand hotel's kitchen and had been a linen closet and ironing room. The room was just large enough for Burston to fill with a smug attitude when he saw it:

"Throwing good money after bad," Burston said.

Pammy was having a hard time liking Burston these days. First of all, he was drinking heavily. It seemed to come in cycles. Lately, the two cocktails before supper had become four for him and, with each stiff drink, he became more bitter. Pammy had tried to speak to Burston about it without getting into an argument. But Burston drew a line at the topic. What he drank was not her business, he said. Some resentment was building up in him. Pammy could feel it in the deep, harsh thrusts of his love-making.

"What's bothering you?" Pammy asked Burston after an angry coupling during which Burston accommodated his needs with no regard to her own.

But Burston only caught his heaving breath, rested his forearm over his eyes, and began to snore.

***

Tommy had granted Sissy's every request. He'd had the room painted, ordered new shades for the windows, had several cribs brought in, and sent for his custodian to set up the other furniture purchased with money from Grandma O'Neill's bequest.

May 2, 1905 at 7 p.m. when the new hotel crew finished their first day of training for the upcoming season, mothers of nursing infants were invited to the new Mothers' Care Center. The women, four of them, walked around the cheerful room, noting the line of white rocking chairs, the bathinnettes, changing tables, toys, cribs and other amenities, the likes of which none had ever enjoyed for their children.

Pammy welcomed them, introducing herself and Sissy, as well as Nuna about whom she said:

"We have invited our neighbor from Ke'was End because of Miss Shellfoot's vast knowledge of home remedies for the needs of women. My sister and I have partaken of Miss Nuna's products with great success. We know it is difficult to get to her at Ke'was End, so we've brought her to you. Please feel free to chat with any of us while you look around. We'll show you how to use the bathinettes and what we have planned for the diaper area. We have designed the room for newborns but we will adapt it as their needs change. We want you to go to your jobs in the hotel worry free, coming to nurse your babies on a schedule."

The women seemed confused at first as they sat in the rockers and lifted the small hoses of the bathing tables. One mother found her way to Nuna. Pammy noticed them sitting in a private spot where the woman was baring her breast to show Nuna a scabby, engorged nipple. Pammy made a mental note to order privacy screens and to keep some of Nuna's poultices on hand for just such conditions.

Pammy turned to see Sissy chatting with a woman who was touching and cooing at Sissy's pregnant belly, saying she was sure it was boy from the way Sissy's navel protruded. Pammy walked up to them, reaching her hand out to say hello, only to hear the question that pained her the most:

"And you, Mrs. Bakker, do you have children?"

"I do not," Pammy said with a forced smile. "But Miss Nuna assures me I will."

In all, it was a great success. Sissy took pertinent information from each mother about their babies and their work schedules. She told them someone would always be available in the nursery because there were several community volunteers: Mrs. Stoli, the principal's wife; Eula Morely from Ke'was End, and others. "I will put a schedule together from the information you gave me today and post it on the door so you know who will be in the nursery and when. Miss Nuna will always be here on Wednesdays, available to you whether you're working that day or not. We haven't gotten a telephone wired up to this room yet, but that's coming. Please, we are here for you so don't hesitate to let us help you. We're all pioneers in this, but we can do it together, and hopefully be the seeds of a program that will help all Corycian mothers."

The women enjoyed tea breads Eula Morely had sent along with Nuna for the occasion, and sipped coffee while growing comfortable in the space. Sissy glanced at Pammy and they held each other in a long look of satisfaction.

Before Nuna left, she said to the sisters: "Great spirit be a mad-uh. She feed us; we feed dem. 'Round and 'round. Dat's de way. You helps dem, don't ya know, so you helps alla us, all-a-wanna."

***

One month later, as easily as she did everything else in Pammy's eyes, Sissy gave birth to Samuel Thomas Lawson.

A few weeks after the boy's birth, Sissy and Tommy showed little Sam off to friends and family who had gathered on the green lawn overlooking Union Harbor behind the Lawsons' sprawling clapboard house. The day sparkled in the calm pools of a blue bay dotted with white vessels and prisms of sunlight. A buoy bell clanged in the distance.

Sissy wore a shirtwaist of soft, peach organdy. Tiny buttons lined its bodice with thin pleats on either side. The fabric fell from Sissy's already narrow waist into a gathered skirt. Her hair was held back from her face with a length of peach ribbon. The new mother held her son in her arms. Her dress swayed while she rocked him.

The baby's little hand reached up to stroke his mother's face.

Sissy's older sister took it all in. "She's a damn Madonna in the flesh," Pammy thought, hating herself. She turned away and walked over to Burston. He was pontificating about something to her uncle, Conor McElroy, who claimed he'd come from

Manhattan to represent his brother, the father who had spurned his daughters.

"He's a stubborn man," admitted Uncle Conor who had given the women in marriage when his brother would not. "If Sissy would agree to baptize the boy in the Catholic church, all would be forgiven." Conor stepped back to let Pammy join the conversation. He finished his part with:"But you know these girls, Burston. Both of them, since they were little tots have had minds of their own." Uncle Conor laughed and clinked highball glasses with Burston who said:

"The way I've heard it, dearly departed Grandma O'Neill is the one responsible for all their suffragette business. Do you know what your nieces are up to at the Strand? Tell your uncle, Pamela. Tell him how you're saving the street rats of Corycian Island."

"You tell him, Burston. You only believe your story anyway," Pammy said, leaving to walk toward the house, then running up the broad white steps to the rear porch, and bumping into Nuna at the top.

"I jus' be takin' in a bit a shade up here," Nuna said, seeing the tears in Pammy's eyes. "Let dat sad come now," she patted Pammy into a soft embrace."Wash dat hurt outta you. Shhhh. Bebes be comin' for you. I sees bebes. Dey be here soon."

Pammy composed herself and turned, leaning forward with her hands on the porch railing: "Burston seems so weak to me, Nuna. Maybe I chose the wrong father. Something's changed in him or is it me? Am I just a barren old bitch to him now?" Her body heaved while emptying a load of stored up sadness. Pammy sat down in a wicker chair and allowed herself to cry. She tried to explain."I thought falling in love was easy, so marriage was easy, and becoming a mother just happened. I took it all for granted and went off on some crusade about being a liberated woman."

Nuna sat next to her and listened. She took Pammy's hand and nestled it in her own on the lap of her white muslin skirt. Nuna heard Pammy's spirit story.

"I'm not a liberated anything, Nuna. The 'new woman of the new century' I speak about isn't me. Inside, I just want a happy

SUZANNE MCLAIN ROSENWASSER

home. A happy family. The truth is: My husband is turning into a drunk and I'm just a nag."

"You no such t'ing," Nuna said, crossly. "I sees you. I sees who you be."

"You don't see me when I'm picking at Burston until he has to drown himself in drink to shut me out."

"If dat man be doin' what you say, it be him doin' it *to* hisself *because* a hisself. No two ways 'bout it."

Pammy had calmed down. She spoke softly. "I married Burston because I thought he could give me everything I wanted, but when I'm left alone with him in our home, I feel as if he provides nothing." Pammy put her head in her hands. "Oh, Nuna, I'm such a fraud. I have the nerve to talk to other women about liberating themselves while I'm the one who is waiting for her man to save her."

"None 'a us is free, Pammy. We all gots t'ings dat twist and pain us."

"Even you, Nuna? You seem to know how to hold on."

"Maduh Eart' be keepin' me up. Same maduh be keepin' at you."

***

Later on, Sissy held the crook of Tommy's arm which cradled their bundled baby. They stood at a loamy place on the dunes where they had buried the child's placenta, its life-source. Tommy turned to look at the assemblage. He became emotional, cleared his throat, and spoke:

"This was Sissy's idea. My beautiful wife did a bit of research and discovered that it is a custom of local indian tribes to bury a child's placenta in the earth upon which he was born. To mark the spot and to bind the child to his homeland, a tree is planted there. I look around at the many magnificent trees of our home and wonder about the mighty men and women who grew alongside them. May our little Sam join their glory."

Handing the baby to Sissy, Tommy placed a young maple sapling on the mound of dirt that covered the placenta. He spread the roots and covered them with dirt until the tree stood on its own. Tommy spoke again: "So we place little Samuel's tree of life, which kept him nourished inside his mother, back into the womb of Mother Earth." Tommy cleared his throat of emotion and went on. "Sissy and I also want to acknowledge Mrs. Shellfoot who is here because she has a stake in this little boy of ours and even deeper roots to this island. We can't think of a more appropriate person to honor as we celebrate. Thank you Miss Nuna, from the bottom of our hearts. I'd like to add: now as we have the joy of holding Sam's life in our arms, I know why helping the mothers of Corycian Island was so important to Sissy and Pammy. So thank you to them - and to Grandma O'Neill for making sure all Corycian babies have a healthy start."

As Tommy spoke, Nuna reached for Pammy's hand and held her fingertips till a soft charge passed through them. Pammy turned to her right and looked at Burston. Her husband's eyes were downcast, and when he glanced back at her, she saw those blue eyes ask for her forgiveness.

Later that night when Pammy and Burston were alone in their bedroom where the charge from Nuna's fingertips had sent them, Burston said: "I can be a cussed fool, Pamela."

This admission didn't come as news to Pammy. She'd heard it before. It was Burston the Penitent who spoke, another of her husband's personalities. Burston the Penitent loved Pammy with his whole heart and his simmering loins. He brought her to orgiastic ecstasy and felt himself cleansed by the power of his ejaculation. Burston the Penitent fell into a baby's sleep after their love-making, still ignoring Pammy's question:

"What's troubling you, Burston?"

Burston the Penitent just couldn't admit that he felt small. He couldn't tell Pammy that he'd become the tiny man he always feared his father was, living in a tiny place, running a tiny excuse for a newspaper. He couldn't tell her about the hole that gnawed at his insides every morning. He couldn't tell her about the anonymous letters he'd started receiving from some islander accusing him of just those things, writing that Burston's editorials lacked courage, saying they revealed Burston's small mindedness and his desire to be a big fish in a little pond.

Burston knew critical letters were part of the business and they'd bounced off him before; they'd even been a source of humor between Clarence and him.

But these particular letters Burston kept to himself. They were written on fine vellum with a prep school penmanship that struck Burston's rawest nerve. The letters usually arrived on Fridays after the Thursday publication of the paper. The last one accused Burton of buying the town's affection by secretly subsidizing a center at the Strand Hotel "for women too weak to care for their own." The letter writer ended with the snub:

"You are the smallest of men. One who buys a voice in his little town to be heard, then says little or nothing that matters."

Burston shuddered with worry about the truth in these missives. He was afraid of taking positions on town issues in print and it showed. He avoided confrontation because he couldn't bite the hands of the advertisers who fed the newspaper. Looking through the archives, Burston saw that his father achieved some delicate balance he couldn't attain. The letter writer said it was because Burston's father "was not a little man."

Burston couldn't tell Pammy that alcohol made him feel bigger, like he was in control, and like he mattered. He couldn't tell Pammy any of these things because he was afraid she already knew them.

1906

Ke'was End
"Our daughta be de color of autumn."

Closing the front door behind her, Eula Morely listened to the quiet of the foyer and drew upon the peace in the shafts of light cast through the jingle shells of the window. Eula took a deep breath and relaxed before reaching up to refasten the twist of her hair. Smoothing the flat panel of her dress bodice, she walked to the kitchen where Nuna was turning up the gas under a kettle of nearly boiling water. Eula opened a drawer and removed a fresh, white apron. She shook it out and said while putting it on:

"I know Adelaide Coeur brings us business, but she wears me out when she comes here. It relieves me so when she goes back home. And I know I'm not the only one who feels this way. Am I right, Nuna?"

"I be holdin' my tongue when dat womens 'round, and I best be holdin' it whens she gone. She wear spirit out, dat one!"

They both knew Adelaide's recommendations had provided them with a full house that summer. And what a full house it was.

A completely tattooed, weightlifter from Appalachia, of mixed Native American and Asian heritage, took over a suite. He practiced the Japanese tradition of Reiki healing on a bed of smooth, crushed crystals handed down from his maternal ancestors.

Another of Adelaide's referrals took the suite next to the Reiki healer. She was a Bohemian lady from Brooklyn who read tarot cards. It turned out this practice was so popular, word of the tarot reader reached the mainland. Henry had to rope off a field to accommodate the increasing number of automobiles and wagons arriving daily.

The tarot card reader encouraged Eula and Nuna to lease rooms to her brother, a medium.

By the end of July, the Captain's house was rented out and earned steady money. The spiritualists were perfectly happy to have kitchen privileges and to take on jobs around the small farm. Things were running so smoothly that even Nuna began to doubt her intuition the year before about trouble coming their way.

Adelaide Coeur sent customers as well as prospective tenants with letters of introduction through the end of August. An old woman took Nuna's smallest cabin in front of Henry's Fish and Produce Store for three weeks. She was a palm reader, one Adelaide introduced as the "Toast of Lily Dale," due to her profound ability to offer a vocal link between herself and spirit.

The woman's name was "Schultzie," Schultzie Farnsworth, a name she refused to explain, saying: "I'm an old woman who is done explaining myself!" This was followed by a hearty laugh.

Schultzie was a delight, holding guests in her spell while she told wonderful stories in the parlor where the Captain's guests were invited to gather for an afternoon sherry or tea.

As for Schultzie's palm reading skills, well, the gravelly voiced, husky, black woman drew regular complaints from clients. The people stormed from sessions complaining that Schultzie had fallen asleep during a trance and was snoring like a bull to prove it. However the more transcendent clients, those who believed this was indeed Schultzie's method, were satisfied. They discovered that upon awakening, the medium traced paths in their "palm stories" from her "spirit dreams" which only the client could have known.

Once Schultzie told a young man his mother had made her sit down and sing "Calling To Her Boy Just Once Again" during a dream. The client began to weep. That was a song his mother sang to him. He said he heard the melody while Schultzie was entranced.

News of successful encounters with the great beyond spread quickly during these spiritualist-fueled times and even the Strand began to transport people, upon request, to and from sessions at the Captain's house.

The business was a financial windfall. Practitioners of the spiritual arts leased rooms for a minimum of two weeks, agreeing to pay an additional 20 percent of the fees they earned from clients. Nuna and Eula kept a strict accounting of the arriving clientele.

These details were in compliance with the agreement laid out by Adelaide Coeur who came to Ke'was End to collect her ten percent share every four weeks in season. While there, sleeping on a cot off the kitchen, Adelaide held séances in the front parlor for clients and began to lead walks to, what all visitors now called, "The Mound."

Neither Nuna nor Eula was entirely comfortable with Adelaide's distortion of the truth about the hill of graves in the woods. Nuna, in particular, had become certain Adelaide's intentions were much more earthly when she noticed how eagerly Adelaide counted her financial share upon each visit. The money seemed less important to Nuna than the privacy they used to have, but she knew how the income eased the everyday situations of maintaining their properties which would surely have been lost if their venture had failed. So, Nuna went along tending her garden with her daughter's help and visiting the Makiaweesug on her own time. She thanked them for the spirit story of Bay, for the calm aura of her child's nature, and the warmth in her sweet face. As Nuna told Bay's father in prayer:

"Our daughta be de color of autumn and de peace of a pretty day."

Bay, at 11, was a quiet girl. She didn't have real girlfriends at school and seemed to favor being with her family.

"Judah's friend enough for me," Bay told her mother when asked if she would like to have a girl from school visit. Nuna began to watch more closely after that. She saw that Bay and Judah were inseparable.

Judah, 13, worked in Henry's store after school and fished the sound with Henry in the summer. He was a fine-looking boy, growing tall with thick, blonde hair and sky blue eyes.

Nuna followed the path to the beach through an arbor of sun bright, green leaves toward the northeast side of the cove. The air was warm and dry. From a slight rise, she could see the straight rows of Ezra Goldsmith's garden, all sorts of vegetables standing tall in the sun, waiting to plump to a ripe harvest. Nuna closed her eyes and inhaled the salted-fresh air. She exhaled and scanned the shoreline where she saw a man sitting on a rock, reading. Upon closer look, Nuna realized it was Goldsmith himself.

The Shellfoots and Morelys had welcomed Ezra Goldsmith's arrival when he purchased the cottage several years ago but, beyond polite nods, they hadn't been too neighborly because life intervened. Their children were born, their husbands drowned, and the young widows opened the guest house.

"Dat be a longtime gone by," Nuna said softly to herself. Her shame rose to redden her cheeks. Ezra's back was to her. His thick, grey hair curled at the nape of his neck, with frizzles lapping the small, round cap he wore.

Nuna walked into his view. "Mr. Ezra?" He turned slowly and his face broke into a welcoming smile. "I be Nuna Shellfoot from de shell road," Nuna said holding out her hand.

"Of course, of course, Mrs. Shellfoot," Ezra said as he stood, warmly closing Nuna's hand in his two soft paws, one still holding a prayer book. Nuna had to crane her neck and shield her eyes from the sun to see the man's face. Ezra bowed his head slightly then, and colored at his own shame: "I am so sorry that I haven't been by to say hello. I am a shy man," he said abashedly, then: "Oh no, I'm so sorry, I...." Ezra looked at Nuna squarely and said: "I am glad we are together now and...I...well...uh...you see, I believe you've met my brother."

"De one who be at de Captain's house a time or more?"

Nuna saw the furrow of Ezra's sunburned brow deepen. His voice held concern when he said:

"It seems one evening as a guest at the Captain's house, he got on his high horse, and ...well... my brother Autler considers himself to be a scholar of the truth, Madam. He eschews many of the old beliefs, my own included, as well as most modern ones.

A psychology degree allows him to assume facts he has never attempted to learn. I assure you, of spiritual matters, he knows nothing," Ezra Goldsmith's eyes laughed with his smile.

"My mama say: 'Even a bazodee-head can't know nothing.' " Nuna smiled at her own joke.

Ezra threw his head back in a huge laugh that came from his shoulders and engaged his whole face: "Now I know we'll be friends. A bazodee? Is that it?"

"Dis be what de Bims say for de ones who don't see no'ting but where's dey be."

"Ah, I like that, Nuna - may I call you Nuna?" Ezra asked.

Nodding, Nuna said, "Yes."

"That was me before I bought this place. A bazodee. Partners with Autler in legal deceit." Ezra helped Nuna step down toward a fallen tree and indicated she sit on the shaded end. Ezra sat on a rock across from her and continued to talk while Nuna arranged her cotton skirt and retied the leather string holding her hair over her shoulder. She caught herself, caught hold of her wish to pretty herself up in the moment. Nuna thought: "Spirit be playin' wit' me," she smiled at Ezra's kind face and met his hazel eyes which seemed to be in sync with his words:

"I was a lawyer....am a lawyer...I don't practice the law anymore. At least not those laws....I'm sorry, I don't get to talk with other people too often. Poor Gracie Williams at the Post Office gets the brunt of it when I go into pick up my mail. I talk her ear off. I hitch a ride with Henry now and then, so I've talked his ears off, too. I'll try not to do that to you, but there's so much I want to know." Ezra stopped. "I'm a decade or so older than you, but we both come from ancient traditions and well...here I am."

"I be 30 years now, but my grandaddy say I be dat at six."

"Yes, age is relative, isn't it, like time?" Ezra paused, then said. "I've thought about this for so long, Nuna, and this is an awkward start, but hear me out. There's a lot of praying that goes on in the legal business, and not just from the victims either. The accused and the lawyers, the juries and the judges - they're all praying just as hard. And you know what? Their prayers are the same. 'Help me win, God. Help me win.' That's why I quit the law. Whoever shows up with the best story wins. God has nothing to do with it."

"How you comes ta here?" Nuna asked.

"I had enough money to buy myself the life I wanted."

"And what dat be?"

"Hmmm...well, a place where it is easier to find God. I had looked in a temple where God's name isn't uttered aloud. There, I prayed in silence, thinking: If God's name is too sacred to be spoken here, then is God too sacred to be found?

"Well, I didn't believe that, Nuna. The God I seek answers to that name and many others. I found God here, Nuna."

Nuna looked down at her hands which lay calmly, one on the other, in her lap. She had begun to hear the osprey while Ezra spoke, a voice she hadn't heard since Ahane's death. Nuna didn't have to look from Ezra's face to know a large fish hawk flapped its wings in circles above them, blessing them. Then Nuna's black eyes settled softly into the kind orbs of her new friend. She said:

"My faduh tole me spirit be wit'in you and wit'out you."

***

Corycian Island Town Center
"The Titans who name our shores."

THE CORYCIAN ISLAND READER
Vol.13, No. 15 May, 3, 1906
Editorial
Corycian Island Population Tops 800 in Census

The release of the most recent United States Census confirms that the population of Corycian Island grew from 623, the count in 1890, to 859 in 1900. In the six years since, 23 Islanders have arrived and three left us. That brings the total number of year-round residents to 879, by our count.

With this increase in population has come a welcome demand for services, requiring the ex-

pansion of our Town's commerce center. Stand
at the top of the marble steps to our new Town
Hall and look out at the expanse of our little
hamlet. Survey what tax dollars have done for
us and complain no more about what it costs to
live in paradise.

Burston Bakker took his own advice and stood at the top of
the Town Hall's steps looking over the island's center. Tommy
Lawson was at his side. An expanded post office stood next to
an enlarged public library. Dilly's Market, just before the traffic circle, had spruced up its appearance with landscaping and
a macadam parking lot. Continuing east, the renovated school
building faced a newly painted Presbyterian Church

"The school sure looks impressive," Bakker said. "Two full
stories and a gymnasium. When we were kids, Corycian couldn't
have imagined such a grand school. Hell, the kids worked in those
fertilizer plants or some place. Only a few got to school at all."

Tommy nodded. He said: "Or they worked on fishing boats.
How about Narly Cotts? What was he, nine? He got dragged into
the ocean by a net before anyone noticed he was gone."

"That was when we were in the third grade, " Burston said,
"because another kid from our class - Roddy something -drowned
in Fresh Pond during the ice harvest that year, remember?"

"Yes. I still dream about his dead, frozen face. I was down
there getting ice with my father when they cut him out of the
pond," Tommy paused at the memory and then shook it from
his head: "Well, now that the factories have closed, more young-
sters are coming to school."

"That's an interesting fact," Burston said. "I had a long chat
with George Stoli the other day who says a record of 88 students
showed up on opening day. Stoli attributes it to the new school
building. I don't know. I think it's Stoli. He's damn good, Tommy.
He's a strong leader with modern ideas. Mind crossing over to
Marmie's? I just need to pickup a pack of smokes."

Marmie's Luncheonette shared a parking lot with the Presbyterian Church and a delivery driveway with the newest busi-

ness in town: "Fogarty's Family Funerary and Memento Mori Photographers, Inc."

The latter was currently the big topic at Marmie's among the local workers who sat on ten swivel stools, coveted seats at the gleaming bar of Marmie's chrome soda fountain. The bell on the door tinkled when Bakker and Lawson walked in, triggering ten heads to turn left and assess who'd entered. In this case, each went back to his coffee cup. The conversation picked up where it had paused. The person on stool #1 looked into the long mirror behind Marmie and spoke to the person on stool #10 by talking to his reflection:

Stool #1: "Yeah, they prop 'em up. The corpses. Prop 'em up like, you know, like regular. I seen the one took of the Bolton boy and his kin. He was dead and standin' straight. Held his head up with string, they did and my cousins says they even painted eyeballs on him in the picture. You can tell lookin' at it somethin's gone wrong."

"That right there's what gone wrong," Stool #10 replied. "And people's sendin' their dead kin over ta there, too. Wakin' 'em in that house right there instead a their own death rooms at their own house like they'se been waitin' to use all these years, don't ya know."

Stool #1: "I got one a them death rooms afront a my house. My old lady made me build it on when she said our time was comin' soon. Damn room. She won't even let me sit awhile in there till I'm in use of its purpose. And I won't be doin' much sittin' then."

Marmie walked over to the cash register and handed Bakker a pack of Lucky Strikes before he even asked for them.

"What's that fish wrapper a yours goin' to report on this week?" the sassy 60-year-old teased the newspaper man.

"Oh, you know, Marmie, the usual talk of the town," Bakker teased.

"Well that's bein' reported on right here, no need to waste paper on it," Marmie said.

"Can I quote you on that?

"Do and you die, newspaper man." Marmie threw this over her tall shoulder and returned to work, ladling batter on the grill while telling a complainer on stool #4:

"I ain't your wife, Donny K. Shut up or get off my stool."

Bakker and Lawson walked out of Marmie's and stood looking at Fogarty's. A simple white clapboard cottage was surrounded by a white picket fence. Only its discreet sign, hanging across the front porch, gave reference to its services.

"I'm not sure what to make of this photography trend," Burston said. "Although, I understand in the city, waking one's deceased in a funerary rather than one's death room is the current mode."

"Yes, Sissy had me laughing about that at dinner last night," Tommy said. "In Manhattan those crazy McElroy aunts insist on calling the front death room, a *living* room now. Something one of those women's magazines started to promote, apparently. Uncle Conor told Sissy the aunts make them all sit in there after dinner each night, but everyone's so uncomfortable because no one in there is dead."

Enjoying a laugh, Burston offered a cigarette to Tommy, took one for himself, and stopped to light them both. The men drew the smoke up through the tobacco, looked across the road at the school, and exhaled.

"So, you like Stoli? That's a surprise," Tommy said.

"I'm not saying I've changed my view on why children of means require private school education. I do, however, think the town did a fine job choosing Stoli. He has a genuine interest in leading this school into a new century and he's a bit quirky. I think there's an art to teaching that calls for a bit of quirkiness."

"You're referring to the paper sack, I assume," Tommy said.

"Well, yes. That and all the walking everywhere. I asked him about that. He said he walks for visibility, so islanders can get to know him and stop to talk if they have a concern about the school."

"Did you ask him about the paper sack?"

There was hardly a person on the island who hadn't seen George Stoli and taken note of him; not just because of his youthful, good looks and shock of thick white hair, but because of the ever-present, paper sack. No one knew what was in it, though there were few who didn't speculate about the contents:

"Was it the same sack day after day all these years" islanders wondered? "Was there school work in it? His lunch? His bible? His good shoes?"

The bag was large and often appeared heavy enough to require both arms, while other times Stoli rolled the top of the sack down and carried it with one hand. When he stopped to chat or to give a tip of his hat to passers-by, Stoli shifted the package to the crook of his left arm.

Spectators also noticed that upon arriving at school, Stoli placed the brown paper sack on the window sill behind his desk where it could be seen as clearly from the outside as from any vantage point inside the room. Islanders talked about it whenever they saw Principal Stoli walking by or whenever his name came up over coffee at Marmie's.

One Scaler said he'd stopped his car to give Stoli a lift during a rain storm:"I kept my eye on that sack. It's something square, not books though because the bag was all wet and there weren't no sharp edges. And it weren't his lunch or anything because it was 5 p.m. And here's the other thing he does. I've given him a few rides now and I seen it each time. When Stoli gets out, he shifts that bag to his left arm, then he raps his knuckles two times on my car hood." The Scaler hit Marmie's counter with two sharp raps. "No 'Thanks to ya,' or anything, just that." The Scaler knocked the counter again. "And I'm not the only one to take notice, ask Otto what Stoli did on his car hood. Go on and ask him, he'll tell ya' the same damn thing."

The other coffee-drinkers shook their heads in wonder. Now that the school had become a community center, a whole new mix of islanders provided each other with backstories, both fictional and real, about George Stoli. His father had been a teacher at the Corycian School, thus George understood that sense of mystery teachers hold for their students. Stoli knew he was the object of town scrutiny and didn't mind because it fit right into his philosophy of education: "Always keep them curious."

In addition to his duties in administration, Stoli taught high school history classes; he was a batting coach and, occasionally, a drama director. He was an emergency volunteer, and often rode with firemen to the blazes that consumed wood-frame houses in the winter.

Stoli also wrote regular columns about education for Burston Bakker's newspaper. The issue that followed the new school's 1906 opening contained George Stoli's welcome across two columns:

THE CORYICAN ISLAND READER
Vol. 13, No 35 September 9, 1906
A Corycian Island Education
by George Stoli, Principal of Corycian Island School

As we open school for a new year, I promise that in these hallowed halls your children will be given every opportunity to learn about how to live a life of enrichment from those who have learned it before them - in history, in literature, in mathematics, in sporting teams, and - with the wonders of it all - in our modern, science laboratory.

Let us all promise today to build a community that respects education so greatly that we never miss the opportunity to learn from each other. Let us promise to praise our students, our teachers, and our parents in our homes and in our community.

Our neighbors will be in this building loving and tending your children for part of each day. Lenox Garner and Jackie Sakaate have some wonderful recipes they'll be fixing for lunch. Frank Herbert has himself a full band this year - excluding baseball season, of course - and I hear from the Drama Club that the seniors want me to direct a play come spring. That's just a quick round-up of the highlights for the year to come.

So, let's make one last promise. Let's promise
a lifetime of discovery and growth for everyone
in our town who walks through these doors and
feels the power of learning. Let's promise our
children the strength of the Titans who name our
shores.

George Stoli grew up with his students' parents, so the fact
that Corycian was an unusual place hadn't occurred to him until
he went to college on the mainland. It was a startling discovery.
Just a ferry ride away, the world was a very different place where
people didn't know everyone they saw.

Stoli rode the ferry and a bus, round trip, to Bay Hampton
College each school day. During class breaks, he walked around
nodding to those he passed, rarely receiving nods in return. It
became a social experiment that led him to put the large head of
a sunflower into his lapel or to tuck a nosegay of wildflowers into
brim of his cap.

He observed the change. People not only noticed, often they
even smiled. Frances Nolan, the future Mrs. Stoli, was one of
them. Stoli's experiment led to his conviction that being interesting oneself aroused interest in others. As the Superintendent and
Principal of the Corycian Island Independent School District,
Stoli strove to keep his students and the town interested.

Consequently, George Stoli greeted every student who entered the school each day by name. He saw a bouquet of human-
ity smiling at him and wondered if there was any other place on
earth where such a delicate balance held on.

Of course as the school's head, Stoli was aware of the petty
complaints involved when children from the west side of the
island - who lived in the gracious homes around Calliope Point -
found themselves at lunch with children from, well, nearly every
other side of the island.

Bias usually came from someone like the stern-faced and
prim Calliope mother who told Principal Stoli:

"My family is required, at great inconvenience, to live on Cory-cian for six weeks of the school year while our Fifth Avenue home is being redecorated. This is not my choice Headmaster Stoli..."

"I'm the principal of the school, Mrs. Stockham. Just 'Mr. Stoli' is fine..."

"Well," Mrs. Stockham sniffed, "*I* don't think it's fine. I prefer Headmaster Stoli. A man should be titled properly. It distinguishes him from the simple 'misters.' A school is only as public as one's leader makes it, Headmaster Stoli."

Mrs. Stockham went on: "As I was saying, I will require that Charlton be in a classroom without colored children in it. He is a sensitive child..."

"Corycian Island is an Independent School District that does not discriminate among creed or col..."

"Enough, Principal Stoli. I am aware that Charlton needs to be with other children, just not colored ones. What will that entail. Get to the point."

"It will entail private tutoring for the lad, Mrs. Stockham."

Stoli didn't have to go around in these circles very often, fortunately, but he stood strong when he did. Of course, he had to break up a slapping fight here and there among kids from different ends of the island. He'd certainly heard names thrown around that the kids must have picked up at home and he dealt with each case that came along by talking with the families. So far, his efforts seemed to be successful.

Stoli attributed this to having inserted himself into the culture with his daily walks and that mysterious brown paper bag.

Scalers knew Stoli; they recognized idiosyncrasies and identified with them. The locals knew what to expect when their children went to "Stoli's School" - that's what they called it - and those who couldn't accept its culture, sent their children to private schools on the mainland.

Calliope Point
"East side, West side"

Following a trouble free pregnancy, Pammy McElroy Bakker gave birth to a daughter on September 14, 1906. She telephoned Nuna with the news, and joked: "*And,* after all that, those were girl bebe seeds!"

"Well, dat whole t'ing 'bout me gettin' boys ta come nevuh be true, anyways," Nuna replied with a laugh.

Barbara Joy Bakker was nicknamed "Babs" from the start. She was a tiny little girl, six pounds 4 ounces at birth, and 20-inches long. Her lungs were in fine wailing shape, a fact she shouted often.

Once again the families celebrated with friends, as they gathered to witness the ceremony of Babs Bakker's tree of life. It was almost sunset and the water below them lapped quietly. They heard the chink-chink of boats and buoys.

All eyes were on Burston who felt foolish as he placed the newspaper wrapped placenta into the hole Tommy had dug earlier in the Bakker's rear garden. Burston skipped the part where he was supposed to spread the bloody pulp over the earth so its branching veins stood out. He took a trowel and covered it quickly. Then he stood to speak, looking above Pammy's head and out to the others. He was a wordsmith who couldn't find spoken words in front of a crowd. Too many people were sizing him up. What did they see? Burston wondered.

"Well…" the new father said, with a pause. "That takes care of that, little Babs. We plant this tree for you to represent the heights you'll reach some day." He shoveled more dirt into the hole and took the trunk of a Japanese maple tree from Tommy. The two of them, with Judah Morely's help, packed the soil around Babs' tree, the leaves of which absorbed a golden glow. They all stepped back to admire it.

"That's a damn fine tree your daddy picked out for you my little love," Burston said with a brush of his hands.

Then turning to everyone else, Burston threw out arms and bellowed: "Who wants a drink? A drink to my daughter and her beautiful mother! Come on up to our place. Have a drink on me," Burston started for the Bakkers' house.

Tommy Lawson saw the dismay on his sister-in-law's face. Pammy, happy as could be a moment before, now looked as if she was on the verge of tears. A few drinks were all Burston had planned. Pammy had expected a party. Tommy said the first thing that popped into his head: "A drink? Hell, no. Burston's kidding! We planned to have a celebration at our place, all compliments of our host Mr. Bakker of course," Tommy winked at Burston. "Champagne and gourmet fare for everyone! Up we go!"

Tommy and Sissy led the group into their house through the back door off the kitchen. Tommy disappeared into the basement and came up with three bottles of champagne and a ukulele. Sissy took Grandma O'Neill's crystal goblets out of the breakfront. Tommy popped a cork and everyone cheered. He poured the wine from glass to glass and Sissy handed one to each guest.

"First, the toast, " Tommy said, "and then, as a special treat, I'll crank up the pianola for some singing and dancing. I'll not have a niece of mine coming into the world without a good song sung in her name!"

Burston, as surprised as anyone, felt a stab that the Lawsons knew he wouldn't think to plan a celebration for his daughter and his wife. His toast was spoken with a full heart:

"To Barbara Jean Bakker, my daughter. Long may you reign. Long may you love, live, learn, and become…" Burston turned to Pammy, "and become as smart, beautfiul, and provocative as your mother."

Everyone laughed and cheered. Soon ragtime hits tinkled from the player piano and Tommy made sure each female had a dance with him. Then he and Sissy, who made dancing look easy, showed off all the popular moves: the Turkey Trot, the Castle Walk, and the Two-step.

After the applause, "In the Good 'Ol Summertime" waltzed out of the piano and Tommy insisted Pammy let go of Babs, so she could dance with Burston. Tommy handed the baby over to Sissy, picked up his ukulele, and plinked out the tune.

Eula held Bay Shellfoot's hands, counting aloud while dancing along with her: "One, two, three- one, two, three." They
glided around the room. Eula passed Bay over to Judah when
the "Sidewalks of New York" began. She looked around. It was a
very happy time, Eula thought. Even Burston Bakker had a smile
on his face.

Nuna walked over to Eula and said: "Eas' side, Wes' side....
"Dat's what dis island be nowadays."

"Well," Eula replied, "there are really four sides when you
think about it with the campgrounds and the convent."

"And alla dem seems ta be one-sided summa de time," Nuna
laughed. "How dat gets to be?"

"Time just pushes things by, don't you think? I mean, look
at Judah and Bay. We watch them every minute, but we never
notice the changes happening."

The women listened as a tipsy Tommy led a sing-a-long.

Eula said: "Were we ever really all-a-wanna, Nuna? At Ke'was
End, yes, but on Corycian? Seems to me there are a whole lot of
differences when you get a look inside houses like this and the
Bakkers. Not just now. There always have been."

The women saw Burston hold his arms out to Pammy,
who with their child in her arms, rolled into the her husband's
embrace.

"We still all-a-wanna," Nuna said. "Just summa us don't
know it."

"I have to say I don't feel very all-a-wanna at the moment,"
Eula replied, leaning against the wall and watching the dancers.

"All-a-wanna be inside, too" Nuna said, knowing that was
hardly enough to fill the gap in each of their lives.

"The truth is, Nuna, I don't know any more than I did before we went into the spirit business. I know things happen that
people believe, so I believe because they do. But mostly, I believe
because you do."

"Believin' t'ings don't count much. Summa de peoples believes we witches. Now dat don't mean a t'ing. Believin' gots ta be
part of who you is. *T'inkin'* believin' don't work no how."

"These past years have made me feel like an old woman, and I'm only 31."

Nuna looked over at her friend, saw Eula's beauty, and knew her loneliness. She said:

"Summa de time, Oonuh disn't be enough."

"I tease you about never leaving Corycian Island, Nuna, but the truth is, as different as our lives are from these up here at the Point, I know we breathe the same air. Over on the mainland, I see how many people there really are in the world. They move along like they have nothing to do with me. Here, at least I feel rooted to land and family, but..."

"I sees t'ings, Eula," Nuna, the Runapewak storyteller said. "but not for de peoples right by my nose. We all's lonely - you, Henry and me - even Ezra down on de beach, dat's why we all-a-wanna, too."

1907

Corycian Island Town Center
"What in the Lord's name for?"

Hansen Ratliss had a new title: Chief of Police, as bestowed by the Town of Corycian Island which now employed two part-time rookies to assist the Chief in the growing needs of island civilians. These included vehicle accidents, disorderly conduct, and personal complaints, ranging from barking dogs to suspicions of satanic activity at Ke'was End.

Calls about the Morelys and Shellfoots became increasingly annoying to Ratliss. He knew these women; he knew they'd started a venture to survive and found themselves doing better than they could have imagined.

"Free enterprise," Ratliss said to the shouting callers who demanded he raid the place and chase the "devil-worshippers" off the island. "This is America. I've been to Ke'was End many times. They aren't doing anything at Ke'was End that isn't being done in another way at the Believers' Camp or St. Anthony's convent."

His comments, repeated over and again, earned Chief Ratliss some satanic labels of his own from this Scaler or that Calliope villager. Ratliss began to find odd animal parts around his apartment above the police station, most notably a dead kitten strung from the rear view mirror of his prized Maxwell truck.

Ratliss took the trespass as a positive, Remie was getting reckless. He also suspected it was Josiah Remie, at least he and his cohorts, who had begun to make anonymous phone calls to the police station claiming that Nuna and Eula were: "whores for satan," "fascist whores," and "half-breed whores." The calls were being placed from the mainland according to the island's switchboard operator. Ratliss checked with the deckhands on the ferry to see if they remembered Remie or Wesley leaving the island on the days the calls were made, but no one claimed to have noticed.

After the latest slandering phone call, Ratliss ranted to his secretary, Karen Moultrie, who was getting used to his spiel:

"Whores for Satan! Can you imagine Nuna Shellfoot and Eula Morely being whores for anyone? And no one else is whoring down there either. Trust me. I have people looking things over all the time, and besides, Henry Shellfoot would kill anyone who desecrated that land in the slightest, even his own relatives. No, what those women are doing at Ke'was End is taking place all over New York from what I can tell. You know better than anyone, how I've talked with other towns about this spiritualist thing. Just yesterday when you dialed up Riverhead for me, the Chief said he's got a church where the preacher handles poisonous snakes, saying they're the spirits of the dead."

Karen Moultrie's dark brown eyes grew wide: "What in the Lord's name for?"

"Exactly! In the Lord's name! That's what-for, if you can believe it," Ratliss replied. "They're lunatics, I guess, but then again, they think we're the crazy ones for living on this floating rock, so...it's a wild business being on this side of the picture, isn't it Mrs Moultrie? I told you when you took the job you'd hear things you'd never heard before."

Chief Ratliss smiled wryly and shook his head: "I don't know what's going on. But the people residing at Ke'was End are legal landowners, practicing legal businesses - and I don't see the devil anywhere near - and more important is that neither do you who has known these folks all your life."

Ratliss still hadn't caught Remie in his random acts of trespass and destruction which had now been perpetrated at every corner of the island.

Yes, every corner.

West at the home of a Calliope Point bigwig where dead mice were found hanging by their tails from every bush and shrub one morning.

East, where dead chicken parts were left in a circle around the Captain's Guest House and dozens of dead rats were thrown around the entrance to Ezra Goldsmith's cottage, also at Ke'was End.

All these annoying incidents, in addition to the recurring violations at St. Anthony's, even included a visitor at the Believers' Camp being victimized.

Josiah Remie, of all people, had filed a complaint on behalf of a visiting Believer. Remie said the man was brought to the door of his rented cabin by an insistent knock in the wee hours of the morning. When the guest opened the door, no one was there. This happened three times within a two hour period, according to Remie's report. The third time the visitor opened his door a maggotty, dead rat, made to swing from a rafter outside the door, hit him in the face.

The Chief was smart enough to see through Remie's attempt to hide in plain sight, but he had missed Remie's visit to the station, so Ratliss had to rely on Karen Moultrie's report which was matter-of-fact.

"Did Remie smell of alcohol?" Ratliss asked.

"Of course," is all the harried woman replied, answering the ringing telephone and handing Ratliss the report Remie had signed with a scrawl.

"Corycian Island Police Department," the secretary said. "Yes there's a town over here, M'am. That's why I'm answering the telephone."

As soon as she ended that call, the phone rang again, so Ratliss read the report written in his secretary's fine penmanship. She quoted Remie's story about the camp's visitor and the rat. Then wrote:

"Mr. Remie said he heard about some Scalers in a group called the 'Keyclose Clan' doing things on the island. He went on to say: 'I heard they're doing these things to people. Sometimes it's just annoying people, but usually its you-know-what-kinda people.' "

"And what kind of people would that be, Mr. Remie?" Mrs. Moultrie had asked. The complainant replied: "Them who's not like they supposed to be, and you know damn well who I mean, cause you probably is one."

Karen Moultrie's notes ended: "Mr. Remie signed his complaint without reading it or making further comments. He left the station at 4:32 p.m."

Ratliss sat back in the chair next to his secretary's desk. He waited for her to end another call. He put his feet on the rim of a metal trash can. When she put receiver in the cradle, he said:

"Remie just loves to hate people. I wouldn't let him bother you. One day he told me I wasn't a Scaler, so I had no business being here. He thinks he owns the island. But he's a difficult guy to catch breaking the law. I hear he doesn't sell whiskey as much since he got the Camp job. Besides, if I bust him for that, I'll have to bust half the island, including old Miss Lottie who makes some darn fine elderberry wine," Ratliss laughed.

"Anyway, I'm sure you being part Runapewak bothers Remie. That's why he said those things. For me it's being a mainlander. It's something for everyone Remie knows...so, I'll do the best I can to get down your way or to borrow the eyes of your neighbors for awhile. I'm sure Remie will be up to his old tricks."

Later on, Ratliss thought about Hector Wesley who didn't seem especially bright, but was clearly Remie's accomplice; however, the two of them were crafty and knew the island's woods inside out. It was easy for them to sneak around these places. Remie needed Hector Wesley to carry all the junk they brought with them. The hulking Scaler was just a tool for scrawny Remie.

Pipers' Cove
"You can't be Keyclose and kills white people."

Josiah Remie was in a foul mood the night after dealing with Karen Moultrie at the police station. He'd gone there to taunt Ratliss. That Moultrie woman hit a nerve and Remie drank a large quantity of moonshine to calm it down.

"Damn indians," Remie said to Hector Wesely who sat next to him on Shell Beach off Pipers' Cove. "That woman in the police station acted like she was some kinda hot-shot, fillin' out that form with my words, like she did. This damn town'll hire anyone who got graduated from Stoli's school.

"Anyways I say we should spend our time on Moultrie and her kind," Josiah said, talking to Wesley, but not really: "Where's that indian live anyhow? Over there by the jew Goldsmith, I think. We could get 'em both in one night."

Remie paused to drink and Hector responded:

"We can't go after her. She knows she needled you at Ratliss' place, Josiah, and by now, Ratliss knows it, too. And besides, she's pretty smart. I think she mighta got A's when we was in school..." Hector saw the scowl on Remie's face and knew it was time to change the subject: "I told you 'bout all them weirdos I been drivin' over to Ke'was, remember? Like that guy with all them tattoos...well..."

Remie's scowl began to contort while his face reddened. He cut Hector off:

"I'm tellin' you Hector, it's time we got busy stoppin' all this that's goin' on here. There's people in Georgia stringin' up undesirables from trees for everyone to see. All we's doin' is scarin' people."

Hector looked strangely at Josiah who'd crossed into a whole new territory of talk - this was Josiah's voice when he was liquored up and mean.

"I'd really like to kill one a them down there on the east end," Josiah said. "And I'd kill one dead if I heard from Jesus about it," he slurred.

Hector paused to figure out a diversion technique. Nothing came to mind, so he said: "Well, you can't and that's all there is to it, Josiah." Then Hector laughed like it was a big joke: "Let's kill one of them nuns if we're gonna kill somebody."

"For damn sake, they's white. You can't be Keyclose and kill white people," Josiah said with brewing anger.

"Jews is white, Josiah, and Keyclose's kills them. You says so yourself," Hector replied trying to assess if Remie was too drunk to coordinate a left hook which had caught him unawares before. But Josiah replied in a surprised tone: "Are not white at all. Jews is Ay-rabs," and then with a click of thought Josiah wondered aloud: "Was Jesus an Ay-rab?"

"Who the hell knows," Hector said, shifting his seat in the sand and leaning back against a rock. He reached across to Remie: " Gimme that jug. You know what' s funny. You say I'm too dumb to be stupid... but you don't even know your kid's name means King of the Jews."

Josiah's head was lolling around while he tried to understand what Hector was saying. "Yeah, your kid's the King of the Jews and Jews ain't white you said."

Josiah jumped to his feet and threw a fisted hook at Wesley's head. Hector grabbed Josiah's wrist before the small man connected. Hector stood above Josiah and looked down. Hector's fat hands formed tightfists. He spat at Josiah's purple face, saying:

"And for the last time, you ain't the boss a me."

Coyrcian Island School
"They call you names."

It wasn't easy at school for Judah and Bay when their mothers leased the Captain's house to spiritualists. Other students teased them, making ghoulish, ghostly noises at them or worse, passing a sketch of them around at recess with "Spawn of Satan" written beneath.

Bay and Judah defended each other, discovering a bond in the process which worked until Judah was a teenager.

Then Eula got a call from Principal Stoli to come to school immediately. Judah had been in a fight.

Henry dropped Eula off at the school in the used Rambler purchased with profits from their businesses. On the driver's door, a sign identified: "The Captain's Guest House and Henry's Fish and Produce Store" in white-painted script, another of Henry's talents. The entire trip across Old Post Road to the center of town, Eula kept saying:

"How could it be, Henry? If there's one way this family is Quaker, it's in our belief in peace. I raised him like that, Henry. You were there, you know!"

Henry couldn't do much more than nod and repeat the good things he knew about Judah Morely, which were many. When they got to the school Henry said: "I gots only one thing to say, Eula. You wait till you hears from Judah."

Eula entered Stoli's office to find Judah sitting there with a bloody nose and a quickly bluing cheekbone.

"Are you all right, Judah?" she asked.

"He'll be fine, Mrs. Morely," George Stoli said. He was standing with his hand on Judah's shoulder. "Tell your mother what happened, son, and let me add, Mrs. Morely, I was right there and know this to be the truth."

Judah spoke with hesitation, but all the years of hearing his mother and Nuna called names without telling them about it, and trying not to hit someone, had finally come to an explosive peak.

"There are these people, boys, mostly... who don't like us...."

Even though this wasn't news to Eula, the rest of what Judah had to say was."They call you names. You and Nuna." Judah looked at his hands. "They've been doing this since Bay and me was...uh...were... kids. They say you're...devil whores...and things like that. Bay always just turns her back to them and...I know what you said...so I do, too...or did...I just got so mad this time."

George Stoli squeezed Judah's shoulder. Eula was kneeling at the side of the chair, blotting Judah's tears with her handkerchief. "I didn't know...Judah...I didn't have any idea..."

Stoli interrupted. "Today, one of the young men who calls these taunts at Judah didn't know I was within earshot. I heard what was said, and I saw Judah move to defend himself when another boy threw a cross-punch right to Judah's face. The offending boys are too young to be charged with assault, but I've had them taken to Chief Ratliss's office. We'll give them a good scare, if nothing else. I wanted you to hear this from Judah, Mrs. Morely. From what he tells me this is something he and Miss Shellfoot have endured for some time now. I will do my best to see that it ends. I will be placing a telephone call to the parents of all the students involved. I'll also call Bay Shellfoot's mother, but I'd appreciate it if you would discuss this with her, too. I promise you, Mrs. Morely: I will not run a school in which cowards hide behind name-calling and assumptions. I hold my staff to higher standards and will certainly see that they become far more watchful, intervening before confrontations occur."

The Strand Hotel
"Well, we're women and we live everywhere."

Nuna said "bebe spirit seeds" grew at the same time in Pammy and Sissy that winter because of their gifts to all the mothers of Corycian Island.

"You brings all-a-wanna back to dem," Nuna said.

It was true. The blended team of island volunteers had gone a long way toward engendering a new sense of community among Scalers and other islanders which started with females.

An easy and comfortable atmosphere settled on the Strand's nursing mothers who rocked their infants during breaks while helpers sat on the floor playing with crawling babies or toddling ones.

The women enjoyed tea and they shared in some gossip or heard from Pammy about a topic common to all, the rights of women.

A very pregnant Pammy Bakker sat at a table in the kitchen off the babies' room one afternoon. Three mothers sat across from her. Nuna Shellfoot tended to a pot of steaming water, and Sissy Bakker, equally as pregnant as Pammy, gathered bags of dirty diapers to be cleaned in the hotel laundry.

"An old friend of mine from school sent me the most incredible newspaper article," Pammy said to the women. "Do you know that women in Colorado state have the right to vote? It's true. They've been voting for years."

Pammy expected the women to be more aghast than they were, but the faces looking back at her were tired and self-absorbed.

"Did any of you hear what I just said? Women in a U.S. state have been voting in national elections for years and we're only just finding this out. I want a voice in what goes on in this country, don't you? I want to vote, don't you?"

Sissy, still at her job, said: "Yes, but we don't live in Colorado."

"Well, we're women, Sissy, and we live everywhere."

One of the mothers at the table began to nod in agreement. Pammy went on:

"Men don't have any idea what we want. Much less what we need or what we can do." Everyone laughed and agreed.

Nuna turned from her task with the teapot and said: "Mens don't be wantin' ta know."

"I believe you're right, Nuna," Pammy said, fishing in a pocket and pulling out a long column of newsprint. "Listen to what men want to know about this woman, a former New Yorker by the way. Let me see if I can find her name. Yes, here it is...a Mrs. Tiller. She's a delegate from Colorado to the Democratic Convention. Can you imagine?"

"I don't know what that is," a mother sitting across from Pammy said.

"The Democratic Convention?" Pammy said. "Oh. That's where Democratic *men* decide who is going to run for President against the *man* the Republican *men* pick. But this year, the Democrats in Colorado have to send *women* since there has to be equal representation from the people who vote in a state."

"So what did the men want to know about the woman," the same mother asked. "You started to read it and then I cut you off..."

Pammy said: "The man interviewing Mrs. Tiller wanted to know if being a suffragist interfered with her household and maternal duties. Boy, did she have an answer. I'll read what she said:

'Of all the ridiculous ideas. It is just the other way. An interest in the questions of the day brightens a woman, takes her out of her daily rut of dishes, dusting, and sweeping and gives her a common bond of interest with her husband.

"She can help to make conditions right for her children and can guide them with more wisdom. Then, too, a child must naturally respect a mother more when that mother is allowed a voice in the government. Woman suffrage is bound to spread and it makes one feel proud to live in a state that early recognizes the justice of giving women the ballot.' "

"How old is she?" the curious mother asked.

"Well, 30 or so, around our ages," Pammy replied. "She has nine children."

"She's either got wads a money or a bunch a spinster sisters to take care of that brood while she's off galavanting..." another piped in to a round of agreement.

Then a woman who was quiet throughout the conversation said: "She gotta be rich, I agree, but I don't buy the galavantin' thing you said. It ain't galavantin' if she's fixin' things for kids down the road. My Ned grew up workin' in them fish oil factories that was here. The young ones died all the time in those vats. The resorts shut them filthy things down, but women who watched their kids dyin' shoulda been the ones."

Another mother added: "They stopped takin' kids at the lima bean cannery here. They has to be 13 or 14 now. That boy from Ke'was got his arm cut off, don't ya know, so's they changed it."

"Well, when women get the vote here in New York," Pammy said. "We'll make a lot of changes to protect our children. But it's clear we have to change men or change will never happen."

Calliope Point
"What you see as weakness, I see as strength."

Sissy and Pammy's sons, Nathaniel (Nate) Lawson and John Burston (JB) Bakker V, were born within two days of each other in December of 1907.

Burston buried JB's placenta in the softer soil closest to the edge of the cliffs overlooking the harbor next to where Tommy had lain Nate's. The wind whipped too hard for the others to join them, so the fathers - fortified with brandy, twin sugar maples, and a large torch - struck out at dusk to perform the treasured ritual.

Sissy and Pammy, holding their newborn sons, stood at the large second story window with Sam and Babs clinging to their legs. Their eyes followed the sky from the torch, until it stood still, flaming in the fading light at the spot where Burston and Tommy were.

"It's god-damned freezing out here," Burston said, swaying as much from inebriation as the wind. "Figures this is an indian tradition - who else would come out here to bury body waste in sub-zero temperatures for Chrissake."

"You better not let Pammy hear you say that," Tommy said, while Burston took a long drink from the flask. "I'm just going to dig that hole a bit deeper. I don't want to find these things after they're dug up by some critter."

"See?" Burston said. "You're as disdainful of this stupidity as I am."

"Actually, I'm just being practical. And I don't disdain the ritual, Burston. I'm far more broad-minded than you."

"Yes, I see that more every day. Sometimes you remind me of a woman, but far less educated," Burston said.

"Yeah, yeah..." Tommy answered, "so you say whenever you're tight and nasty. That's your big insult. Anyway, what you see as weakness I see as strength. I admire women and I'd choose to be a woman over your pompous, manly ass any day."

"Bullshit, Lawson, you kiss pompous, male asses like mine every day at the Strand, and you also give your maids babysitters," Bakker snarled. "You voted for Bryant in this election didn't you? You swallowed his 'governing by the people instead of the elite' bullshit. I'm sure my erudite wife talked you into that nonsense."

"Time to shut up, Burston. Probably time to quit with the brandy, too. It's making a fool out of you. Now, turn around and wave to your wife. She thinks you're doing something sacred out here."

1908

Ke'was End
"Sorcery and high jinks"

The taunts at Judah and Bay from their classmates didn't end. They just took place off school grounds with greater intensity. Slowly and almost without notice first Judah, and then Bay, stopped going to school. George Stoli spoke on the telephone with their parents several times, but neither Eula nor Nuna knew how to force grown children to change their minds.

Stoli took a walk down to Ke'was End where he was told by Judah, most politely, that he worked in their family businesses now and was finished with school.

Nuna tried to convince Bay to go back, but the young girl refused.

With Bay home to help, Nuna stepped up her work. She taught Bay how to dry and mix herbs for the products she sold in Henry's store. They brought treatments for engorged milk ducts and other new mothers' ailments to the Mothers' Care Center, and also tended to a few local women who telephoned about any number of female needs.

Soon Nuna realized, some of her clients were from the mainland and when she said it to Bay, her daughter laughed:

"See? You're a regular miracle-worker, Mama."

One woman told Henry that she had purchased a few ounces of Miss Nuna's special "Herbal Honey-Butter" at the store. She said:

"You know, I mixed a bit of that honey-butter of hers into my husband's afternoon tea. From then on he's been pleasant as can be. It's the first time since the 1890s. Now he drinks two cups a day. Please tell Miss Shellfoot she gave me my marriage back."

Henry's tickling laugh tee-hee-ed through his gapped teeth when he told Nuna the tale. He said: "I'll *bet* that lady gots her marriage back and then some."

However, there were locals who subscribed to more traditional beliefs, and they weren't laughing about the changes taking place at Ke'was End. In conversations with each other many were unhappy with the "sorcery and high jinks," as Josiah Remie called the goings-on when talking to his fellow Believers.

Discussions around island family dinner tables turned to topics of spirits and the afterlife. Locals whispered about the spirits of long-dead Scalers appearing at Ke'was End séances. The story that everyone heard involved the spirit of a deceased bayman who told a man at the table: "You owe me." Reportedly, the recipient of the message, sat stock still while he heard the declaration repeated three times; then he stood, toppled his chair and ran from the house.

There was also a rumor about the local mortician, Fogarty, who'd never been seen to smile. Attending a séance, Fogarty had laughed like a hyena. When asked about it, Fogarty claimed his dead brother had tickled him beneath the table and wouldn't stop, just like he had done when they were kids. Fogarty also added to his story: "I have a special relationship with the dead." The comment ended most conversations.

But the most damaging rumor concerned a total lie about a despondent islander who committed suicide. The gossips said the tarot card reader at Ke'was End had dealt the Ten of Swords to the forlorn lover, clearly indicating that doom awaited him. The young man hanged himself in a barn the day after his visit to the reader.

After the young man's funeral, (which followed a photo session with the deceased at Fogarty's), chicken guts and dog manure started showing up around the portals of the various houses at Ke'was End.

Henry told the women he would deter the trespassers. He said:

"Don't you talk to no one about what we found. Them kinda folks hears things, and I be trackin' them with silence. The indian way. Mr. Ezra's gonna help me."

Fish Oil Factories
Guano and Mossbunker Mash

Before Corycian Island was discovered as a respite for the weary, it housed huge and smelly factories at points along its shore where fish oil production was the mainstay of the island economy for generations.

Prior to the turn of the century locals seined mossbunker, slimy fish indigenous to the area, and boiled the bunker with bat guano. They pressed the resulting mush to extract an oil known in the trade as "Long Island Shit." The Westside Ferry Company transported containers of the thick oil to a depot on the mainland where it was processed into fertilizer.

Since production of fish oil took place in dozens of factories along the entire coastline of Long Island, an odor emanated that was putrid enough to keep all but the most hardy away from the long expanse of beaches in the 1800s.

Nonetheless, the fish oil factories fell like dominoes when the earning-power of the beautiful Long Island shorelines became obvious. Sprawling mansions and resorts appeared from Manhasset Bay to Montauk Point. The shit factory on Corycian Island was the last to be demolished in 1885. However for decades afterwards, a horrific odor wafted through the island air like a moldy spirit each fall. Islanders knew it was from the old ones who still boiled mossbunker and guano to enrich their soil, but also to disturb the greedy who'd cost a culture its livelihood.

Nuna Shellfoot kept a pile of guano and mossbunker mulching out by the Sound and when it came time to boil the mush, the smell chose its path.

Nuna waited to light her pot until a north wind blew in the direction of the evil she felt coming their way.

Pipers' Cove
"No how, don't ya know."

Josiah Remie didn't pay much attention to what went on with Ruth and their boy, Inri. As long as Josiah's meals appeared on time and Ruth let him fool with her on occasion, he put up with having a wife. As for a son, well: "Better said than done" was the thought Josiah kept repeating when the three-year-old acted like such a baby all the time.

Ruth said: "All he wants you to do is notice him. Have you ever even hugged him?"

To himself Josiah thought: "God damn women! It always comes down to somethin' like that, no matter what's being talked about. Goddammit."

To Ruth, Josiah said: "Did I have anyone hug me? No! and I'm a man because a it. You bet your sweet rear-end I never did. No how, don't ya know!"

Josiah had become more fueled with the belief that he possessed an invisible control over the forces he opposed, on the sheer fact that he hadn't been caught in his many misdeeds. This empowerment propelled Josiah to work even harder, assuming the Believers' pulpit with a rallying cry to protest, in his words: "The town's support of the witches at Ke'was End and other points of Corycian Island."

Josiah's small group appeared at a Town Board meeting. One of them spoke of the town's need to do "something about those crazies on the east end," but it was really the speaker's next comment that received newsprint in "Town Whispers This Week," a tongue- in-cheek tidbits column in the *Reader*:

> "At a recent Town Board meeting a member of the Believers' community reported this new information: 'It is obvious to all who know the good souls congregating at the Believers' Camp that the holy spirit who dwells on Corycian Island clearly prefers our refuge at Pipers' Cove.' Hmmmm, so where does that leave the rest of us?"

Beyond that observation, little else the faithful did at the camp attracted attention from the majority of Corycian Islanders who continued to worship wherever they chose. Remie tried to make the Believers' Camp more appealing to locals by ramping up its shouting ministry. He invited a devotee of famed evangelist Billy Sunday, named Billy Newday, to preach at the dedication of a new chapel at the Believers' campground.

The advertising for the preacher's appearance and the buffet served after the opening of the chapel drew many, none of whom were discerning enough to notice the irregularity in Newday's name, and few whoever came back to the services again.

The preacher's inspiration was directly from Billy Sunday's message which involved screeching about "the devils of places called spiritual, right here in your midsts" and encouraging those gathered to root out the "peanut-brained, weasel-eyed, hog-jowled, beetle-browed, bull- necked, hog owners" who threatened their very souls.

Presumably, Newday meant spiritualists and Catholics, but not much came of it, other than small protests. After the condemnation, four people from the camp appeared at the corner of Post Road near the Captain's Guest House, bearing misspelled signs:

"Beloved: Believe not in every spirit." ~ John 4:1 "
"Beware the devils of things called spiritual."
"Holey Spirit dwells at Piper's Cove."
"Thou shalt not worship false profits."

Near the gates of Màthair, a young cousin of Hector Wesley's, who was paid $1 for four hours, also walked with a sign. An arrow pointed toward the house, the words read: "Witches here. Beware!"

Chief Ratliss explained to the nuns, the Morelys, and the Shellfoots that as long as people stayed on public property, they had the right to free speech; adding, if the group caused civil problems, he would roust them out.

To Josiah Remie's dismay, it became apparent that the protests drew attention to The Captain's Guest House, and therefore, created more business for them. He pushed the protestors toward other tasks of faith in action.

1909

Ke'was End
"I only deal in silver dollars."

Eula and Nuna sat on the rear porch of the Captain's house, fanning away the still heat and bemoaning the fact that a water pipe had leaked through the plaster ceiling of the living room. The repair bill was significant and their seasonal rents had been collected. They looked up upon hearing the familiar crunch along the shell road and saw a covered carriage drawn by a sorry-looking horse and driven by a broken-looking woman. It was mid-August.

They watched as the woman climbed from the wagon, hitched the horse up to a post in the parking area, and then stood there waiting for a man to disembark. She followed behind him as he lumbered up the path to the house.

"That back there's Tereza," the man called out when he was still 50 feet away from the porch. "She's a fortune-teller and what not. I'm Rollo Lavidas, how'd ya do. We're here to rent a place and make some money for alla us on account of Tereza's gift and all. And here's this from that Core lady."

Lavidas reached the porch. His steel gray beard held bits of food. His teeth were brown with tobacco stains. His belly hung over a makeshift belt holding up his pants, and a thick, silver medallion hung around his neck from a chain. There was a hole in the middle of the shiny disk. Lavidas spat and stretched his pulpy hand forward with a dirty, folded paper in it.

It was a letter of introduction from Adelaide Coeur naming Tereza Lavidas but containing no mention of a husband.

Eula returned the letter to him. She said: "We haven't any vacancies, I'm sorry."

"I only deal in silver dollars," the man said, ignoring Eula, and shaking a jingling pouch in Nuna's face. "Here's a hundred for that cabin over there till fall comes," he pointed to the empty cottage by Henry's store. Nuna stepped back, saying nothing.

"I never know'd a injun who said no to silver," Lavidas said, jingling another pouch. "You two ladies in this place together I hear, so how about $20 more just in case we break something."

Nuna was about to say her cottage wasn't for lease, but apparently Eula felt the power of the money. So, without consulting Nuna, Eula said: "All right. I make the financial decisions. But you'll have to take it as is."

The man laughed gruffly. "I see you have the good sense to hear the ring of a silver dollar, little lady. How else can a body be sure to get what's paid for, you see? Paper is nothing but paper."

And, with his arm outstretched, he crumpled up Adelaide's letter.

Later that day Nuna had pushed her original feelings aside. The man and woman had moved into the cottage without incident, and Eula had already scheduled a handyman to fix the water damage in the main house.

By early evening Nuna heard herself laughing. Bay and Judah had never seen $120 in one place. One by one Eula dropped the silver coins into a large glass jar on Nuna's kitchen table. "I'll hold out the money to fix the pipe and the ceiling and let's put the rest aside for a celebration. We need a celebration. We'll leave the jar right here near the bread box."

When Eula lifted the jar a tremor shook Nuna's shoulders. Eula saw it.

"What was that Nuna?" she asked with concern.

Nuna just shook her head and waved Eula off in dismissal, but she began to notice her hands stayed cold despite the heat that summer.

The Lavidas couple became an object of attention for Eula and Nuna within two weeks. The wife, Tereza, seemed to speak only to those who paid to hear what she saw in their palms or in their tea leaves, and Lavidas was heard more than seen. He shouted at Tereza when he was drunk and never at the normal hours kept by all the others dwelling nearby.

Henry said Lavidas bought moonshine from the locals and always paid with his silver coins. He also said that the large man had been thrown out of the two local bars that were open all night when he became "rowdy," as Henry called it. "I doesn't like that man, Nuna. No matter about pipes bein' fixt. That man gots bazodee writ all over him. He don't like us much neither. Ray Moultrie heard him at the R U Inn talkin'. That man say he stay down this way 'cause he a gypsy and we thieves, so we all in it together. He even say 'all-a-wanna,' Nuna. Then that man laugh like he's makin' a dirty joke, Moultrie say."

Henry's news stuck with Nuna. She wanted to tell Eula they had to get rid of Lavidas, Tereza, and the money, but she didn't know how. This time waiting to hear from spirit was a bad choice.

***

The last week of summer, Lavidas' curses rang through the air with enough anger and volume to draw Bay and Nuna to their back porch. Henry saw them and came over to say he'd already been on the telephone with Chief Ratliss. Just then they heard Tereza call Lavidas "a cussed fool" before she appeared on the front stoop with the hulking man behind her. Lavidas grabbed Tereza's arm, slapped her face, and pulled her back into the cottage, casting a vicious snarl over his shoulder at the Shellfoots.

Ratliss arrived, walked right up to Lavidas' entryway, and called out his name. Lavidas jerked open the door with force and shoved Tereza out.

"Tell them whether I beat you. That's what they're here for," Lavidas said standing on the stoop.

"He did not beat me," Tereza said, casually covering her jaw with her hand. "He's loud and ugly, but he did not beat me."

"Is there a law against shouting in America?" Lavidas asked with a smirk on his face.

"Actually, Mr. Lavidas, there is. You're disturbing the peace of your neighbors," Ratliss replied.

"My neighbors? You mean these injun thieves? Do you see how they're stealing money with their lies down here, Mr. Police Chief?

How much do they pay you to leave them alone, huh? They squeezed every last dollar they could from me. Ask this one, she was there." His fat finger pointed at Tereza, who stood where she'd landed. Her head was defiant, but a hand still covered her chin.

Nuna had had enough. "Dat man hits her hard. We all sees it."

Ratliss said: "You've caused a lot of trouble on this island since you got here. When is his lease up, Mrs. Shellfoot?"

"Dis be de last week."

"In that case, prepare to leave by sun-up tomorrow." Ratliss said. "You've worn out your welcome here. Is that agreeable to you, Mrs. Shellfoot?"

Nuna nodded. Lavidas looked at her with anger so strong that it curled his lips and inflamed his eyes. He said: "I never shoulda trusted a bunch of molo half-breeds. We'll be gone, soon's we do what needs to be done first." Nuna told Eula about the whole scene later. "Dey's t'ings 'bout dat man I disn't abide, is all. He gots too much mean in him."

That night fierce thunder cracked and sharp rain fell disturbing Nuna's sleep. She felt the shame of being entranced by money instead of listening to her body scream with warnings from the moment that Lavidas man arrived. Nuna tossed and turned, sure she heard footsteps, but then certain the sounds were branches blowing about in the storm. That filthy man would be gone tomorrow. And just as Nuna felt herself falling asleep, she startled awake to the pressure of a hairy hand stifling her mouth and another hand holding a knife to her throat.

Too frightened to move, Nuna realized it was Lavidas. The huge man tore at her clothes, drooling from his contorted mouth as it hovered above hers.

"I tole you I got one more thing to do before I leave, you injun whore. One more thing. You scream and then I got two things cause I'll kill you."

The huge man's heaving chest had pushed the air from Nuna's lungs. He raped her silently, gorging himself into her tiny body while the charm from his silver chain slapped her face. Nuna couldn't breathe, much less scream. Then she saw her daughter appear above Lavidas' head with a fish knife.

Bay plunged the blade into the beast's neck; once, twice.

Lavidas jerked his head back and Nuna gasped, gripping onto his silver chain and twisting it into a noose around his throat. With the man's blood dripping into her eyes, Nuna squirmed away. She picked up Lavidas' fallen knife and stabbed at the hulk herself, though it was clear the man's breath had ended with Bay's thrusts and Nuna's fierce torque of his jewelry.

Covered in blood, Bay and Nuna looked up from the murdered man's body on the floor of the bedroom and saw Henry Shellfoot standing in the doorway with his shotgun. Henry had tears rolling down his cheeks: "I seen that man creepin' around, Nuna. I grabbed my gun and missed gettin' here in time..." Henry held the two trembling women, patting their backs while staring at the bloody corpse on the bedroom floor, a flaccid penis as dead as the body attached to it. "Hush-hush, it be over, for now...you let's me fix it."

But it took the three of them to drag and roll Lavidas' body, wrapped in a tarp, outside into the teeming rain. They took it off the path and through a trail of mud until they got it to the base of the hill of graves. They covered the body with muck, shells, and fir branches before running to the beach to rinse themselves in the cold bay. Then they scrubbed the blood from the cabin, not speaking at all.

Henry made sure the women each got enough water for a hot bath and he put a large pot of bean soup on Nuna's stovetop to heat. He stoked the fire in the wood stove, drew the curtains, and told Nuna and Bay:

"You takes care a each other and I takes care of the both a you. If Eula come by, I be tellin' her you got the grippe. I'm 'bout to fix you a bowl a soup. You know my soup fix everything, right?" Henry forced a smile.

But Bay and Nuna just sat at the table. They stared at the wood crackling in the stove. Henry leaned on the table and said:

"Listen. We done what has to be. That man was gonna kill you, but for a little luck. I sees a thing that ain't right in Nuna's window. I grabbed my gun and run. I wisht it was me that kilt him, but I seen it too late."

They were quiet for a long time, until Nuna said:

"Well, we saves us. We saves us, and dat's everyt'ing we got."

***

The day after the rape, Lavidas' wagon and his wife departed. The ferry workers assumed that Lavidas was in the back of the wagon sleeping off another of his notorious drunks.

Apparently the jar of silver coins left with Tereza Lavidas since it was never seen again.

The whole night had been like a dream to Bay. She was asleep when she heard strange sounds coming from her mother's room. She rubbed her eyes as she walked through the kitchen toward the noises. Then, feeling disturbed, she picked up the fish knife. Fear seized hold of her. In her mother's room, she raised the knife and brought it down with only thoughts of Nuna. What followed, she couldn't recall. She held on to that while deciding if not knowing was a blessing or a curse. But Bay said nothing. She remembered falling asleep with her head on the table, Henry carrying her to her bed, and hearing her mother tell him at some point:

"Dat bad man's body disn't be stayin' where he be, no way. Good spirits be in dat place."

Now, Bay's dreams were of an open-mouthed Lavidas swirling in the bay, but it was never all of him. The rest she saw bubbling in a stinky batch of guano and mashed mossbunker being boiled by Nuna and Henry in front of a bloody sea.

Following the incident, Nuna and Henry had lit the fire under their annual autumnal brew a few weeks earlier than usual. It bubbled incessantly in the large cauldron out back. A putrid, yellow vapor arose in a ribbon, curling toward the sky and twisting its way across the water.

Bay watched from the rear porch and saw Nuna and Henry laboring over the steaming pot in the distance. Nuna said when these batches were finished, they were dumped into the bay.

"Salt water heals, don't ya know." It was a prompt delivered to introduce the topic of what happened so Bay would talk about it. But none of Nuna's attempts worked. Bay didn't have words beyond her dreams.

Eula saw a change in Nuna and Bay, but it was Judah who mentioned it.

"What's happened, Ma?" he asked Eula when he came in from chopping wood, "Nuna and Henry are cooking that mash like it's going to fertilize the whole island and Bay keeps telling me she's tired, or cranky, or not feeling very social, or whatever the heck she comes up with. It started right after that palm reader left with her fat, drunk of a husband."

Eula, who was paring apples for a pie, nodded, paused, and said:

"You know, Judah, that's exactly when it started."

"So you've noticed it, too?"

"Well, it's hard to miss the fumes from the boiling mash," Eula smiled. "But what would the Lavidas people have to do with that?"

"Maybe the wife told Bay something bad about her and me in the future. Do you think, Ma? Maybe she said something bad to get even about having to leave and Bay listened to her."

"Slow down, Judah, maybe Bay *is* just tired or cranky. Give her some room. Girls like enough space to be themselves from time to time. Give Bay that. She's only 14 years old, Judah. She has some growing up to do."

But Eula knew something bad had happened, and now that she thought more about it, Judah was right about when all this started.

"Nuna, I can feel a change in you and Bay. Did something happen with the Lavidas people other than what you told me?"

"Dey be gone, Eula, and dey takes dem coins wit' dem. Dey be bad for us here. Me and Bay's workin' on gettin' dat bad spirit from alla 'round us, dat's all. Summa de time de bad ones takes alla de good wit' dem for a whiles."

But Eula knew Nuna wasn't telling her the whole truth, mostly because she saw a look on Nuna's face she had never seen, and she'd been looking at Nuna's face her entire life. Eula ventured a prayer to Father Sky on a fall night when the cold was needle sharp and the heavens were cyrstal blue.

"Help her," Eula whispered with her head turned up and her body filled with prayer."Help her. She believes help is in you."

When Eula thought about it later, she assessed her plea as a reprimand as much as a prayer.

Goldsmith's Sukkoth
"Man only took form after he existed in the Holy One's thoughts."

Nuna found herself walking toward Ezra Goldsmith's cabin on a bright afternoon. She couldn't explain why, except to acknowledge that she felt drawn there and she hadn't felt much other than the burden she and Bay carried each day.

Lying to the Morelys was the hardest part because it seemed to silence Bay even more, no matter how Nuna tried to explain the lie:

"Dey be stories dat disn't get tole, Bay," Nuna said when Bay wept about the distance she was putting between herself and Judah. Nuna held Bay close: "Judah be wantin' ta fix dat hurt for you. Dat's what mens do. Dey's no fixin' dis by him. Jus' us and Henry. We gots de fixin' ta do."

Walking to Ezra's, Nuna paused at the end of the path and eyed the remains of his harvested garden and the few gourds that had popped up during a week of warm weather.

Just beyond, Nuna saw what appeared to be a structure, and then she remembered Ezra telling her about the Hebrew tradition of building a Sukkoth, a temple to honor one's ancestors in gratitude for a good harvest.

Nuna approached carefully, in awe of its fragility.

The Sukkoth was constructed from the flowers, fruits, vegetables, branches, vines, and stalks of Ezra's robust gardens.

Sturdy bamboo poles were interlaced with woven ropes of vegetation. Corn stalks were threaded through lattices between stripped stakes of green bamboo to create a covered roof. Clipped and fading, long-stem roses in every hue bordered the outside of a willow-branch fence around the Sukkoth's base. Huge sun-flowers glowed in a patch at one side of the hut and maple trees glowed with branches of hot pink and orange leaves along the other.

Beauty lit itself in front of Nuna's eyes with such force that the tears she'd held in for Bay's sake finally broke loose. Nuna slid down the trunk of a Ginko tree and stared up at the glowing yellow of its crown, feeling a flow of grief run from her body.

She looked again and saw Ezra's hand reaching out.

"Come, my friend, sit in the Sukkoth." Ezra pulled Nuna up and tucked her small arm in the crook of his large one. Ezra patted her hand. "Whatever great sorrow you have, it will be borne away by the spirit of renewal in the harvest house."

They sat on woven mats that kept the cold ground from chilling their bones. Ezra handed her a clay mug of hot tea poured from a thermos.

"I knew you'd come soon," he smiled, "so I kept the kettle on."

They sat in silence while the sun threw a blanket of goldenrod light over Ezra's yard. He spoke first:

"Do you know the Old Testament at all, Nuna?" he asked.

"Summa it. Captain Morely reads it to Eula and me summa de time when we be girls," Nuna said smiling. "He be readin' and gettin' mad at de same time."

Ezra let Nuna's memory fade before speaking:

"Well, the Hebrews believe the Sukkoth comes from what God told Moses in Leviticus: 'On the first day you shall take the product of hadar trees, branches of palm trees, boughs of leafy trees of the brook'... and on and on... 'in order that future generations may know I brought them out of the land of Egypt. To me," Ezra said softly, "the Sukkoth praises the Holy One who created spirit first. Man only took form after he existed in the Holy One's thought. My Sukkoth praises the beauty of that thought. It is man who causes pain and spirit which lifts man back to the Holy One, out of the land of Egypt and sheltered with the fruits of glory. Spirit is in all things, like those that form this house of praise."

Ezra waited in silence again while Nuna and he sipped their tea. When he spoke, he nearly whispered: "I know evil befell you, Nuna. I don't know in what way it came or how deeply it hurt, but I know it will envelop you if you don't reach for spirit again. Return yourself to the Holy One's thought. Find it in your Oonuh as you say. The Sukkoth reminds us that we are part of this harvest, part of the seed, part of the soil. We can disintegrate into ugliness alone and grow again in beauty together."

Nuna didn't speak. Her tears fell too hard. They were jagged, flooding tears pumped by shuddering sobs. Ezra sat quietly, reaching out now and then to pat her as one would a small child. "There now," he said. "There, there."

Nuna's weeping slowed. When she was able to speak, she said: "Dis bad t'ing shake me em'ty."

Ezra poured more tea into Nuna's cup and sat. "If spirit is everything, Nuna, then God is in the bad as well as the good. That's the great puzzle, isn't it? No matter what our belief is. No matter how many houses of praise we build or Makiaweesug we meet. We still seek the answer to why? Why is there so much pain? Why would Mother Earth allow her children to be hurt so deeply?"

1910

Màthair
"Will there be more dilly-dallying on your part…"

Hansen Ratliss hated answering the telephone in the police station and he believed it rang twice as much when Karen Moultrie took her break, (walking around the center "to get herself a breath of normal air"), each work day rain or shine.

In the last ten minutes, Ratliss had heard from a Civil War vet who called to say he saw a man he believed to be a German spy on the ferry; a woman who said Nuna Shellfoot had cast a spell on her; and a mother who said her son, a police department rookie, was "*un*capacitated" and couldn't work his shift.

Ratliss stared at a new call coming in that had a great, ringing urgency. Six long bells later, the Chief answered it:

"Ratliss here," he said.

"Chief Ratliss, Mother Augustus of Màthair speaking."

"And how are you, Mother?" Ratliss said, smiling at that word and shaking his head. He hadn't heard from her since Hector Wesley's paid protestor quit.

"I am not well at the moment, thank you," The Mother Superior said. "Ray Moultrie delivered our dairy provisions this morning and noticed a lewd remark scrawled on the fence by our gardens."

"Lewd, Mother?"

"And blasphemous, Chief Ratliss."

"I see. May I inquire as to what the remark says?"

"I have Ray Moultrie here to tell you. I'm handing the telephone instrument to Mr. Moultrie now. He has my permission to repeat the lewd remark to you. Here he is."

Ray Moultrie took the phone and nodded his head at the nun. He felt very nervous, but he knew Ratliss through his wife, Karen:

"Chief?" Moultrie shouted into the phone. "Ray Moultrie here to report on the words I saw."

"Yes, Ray?" Ratliss said.

Moultrie cleared his throat and said: "Ok... then, it says.. you might want to block your ears or something, Sister."

"Mother!" The nun and Ratliss interjected at the same time. "Uh...right," a startled Ray said. "Well...'Whores of Babylon,' with a arrow pointin' at Màthair. That's what it says. It's big. Maybe two-foot tall letters. But most is spelled wrong."

"Thank you, Ray. Would you put Mother back on."

"Uh, sure Chief."

The nun took the receiver and spoke without a pause: "Will there be more dilly-dallying on your part in pressing charges against these trespassers, Chief Ratliss?"

"I wasn't aware of any dilly...any of that. We have suspects in all the cases you've reported, Mother, but we have no proof. We need proof to apprehend people."

"Well, I suggest you go to your suspects right now, Chief Ratliss, and see who among them is soiled with blue paint."

The telephone line disconnected.

Ratliss cranked up his car and drove over to the Believers' camp. It was early May, so the campgrounds hadn't opened for business. Ratliss expected to find Remie readying things up. When he didn't, he crossed over to Remie's house and knocked on the door.

Ruth Remie appeared when it opened. Ratliss hadn't really seen much of her before, but he was surprised at how old she was with sunken eyes and toothless gums.

"Good day, Mrs. Remie," the Chief said. "Is your husband at home?"

Ruth had her right hand on her bony hip. She threw her chin up and said through the gaps in the teeth that remained: "I don't see him enough to know where he is, thank the Lord our God." She closed the door.

Ratliss took a look around the camp. He didn't find Remie or any blue paint. He drove away wondering if the loss of Ruth's teeth was due to her husband or poor nutrition. Then he noticed a house just above Pipers' Cove. It was a large log cabin that had a door painted robin's egg blue. Ratliss got out and knocked. The owner called for Ratliss to come in. He was a very elderly man who could barely stand from his chair. He lived there alone. He painted the door a decade before. He said the paint cans were in his barn. They weren't.

Ratliss drove over to Wesley's house where he found Wesley and Remie. They were sitting on two old chairs in a tangle of weeds at the front. Remie moved the whiskey jug behind a rock when he saw it was Chief Ratliss getting out of the stopped car.

"What can me and my friend, Hector here, do for you, Chief?" Remie said, standing up and walking toward Ratliss.

Remie reached out to shake Ratliss' hand. He'd never done that before and Ratliss noticed Remie's right hand was clean up to his wrist. The Chief thought he smelled kerosene. He said:

"I was just coming by this way and thought I'd see how the camp is doing. Getting ready for the season are you? Cleaning and painting and such?"

Hector Wesley came up to stand next to Remie. He nodded at the Chief and shuffled his feet. Remie answered Ratliss:

"Yeah, Hector's been paintin'. See that fence right there, the white one? He painted that once, didn't ya Hector?" Remie laughed at his joke.

Ratliss allowed Remie to think the sarcasm was beyond the Chief's ken and continued. "And a nice job you did painting that fence, Hector," Ratliss said, slowly, looking Wesley in the eyes and watching him look away. But Ratliss didn't see any blue spots on Wesley either. "So listen," he said, putting his spit-polished black shoe up on a rock and leaning forward on his thigh. "I need your help."

Remie looked at Ratliss from the corner of his eye and scowled. Hector sidled in to hear better. Ratliss went on:

"I know you're a man of faith, Remie and I respect that. So I'm confiding in you and your friend here." Hector nodded. Ratliss continued. "There's some tom-foolery going around the island that just isn't christian. I'm sure it's only two or three immature boys doing childish things. You know how that is. They can get pretty wild before they grow up." Ratliss paused again. Remie shifted his weight from one foot to the other and tried to make sense of what Ratliss was saying. He wanted their help?

But Hector was already talking:

"Yeah. Yeah. You want us to keep our eyes out, right? For these two boys...or three. Yeah, Yeah, Sure we'll do that. Like posses, right?"

"Sure," Ratliss said. "That's it, we'll all keep an eye out. We'll be the adults here and teach these juveniles how to be men. So if you see anything or hear anything, let me know, and let's keep this arrangement to ourselves, ok? Check in when you've got something."

Ratliss got in his car and left. He really wasn't sure where his story about the "tom-foolery" came from, but he knew it confused the hell out of both of those dimwits and that was enough. Then, he decided to send one of the rookies over to Màthair to tell Mother Superior the case was still open.

Meanwhile, back at Hector's place, Josiah Remie stared at the departing motor car and said:

"There's something about all this I don't like. First off, ain't posses for sheriffs? And second who is that Tom somebody he said is goin' around the island? Is he a rich boy? Them rich boys cause all kinds a trouble some times."

"Oh! So you doesn't think he mean us, like calling us little boys in code and all?" Hector asked.

"He said that Tom guy's name, Hector. How clearer can he get? Be on the lookout for him, ya hear me? We can go along doin' what we do and be reportin' about a rich boy named Tom. Got it?"

Pipers' Cove
"Must have a curse on it!"

Ruth Remie, at 42, had buried her parents, lost all hope for her marriage, and found that her son, the one light in her life, idolized his father whose abusive neglect of his family led to Ruth's loss of teeth, since she sacrificed her portion of the spare food available for Inri.

But her seven-year-old blamed his mother for her position and studied his father by working at his side, handing Josiah tools to replace a rotted board at the community center or to reglaze a loose window pane in the barn.

Inri believed his father's ability to fix things was directly related to Josiah's personal relationship with Jesus. Every summer of his life so far, Inri's chest swelled with pride when Josiah appeared as Jesus and proclaimed the Beatitiudes.

Inri's father-worship led him to feel flush with a desire to be with Josiah on a beautiful day the last week of school in June. So the little boy walked off the playground at recess and ran through the woods toward Pipers' Cove. It was an easy cut and since no one was his friend, no one missed him. Inri leaned against a tree to catch his breath. Nothing happened. Noone came after him. For a moment Inri felt the pain of that kind of invisibility, but he pushed it aside. He wasn't entirely sure of the right paths and found himself in an unfamiliar area of thick undergrowth and enormous hardwood trees. It felt dark, though Inri could see bits of blue sky shining through the canopy above. The boy's heart beat fast and his head was unsure of which way to go. Then the familiar voice of his father hit him and Inri felt a rush of relief. He saw his father through a thicket of bushes near an old lean-to shack. Inri started to call out to Josiah, but something about his father's appearance made the boy crouch lower in his hiding place to get a better view.

Josiah fumbled with the buttons on his fly, preparing to pee in the bushes. He wove around unsteadily, having a terrible time of it. Finally, he leaned forward, held on to a skinny tree trunk with his right hand and his penis with his left while talking to himself: "I pee like the strongest horse on this fuckin' island, my friend. Hell, any horse anywhere, goddammit." His bladder appeared to doubt this because only small spurts of urine were visible to Inri. Josiah waited, straining, but still not producing a race horse stream. "Fuckin' moonshine," Inri heard his father say. "It dries me all up."

Then Josiah vomited with an outrageous gag that spewed the contents of his stomach onto the foliage between them. Inri almost wretched himself.

"Shi-i-it!" he heard his father say and saw him wipe his mouth on an old rag drawn from a rear pocket. As Josiah worked on maintaining his balance, he buttoned up his fly. Then Inri saw his father pick up a Mason jar filled with an amber liquid. He swilled a gulp, swished it through his mouth, and gargled with it before spitting it out. Two beats passed before Josiah took a longer swig and swallowed.

Inri watched Josiah grimace with the burn of the whiskey making its way down his gullet. Josiah's shoulders heaved twice, like he was going to throw the whiskey up. He gagged and held his stomach with his free hand, trying to control the turbulence. When it appeared the whiskey was there to stay, Josiah took another long swallow from the jar.

A stick cracked. Inri heard footsteps and a voice coming from the far side of the lean-to. A man appeared whom Inri recognized as Hector Wesley.

"I hear'd you wretchin' all the way back at my house, Josiah. You okay?"

"Will be in a minute," Josiah said.

"I'll just go into the still and get started myself while you do that," Hector said, moving into a shaft of sunlight that shot a beam from a large silver disk around the man's thick neck.

"No you will not, Hector. No one touch that still but me," Josiah wiped his mouth on his sleeve, spit twice, and reached into his front pocket. Turning around, he looked at Hector, and withdrew a wad of greasy, dollar bills.

"Where'd you get that thing hangin' on your neck?" Josiah asked as he counted his money.

Hector held the silver disk out for Josiah's admiration: "It's something, ain't it? I cut it outta a tuna I caught with the fleet. Captain said 'finders, keepers,' so here it is. It's a silver dollar with a hole in it. See?" Hector held it up higher.

"Humph," Josiah said. "Must have a curse on it."

"Why you goin' and sayin' that?" Hector whined.

"Well, numbskull, think about it. Fishes doesn't wear silver neck chains. It got there for some bad reason." Josiah rolled the cash and stuffed it back into his pocket. "Bring them jugs over to here. You knows I don't do no heavy liftin' " he said, walking into the shack.

Inri crept up close to the rear of the ramshackle structure. He heard Josiah say:

"I'd get rid of that cursed thing 'round your neck, if I was you."

"Well, you ain't," Hector said.

"It ain't worth a damn thing 'less you melt it down for the silver. This way it ain't nothin' but a dollar with a damn hole in it, and what could be more cursed than that?"

Inri scurried to another clump of bushes when he realized Hector Wesley had slammed the door to the still and was heading back where he came from, holding two empty jugs. Josiah came out and called after him:

"Don't know what you're wastin' a trip for? You'll be back soon enough you old drunk."

Inri watched his father glug from the jar and listened to his angry mutterings for awhile longer, but the boy left when he realized he wasn't going to see the father he thought he had ever again.

The next day, Inri stopped joining Josiah in shared tasks. As it turned out the great Jesus-Father Inri knew at the Believers' camp was a sinner like everyone else.

Inri's life took a different turn that summer. The younger children of the visiting Believers began to follow him around like he was some kind of leader, a position Inri hadn't experienced. It empowered him to dare the others to do dangerous things..

"I got matches. Let's go burn them ants," Inri said to a little boy who looked like he'd never had dirty knees.

"Ants was made by Jesus, too, ya know," the boy said to Inri.

"And so was matches," Inri replied.

The boy heard logic in this and nodded his approval.

"You've got pockets," Inri said handing over the matches. "Put these away so no one sees 'em. Follow me."

The fire Inri started in the dry grass at the edge of the woods was quickly doused with water from a garden hose. However, the visiting boy stuffed the matches back in his pocket and ran when he saw the flames spread.

Inri told Josiah, who arrived minutes later, that the boy lit the fire.

"He's got the matches in his pocket," Inri said. "Tell his father to look for 'em. You'll see."

The boy's father, upon learning of his son's transgression, pulled the youngster out to the back of their cabin, grabbing a large wooden spoon on the way.

The thwack of the flat wood against the boy's calves, followed by his screams, resounded through the campgrounds for 10 minutes.

Calliope Point
"Year-Rounders Only Party"

August of 1910 Tommy Lawson stood with Sissy on the back lawn of their home. They saw the Westside Ferry crossing the Sound toward the mainland. Departing guests hung at the sides of the flat-bottomed boat, looking back at their summer haven.

"I know how they feel," Tommy said. "Especially the kids. I never could leave this place."

"You never thought about living elsewhere?" Sissy asked.

"Well when I thought about it, I got deeply sad. Like a kind of grief, I guess. So I never left."

"I had that sensation on my way back to the city after meeting you, Tommy. It was as if I'd passed through some veil to a better place and, when leaving, I feared I might never find my way back. You're right. It was grief, a longing for something that seemed unreal."

Tommy responded with another memory: "Every year when we were kids, after the final summer ferry full of tourists left, my father held a 'beach bake' to celebrate the day islanders got

Corycian back for nine months. It was the second weekend of September every year. The whole island came. Those are some of my most happy memories from childhood."

"Why didn't your father continue them?" Sissy said.

"Hmmmm, I forget you didn't know my father. Not much of a partier when he got home from the war with Spain. My mother said war robbed him of his joy. He had horrific nightmares and I guess the hootch helped. He partied plenty by himself and then screamed during his sleep every night…hmmm, it's best not talk about my father, ok? It just spoils beautiful moments… I was about to say: Let's have a beach bake. We'll reinstitute a good part of his legacy. I'm sure he'd like that"

"Great idea," Sissy said. "What can I do?"

"Well, start by inviting every year-rounder you know. That's a rule, year-rounders only. Many of the old ones will remember the beach bakes. Those days are part of the lore, I'm sure. We need the old fellows because I'm a little rusty on the details about laying out and digging the pits."

The next day, Tommy gathered his staff:

"Who here remembers the beach bakes my father used to have?" Tommy asked.

Hands shot up around the room. Voices called out:

"My folks talk about 'em all the time."

"My mom digs a small pit to roast fish and says it's what they did for the whole island back in the day."

"You gonna have one, Tommy?"

"That's just what I hoped to hear," Tommy said. "I'm launching the rebirth of the Lawsons' Beach Bake."

Cheers went up from his staff.

"Spread the word," Tommy said. "It's for year-rounders only, the second weekend in September. Come talk to me if you know what it's all about so we can plan, and talk to others so they can be up to date on what it takes to pull off a beach bake. Make sure you tell those you invite that we're celebrating all Corycian Island year-rounders who worked to make this a record season. At the Strand, 1910 is a year to celebrate. You know why? Because it isn't 1909! Remember 1909? Can we ever forget '09?"

In 1909 a State Senator died in the bed of a female guest who was not his wife. The woman, upon realizing the Senator slumped on her body was not relaxing after his orgasm, screamed like a jungle parrot. Her squawks awakened the Senator's wife, aslumber in the room she supposedly shared with her husband down the hall. The death was handled discretely by the local and national media.

Also in 1909, a freak bolt of lightning struck a bathhouse on the Strand's beach. The crack scared and scorched female guests changing into their bathing attire. Several nearly naked women ran from the bathhouse to the safety of the beach. The *Reader* did carry this story in the police blotter:

BLOTTER
(cont'd from p. 2)

> Lightning struck a bathhouse at The Strand Hotel last Monday startling those who were in use of the facility at the time, some of whom were exposed to the elements.

News about the rebirth of the Lawsons' beach bake rang through the town in record time. Workers talked among themselves about what to do and what to bring. The plans were big -huge - considering there were still tourists lingering around the last edges of summer who required service at the Strand and elsewhere.

Nonetheless, the preparations continued and islanders showed up at Union Harbor to make the feast happen. They dug long shallow pits along the beach, dragging in rocks and baskets of seaweed to lay under grills racked above burning coals. On the appointed morning islanders arrived from all over Corycian, fresh from the last day of a heavy summer workload. They readied the beach for the party, sending children with buckets at low tide to scratch sandbars for clams.

Just before the sun set, the entire group gathered "to cast the seine," an amazing sight and an age-old tradition. The young and the old, Scalers and otherwise, held one side of a voluminous net while two fishing boats towed the other side out toward the horizon. Slowly, the net dropped deep into the water. Minutes later, with great care, the boats turned, heading back to the shore, towing the net as it filled behind them. When the boats were at the shoreline, islanders - dozens because it took that many - took hold of both sides of the seine and hauled the heavy catch to the beat of a syncopated call.

At Tommy's beach bake, Henry Shellfoot "called the seine" by beating a kettle drum used by his forefathers at the old Bakker homestead. The booms heralded over the water, each note keeping the leaded-line low and the corks afloat. All-a-wanna, the islanders worked to unfurl the bounties of the sea.

"Pull--(boom)--Turn--(boom)--Pull ---" Henry called. The haulers grabbed hand over hand, turning the net as they yanked on each beat. "Pull-- (boom)--Turn--(boom)--Pull---"

At last, when the net was on dry land, fish spilled out as they had generations ago, blessings from Poseidon for the workers who had produced another summer of profit, prophecy, and paradise on Corycian Island.

The partiers brought casseroles of late harvests, loaves of bread dough, and every color of potato, ready to bake.

They placed these foods at a deeper end of the beach pits where the coals burned more slowly. Several fruit pies prepared in iron skillets sat next to rows of seaweed wrapped fish and cobs of corn. Pots of shellfish stew bubbled alongside. Some men tended hotter coals, readying them to grill venison steaks, whole chickens, racks of clams, oysters, and lobsters.

Henry brought along his special catch of fresh tuna. At a section of the grill pits he manned those steaks himself, serving them with his characteristic cheer when they were cooked just right. Lifting one, just charred, Henry placed it on the plate Karen Moultrie held out to him:

"And hello to you good lady," Henry said, adding his tickling laugh. "There's a piece a fish like you never tasted before, don't ya know. Tee-hee-hee."

"It's nice to see you Mr. Shellfoot," Karen said, "outside the store, and all...the tuna looks lovely. Isn't this a wonderful night to celebrate our home?"

"All-a-wanna, Miss." Henry said. "That's what Nuna say. All-a-wanna, what life be all about."

The two neighbors looked around them as night fell over the beach. Smoke rose from the pits with the sounds of laughter, music, and waves. Sitting on the rocks near the bay's edge, a trio played "Down by the Old Mill Stream" on ukuleles while an audience of happy islanders joined in. Little children, worn from a day of sun and an evening of wonder, slept on the beach, curled under blankets and a starlit sky.

"Nuna say the stars is part a us," Henry said to Karen Moultrie, as he looked above the horizon. "She say we comes from them, but they here because a us, too. We all connected to the stars. I like that."

"Makes you feel larger somehow, doesn't it?" Karen Moultrie said. "I think if I couldn't see the stars any more, I'd die. They are my proof, you know, Henry? They are my proof that God exists."

Henry laughed. "And we proof for God, too, don't ya know."

Hansen Ratliss and Burston Bakker marveled at the commingling of the islanders from their viewpoint on a rise above the beach.

"I've even seen a few priests from Màthair here," Ratliss said, looking out over the crowd. "It makes me wonder where our troublemakers are. You seen Remie or Wesley?

"Sometimes, I think we only find out where they've been."

Ratliss and Bakker continued to chat talking about the people they saw and drinking from mugs of beer they'd pumped from a keg. Had they been more observant they would have noticed that one Remie was there: Inri.

But Inri's presence went by undetected. He had followed his father and Hector to the Strand, and then lost track of them. Seeing the fires on the beach at Union Harbor, Inri climbed along a shelf of the cliffs and stayed hidden by the cedars and the night. The boy sat on a rise just above the beach and watched the scene unfold like a dream.

He looked for his father and Hector, hoping to find them among all the neighbors. He saw the Ke'was people, the Strand people, even Marmie and the school people, but no one to whom he was related.

Hours later, in the same spot, Inri slept. He dreamed his mother arrived. She was dancing with his father who held up his hand and waved for Inri to come join them.

***

Cleaning up the beach the next day took several hours. The pit's waste required proper disposal and the beach had to be restored to its original condition. More than enough people pitched into help and when all was done, Tommy shook the hand of each, saying:

"Same time. Same place....next year."

"Isn't he a wonder?" Sissy said to Pammy. "He pulled it off. I knew he would."

"It was perfect," Pammy said. "The perfect party."

They scooped their sleeping children up, wrapped and ready to go, handed them over to their fathers, and climbed up the beach to their homes.

PART TWO (1915-1928)

1915

Ke'was End
"We will be at each other's side forever in body and spirit."

Bay Shellfoot and Judah Morely were married in a ceremony of mixed traditions on September 18, 1915. Bay was 20 and Judah, 22.

The couple pledged themselves to each other in the Quaker ceremony. It was late in the afternoon. They stood, silently, at the middle of a circle of relatives and friends in the Captain's wildflower field below the arms of a knotty, old American Plane.

When the hush settled, Judah declared his vows to Bay which she repeated to him:

"In the presence of God, and before these our families and friends, I take thee to be my spouse promising, with divine assistance, to be unto thee loving and faithful, as long as we both shall live."

Bay and Judah signed a marriage certificate, then pledged their troth again "in the eye of spirit," enacting Native American rites with "The Circle of Seven Steps."

Henry and the other men built a bonfire to honor spirit. Henry said, as he lit the wood:

"For those who comes before that gives life to these who comes now, this is the light that calls blessings from the ancient ones."

Judah took a step toward the sacred flame. He reached back and took Bay's hand, drawing her to his side while each spoke at the same time: "We will be at each other's side forever in body and spirit."

Bay took the next step, moving clockwise around the flames. She reached for Judah's hand, drawing him around to step in front of her, and said: "Our love will always grow."

With each step, the couple exchanged a promise and with the last three, a small gift. From Bay to Judah, a polished stone from the Ke'was beach to bring strength; a dove's feather from Judah to Bay to bring harmony; and kernels of corn - from Bay's hand to Judah's hand and back to hers, to bring fertility.

The last step was for the newlyweds to reach out and draw their parents in next to them; then Nuna and Eula each drew in a loved one; the loved one drew in another, and so on until all formed a circle around the fire. Silence fell. The faces turned toward Judah and Bay. Henry snapped his fingers softly, and every head bowed, while each heart silently sent abundant blessings to the bride and groom.

Judah filed the marriage certificate with the Town Clerk of Corycian Island the next day. As required by law, a public notice appeared in the Town's official newspaper:

THE CORYCIAN ISLAND READER
Public Notices

To whom it may concern, the following marriage licenses were issued and certificates of marriage were filed with the Town Clerk as of September 23, 1915: Sylvestri Malone to Mary Catherine Duffy at St. Anthony's Chapel, Rev. Anthony Daniele, officiating.

Bay Shellfoot to Judah Morely at Ke'was End in a Quaker ceremony.

Pipers' Cove
"They're comin' over to here soon, straight across the ocean."

"Those Morelys never did care who they married," Hector Wesley said to Josiah Remie on a chilly night. Hector had just read the Public Notices in the *Reader*. "My daddy said old Ephraim Morley took up with a indian woman when his Quaker wife croaked. Them and Nuna Shellfoot's people were big friends. Always been that way with indians and the Quakers out there - with alla them fornicating with slaves back in the day, too, don't ya know."

"Stop talkin' like I *don't* know, Hector. I was borned here, too."

"Yeah, but nobody ever told you nothin'."

"What in the hell d'ya mean by that?"

"Don't get all riled about it, Josiah. You said yourself your pa was drunk alla the time and your ma never talked to no one at all, least a all you."

"Yeah, I says that, but what's it got to do with what you sayin'?"

"What'd I say?" Hector asked.

"Bout that indian and all," Josiah said, dismissing his lack of attention with a swig from a jug. They leaned against the outside of the still's frame. A small fire burned at their boot tips to keep them warm.

"Oh," Hector said. "Yeah so, well...but...anyways... those two didn't get married in a church."

"What two?"

"The two's that a indian and a Quaker now down there at Ke'was End. That's what I been sayin'- See? Always has been that way with the indians and them Quakers. They just says they'se married and that's it. No bands announced, at all. They'se heathens down there, Josiah. You're righter 'n right on 'bout this. Total heathens and witches, just like them nun-whores."

Josiah passed the moonshine to Wesley. Getting Hector dead drunk was the best way to shut him up, Josiah thought. He let Wesley take a long drink. It was time to change topics.

"Yeah, so, I'm thinkin' maybe it's the day for Inri to go by his middle name because a what I didn't know and all. You know about Jesus and the cross and all, like you said. If people thinks he's named for the king of them Jews he could get hisself into trouble. I started calling him by Raymond - but he don't like it one bit. He don't answer me, and then when I tells them at school to do it, they says he walks out when they trys to call him it."

Hector sat very still. Josiah never talked about his family, but he blabbered on:

"So I was thinkin' Raymond's nearly a man now - bein' just about 12 and all - and I think we should teach him a lesson about Jews. Then he'll want to start bein' Raymond real quick. You see, I read that Henry Ford thinks its Jews that started this war over there in Europe. German Jews, he says, and you know why? So to kill all the young male species so no more babies'll be born to us Believers. And they're comin' over to here soon, straight across the ocean, and I says we stop them right now on Corycian. Stop them right in their tracks, and show Inr ----er --.'"

"What're you talkin' about, Josiah?"

"I'm talkin' about the Jew on Ke'was End - that Goldsmith one - and there are more; a few over past Sirens' Beach, summer people, and I got someone in Town Hall lookin' things over for me. They change their names, don't ya know, but the Town Hall people has ways of makin'things come up."

"Hold on, Josiah. You're doin' that very thing with Inri - changin' his name and all? Maybe doin' that will make *his* name come up..." Hector said.

"God dammit, Hector, you always gotta make everything so confusin'. You think too much is what you do. One's got nothin' to do with the other. Now listen. Here's what to make sense about: Henry Ford is a good man. He invented the god-damn Model T didn't he? Why do you know what his invention's done for the message of the Lord Almighty? I had a fella from a Pennsylvania camp call me about my Sermon on the Mount. Says he heard it from a family that spent the whole summer in their Ford automobile driving from one Believers' Camp to the next to hear Jesus' message. They talks 'bout my Sermon on the Mount at every stop, sayin' it was the highlight, the Pennsylvania man told me. He was wantin' to know all about how I do it and all. I got somethin' here, Hector, and Henry Ford and me won't be lettin' Jews get in our way by startin' wars."

1916

Ke'was End
"The union of man to the power of spirit."

Ismy "Mystifier," born to Bay Shellfoot and Judah Morely, arrived one month earlier than expected on May 24, 1916. She bore herself smoothly into the world with birds singing outside the window by her birth bed. It became the family story about Ismy's pace of life from then on. The baby's middle name - "Mystifier"- was derived from a Runapewak tradition. This was a name only to be whispered.

Nuna and Ahane had given the newborn's mother the silent name of "Inspirier" because Bay had opened them to a new wisdom.

Now Bay and Judah's child was Ismy "Mystifier," honoring the mother-child connection to the heart of Mother Earth; the unidentifiable union of man to the power of spirit.

Ismy had beige skin, blue eyes, and patches of blonde hair. "Mystifier," Bay cooed softly at her nursing daughter sometimes. "Mystifier, from what spirit seeds did you come?"

Ismy's blue eyes shone back at her mother's brown ones. The baby had one dimple in her right cheek. It flashed when Ismy pulled away from Bay's breast. She reached her tiny hand up and touched her mother's face. Judah's heart filled when he saw the tenderness.

"It's...I don't know....overwhelming, the awe, I mean. I can't find the words," he told Bay when he first held them both in his arms.

"Do you see how she looks like you, Judah?" Bay said. "With that blonde fuzz on her head and those blue eyes."

Judah cried for 24 hours, the joyful tears just fell as he moved from task to task, helping to tend his daughter and his wife.

One night when Judah thought Bay was asleep, she saw him standing by the window. He held wee Ismy in his arms, rocking her softly, stroking the soft down on her head, and drying his face with the edge of her blanket.

***

THE CORYCIAN ISLAND READER
Vol. 18, No. 40 August 15, 1916
Editorial

It is said that Americans are isolationists who are wary of involvement in Europe's war. Corycian Islanders understand isolationism better than most. Here lives a community born in a tradition of true neutrality where one's reputation speaks before all. Here is a place where one's home is known and respected. We live apart from, yet within our United States. We are from here and from there.

Right now those from whom many of us are descended, are tearing each other apart in the muck and the mud of France, and we, Islanders so far from their shores, can no longer ignore the turmoil.

We must take a stand. This is evident in our taverns, our living rooms, and our newspapers where we've argued over the fate of the *SS Lusitania* for one year, and Woodrow Wilson's grip on neutrality for two.

We ask ourselves: Is it a war that threatens our shores? Meanwhile, smug and powerful forces in industry, banking, and commerce think war is healthy for our economy. So, is it a war for profits?

Is this what the Americans who are going to give their lives for war want - to enrich the American economy?

> This publication supports Wilson's campaign
> cry for "Peace and Preparedness." Wilson's call
> for an army to stand ready on our shores accom-
> plishes this goal.
> If we succumb to war, what peace is there when
> we've sacrificed the lives of Corycian Island sons?

Burston Bakker's editorial provoked a reply from his anonymous critic. The private letter, again written on fine vellum
stationery in beautiful cursive, said, among other things:

> "So, have you finally developed a spine, Mr. Bak-
> ker? Are you at last willing to join the big brains of
> your generation who know a decade of Christian
> humanism awaits and promises a new social
> order of austere self-discipline. It is for America
> a man must work to succeed. For America on
> American soil."

The newspaperman flattened the letter out on his desk when
he finished reading it. He stamped it received, waved the ink
to dry it, then initialed and dated the stamp and filed the three
clipped pages in a folder marked: "Anonymous and Personal."

Burston Bakker sat back in his chair and wondered why this
letter, approving of his editorial remarks, made him feel worse
than the ones that called Burston a "petty, little man."

Calliope Point
"The tiniest of minds."

Pammy Bakker held the latest edition of the *Reader*. It was
folded open to the editorial. She fumed silently. She wasn't going
to let Burston Bakker think her opinion didn't matter, or worse,
that she shouldn't have an opinion other than his. The dismissive
message he gave to her, by printing this editorial without passing
it by her as he had with every op-ed piece he'd written since they
were first together, hurt.

The screened door to the kitchen slapped behind Burston when he came in early, the one night he was sure to sit down with the family since the paper was on the stands for the week. The children ran to get their due attention and Burston listened to their prattle as he went about hanging up his coat. When he came into the kitchen, he saw Pammy holding the *Reader*. She looked over the top of the broadsheet and said:

"You have a high and mighty attitude, Burston Bakker."

"Could I get a drink before you start ripping me to shreds, Pamela?" Burston replied, shooing the children to another room and heading for the liquor cabinet.

However, Pammy had been waiting to take her verbal shot all day and spoke to Burston's back.

"You forget that I grew up in New York City. I know a little something about industrialists, bankers, and salesmen - the ones who make the world spin, by the way - and what they have in common is money. Do you want to lose your protected Island, Mr. Big-Fish-in-a-Little Pond? If you do, let the Germans win this war. Keep your precious little self out of it and see what happens. And by the way, your deliberate innuendo about Jews can be deciphered by the tiniest of minds."

"So now you want to take on Germany and the Jews, do you Mrs. Bakker?" Burston said with a sneer. "You've taken on all the female causes around, and now you want to take on Germany?"

"Alcohol makes you snide and cruel, Burston."

"It's easy to call for war, Pamela, when your own son is too young to fight."

Piper's Cove
"Henry Ford's a industry-list."

The August sun bore down on Hector Wesley and Josiah Remie who sat on the bollards by the Piper's Cove boat ramp at noon. Josiah fished a copy of the current *Reader* out of a trash can and mumbled to himself while he read.

Hector thought the heat might be making Josiah drunker than usual because he was angry about something. His mumbling sounded angry, anyway. So Hector said: "D'ya have to read that thing. It always gets you riled."

"A little more readin' wouldn't hurt you none, dumbass." Josiah held the paper close to his nose and read some of Bakker's editorial aloud. It was slow going, but the reading gave impact to Burston Bakker's opinion:

> "We ask ourselves: Is it a war that threatens our shores? Meanwhile, smug and powerful forces in industry, banking, and commerce think war is healthy for our economy. "

"Hear that, Wesley?" Josiah said, snapping the newspaper in Hector's face. "The god-damn *Reader* agrees with Henry Ford. Ol' Henry knows the Jews is 'industry, bankers, and commerce.' And so that's what the *Reader's* sayin' underneath. Bakker's sayin' Jews is power-filled and makin' decisions - underneath it all - pushin' at us to fight. Do you want to die for Jews to get rich, Hector? I don't, that's for damn sure."

"Now, right there that you said don't make no sense, Josiah. Henry Ford's a industry-list, ain't he? Makin' Fords in a factory and all, right? I know things you don't think I know, ya know. You got a muddled brain and besides, you ain't goin' to war. 40s too old, unless they make you type letters or somethin'."

"Why you always gotta harp on that, Wesley. I could beat the crap outta you and any Jew who shows up at my door. I'm stickin' with my people, don't ya know! Bakker's Dutch from way back and so are my people. Bakker and me are like brothers and Dutch is just about German almost, so I know what I'm talkin' about."

Ke'was End
"Who you t'ink wrote dat old test-a-men?"

Ezra Goldsmith read the editorial of August 15 in the *Reader* and noted the antagonism behind Bakker's carefully chosen words. He put the newspaper aside and wondered to himself what it was that made humans so ready to declare superiority over one another. It is all so wrong, Ezra thought, no matter who does it. Clearly, the Jews calling themselves "The Chosen People" is no worse than the Believers promising theirs is the only path to salvation, and the Catholics saying heaven belongs to them, and so on and on.

"As if God deals in such matters," Ezra said aloud, walking toward his garden, imagining the Sukkoth he would build to honor the spirit of his ancestors this year.

"The ancestors who are all-a-wanna," Ezra whispered, thinking of those who brought him a new understanding about Mother Earth and Father Sky. It came one day as he and Nuna walked along the beach.

"Who you t'ink wrote dat Ol' Test-a-men, anyway?" Nuna asked Ezra when she saw him tuck his prayer book into a pocket.

"Man wrote it," Ezra said. "Of that I am certain, but I also have no doubt that God is in man, hence, you see like all questions of the infinite, it is an unanswerable one. So, since Jews are taught not to accept without proof, I have to say...I don't know who wrote it."

"Hmmm, dat be a long way a sayin' so. You be readin' it alla time," Nuna said. "Seems ta me you missin' de proof in de eart' you be standin' on. You too stuck in dat book to sees it."

"A Rabbi, I'm not," Ezra chuckled, "but you, my dear friend are the wisest Reb I know."

***

Bay saw a new life in her mother whenever she talked of Ezra Goldsmith. She teased Nuna about it. Her mother brushed it off:

"Summa de times I t'ink your daddy sends me Ezra. He be de first friend I has since Eula and de first man-friend since Ahane, but I disn't want a man likes you be t'inkin' Bay."

Nuna had the same conversation with Eula who laughed and said to her :

"I see you flirting with each other, Nuna. Friends don't flirt."

168

"Sure does, too. Just not so much whens dey be to-geder so long likes you and me be. Dat's how you knows friends. De Oonuhs gets to flirting."

Laughing, Eula said: "Well, he's a good man, Nuna. Henry likes him and that's always a great indicator of someone's worth."

Over tea that day in the Captain's kitchen, Nuna told Henry, Eula, Bay and Judah about Ezra's plan to build a harvest house to honor them all as neighbors. "We be building dis house to Mudah Eart' and Fadah Sky wit' de last of de gardens, see? We be sayin' prayers dis way. Bein' great-filled dat spirit help us. So, puts de stalks and t'ings over ta here and den we bring dem over ta Mr. Ezra's one day and you be seein' what comes."

The second week in September, the families of Ke'was End learned how to build a Sukkoth with Ezra Goldsmith. The resulting structure was twice as large as any Ezra had erected before, and all of them enjoyed sunny afternoons within it, drinking tea, laughing at baby Ismy's antics, and sharing stories that bound them together in the family of man.

Pipers' Cove
"Be that as it may..."

Josiah and Hector, men on a mission, took a rest at Nanny Hill, a goat pasture just west of the Believers' Camp. They wore white robes, surreptitiously on loan from the Believers, and carried coned hats which Josiah had modeled after a picture he saw of southern klansmen in a Long Island newspaper.

"The newspaper said there's Keyclose types everywheres, now. We got brothers, out there, Hector," Josiah said. "And I have to gives you credit for bein' right about one thing. Them nuns oughta be regulars for us. Devil-worshippers, is what I hear, so we're gonna dial up the action over there at their place."

"That's exactly what I mean, Josiah" Hector said, empowered with an acknowledgement he received rarely from Remie. "I'm tellin' ya, I was draggin' my nets out thatta way on a Sunday, early, and they was all out there in back of the house. You seen they fixed that statue, right? I saw 'em all through my binoculars.

It wasn't even dawn yet, and they was all out there in a big circle. And I remember when 'cause it was Easter morning and it was damn cold out. There was priests there with 'em, too. They was all on their knees, and they stays like that a long time while a priest walks around 'em. It's just like I said, they got somethin' going' over there. Really creepy. And definitely not very Christian, don't ya know."

Josiah passed a flask to Hector who held it up with his hand in testimony: "I know. I know. I'm not much for goin' to church now, but my mama had me goin' up there to the Calv'ry Church on Old Post Road more'n twice a week till she died."

Josiah couldn't hear a word of the story, but he knew it by heart because Hector repeated it whenever Josiah gave him space to talk.

Remie needed some time to think so he let Hector rattle on about his years of servitude to the Scaler who opened Calvary Church in his barn after claiming himself a pastor with a framed certificate to prove it. The new reverend was a charismatic fellow to whom many women seemed attracted which Hector couldn't help but notice. This is the point Hector was at in the retelling: "Be that as it may be..." Hector continued.

"Ok, enough of that," Josiah said. "Them nuns and priests is pagans for sure if they're chantin' at the sun on their knees. I been readin' enough of the Bible to know that. It's reason alone to give it to them good, but first we got other fish to fry. Here, now. This here is somthin' to get riled up about. Inri - er...Raymond...come home from school and says he heard about a house that Jew off Ke'was builds to them idols."

"Jew idols?"

"Sorta like that Virgin statue behind the nun's place over there that you saw them all laudin' at on Easter. Anyways, it sounds to me like this Jew has built hisself a temple and you know how Jesus tore up temples. It's because that's just plain breakin' the very first commandment, about idols and all. And maybe the second one, too, don't ya know. Name one place where you or me's been to worship that has a idol in it. Notta one, that I can think of. I mean that we been to, not them heathen Catholic ones."

Josiah gave them each a minute to swallow a few more gulps from the flask and to reflect on his plan while a cool breeze washed over the field.

Standing, Josiah picked up Hector's pointy hat and handed it to him.

"This flap goes in front so the eye holes hit your face right," Josiah said. "Don't put it on until we are in service of our mission. That's a pledge we gotta make. We stand with the Grand Wizard when we put the hats on."

"Who's the Grand Wizard?" Hector asked.

"I'm not sure we're privileged to know that," Josiah said with a reverential slur.

There was some sort of solemnity in the moment and Hector couldn't help but feel a strange pride in receiving the hat from Josiah's hands because, there on Nanny Hill under the influence of stars and moonshine, Josiah held on to the hat for a second longer than he had to and, clearly, a moment was exchanged.

By the time they got to Ke'was End, they were more than a few sheets to the wind.

Josiah kept telling Hector to shush, even though Hector hadn't said anything for the last mile. They walked through the woods so no one would hear them crunching oyster shells along the road. When they got to Goldsmith's weather-beaten cottage, Josiah signaled Hector to don his hat.

Then the two crept from tree to tree toward the back of the house until Josiah heard laughter. His hand shot up to stop Hector. He motioned for him to crouch down behind a thicket of bushes and remove his hat.

Before them, about 100 yards away, the Sukkoth was glowing with candle light. Josiah counted six people in a semi-circle, sitting on pillows and bales of hay, smiling at a baby.

For a moment, Josiah thought he was having a vision of Jesus' nativity scene. He looked over at Hector whose drunken mouth was hanging open and whose eyes were fixed ahead on the creche-like Sukkoth.

"What'd I tell ya?" Josiah said to the stoned face in front of him. "And it's even worse than I thought with those witches Morely and Shellfoot bein' part a it all."

He sat back and prepared to take a hit from the flask, but Hector poked at his shoulder with his finger.

"And look," Hector said. "I'll bet they're drinkin' that tea I hear Shellfoot sells to sex people up with. I wouldn't be surprised if we saw them gettin' really heathen if you know what I mean."

"Well, I'm not waitin' around to see any of that goin' on," Josiah replied. Then he startled at the sound of the group saying "good night" to one another.

"Get down, Hector! And tuck in that cursed dollar hangin' around your neck. It's catchin' the light."

The trail back to the Captain's house was far enough away that neither of the klansmen was spotted by the Shellfoots and Morelys heading home, talking in happy tones to each other with a few expressions from the baby that set them all into laughter.

Josiah looked back at the Sukkoth. Ezra was putting the candles out, and when the last was extinguished Ezra stepped out into the moonlight and looked toward the sky.

"Thank you Father Sky," Ezra prayed with his arms outstretched and his head tilted up toward the universe. "Thank you for this beautiful night. Thank you Mother Earth for this rich harvest - and thank you Makiaweesug for bringing me the spirits of these friends who have made my life whole again."

Josiah was too far away to hear Ezra's prayer, but he told a very drunk Hector:

"See that? What he's doin' there? That's part of what Jews do. Incarnatations and stuff. Uh-huh. We got ourselves a problem that needs to be dealt with right here. Yes we do."

"Let's just set it on fire," Hector said.

"No, then they might think it was on accident."

When Josiah and Hector saw the lights go out in Ezra's cottage on the other side of the thicket, the two sots donned their pointy hats, pulled down the masks, and set about tearing the Sukkoth to shreds.

***

Nuna came upon Ezra the next morning. He was standing in the midst of the destroyed autumn house. There were corn stalks strewn everywhere amid bamboo supports that had been snapped in half. The squash was cracked open on the ground and Birdie-flower petals were visible among crushed sunflowers.

Ezra looked up at Nuna who had stopped on the rise when she saw the destruction. He spoke to her quietly:

"They're here now, Nuna, my friend. Those bad spirit seeds you told me about. How strange that they appeared after such a beautiful evening. One might think the Sukkoth would have been protected by that night alone."

Nuna's heart pounded in her chest. Ezra was talking to her.

"I'm not going to get Chief Ratliss involved with this, Nuna, but I'd like to talk with Henry about how to be more vigilant. Evil has rooted itself here, and it is always people like us who get hurt."

The two words - "like us" - rang through Nuna's head.

"Us and dem never be a good way to live side by side," Nuna said.

1917

Ke'was End
"I'm a grown man after all."

On May 18, 1917 the U.S. Selective Service Act authorized the registration and draft of males between the ages of 21 and 30. Twelve men from Corycian Island were eligible, including Judah Morely who was 24-years-old.

Eula and Bay were aghast when Judah came home from the recruitment office.

"What do you mean you didn't tell them you were Quaker?" Eula said with a terrified tremor in her voice.

"Because it isn't true. I am of Quakers, not a Quaker myself. We just say it Mama, we don't do it. Besides, our country has called me and I believe service is a citizen's duty."

"But Judah," Bay said, with Ismy in her arms, the baby's thumb in her mouth, and her head on her mother's chest, "they would have given you a job if you'd told them. They just wouldn't have sent you to the front." Judah reached for her. She backed away and Ismy let out a fear-filled shriek. "You have responsibilities here, Judah. Right here. Nowhere else. Why didn't you talk to me first?"

"This is what I had to do," Judah said. "For myself, as much as all of you. I didn't want the weight of your pain until after it was done, and I'll carry that with me. I've accepted that, Bay."

***

Judah trained at Camp Upton in Yaphank, Long Island. He had been to the mainland many times, but never this far up-island. He may as well have been a continent away from Ke'was End. He trained for six weeks and prepared to join General John J. Pershing's American Expeditionary Force to France on June 24th.

175

Bay walked to the post office every day with Ismy. They mailed a letter to Judah, or pulled one from him out of their mailbox. Bay breathed sighs of relief when a Long Island postmark indicated that Judah was still just across the Sound. Then a letter came telling her he was leaving for France in two weeks. In the last one with a Long Island postmark, Judah wrote that he was shipping out that day.

In July, Bay turned the small combination lock on the door of mailbox #444 and withdrew an envelope postmarked "France."

She held it in her hands with Ismy in her arms and felt a slow apprehension snake up her spine. Ismy grabbed at the paper, but Bay ignored her.

She walked over to a bench on the lawn outside and sat. She gave Ismy the envelope to distract her. Bay unfolded the letter, holding it to her heart before she read it.

"Dear Bay -

I never in my life thought I'd be writing you so many letters and then never thought again that one of them would be coming from France. And I guess I have to add: I never even considered the feelings of shooting at someone in a war and I can tell you, Bay, I'm not happy about it. I didn't know what war was when I left to fight one so willingly. It's hard for me to say that, but it's true. I wasn't here for one day before I realized I'm not the killing kind even though my Sergeant keeps saying we're killing machines. I know I'm just gonna have to aim and shoot or get shot at when the time comes. Please don't let anyone know I'm scared about it. I'm a grown man after all - but that's part of it because I'm scared of losing you, Bay - and Ismy, Mama, and Nuna. They keep telling us we're fighting to protect you, but these guys never did anything to us. I mean....oh, who knows what I mean. I'm just plain scared of being

so far away from home, and not so sure if claiming myself a man has anything to do with killing
another man. I can tell you this, Bay, cause I know
you'll love me anyway. All my life I've told you
my secrets. I close my eyes and feel your breath,
Bay. In my dreams I hold myself inside your body
as strongly as I held you those nights at home.
We're part of each other. Closer than ever, and
Ismy is our proof of that. There's too much love
in Ismy for me to believe it's right to kill another
parent's child. This fool's journey is taking me to
a place called St. Mihiel. It's as hard to say as it
is to write. I'll be marching soon so won't get a
chance for a letter. Let this be the one to hold on
to for a time, but don't show anyone, ok? I want
it to be ours, Bay. Just ours. I love you, you've
always known that. I didn't always have to say it
out loud; you heard me say it in my head every
time I saw you, every day of our lives. Hear it now,
Bay, I'm calling over the sea. Feel me in you. Feel
me love you.

Judah."

Bay kept the letter, neatly folded, next to her heart. It was
worn with her reading of it. Two months had passed since she'd
received a follow-up. Bay kept mailing letters every week, and at
first she knew her mailbox would be empty, but as time passed,
opening box #444 made Bay's hand tremble.

Meanwhile, Judah was dug into a muddy trench in the
Northeast area of Ypres behind a battery of tanks led by Colonel
Patton. They were preparing to attack a battalion of retreating
Germans. When the battle began, Judah prayed because every-
one around him was praying while bullets flew over their trench.
He shot at shadows, shouting his prayer:

"Don't let me kill someone. Just let me get back to Bay. Let me live. Please. Even if it isn't right how I'm asking. Please. Just let me live."

And Judah did live through that battle and survived again for another nine days of warfare. On the tenth day, he was gassed by the Germans in the Argonne Forest and then cut in two by a machine gunner, prayers or not.

***

Two Scalers, veterans of the Civil War, were sent by the United States Army to the Captain's house with news of Judah's death.

Eula came to the door and wondered about the strangeness of these old men in Union jackets as she let them into the parlor. She knew them from the ferry boat, members of the crew she thought, trying to reason it all through her head.

"Mrs. Morely," the one named Meyer said, removing his hat. "Is your daughter-in-law at home, Mrs. Judah Morley. Is she at home?"

Bay walked into the foyer. She wiped her hands on her apron. "Hello," she said. "I'm Bay. How may I help you?"

"Mrs. Morely, uh," the soldier bowed. "Both, Mrs. Morelys. We're here on instructions from the United States Army which has asked us to inform you that your husband and son, Judah Morley..."

Their words bounced around the light from the Captain's stained-glass window. Bay took the blow first..."died in battle..."

Bay sat down slowly on a bench, then Eula read Bay's face and knew for sure what the man said. Eula covered her ears and turned away from all of them. Was she screaming? Could they hear her screaming? The room spun. Louder...Was she screaming louder?

Nuna ran to the Captain's house when she heard Eula's screams. She found Bay calming Eula. The grief-stricken women turned at the sound of Nuna's approach. Eula took in a shuddering breath and Bay's brown eyes told of death. Nuna folded her daughter into her arms and felt the pain trembling through Bay's body. "It's Judah," Bay said. "It's Judah."

"Inspirier," Nuna whispered into her child's ear, calling Bay's spirit name to help her be strong. "Inspirier," Nuna breathed the name again, stroking her sobbing child's head.

Bay felt her muscles shaking. She felt her neck straining and her shoulders tensing, but she heard nothing.

Then a screech let loose from Ismy's room where the baby had been napping. The sound cut through the grief and bounced its added truth off the walls.

"Daddddy...Daaaadddy," Ismy cried.

The three women exchanged furtive looks.

"I'll get her," Bay said, barely.

Eula and Nuna watched Bay walk across to the room from which came the plaintive sound of Ismy calling for her father.

"Why all dis grief comin' our way, Eula?" Nuna, who rarely questioned Mother Earth asked. "Our mens got took, disn't it be enough?"

Nuna looked up to see Henry come into the house. He stood in the doorway with a stricken look on his face.

"I sees them two soldiers," he said between coughs from raw emotion and a lack of breath from running. "They tells me...oh, no, Miss Eula...they tells me..." Henry's body sobbed. He was bent over with grief, holding onto his thighs.

"Go to Bay and Ismy," a barely lucid Eula said to Nuna.

Eula walked over to Henry and helped him lean into her embrace, patting his shoulders which seemed to be calming her as well. The two stood still for a moment. Then Eula nodded to Henry, walked out the door, and down the porch steps. She stood at the front of the Captain's house and was struck by how different the world looked and all it took was a knock on the door.

THE CORYCIAN ISLAND READER
Vol. 10, No. 40 October 4, 1917
Judah Morely
Corycian Island Lad Plays Great Part in Struggle
Judah Morely Fought Enemy Gallantly in France

While fighting in defense of our country, and hence the residents of his home, Judah Morely,

U. S. Army Field Artillery Sergeant, was killed in action in the Battle of Argonne Forest, France September 1917. Sergeant Morely was the husband of Bay Shellfoot, the father of Ismy Shellfoot Morely, and the son of Eula Morely and the late Melvin Harkness.

News of the Sergeant's death was communicated by telegraph borne by two, uniformed veterans to the Morely's Ke'was End home. The widow of the deceased and her mother-in-law received the mournful news at the Captain's Guest House.

Sergeant Morely was a true patriot whose heart was filled with the brave love of family and country while he fought valiantly in several battles in France.

Judah Morely was born in 1893 at his family home. He is the great grandson of renowned Corycian Island shipwright, Captain Ephraim Morely, whose impeccable skills contributed to the fleet of the U.S. Naval force in the War Between the States. The deceased's wife is the granddaughter of the last Grand Sachem of the Runapewak tribe on Corycian Island.

Judah Morely will be remembered as a faithful husband, devoted son, and caring father who gave his life for his country, but also as a splendid fellow by the many who knew him well. From Judah's cordiality while serving customers at Henry Shellfoot's store to his gentle ways and kind heart toward his family, neighbors, and friends, his presence will be greatly missed.

Services for the fallen hero will be held at the Corycian Island Founders' Cemetery at Noon October 6th when a memorial stone will be commemorated.

***

Judah's body was buried in a mass grave on the battlefield in France, but Bay knew his spirit had to reside at the cemetery within the site of his family home. So on October 6th the families gathered around a large stone Henry and others had placed inside the wrought iron gates. Ismy struggled in her mother's arms while a veteran read a citation from the United States honoring "Sergeant Morely's gallantry and intrepidity in the defensive sectors of the battles of Ypres, St. Mihiel, and Argonne."

Bay stood, stoically, holding a subdued Ismy. Eula wept quietly, standing by Nuna whose focus was on a large osprey hovering at the side of its nest in the tallest fir tree near the water.

Henry stood behind Nuna with his hat over his heart. Ezra stood with the Moultries, outside the fence. It seemed as if the rest of the town stood beyond them, all around the meadow and in front of the path to the woods.

Nuna glanced again at the osprey who opened her wings slowly, just once. Nuna remembered a shattered egg she had found beneath that nest two weeks before. The dead chick inside had wings and claws. That day Nuna hadn't seen the mother who she assumed was searching for the murdering predator. So Nuna dug a deep hole and buried the little bird, covering the grave with a small pile of stones to protect it from vultures.

At Judah's memorial, only the natural sounds of the earth he loved so dearly spoke. Bay put a bouquet of wildflowers on the stone and touched it as if Judah's spirit was there. The townspeople didn't move.

A breeze blew softly among them, the water crashed against the rocks below, and a few remaining leaves rustled. As if on cue, heads bowed and hands joined in a huge circle around the cemetery. Corycian Island bid Judah Morely a silent farewell. Then people began to disperse as quietly as they had arrived.

The five who loved Judah the most lingered before taking steps back into a world without him. The sky was bright blue and a hot October sun burned through their mourning clothes.

They walked back up the worn path. The osprey left her perch and flew into a wide circle around the periphery of the meadow. The others followed Nuna's glance and watched the graceful bird as she made each go-round smaller, flapping her wings in slow fluid movements, until she flew in a tight circle above them before heading back to her nest, resuming her watchful pose.

THE CORYCIAN ISLAND READER
Vol. 10, No. 41October 11, 1917
Editorial

There are times in the lives of men when we have to stand up and say we're wrong, and this is one of them for the publisher of this newspaper.

Turning my editorial back on the world, I said the United States' entry into Europe's war was wrong and held that course in a variety of opinion pieces for three years.

We mourned a son of Corycian Island today. A brave young man who put country before everything and took off to fight an enemy he knew little about.

Why? I asked repeatedly in these columns, ignoring the simple answer demonstrated by Judah Morely and so many other young Corycian men who answered: "Because I believe in my country."

I felt the roots of Judah Morely's answer deep under the land on which I stood Thursday.

Corycian Island is a tiny speck of life on the world's continuum, but that speck gets its life from every speck connected to it.

As neighbors we held hands and bowed our heads to pray our own silent prayers when Judah Morely's service ended. There was a cosmic power in the linked circle. It was too real to be denied. In that moment, I knew standing alone had

been the wrong answer because in that moment,
standing together imbued us with greatness.

I am a native of Corycian Island, who, at the
age of 43, is only learning the Runapewak word
"all-a-wanna."

All together. All-a-wanna, we weep.

Bay moved into the middle cottage on her mother's property
soon after Judah died. She told Eula that Ismy and she needed a
place of their own. The cottage had been enlarged. It was Henry's
idea. He tore down the back room within days of Lavidas' death,
and in no time had added two rooms and a screened porch.
At least that much of the memory was gone and the place was
cheerful and bright.

Several mornings the sun rose with a warmth that beckoned
Nuna to try, once again, to get her grieving daughter to take a
walk. Nuna knocked softly on Bay's door each time.

"Let Maduh Eart' be 'round you, Bay" Nuna said or: "You
needs summa dis sunlight."

But Bay just shook her head, always saying the same thing:

"Not today, Mama. Would you take Ismy for me? I didn't
sleep much last night."

When the door closed behind Nuna and Ismy, Bay leaned
against it and heard the silence of Judah's absence. He had been
next to her since the day she was born. Bay stood awhile and felt
her way around the emptiness. When she moved from the Captain's house she hadn't brought much, just the required clothing,
a few necessary housewares, and some toys for Ismy. It wasn't a
conscious decision to bring so little, but somehow it defined just
how much of her life was gone.

Bay couldn't go out for a walk because she didn't want to
see how full the world was. She wanted to scream at the flaming skies of fall, to curse at the beauty of the autumnal leaves,
and to run from the cool breezes fluttering over the water. Nuna
said these things would restore Bay, but even Ismy's dear kisses
hadn't done that.

Alone in the cottage, Bay didn't cry. She merely sat at the kitchen table with her head resting on her folded arms. Often, she stared at the same knot in the pine boards for an hour or more. When she heard the happy sounds of Ismy playing outside, she moved into her dark bedroom. Prone on the small bed - just wide enough for one - Bay's eyes were open, but she saw nothing.

As for Eula, the loss of her son dug deeply at the faith she had built in the years since she'd heard from her grandfather's spirit.

Eula had witnessed the joy of guests who emerged from readings, séances, and healings. They seemed far more at peace than they were upon arrival. Eula built her faith on them because they proved her perception of the Captain's message had been right, though she had never dreamed the Captain's house would become a spiritualist colony.

It was something from which she and Nuna maintained a distance. They never partook of the spiritualists' services. Little time remained after minding their personal and leased properties, and besides, the space allowed them to be objective, especially about which practitioners leased rooms. No tricksters. No one who employed spirit photography or used spirit cabinets. No ouija boards.

Until Judah died, the owners' choice was a respected business arrangement. However, death was the spiritualists' medium, and Judah's spirit was apparently moving through their vibrations, so the telephone at the Captain's house rang throughout the fall with well-meaning messages from this practitioner or that one.

The calls came in long after Nuna and Bay had gone home from a day of cleaning and winterizing the last of the larger suites, sealing them off so the family's living quarters could hold the heat onto the first floor. It's what they did every year, with the heavy work handed over to Henry and Judah. This was the second time Judah hadn't been there to help, but the first time he would never be there again.

Eula took the telephone calls and listened to whatever the callers had to say.

"Judah wants you to know he's at peace."

"Judah wants to talk to Ismy when the summer comes."

"Judah wants Bay to know he died instantly. Never knew what hit him."

"Judah is with his father and Ahane."

Eula wrote the messages down on a pad she kept in a drawer by the telephone. She never gave the notes to the intended recipient. She didn't ask herself why. She didn't have to because the messages tormented her at night. If Judah came to them, why didn't he come to her? Why did she have to believe in someone else's belief?

A medium who leased rooms every summer called to say she felt the warmth of Judah reaching out toward Eula. She called to tell Eula about how close Judah was to revealing himself.

Eula waited, but Judah didn't come.

That was the topic Nuna and Eula discussed in the Captain's kitchen. Eula's shoulders were slumped and dark circles underscored her eyes. She had lost weight, making her stricken face look gaunt. She turned a damp handkerchief around in her hands.

"I just have to get used to the emptiness of the family suite at night, which isn't so terrible," Eula said, trying to have a normal conversation but finding it difficult to do. "Bay said: 'There's some crying in life we need to do alone and this will give each of us time to work out our grief.' She's so practical, that one." Eula lowered her head: "I wanted so much more for Judah and Bay. More than we had, Nuna. More time to be in love, I guess. More time to be young."

Nuna struggled to find an answer of comfort, but heard herself say: "Gettin' used to t'ings be what we all doin' now."

Eula went on: "I always thought I'd find more faith in life as I grew older. I'm not sure that's true anymore. How do we start living again? I know that's what Judah wants us to do for Ismy and Bay, but can we? Or have we lost too much?"

"De time afta Ahane and Judah's faduh drown, I tole you: 'Lissen for dat Oonuh in you.' Remember, dat?"

Eula smiled wanly. "Yes, very clearly, and I've lost that, too, by the way. Whatever Oonuh I found is now gone."

"Dat be what I be sayin' to you," Nuna continued. "My Oonuh be gone dat time. It be you dat helped me and Bay. Now, dis time, we be lost all-a-wanna. Bay be holdin' a lotta hurts in her. First her daddy....now Judah - and a whole lotta t'ings elsewise. You and me and Henry gots ta be strong for our Bay and our Ismy. I sees Judah in Ismy and I sees Judah in Bay. I sees Judah in you and Henry, too. All-a-wanna we help."

Nuna reached across the table and took her dear friend's hand, but it would be a long time before they felt much of a life force pass between them again.

Women from the Mothers' Care Center came to the Captain's house with offerings - pieces of their hearts - wrapped in wildflower bouquets, apple pies, homemade wine, and tearful clenching hugs.

Sometimes they all sat around the Captain's long, kitchen table sharing a pot pie or a pumpkin one; a shepherd's pie or cherry turnovers - each one more delicious than the last merely because of the love put into it.

"I ain't lyin' when I say you make the best piecrust on this island, Bernadette Petrie," Henry said on one such occasion. "Why Judah would come home from helpin' you out with somethin' and he'd have three or four of your pocket pies wrapped in a napkin. I'd have to tackle him to get so much as a bite."

Pammy Bakker brought food and comfort to Bay's house a few times over the mourning period. One day she found Nuna having tea with Bay while Ismy played on the kitchen floor.

Pammy sat across from them, noticing how Bay's eyes had lost the sparkle she had seen in them so many years ago. Bay wore what Pammy guessed to be Judah's trousers with a man's shirt tied up at her waist. They all spoke politely with small quips about Ismy's antics, until Pammy said:

"I've never lost anyone I loved, so I won't placate either of you with pretending I understand. I can't even imagine it." Bay gave Pammy a strained smile and Pammy went on: "I suppose I wonder if there is any comfort in - well, you know - since your mother is - well, if Judah's spirit comes to you because you believe those things?"

Bay was very quiet. Nuna fidgeted with a fresh pot of tea, curious about Bay's answer, but Pammy went on blurting into the awkward silence:

"I hope it isn't rude to ask. You see...well..it's just that, I've been thinking about going back to church...the Catholic Church...and well, I'd rather not, you see, because I hate all that pomp and all the rules written by men… but I need to believe in something. Now that I have children and I'm getting older and... well..and now that life isn't all that...well...I need to pray, and I only know how to pray Catholic prayers. But ...oh, I didn't mean to talk about this. Forgive me. Bay, Nuna...I mean to help you..."

Nuna placed full cups in front of each of them."We be helpin' to'geder, Pammy. Friend ta friend."

" I guess I'm asking, is that how you know something's right? Spirit tells you? I mean, if I could experience what you do...spirit - you know communing with souls who tell me...I don't know... who tell me...How... I guess. Just how *to do* living. Catholics only tell me how not to do it."

"Livin' be somet'ing you tells yourself how ta do, and prayin' be feelin'" Nuna said. "Holdin' dem little bebes wit' de heart in you growin'. Dat be prayin'. Doin' right, dat be prayin' too. From what I sees, you be prayin' all de time. But prayin' don't mean gettin' t'ings, don't ya know. Prayin' just brings in spirit ta calms ya down."

Of course Nuna meant these words for Bay, too, who could hardly hold Ismy, much less utter words of prayer.

***

The war cemeteries of France soon held memorials for ten more Corycian Island men who had left to serve after Judah. Seven died from combat wounds, but alarmingly, three died of influenza.

In a steady procession throughout that fall and winter, families walked solemnly down streets to this church or that one. Mourners lined the pathways waving handkerchiefs and crying while the bell of the Presbyterian Church rang a bitter, death knell from its tower, honoring every soldier regardless of creed.

Veterans of other wars stood in uniforms with pinned sleeves or trouser legs, with scarred faces and marred minds, with dreams of their peaceful island and nightmares of lands so far away.

Long after the bells of the church tower stopped ringing, Eula heard the toll of the funeral gongs clanging in her head. Some nights the ghostly rings rumbled through the hollows of the Captain's house and to escape them, Eula pulled on boots and Judah's tweed coat. She wrapped herself in woolen scarves and mittens, opened the front door, and stepped out into the dark.

Henry, who still patrolled the land while Ezra kept an eye on the beach, caught up with Eula on the shell road one night. She told him to leave her be in a tone that made Henry comply, though he talked to Nuna about it.

"Keeps a look out, Henry," Nuna said. "Eula be needin' dat most, just us keepin' a look out on her."

Eula's walks happened with regularity while Henry watched. She always did the same thing.

Tucking a scarf around her neck and buttoning Judah's long coat over her chest, Eula pulled up the collar and breathed in his scent. She left the house and walked, feeling closer to Judah in the open air. She covered two miles ending on Shore Road at Màthair.

The first night, the manse was lit by the moon, its stony magnificence glowing behind a tall wrought iron fence. Eula followed the fence to the far side of the yard. She heard the bay lapping at Sirens' Beach below the berm. She followed the fence to get nearer to a soft glow at the edge of the grass toward the water.

The white alabaster statue of Mary formed from the blur of Eula's vision when she got closer. The statue was tall and made taller by its gray marble base. It seemed to hover in the darkness. The pedestal read OUR LADY OF THE SEAS.

Eula studied the simple garments the lady wore. How the moonlit stone appeared translucent; how the veil fell from the lady's head to drape her outstretched arms at the wrists of her open hands. How the dress was gathered in folds at the bodice which fell in a sultry way off the lady's left knee - held aloft to crush a serpent under her foot. The lady's eyes were cast toward the heavens in some unspoken plea.

Was the lady asking for help to crush the threatening serpent, Eula wondered? Is that her plea? Is that her prayer?

Eula stared at the lady. She heard the waves hit the rocks of Sirens' Beach as a cloud passed by to dim the moonlight. Eula sought a prayer, a message to send to the Lady of the Seas, but all she could rouse from herself was a tear-filled litany:

"I don't know. I don't know. I don't know."

From then on when the night beckoned Eula to search for Judah, she always found herself reaching through the fence with open palms and silent psalms to Our Lady of the Seas.

Again Henry spoke with Nuna about Eula's nightly wanderings. Nuna said:

"I talks ta her 'bout it. She say she gots ta cry till she can't no more. She cryin' for answers, don't ya know, Henry? Like you cries when your Neeley goes and I cries for my Ahane." Nuna paused. "Mr. Ezra say spirit in good and bad t'ings, but still we all wants ta know why, and dat be all we live for, ta know dat some day."

1918

Ke'was End
"A pipsissewa."

The sweet call of spring brought Bay out of her cottage and away from her lonely grief on an April afternoon. Warmed by the sun she walked with a toddling Ismy whose fair-haired curls bounced in the sun. The three-year-old ran head first with her arms flung wide.

How Judah would love to see her now, Bay thought. Then she stopped and examined that idea, exactly what she wanted to stop doing. But since Judah died, her brain kept on with the process. Right now Bay wondered about that thought: "Judah would love to see Ismy." If she had faith, wouldn't she have thought he *could* see their little girl romping in the sun?

Ismy let loose a shrill song of joy, happy to be free of walls. Bay tried to relax in that joy, but she felt vulnerable when she went outside, like her doubting thoughts found their way into the universe.

She told her mother this. Nuna said:

"You has to be trustin' spirit be takin' care a you and Ismy, even de times you don't t'ink so."

"Well, Mama, I thought that when Judah went away, I trusted that spirit would take care of us cause Judah was doing the right thing. But, I'm not so sure Judah was and then I get so mad when I think that way cause I'm sure Judah had doubts, too," Bay stopped, afraid she would reveal what Judah asked her to keep close. Regathering her thoughts, she went on: "Trust just doesn't work for me right now, Mama. My father drowned with Judah's and now Judah's as dead as the two of them, and if you recall, I killed a man. Do you think I ever get that scene out of my head, Mama? Can I ever wash any of Rollo Lavidas' blood off my mind?" She sighed and Nuna winced. New furrows appeared in Bay's young brow. "Seems to me with all those spiritualists on call around here, we should have known not to let Judah go to war. No, Mama. It doesn't look like spirit's watching out for us or anyone else for that matter, so stop telling me that."

"You tries ta make Judah stay. You and his mama."

"Then why didn't he?"

"Some t'ing in him tells him 'go.' "

"Well, that was some bad advice now, wasn't it?"

Once and for all Bay gave up on prayer. She found peace in that. Prayer was just another spiritualist trick. So Bay turned to Ismy and calmed herself in the light she and Judah had created. Though Bay wouldn't have acknowledged it, Nuna knew that was spirit lighting the way.

Running through the spring meadow Bay called out: "Wait for mama, Ismy." The toddler turned, but only long enough to point up to the sprawling arms of the budding oak tree in the meadow.

"Pewitty," Ismy said with glee. "Pewitty."

Bay caught up and scooped Ismy into a hug: "You are a pip-sissewa, little one. Do you know that? A pipsissewa is what your daddy called you: daddy's flower of the woods."

Ismy broke from her mother's hug and, with flailing arms, ran toward the edge of the meadow. Bay chased her, noticing a man behind some shrubs near the cemetery.

Bay's throat choked. Henry told them to keep an eye out for... well...for things like strange men hiding in the shrubs. Bay stared harder, one hand ready to reach for Ismy and the other held at her forehead to block the sun.

Then she saw it was Burston Bakker with his camera set on a tripod near a shrub to get the best angle of the fence around the Founders' Cemetery.

Crouching down, he shot the scrolls and queues of iron which had tiny stones marking children's graves poking though the fence spires. Scanning the graves to find the new stone placed for the fallen hero, Judah Morely, Bakker focused his lens to the right of the large obelisk where a little girl balanced herself on a fallen tree inches from her mother's outstretched hand.

Burston held the girl in his viewfinder and snapped a few shots. He recognized it was Judah Morely's daughter with her mother. He tightened the focus of his camera

Bay wore a shawl over a simple cotton dress that brushed calf-high boots. She had a kerchief tied into a headband. Her brown skin took on a copper sheen in the sunlight. She and Ismy turned toward the clicks of the camera. Bay picked Ismy up and called out:

"That you, Mr. Bakker?"

"Yes, M'am...just over here taking photos for the *Reader*'s Decoration Day issue. I couldn't help but snap a shot when I saw you and - is this your daughter? I was presumptuous. I apologize. You're still grieving this great loss. I didn't mean to interfere. Your husband served most honorably."

Bay looked into Burston Bakker's eyes: "Men say that, Mr. Bakker. They say he served honorably. Ismy and me here, well, we think *he* wasn't served near as well." She looked down so she wouldn't cry.

"Do you mind that I took the photos?" Burston asked, changing the subject.

Without looking up, Bay said: "We've never seen one of us."

"Well, I'll tell you what. I'll develop an extra set for you."

When Burston Bakker processed the film he took at Ke'was End, he was puzzled by the white flecks dotting the photos around little Ismy, and especially by those on the smooth side of the obelisk, and on Judah's Morley's memorial stone. They weren't in any of the other photos he took that day.

Left with no conclusion, Burston cleaned his camera lenses, decided the photos would not transfer to newsprint well, and didn't publish any. He assembled a gift set for Bay because they had an artistic light to them and dropped them off at Henry's store since Bay didn't appear to be home.

That evening, Bay stared at the images with Nuna who pointed at the bright specks so prominent in the prints.

"Spirit seeds," Nuna said. "See dat? Spirit seeds, don't ya know. See dem by de big rock, too? And right by where Judah's be? I bet dat little one, Ismy, be seein' spirit. Dem spirit seeds be talkin' to her Oonuh for sure."

Bay saw some worry lines disappear from Nuna's face while she looked over the photographs, and for a moment even Bay felt a tug to believe again.

But later, making fertilizer for their summer garden, Nuna and Henry burned guano and mossbunker out back, an odor that always made Bay feel only fear.

Piper's Cove
"You never can be too sure of him."

Influenza arrived on Corycian Island mid-September of 1918 taking the lives of two, one the child of guests at The Strand Hotel and, the other, an island child who was cared for in the Mother's Center.

Ted Simmons, the island's one medical doctor and the head of the town's health department, shut down the center at the Strand and called in a task force of volunteers through the island's Red Cross, a small group of wives from the firehouse, to schedule an open forum for the townspeople.

The deaths of the toddlers - and the news coming from Manhattan of the viral nature of the flu felling scores of New Yorkers - brought one hundred volunteers to the meeting. That night, under Simmons' leadership, the group designated the firehouse as a hospital in which to quarantine the ill. Cots and mattresses were brought from all over the island.

The group also put together a complete circuitry of islanders who promised transportation, canned goods, office help, simple nursing skills, and any other work required.

The first public charge of the volunteers was to hand out masks and words of precaution to all the retailers, town and school employees, and anyone else who came in direct contact with their neighbors.

Then, the volunteers spread themselves across the island, knocking on doors to deliver masks to residents, as well as to advise of early flu symptoms: a temperature above 102, a sore throat, exhaustion, a headache, aching limbs, bloodshot eyes, a cough, a violent nosebleed or digestive upsets, such as vomiting or diarrhea.

The ill were removed from their homes and brought to the firehouse for basic care since, nationally, no pharmaceutical solution had appeared to offset this virus.

Henry Shellfoot put himself on call with the Red Cross to do whatever he could to help, and the Captain's house donated the use of its automobile. Henry drove the visiting nurses to critical home cases. A call came in about an islander in need, sending Henry over to pick up the school principal's wife, Frances Stoli, another volunteer.

While driving over to Pipers' Cove, she told Henry what had prompted their trip. "I wasn't paying much attention to what my Blossom was telling me, at first," Frances Stoli said. "She's 12 and has a way of over-dramatizing everything and I had to get dinner on the table. But then I realized she was saying something about Inri Remie, and, well, geez, I always feel so bad for that child."

Henry nodded. Frances continued: "Anyway, Blossom said Inri hadn't been coming to school. Well, that wasn't unusual. I've volunteered at the school enough to know that boy plays hooky more than anyone else. So Blossom said Inri told her his mother was dying and no one cared. I looked right at Blossom and asked her to tell me that again because I was just handing out masks in Pipers' Cove five days ago. I remember speaking to Ruth Remie and she seemed fine, but they don't have a telephone, and that husband of hers is never anywhere to be found when the camp is closed for the season."

Frances talked non-stop the whole way over to the Remie's. When they got there, Henry helped her from the car and said: "You best not be goin' up to the door alone in case her man answers. You never can be too sure of him."

But it was the Remie's 15-year-old son, Inri, who opened the door. He looked very relieved to see Mrs. Stoli, less so to see Henry Shellfoot.

"Are you all right, Inri? We're here to help. I'm Mrs. Stoli. This is Mr. Shellfoot who assists me and will help you while I tend to your mother." Inri looked frozen. "Inri, you remember me from school, don't you? I'm going to ask you to listen to what Mr. Shellfoot would like you to do. We're going to put on these masks while we help you and your mother, so don't be alarmed. After you eat something we'll talk some more."

Henry took a pot from Ruth Remie's kitchen to fill with soup from a cauldron he carried in the automobile on these runs. At the door, he asked the boy to wash his hands and face. When Henry came back in, he saw Inri had only made a half-hearted attempt to get clean. Henry stood his tall self up to the hungry, sneering boy. He looked down at scrawny Inri and said:

"You gotta get alla that dirt off a you before I get a bowl a soup in front a you, young man. That's just the way it's gonna be."

Obviously the boy hadn't eaten, so he put his surliness aside and washed himself with a deliberate abundance of soap at the kitchen sink.

They could hear the delirium of Ruth's fever coming in moans and groans from a bedroom off the kitchen while Inri dried his hands and face with a towel. When the boy sat, his mother's cries were joined by the boy's steady slurps of soup.

Henry found some fresh dish towels and soaked them with water to bring to Frances Stoli. "How long your mama been like this, son?" Henry asked.

Inri looked up from his bowl for the first time with a smirk on his face and a whole new attitude now that help had arrived.

"I ain't your son and ain't you just the driver?" he said.

"I'm the one who drived over here to help you, if that's what you mean," Henry said. "I'm also the one who decides if I needs to leave you soup." Henry went back to folding a few more wet cloths to bring to Frances who answered his soft knock at Ruth Remie's bedroom door.

Inri saw Frances shake her head through the crack, as she reached for the towels. When Henry closed the door, Inri said:

"Four days. She been like this four days." The boy fought hard not to cry, but his fear was too big for his strength. The tears fell as he coughed out the words: "He never was here for none of 'em."

After doing what Frances could for Ruth, she and Henry left Inri with food and their assurances that an ambulance would arrive for his mother soon.

"We saw some lights on in the Coleman's house on the way over. We'll use their telephone to call for an ambulance. Your mother will get good care at the firehouse, Inri. Will you be okay here overnight? Will your father be home tonight?"

The boy said "Yes," lying to both questions.

The next morning before heading out with Henry to check on Inri, Frances called the Red Cross office to inquire about Ruth's condition. The volunteer on duty told Frances that 44-year- old Ruth Remie had died just hours after the ambulance brought her there.

Frances and Henry went straight over to care for Inri. Josiah Remie opened the door when the Model T pulled in front of the house.

"No need to get outta that auto, you two," Remie said with a sneer on his grimy face. "We never asked you to come to our house. My Ruthie might still be alive if you hadn't meddled and taken her away. And as for you, boy," Remie snorted at Henry, "no one said one a your kind was welcome into my house."

"Why, Mr. Remie!" Frances Stoli said. "Mr. Shellfoot..."

"I don't want to hear nothin' from no woman neither. So shut your pie hole," Remie said.

Frances could see Inri in the background, sitting at the kitchen table, head hanging over a bowl of soup, mind numb to his father's rant.

1919

Inri Remie
"Open Windows"

Inri Remie turned 16 in 1919 but he had a hard time convincing people who didn't know him that he was more than 12.

Left to his own since Ruth's death, Inri was unfed and unkempt. He stopped going to school and his father didn't seem to care. The boy ate whatever Josiah left at the house, an abundance of food one week and nothing for another week or more.

Inri was rarely seen around town though he saw everyone else. He had become an observer of all things Corycian Island. His years of creeping around in the dark after Josiah led Inri to the brightly lit windows of others' houses.

The young boy spied on different families by concealing himself in bushes near window panes or hiding in the crook of a leafy tree to observe lives on the second story.

In the summer, with people sitting out on screened porches or living life with their windows open, Inri was especially careful about making noise. There were houses he went back to repeatedly because they were alive with families talking, siblings fighting, friends laughing, and couples making love.

Inri wasn't really sure what was going on when he first encountered a couple having sex. It happened the spring night Inri tracked George Stoli. Inri saw the principal locking up the school on a Friday. The school year was drawing to a close and all Stoli's efforts to get Inri Remie to return had failed. Inri wished Stoli had tried harder. The boy had thought about giving in, simply because of Frances Stoli. But when Principal Stoli came to the house, Josiah pulled out his rifle and said Stoli was trespassing. Turning to leave, Stoli saw Inri standing in the side yard and said: "Looks like it's up to you now, Inri."

Stoli left and didn't come back, so Inri started to follow him around the island. At first the boy told himself it was just to see what was in Stoli's ever-present, paper sack; but after a year or more, Inri knew he followed Stoli to catch him at some wrong doing. Inri learned from Josiah that men have hidden lives.

The scrawny boy cut through the Presbyterian Church cemetery next to Marmie's the spring night he saw Stoli locking up the school. Inri headed straight for Stoli's house, to a thicket of bushes under the open windows of the first floor bedroom. From there he crept to other windows and followed the family through their nightly routine. Inri was enthralled.

Principal Stoli came through the front door and put his paper sack on the floor somewhere. He scooped three-year-old Aster into one arm and hugged Blossom into his other.

It was a scene that caused Inri to sit back on his heels when he first saw it happen, and one of which he never tired no matter how often he saw it. The hugs always ended with Stoli's wife coming from the kitchen. Inri watched the couple kiss, softly and caringly.

The Stolis ate dinner together at a table in the kitchen. While listening to a radio program, they cleaned up as a team afterwards. Then Blossom did her homework while Mrs. Stoli got Aster ready for bed. George sat in the living room by a lamp, straining over the text in a newspaper.

It was on one of those ordinary nights that Inri fell asleep in the shrubs. He didn't resist the urge. Blossom was upstairs. Mr. Stoli was tuned to some soft music on the radio, and Mrs. Stoli was singing a lullaby to Aster. Inri must have been asleep for an hour or more because when he awoke, he thought he was dreaming.

He looked through the bushes at the window and saw a naked woman, backlit from a light in the hallway, walking slowly around Stoli's bedroom where the principal was visible, under a sheet in their bed.

The woman sat on the edge of the mattress, her bare back was to the window. Her blonde hair fell over her shoulders. She bent to kiss Stoli and her hair covered his face.

Inri realized it was Frances Stoli, and though he'd never heard enough about sex to understand it, his own body's reaction to what he saw confirmed what he suspected. Inri hardly breathed while the two moved through his introduction to intercourse.

When it was over, for all of them, Inri felt more calm than he ever had in his entire life, and he fell asleep again, listening to the soothing snores of the Stolis.

The spring night Inri caught the Stolis having sex was wonderful, but it was nothing compared to the times he came upon the family snuggled into the Stolis' bed, talking, laughing, and playing games. Inri liked the game about initials. One person said someone's initials - someone from Corycian Island - and the kids had to guess the name. Inri listened intently. He heard Mr. Stoli say:

"GW" and Blossom giggled out:

"George Washington!"

Little Aster repeated Blossom's answer. Then their mom said:

"No. No. It has to be someone from Corycian Island."

And the kids threw out dumb answers, until enough hints brought someone to shout the post mistress' name: "Gracie Williams!"

Inri's familiarity with so many towns' people made him very good at the game. He played along with them, wishing, just once, that the islander's initials would be "IR."

***

The week of Thanksgiving, the *Reader* published a map rendering the concentration of influenza on different areas of Corycian Island. Josiah Remie studied it in Ruth's kitchen to which he had returned when the Red Cross volunteers finished swabbing it down following Ruth's death.

Few things terrified Josiah more than illness. He had tried to explain that to Inri when Ruth first took sick, but the boy hardly talked to his father by then, so Josiah gave up without too much effort.

After Ruth died, Josiah took down anything that was remotely reminiscent of her and, to add to the insult, drank openly in her house. When the man's body refused to process any more alcohol, Josiah spilled his guts outside the window near Inri's room.

Inri welcomed the nights he heard the loud regurgitations through the walls. That meant Josiah would pass out eventually and at least there was another breathing human in the house for awhile. Inri remembered what his mother said to Chief Ratliss once when he came around looking for Josiah: "I hate him, but he's what we got."

Drunk at 4:00 on a Thursday afternoon, Josiah sat across from Inri at the kitchen table. He pushed the trash accumulating on its surface to the floor and spread the paper out so Inri could see the map on the *Reader's* front page.

"Look at this, boy, and tell me what you see. Look real close now."

Inri looked. He saw the geographical drop of land and stone that formed Corycian Island with grayed areas of various hues. Too excited to wait for Inri to figure the answer out, Josiah said:

"Look down there where that Jew and them witches lives, Raymond. It ain't very gray down there on Ke'was End, now is it? Explain that to me! Mr. Bigman Bakker don't ask that question now do he? Why they only got a little gray down there, Raymond? What do you think this map's tellin' us about that?"

Inri looked back at his father without proffering an answer. Josiah continued: "That's devil protection, if I ever seen it, Raymond. Devil protection for all the worship they gives to him," Josiah said.

Inri finally spoke with an unmistakable strength in his voice: "Stop calling me, Raymond. My name's Inri. I-N-R-I."

Josiah was startled. His son had never spoken back to him. In fact, the very tone Inri used made Josiah turn around and leave the house.

Later on when Inri mulled it over, he wished he had added dammit.

"My name is I-N-R-I, *dammit!*"

Calliope Point
"Perseid Showers"

On a July day in 1919, Sissy Lawson stared out her kitchen window to see the *Barna-Call* bobbing out in Union Harbor.

Every spring, Tommy hauled her out of dry dock to stay moored in the cove, occasionally taking her out with Burston. The families hadn't taken a sail for two seasons. Whenever Sissy brought it up, Tommy said:

"Look Sissy. I have a lot of responsibility at the hotel, right now."

In Sissy's reverie at the window, an idea struck her. The next day, with Pammy's family in tow, she registered the children, ages 12-14 and their mothers, 38 and 40, for private sailing lessons at the Harbor Club Marina, operated by The Strand Hotel. Sissy knew this would drive Tommy crazy. Turning over the helm of the *Barna-Call* to anyone was incomprehensible, but a woman? Tommy's ideas about liberation were limited.

Sissy's plan was to prepare herself to Captain the catboat with a family crew, and wait for Tommy to take charge.

It worked. In the middle of August, Tommy stormed around the marina after hearing about his wife's plans for the first time.

"I knew she was taking lessons," Tommy said to the harbormaster who delivered the news, "but she sure isn't taking out the *Barna-Call*. Not while it's my boat anyway!"

So Tommy arranged to take some time off without letting Sissy know. He had the kitchen staff at the Strand pack provisions enough for eight and bought a Captain's hat at the Harbor Marina.

When Tommy walked into his house, it was full of the usual cousins and no one looked up. Then Sissy raised her eyes and said:

"Tommy?" with a questioning pitch that made everyone look at him. Tommy's arms were full of his purchases and of course, he was wearing the Captain's hat.

203

"I heard when I was at the marina that my crew is ready to sail," Tommy said, and whatever followed was drowned out by the squeals of jumping children and two very happy mothers.

"I stopped by and talked to Burston," Tommy said during the commotion. "He has to cover a town board hearing tonight. There's a big fight going on about the Westside Ferry dredging another slip for a third boat. Those fights can last till midnight, but we're going to try to meet up with him."

Sissy calmed the cousins down so they could listen to Tommy's announcement.

"So here's how it's to be. I'm the Captain, your mom's first mate. Aunt Pammy and Uncle Burston are both Second Mates."

"What am I, Dad?" 12-year-old Samuel asked, trying to contain his boyish excitement in a manly way.

"Well, you, my good man are the Ensign, my right hand, of course."

"And us? What about us?" the others wanted to know.

"Well, my goodness! You're the sailors! Who could go on a cruise without sailors?"

With that, Tommy produced a bag full of white sailor caps, handing one out to each, except Sam to whom he handed a visored, Ensign cap.

"Ok, so listen up, here's the drill: Men...in a matter of speaking of course," Tommy added with a gallant nod to the females, "I got it from the harbormaster first hand." He lowered his voice as if revealing a great secret: "There are going to be meteor showers tonight."

The kids stared back at him. JB, the youngest by two days, asked.

"What's a meteor, again?"

"Why it's a celestial event," Pammy chimed in. "A celestial event of such magnificence that stars light up the whole sky, then they shower down and fall into the sea."

Babs, thirteen and full of drama, whined:

"Are they going to hit us?"

Tommy spoke directly to his niece:

"Meteors, my lady, are really fairy dust, with particles no bigger than grains of salt. They are totally invisible when they get near the water, but I have to be honest, if you're really lucky, they will fall on you. They sort of tickle your arm, like this, or your neck.." Babs giggled. "Yes. You'll be ready for them now. I hear they make you stronger with every drop."

Babs, who was rarely treated girlishly by Burston, was utterly thrilled when her Uncle Tommy put on the charm.

"Miss Nuna says we're all born with stardust in us," Babs trilled.

"Does she now?" Tommy said.

"Miss Nuna says we're connected to the sky and it's connected to us so we take care of each other."

"Miss Nuna is one smart lady, Babs," Tommy said with a hug.

"Sailors," Sissy called sharply, just like the Commodore of the Harbor Yacht Club did when he presented them with their merit certificates for sailing class. "I want you to get yourselves and your mates shipshape. It's 7 p.m. now. Report to the Captain with bags packed at..." she paused, "Uh what would 8:00 be in nautical time, Tommy?"

"Twenty hundred hours."

"Seriously? 20 hundred? I never heard that number...uh..." Sissy said. "But, ok, report to the Captain when Ensign Samuel tells you to. Furthermore, while the first mates get the ship in shape, you sailors will sit on the beach and behave. I will fix you a sandwich, so you will board the cat fed and ready to respond to all orders like the true sailors you are, in full uniform with caps in place."

When they were underway and the kids were settled with a spyglass and binoculars to share in search of meteors, Tommy told the girls that Burston would meet them off Sirens' Beach where they'd anchor.

"How's he going to do that?" Pammy asked.

"I secured the Strand's launch for his transport after the meeting lets out," Tommy replied. "It's a Tuesday night. No one's coming into the dock and if it happens, then they all go for a ride."

They had the main sail of the *Barna-call* up and caught the wind in a zephyr that cruised them around the perimeter of Corycian while the sky faded into a pink, then purply blue.

They anchored off the shore of a small, wooded island in the bay and rocked in gentle waters while the adults set up a midnight feast, and the children swam in a shallow cove.

The moon was nearly full with a cloud of vapor around it, making a golden halo that floated in a navy blue sky pulsing with stars. Nate was the first to climb the ladder back into the boat and wrap himself in a huge towel. He curled under Sissy's arm and shivered, refusing to be tired.

"When will the meteors come," he asked.

"As soon as Uncle Burston gets here," Nate's mother said.

Not long after, the familiar launch from the Strand pushed through the moonlit waters toward the cat. The launch slowed and Burston waved to them from its hull. The skipper approached deftly, deposited Burston, and with a tip of his hat, motored off into the night.

Burston seemed relaxed for a change. He wore a sports' shirt with a windbreaker and boat shoes. He was tan and had a healthy glow to him. He sipped at his scotch instead of downing it. Pammy took notice while they enjoyed small plates of the Strand's delicacies.

"Well, look at that," Burston said pointing to a star that fell above them. That's the start of the Perseid Showers, right there. You all know the story of the great King Perseus don't you?"

"I do, daddy. I know the story," Babs said.

"You mean the story when Perseus kills Medusa?" JB asked.

"Exactly," Burston said. "Perseus kills Medusa and all the scaly, fang-tongued, venomous, slithery serpents crawling around her head."

The children looked up at showering stardust that began to fall in streaks of light shot from milky mists in the sky.

"Tell us more," Sam said. "What kind of snakes?"

"Gorgons. The Greeks called them Gorgons," Burston said. "Keep your eyes up there like the sailors do. The whole story is written in the heavens. See Cassiopeia, that 'W' of stars? Cassiopeia said she was prettier than Posiedon's sea nymphs."

"What's a sea nymph?" Nate asked.

"Ah, interesting you should ask that," Burston said. "Let's ask your Aunt Pammy. What do you know of sea nymphs?"

Pammy tilted her head and smiled softly at Burston. On this night he was Burston the Magnificent, someone Pammy hadn't seen in awhile.

Laughing, Pammy said: "Sea nymphs are beautiful, enticing, young women who lure men into their arms and kill them with their power." The children stared at the constellations and Burston went on:

"Beauty is a treasure not to be trifled with, especially beauty that dwells in celestial majesty. Imagine this: Perseus saved pure beauty. It's what we all should strive for....perhaps, what man was made for, don't you think? That's what the Perseid Showers remind us."

Pammy reached for her husband's hand. The Perseid magic fell around them while Burston rambled on. The children fell asleep, the adults sipped brandy, and the night embraced them all in stardust.

1920

Corycian Island
"That's because a them women, don't ya know."

The new decade brought the Volstead Act, prohibiting the sale and consumption of alcohol nationwide and triggering the earliest business instincts of ancestral rum-running on Corycian Island. Business was so brisk, it took Remie and Wesley away from their pranks.

Few islanders didn't profit from the new law, even high school boys took to boats at midnight, earning $20 to transport cases of liquor. These were unloaded from Canadian, Jamaican, and Panamanian ships and taken to the beaches. There island men helped stack the cases according to whatever number their neighbors had agreed to store in a basement, attic, or barn. The storage fees started at $50 per month.

Prosperity on Corycian Island reigned and every islander, including the Chief of Police, turned a blind eye to the illegality of their gains.

Tommy Lawson discussed this phenomenon with Burston Bakker. "We store at the Strand, you know?" Tommy said. "We're paid a nice sum for storage, and also procure fine liquors for the hotel's use at a fair price."

"I wondered about that," Burston said. "How you're able to keep business going and all. I drink there, for Chrissakes, so I wasn't about to ask any questions. I guess that's what we're all doing."

"There's this generation of young people who are making tons of money," Tommy said. "They want champagne. I have to give them that or lose my job. The investors in the Strand send their friends here and none of them are tea-totalers. And, lest you forget, I'm not a wealthy aristocrat like you, Bakker."

"What if you get caught? Ratliss has officers-in-training now."

"I know." Tommy said. "And both of their fathers have worked for me since day one at the Strand. Besides, Ratliss knows, too."

"Is he on the take?" Burston asked.

"Geez, Burston, turn off the radio. You sound like a gangster. Anyway, not from me. And I doubt from anyone. Ratliss knows how every dollar earned on this island gets passed around from one hand to the next. Did you ever notice how so many of our dollars are marked with some hand drawing? That's locals tracking their money. I'm serious. Hansen wouldn't screw with that economy. He knows the liquor trade is a boon for the locals. But other than accepting a fifth here and there, I'll bet Ratliss doesn't take a nickel from anyone. He's a straight-up guy."

Lawson was right. Ratliss did enjoy a few sips of whiskey after a day of "herding Scalers," as he told himself when he kicked off his boots in the apartment that housed him near Town Hall. He walked to the small kitchen and poured himself two fingers from a Scotch whiskey Tommy Lawson had given him.

"Hell," Ratliss thought, easing into the one comfortable chair he owned. "I know who these guys are. They're out fighting that damn sound for fish in all sorts of weather. Let 'em make a few extra bucks if they can. Besides, it keeps Remie away from that Klan business."

Ratliss, who was 42 and single with no wish to marry, had little desire to do anything to upset the predictable life he led, so he picked his battles carefully. He knew which islanders were aiding and abetting the mainland crooks. All anyone needed to do was sit on a stool at Marmie's for 30 minutes and listen while he ate. Just yesterday, Ratliss heard a Scaler whisper to another:

"Weren't that you I seen on the cove last night, Paulie?"

"Maybe,'" the man addressed said.

"Oh get off it. I seen you, and I been there every night. I get a ten-spot for keeping an eye out." The man named Paulie wasn't interested in replying, so the talker went on: "You seen those two guys from the ships with tommy-guns? What d'ya think? Maybe them numb-nuts thought old Henry Shellfoot might steal it?"

Fits of a staccato laugh came from the talker. Ratliss didn't bother to reveal himself and went back to his breakfast.

The machine gun story was new and the Scaler's scoffing take on the need to guard anything on Corycian with such force was justified. Ratliss certainly didn't have the manpower required to face that kind of artillery. The intimation that Henry was there didn't surprise Ratliss, though. He knew the Captain's house stored barrels of whiskey in its cavernous basement. It was one of the first infractions of the Volstead Act reported to the local police by none other than Hector Wesley.

"I'm calling in a sighting like the Chief asked me to do," Hector said into the telephone when Rosie Griffing, the switchboard operator, connected him with Karen Moultrie at the police station. "There's illegal whiskey activity at the Captain's Guest House on Ke' Was End."

"May I have your name, sir?" Moultrie said.

"My name is Hector Wesley and I seen a crime from my boat. I'm a posse."

"Yes, a posse. I see" Moultrie said, used to strange calls. "Where do you live, sir?"

"What the hell d'ya needs to know that for? Geez."

"I need it to file the report of a witness, Mr. Wesley."

"Robin Lane, then. I'm livin' at Robin Lane now. And I don't know the damn number so don't ask me."

"What did you witness, Mr. Wesley?"

"I ain't a witness. I told you I'm a posse and I seen something."

"Yes, that qualifies you as a witness, Mr. Wesley."

Hector's silence hung in the telephone lines, but his head screamed at him: "A witness? Like in court? Like with a pledge to God and all?" He said aloud: "Maybe I seen something else other than what I said I seen. Yeah, that's what I seen. Something else. Sorry then, and a good afternoon to you." The telephone went dead.

That night Hector and Josiah sipped from the bottom of a bottle of whiskey they'd opened a few hours before. They were lying under a bright moon shining on Nanny Hill.

"Why d'ya s'pose Ratliss never did nothin' about that house we took down over at that Jew's place?" Hector asked.

"I wondered on that myself for awhile, Hector. I think it's that those kinds a people down there cast spells and such. They don't need no police. Don't be forgettin' my Ruthie died real soon after we took that temple down. Then that plague come and near wipes us all out. That's the devil right there."

Hector thought about Josiah's reasoning for a bit and found it faulty: "Yeah well, Josiah, before Ruthie died, Judah Morely got killed, so what you're sayin' just don't make no sense....again, by the way."

"What d'ya mean it don't make sense. What you sayin' don't make sense is what don't make sense, Hector. Morely died in the war. That don't count for witches' spells. My Ruthie died of some kinda bug them witches made come here."

Josiah took three large gulps of whiskey. He was morosely drunk; self-pitying drunk; sick and soul-searching drunk.

Hector said: "The Keyclose's is with the KKK now, don't ya know."

"I hear'd." Josiah said, holding on to his anger. "I'm pissed at what the KKK's have to say about whiskey making folks muddled, and the Believers ain't makin' sense - what with Jesus bein' a drinker and all in the Bible, and now the guv'ment is tellin' us 'No.' That's because of them women, don't ya know. Women don't like whiskey and now they can vote about it. But you see how the mens feels, right? The hell with the whole lot of 'em. I say we do what *we* believe. I mean I give my sweat and blood to the KKK's, to the Believers, *and* to this guv'ment and they all want to take away the one little joy I have in life."

"You're right when you're right, Josiah," Hector said, smiling broadly in his own drunken reverie. "Good whiskey, my best friend, stars, sky, moon. It's joy all right. Hope Lindy lets me ride her good when I get home tonight. Nothing like a harvest moon and a good screw. There's something about the energy Lindy says."

Hector looked over at Josiah who was strangely silent. Josiah's head was bobbing.

"Oh, sorry there, Josiah. You know, about Ruth bein' dead and all."

"Ha I do miss screwin' my Ruthie," Josiah said. "My little woman, Ruthie."

"Anyways," Hector said. "seems to me we're drinkin' *better* now that the Vol- steaders is at it. Hell, Josiah, we never drunk liquor's good as we're drinkin' now. No offense to your personal product and all. And as for the Key-err - KK thing, it's just some-thin' to do sometimes. You know, like you and the Believers..." Hector looked at Josiah who was chewing his cuticles. "I never give much thought to them Believers, Josiah. I just figure it's a cover-job for you. You know, to keep Ratliss off your tail, right? I mean, I seen you out on the bay in them boats at night. You know, when I'm fishin'. Once I saw you on that city guy's big yacht and it didn't look to me like you was goin' for a sail."

Josiah scowled at Hector and spit a piece of cuticle skin just past Wesley's ear. Hector went on: "Ratliss asked me about what I sees out there at night. I said I never seen nothin' bein' far-sighted and needin' glasses and all."

Remie picked at his nails. Hector sipped at the whiskey and didn't speak for a long time, and then it was in a soused slur: "I was just wonderin'... hell, do you ever think, Josiah, maybe we're our own group? Maybe we're just like Scaler Watchdogs or somethin'...like protectors of our home front...like those Scalers during the Big War looking in the bay for subs and all. I mean, you're not a Scaler, legally, but you're spendin' plenty a time in the bay these days..."

Josiah stood up: "Ok. Enough a that Scaler shit a yours...but keep goin' about the group idea, Hector. I like what I'm hearin'. We're like a underground of our own, is that what you're sayin'?"

"Why not? Then our day jobs is like secret identities and our night jobs is missions of justice..." Hector said.

Josiah cut him off:

"That's right from those damn comic books you reads, ain't it? Would ya mind behavin' like a grown-up here. You can't be underground without bein' mature about it. Secret identities, my ass. Nothin's changin' but how we call ourselves. I like that watchdog idea. We can make our own symbol up. And we can drink whatever and whenever we want. Screw everyone else. Yeah, I like it, Hector. Let's drink to October 22,1920 the day the Scaler Watchdogs declared their independence."

***

Chief of Police Hansen Ratliss tried to keep Josiah Remie and Hector Wesley under his radar, but it wasn't easy. The part-timers he hired were not much help. Stirring up trouble with Remie, who provided their families with alcohol, was not in the part-timers' plans. Besides all the nonsense with dead rodents and dog manure at the convent seemed to have stopped. Maybe the twosome was too busy dealing with bootleggers and that was just fine with Ratliss.

Consequently, the Chief missed the gathering in the woods off Pipers' Cove when the two drunks set out to address the devil's protection of Ke'was End. On their way, they left a few dead rats at the Stolis' house because as Josiah said: "That bitch killed my Ruthie. We'll deal more with 'em soon, but for now, let the Scaler Watchdogs shows 'em what's what."

Josiah had decided that destroying the Founders' Cemetery on Ke'was End was the perfect way to send their message which Josiah said was straight from the Bible: "to protect us from the false idols of our ancestors."

This didn't make a whole lot of sense to Hector, but he went along with it because Josiah promised Màthair was their next target.

They were even drunker than they'd been in a while because they had stopped for refreshers too many times on their journey, but they made it to the cemetery by 2:00 a.m. There weren't any lights on in the houses around Ke'was End. The moon seemed so much brighter near the water and the Shellfoot cottages were a lot closer than either Hector or Josiah had remembered.

Disturbed by unnatural noises altering the rhythm of famil-iar ones, Bay awoke. She crept to the window and looked to see what was causing them. She saw two ghostly outlines of white, illuminated by the moon and framed by the branches of an old willow that dripped feathery fronds onto the scene. Bluish-white rays pointed around the cemetery as what appeared to Bay to be spirits jumped beneath them.

The young woman stared at the apparitions. One demon kicked at the fence and another whacked at the obelisk with a mallet, his wild-winged clothes flapping in the air with each swing and moonlight bouncing in a round beam off his chest. Fear drove Bay to the door to call for Henry. She saw him running toward the white forms in the distance. He carried his rifle.

At the moment Hector Wesley positioned his mallet to bash Judah Morely's stone, he stopped. The large tool hung above his head and sweat dripped down the chain of the medallion around his neck. He looked at Josiah.

"Shhh," Hector said in a drunken slur. "What was that?" He felt eyes on him, all around him, eyes, everywhere. So Hector ran and Josiah followed as closely as possible. Henry, just reaching the fence, shot his rifle into the air. Hector Wesley jumped as if he'd been hit. He was breathing so hard that even when he realized he hadn't been shot, he didn't notice he had dropped his hat.

Ke' Was End
The Founders' Cemetery

Burston Bakker came over to the cemetery to take photos after being notified by Ratliss. The place was a mess. The small stones marking children's graves had been smashed to chalk dust. Chunks of shale had been knocked from the obelisk. The graceful iron fence was bent and broken.

Ratliss walked through the debris, aghast that any islander, even Josiah Remie, could stoop so low. Ratliss pointed at things he wanted recorded and Bakker took photos. At the snap of a twig, they looked up and saw Bay walking over towards them with Henry, Nuna, and Eula who held Ismy's hand. Ratliss strode over to meet them. "Thanks for coming here to talk," he said. "I thought we'd start at the scene."

While everyone nodded their heads, Ratliss flipped open his notebook.

"I think you know, Mr. Bakker here," the police chief said. "I'll take the notes, and then the two of us will talk about how much to reveal in the newspaper. I don't want to risk letting these fellas know we're on to them. So, Henry. You said you fired your rifle into the air, would you show me about where you were when you did that?" Ratliss waited for Henry to take his position by the cemetery fence. "And, ladies, where were you at this point?"

"Well," Eula said. " I was a ways behind because I didn't come out till I heard Henry's rifle go off."

Nuna said: "I be seein' to Ismy, so I be in Bay's house."

"All right then. I'll get back to you later." Ratliss addressed Bay. "Where were you when the rifle went off?"

Bay took her spot a distance behind Henry. Ratliss nodded to Bakker to get his camera ready, explaining: "I study these photos for indicators that help me understand the whole event. They will not be used publicly, I assure you. Now if you'd each tell me what you heard or saw before you got to these positions. Mrs. Morely?"

"First off," Bay said. "I heard a loud laugh and when I went to the window I saw a white thing running all about, swinging at the fence and the stones."

Bay finished her story and then Henry told what caused him to grab his gun. He said: "I know'd they was mens. They was real drunk and troublesome lookin' in these white clown hats like, with masks."

While Ratliss questioned Nuna and Eula, Burston noticed Ismy playing in the debris of the shattered memorials. The little girl toddled up to a wildflower bloom and squatted close to it. She pulled the stem with two hands until it succumbed, when she fell on her rear. She brushed herself off and took the flower over to a toppled gravestone: "You be better," Ismy said and Burston snapped a photograph.

Chief Ratliss confirmed that both eye witnesses agreed the men were wearing some type of white robes."Or somethin' like that," Henry said. "Clown hats and choir robes. Ain't that a crazy thing?"

***

Hansen Ratliss had already expressed his feelings about Remie and Wesley to Burston Bakker on past occasions of island vandalism. Ratliss and Bakker shared a common sentiment: The two men were misfits making trouble. After the cemetery destruction, Bakker sat in Ratliss' office at the station with the door closed and said: "I tell you, Hansen, I'm still wary of getting mixed up with people I know nothing about and share little with, but I'm respectful of most everyone. Things aren't that way these days. Far from it. I've read about this southern klan and I don't like it. I don't like vigilantes of any kind. It's un-American. Do you suppose that's what's going on here?"

"I don't know what you've read," Ratliss said cautiously.

"Why, these klan buffoons are killing people for nothing down there, Ratliss. They're killing people for what color they are or what God they believe in. I've never heard of anything so ridiculous. Treat a man with respect and he'll respect me in return. That's the way. It isn't easy and I spend my life trying to learn how to do it, but heavens, what kind of people make these ugly threats."

Burston reached for a large file that he had brought. "Here's every unsigned letter we've gotten at the *Reader* since I took over. Plenty of them are aimed at me, others at everyone else on the island. Match these to the ones you get here at the police department and we might have a solid clue to use against these fellows."

The Chief walked to a file cabinet and pulled out a stack of similar letters. A few used the same salutations: "To Who it maybe concerns" and the content put forth the same complaints to the *Reader* and the police about "Half-breeds, catholics, and jews taking over Corycian Island."

"Remie and Wesley," the Chief said. "I've compared the handwriting to town documents they've had to sign. It's clearly them. The writing is done by Hector Wesley, not sure Remie has that skill." Other indicators included the fact all the letters contained similar diatribes full of insulting ramblings and ignorant errors. "Hore" appeared 12 times with mis-spelled references to Ke'was End and Màthair. "But there aren't any threats," Ratliss said. "I brought them up to the town attorney who looked them over. He said we could ask Gracie Williams at the post office who's mailing them, but you know Gracie. She'd want a search warrant or something. We know who it is. We know where they're focused. I have people watching things out at Màthair and Ke'was End. I'd be happy for you to take a few drives around there if you're up at odd hours. Ask Tom Lawson to make a few rounds as well. We just need to catch them in the act and we're rid of them."

**

Henry found a white conical hat in the woods two mornings after the destruction. He brought the hat to show Ezra. "You ever seen anything like this," he asked.

"Where'd you find that?" Ezra said.

"In that thicket out front. It was caught on a branch. One a them clown hats, don't ya know," Henry said, holding the hat up with his fist in the top and pulling down the mask.

Ezra rubbed his tanned hands together as if they were cold, then stroked his beard before he spoke, pausing again, while trying to find words for the unthinkable."I've seen photos in the newspapers of men who wear such hats. They are men who hate people... jews, negroes, catholics, and I don't know who else. Let's hope I'm wrong, but the sight of the hat raises fear in me."

Later that day Henry and Ezra turned the item over to Hansen Ratliss when the Chief came to the store at their request.

"Ezra, here, says there's some clan-something or other wearin' these hats," Henry said.

"Yes, Chief. Henry found the hat in the woods beyond the cemetery. Do you know about these clan people?" Ezra asked.

"I've heard of them," Ratliss said, taking the hat and wondering what to say about it. "I'll see what I can find out. I ...uh...I believe there is some activity with them and their...uh...with people like these...uh... this... on the mainland." Ratliss didn't want to increase the fear he sensed Ezra Goldsmith felt. The

Chief asked a few questions about the discovery, thanked the men, and walked away, holding the white hat while a deep chill ran through his bones.

***

Burston Bakker studied the photos he took of the Shellfoots in the cemetery. He had to handle its destruction carefully in the newspaper. The editorial wouldn't be difficult to write and Burston knew what two photos to run. But he had asked Tommy Lawson to stop by the office. Tommy had taken Pammy's place as the voice of reason regarding the *Reader's* editorials.

Tommy took a seat at Burston's desk. The newspaperman told him about the cemetery destruction, the conical hat, and the KKK. Tommy listened and said:

"I'll admit to knowing very little about this klan business. I know Remie runs that old still. I see him hanging around the Strand's kitchen at night. As long as none of my guys are drinking while they work, I don't bother with him. I don't hear anything about any Ku Klux Klan, though."

"Well, it's a nasty group of hate mongers, Tommy."

"I hear most of the talking that goes on in the back rooms of the Strand, Burston, and I've never heard anything about it. Hell, these islanders have been sleeping in each other's beds for so long, they wouldn't be able to figure out who was in the group and who was out!"

"I thought that, too, but the spiritualism thing is new to the island, Tommy, and the hoity-toity city people are something new to deal with, and there's been trouble over at the Catholic place, too."

"Well, I've definitely heard that Remie rails against palm readers and boogie-woogie at camp services," Tommy smiled at the thought.

Burston laughed and said: "As for the Captain's house, well I hear stuff from Pammy but what else do you know about what goes on down there, Tommy?"

"The Shellfoots and Morelys are good people. I've never known anyone to speak ill of either family. There are curious people working down there, that's for sure. But I have guests asking for a lift to the place all the time and I've yet to hear one of them claim fraud."

Burston pulled open a desk drawer and withdrew two glasses and a bottle of scotch. While pouring, he said: "Sometimes I think the spiritualism thing has moved masses of people toward an epidemic of delusion. There's just been so much death and grief since the war and the flu epidemic. People can't resist the assurance of an afterlife."

Burston slid a glass over to Tommy who took a sip and replied: "Yes, and it's young people who've died in great numbers. All that must have an effect on the surge of the practice across the country, as I've read. But as far as I know, the Shellfoots and Morelys don't practice any sort of...well, whatever you want to call it." Tommy paused. "Look, I've heard people say that Ke'was End is an evil place and there is no point talking about it. On the other hand, I've heard from folks, who've actually gone over there. Simply said, they see things and hear things that make them feel better.

"I remember this one fellow who stayed the night down there and came over to the Strand for three days to 'get over it.' It wasn't like he was all torn up. No, quite the contrary, he just wanted to 'savor the feeling', he said. He'd smelled his dead mother's cabbage soup cooking when he walked in, he looked all around but only the smell was there. It was as if a cauldron of soup was boiling beneath his nose. He was as sober as could be when he told me this, and you know, it makes me feel silly saying it, Burston, but there was a light around him - a sort of glow."

Tommy went on: "You've heard about the indian spirit child, right? The one they say appears at that mound of dirt and bones out there? I talked to old man Goldsmith about it once. You know him, in that tiny cottage on Triton Road down from the Morelys' - Goldsmith?" Tommy saw Burston's blank face. "He's an interesting old fellow. Anyway, Goldsmith walks around out there by the jetty, a favorite place of mine, and we talk from time to time. This is something: He records every day of his life in journals. I saw them once when I stopped by in the winter to see if he needed anything. He has the journals stacked around the house in dated order. I'm telling you, Burston, if there's one there are a thousand of them, and this old guy can just go to a pile and pull one out to prove a point he's making about some date.

"I'm getting a bit off topic here, but that end of the island *is* mystical. It's the side that was first inhabited you know. Goldsmith told me. He said the natives were safer there. It's the side where the island's ancestors are buried, so the natives believe the land is sacred."

Bakker freshened their drinks and handed Tommy two photographs. One was of the crumbled headstones in the Founders' Cemetery and the other was of Ismy. She was dressed in a light frock, bending over to place wildflowers on a tumbled tombstone. A clear white aura pulsed from the girl. The rays were unnatural to the light of day.

Tommy said: "That's Judah Morely's daughter, isn't it?" Then he pointed to the base of the mound which loomed in the distance beyond the toppled fence and asked: "Who is this?"

Burston hadn't noticed before, but in the photo there was another image, not unlike the light specks in the photos he had given to Bay Shellfoot in May, except this time the specks formed a small, translucent shape.

Burston stared and Tommy spoke: "In case you were wondering what the connection of the photo to old man Goldsmith's journals is, I'd say it's that strange light. The old man showed me entry after entry in his diaries, Burston. He's not a man who deals with trifles. He calls it "spirit" that speaks to him and he records it."

"And this spirit says what?"

"Always the same things: 'We are them' 'You help them' 'Be with them.' Goldsmith responds with 'mitzvahs,' that's what he calls them. That means good deeds. He finds people who need a hand with something and then he helps them, usually without them knowing."

The men looked again at the two photos, one of destruction and the other of hope.

"Publish them both," Tommy said.

So, Burston ran a photo of the rubble in the cemetery across five columns of the front page on the top half of the weekly broadsheet.

THE CORYCIAN ISLAND READER
Vol. 13, No. 42 October 15, 1920
Desecration and Destruction Occurs at Founder's Cemetery

Gravestones honoring Corycian Island settlers and veterans of American wars were destroyed in the middle of the night last Tuesday in the Founder's Cemetery at Ke'was End. The two suspects, believed to be islanders, were observed running from the scene by eye witnesses. According to information obtained by Corycian Island Police Chief, Hansen Ratliss, it was 2:00 a.m. when the residents of *(cont'd page* 3*).*

On the Op-Ed page, Bakker ran the photo of Ismy laying flowers on the broken stones. The child's aura and the light behind her couldn't be missed. the *Reader's* editorial appeared under the title:

What is it we see?

"The beauty of Corycian Island has always been in what we don't see as well as what we do.

Corycian islanders are a people born of miracles. We see them everyday with each glorious rise of the sun and hear them in every call of a loon. A whisper in the breeze reminds us of someone, now gone, who loved to sail. In the curl of a wave the mind's eye sees his childhood at the beach. The smell of a lilac brings the image of a mother who passed long ago.

We've been gifted with a lack of sight in the visions of mainlanders who see differences first, causing them complications and endless angst. Here, we are often told of our similarities to this ancestor or that one. We've lived side by side, seeing, helping, and supporting one another, until the other night when a menace among us appeared to destroy all that we honor in ourselves.

These are the graves of our forefathers. It doesn't matter who you are. Once you moved your life here and dug into the soil, you became a part of this place and therefore, a part of those who came before. It's a lesson we all have to learn to live here: We are them.

This heinous act is a desecration of ourselves, and if we allow those among us who are responsible to remain unidentified, then we may as well have pummeled those memorials to pieces with our own hands."

The day after the *Reader* came out, forty islanders arrived to restore the Founder's Cemetery.

The workers divided themselves according to skills and began to work. One group set out to replace the broken adornments of the wrought iron fence surrounding the large plot, including the once beautifully scrolled tree welded into the gates. Others worked at mapping out the original areas of internment, matching the names with the plots, and returning broken pieces to their original stones.

Burston Bakker and his family toiled alongside their neighbors. Repeatedly, people spoke to Burston about his editorial:

"Thanks for that, Bakker. You said it for all of us," one man said with a pat on Burston's shoulder.

Another said: "See what those mighty words of yours did, Bakker? They got us out here, don't ya know."

But perhaps Burston's greatest compliment came when he noticed Nuna Shellfoot was beside him. They exchanged greetings and Nuna said: "Dis be what de picta say, Mr. Bakker, de one wit' Ismy. Dat blink you sees? De spirit seed? Dis be what it say." Nuna held up a shard of polished stone that had been skimmed from the obelisk at the center of the cemetery. It bore the hieroglyph of the Runapewak people, hand in hand. "You help dem. Dat why dey comes. Dey be all-a-wanna strong."

In the flash of a moment Burston felt a sense of his best self. He had an unopened letter on fine vellum stationary addressed in a prep school cursive in his breast pocket. He excused himself from Nuna Shellfoot, walked out of the cemetery toward the woods, and stopped just beyond a few trees. Using a flat rock he dug a deep hole into the soft earth, tore the envelope and its contents into tiny pieces, dropped them into the hole, replaced the dirt, and stood up. Burston turned to leave and looked straight into the eyes of Ezra Goldsmith.

"Good day. Mr. Bakker," Ezra said. "That was a fine editorial you wrote this week. I have to say, you had me worried for awhile, but you seem to be coming around." Abashedly, Burston brushed dirt from his hands, still surprised at Goldsmith's presence. "Is there something I can help you do here?" Ezra asked. "I have a spade since I'm on my way to help at the cemetery."

Burston laughed. "No, Mr. Goldsmith. You've helped me already, in a way. Let's just say I was doing a 'mitzvah,' you know? A mitzvah for myself."

As they walked from the woods, Ezra Goldsmith clapped Burston Bakker on the back and said, heartily:

"Yes, my friend, a mitzvah for yourself. That is where every mitzvah must start."

Calliope Point
"It's a big world over on the mainland."

When Babs Bakker turned 14, she had been the bossy Queen of the Cousins, a self-appointed position, for years. She was tall and thin like the McElroy side of the family while her brother, JB, and her Lawson cousins - Sam and Nate - were still a head shorter than she.

The four of them spent hours together every day of their childhood, but that was about to end since Babs would be the first of them to be sent to a Connecticut boarding school. Miss Porters' in Farmington.

Pammy didn't want Babs to leave the Corycian Island School, but Burston put his foot down saying it was a new age and Babs was entitled, in Burston's words, "to have a broader world view."

"What does that mean, Daddy?" Babs asked.

"It means there's a big world on the mainland, and you need to get to know what's going on over there, so you can evaluate life here."

"Is that why Uncle Tommy is so keen on Sam going to Choate?"

"Well, yes," her father answered. "I think your Uncle Tommy always felt bad about not going away to school."

"Why didn't he go?"

"Well, Barbara Jean, his family couldn't afford it. Boarding schools cost a good deal of money."

Babs loved her father's precise explanations of things. She knew he favored her over JB who, according to Burston, never did as he was told. Babs thought her mother babied JB. Once Babs had overheard Burston tell Pammy:

"A man needs to learn what he believes."

"When he's a man, he will have learned, Burston," Pammy had said. "He's just a boy. Leave it alone."

From Pammy's point of view, Burston's attitude toward JB was annoying, but Burston appeared to be drinking less, so his cutting remarks weren't as frequent. Currently, Pammy's annoyance flared when having to listen to her newly enlightened daughter.

"JB can be such a dullard," Babs said to her mother one day.

"Oh Babs, just because JB hasn't the same interests as you doesn't mean he's a dullard."

"You sneer at everything I say, Mother."

"That is just not true, Barbara Jean. You and I share many of the same opinions. You just refuse to acknowledge that."

"Well, your opinions sure proved themselves wrong in the national election, in case you didn't notice. As for mine, well, I was for Harding, all the way."

"You were for Harding because your father supports him," Pammy said. "For my first official vote, I chose to think for myself."

"Perhaps," Babs said, enjoying the spar and turning it to a more likely win for herself: "But I am not a snob."

Pammy knew Babs was picking a fight. She was very good at it now that her hormones raged against adults. Her "brazen mouth" - Pammy's words - was one of the reasons Babs was going to boarding school. Pammy called Babs "will-full, stubborn, and fresh" during one tirade, and "ungrateful, obnoxious, and spiteful" in another.

Pammy had promised herself not to be baited again, but Babs' remark got to her: "How can you say that? How can you say I'm a snob?"

"You make yourself look good because you volunteer at the Care Center and you get women to the voting booths," Babs said, "but once I heard you say to daddy that you only volunteer at the care center because you love babies."

"Oh my goodness, Barbara Jean. I was kidding - that was a throw back to something daddy said to me years before you were born. Yes, I love those babies, and their mothers, too. That's just totally off the subject."

"No it's not. When was the last time you had any of those mothers you love so much over here?" Babs shot back. "Or when was the last time you sat out on the lawn drinking spiked tea with them like you do with your Calliope friends? You talk *at* those women when you're at the Care Center not *to* them. It's all about whether they like you, don't pretend you like them."

Pammy never knew a girl to be as outspoken as her own daughter, certainly not one this young. She had allowed Babs to choose books from the extensive library in the Bakker house as soon as she realized her daughter was doing so anyway at age six. Babs started reading with *The Secret Garden* and had graduated to Edgar Alan Poe by the fifth grade. Pammy told Burston she had been too permissive as a mother and she was paying the price. Burston said the child was smarter than the two of them put together and needed to be around girls her own age who challenged her.

"Since when did you become a suffragette?" Pammy asked.

"I guess when I realized it was give in or perish," Burston laughed. "It just makes sense to put someone as bright, articulate, and self-informed as Babs into a stronger learning environment. God knows her brother won't have that chance. Not that George Stoli doesn't run a fine school. Babs wouldn't be fighting us so hard if he didn't."

One night Burston escaped to read *The New York Times* in the library after dinner. Babs leaned on the frame of the door. She had her arms folded and her dark, brown hair framed a furious face.

Burston barely looked up and said: "I've told you before Barbara Jean. Boarding school will be good for you. Look what it's done for your cousin, Sam. One year under his belt and he's twice as confident as he ever was. Boarding school builds character. You'll meet all the right people to rely on later in life when you need a hand up. You're a smart girl, much smarter than the girls at Stoli's school. You win the language and math awards for your grade every year, and you've skipped a grade already. You'll be home for holidays and you can see your island friends then."

He folded the paper onto his lap and listened to her reply.

"It's not my island friends I'm going to miss," Babs said. "It's you and the boys and Aunt Sissy, but not Mother. I won't miss her. She's always belittling me."

"You're too much alike to belittle each other, little lady." Burston reached from his chair to grab Babs' elbow. He pulled her down into his lap. Babs put her head on her father's shoulder and felt the boom of his heart beating beneath his broad chest. "You are way too grown up, sweet girl," Burston said, speaking with less command. "I might say, you brought this on yourself with all that reading and showing off about how much smarter you are than your parents and your teachers. George Stoli agrees that you're ready for more challenging work. I want you focused on the years ahead in high school and college. Why you could take over the paper when I'm ready, Barbara Jean. Your brother doesn't seem interested in writing skills. But the job's meant for you. You've shown me those journals of yours. I suspect writing is in your blood."

Babs made her own journals out of blank newsprint her father brought from work. She filled them with vignettes of what she saw during her days on Corycian Island - five or six sentences, jotted down here and there. Some dated, others not, like:

"Drove past the windmill off Old Post Road with Daddy. The sun was setting behind the tower, making the turning blades burn pink, a Dutch masterpiece came alive!"

"Johnny Goodroy, the only boy taller than me in the fifth grade, is smart, but gets the worst grades because the boys call him a fairy if he reads during recess. I have heard Johnny tell the teacher he doesn't know an answer that he's told me the day before when we talked about that very subject. Why is it some people hide what makes them interesting to begin with?"

When Babs showed the journals to her father, she asked him to read a few entries and tell her if they were dumb.

"That's what you said to me, kitten," Burston told Babs. "You asked me to tell you if they were *dumb*. I want you to start asking me how smart what you write is. *That's* why you're going to a higher achieving, educational facility!"

Babs' arguments with Pammy about boarding school ended that night, as did her reign as Queen of the Cousins, although on holidays the boys were so glad to see her again, and they willingly subjugated themselves to Babs' orders.

Hansen Ratliss and Josiah Remie
"I believe I have your hat."

The Corycian Island Town Board authorized Hansen Ratliss to align his department with other mainland police departments. As a result, the Chief had the opportunity to send his two part-timers off island for official training. This would, hopefully, lead to their designation as full-time Corycian Island police officers. Some day.

The need to increase the force had become obvious before the U.S. entered the Great War. Then Scaler fishermen had scouted the Long Island Sound for German submarines. Ratliss had handled their assignments as well as their reports. He worked night and day until he was allowed the two part-timers to help out.

Ratliss had more time to follow Remie now, mostly at night when the rest of the town was quiet. Ratliss knew that was when Remie was on the prowl and if Remie was out, Wesley was at his side. However, little of what Ratliss discovered when trailing Remie surprised him. He saw the wiry little man meet a bootlegger on a beach east of Pipers' Cove and watched Remie make a transaction to buy six boxes of whiskey. Ratliss had seen the large bootlegger before, and the boxes he was trading, at the time, had brand names. Remie was buying some no-name swill, but he probably didn't know it. Neither would his clients, Ratliss reasoned with a smile. But Ratliss didn't want to pin an alcohol violation on Remie, so the Chief waited for him to get the itch to play his stupid games again, and he kept the conical hat Henry found at the ready.

Ratliss saw Remie where he least expected to see him - at the Founders' Cemetery, on another day planned by the community to continue the restoration. Remie led a group from the Believers' Camp. They got right to work with Remie hiding among them, keeping his head down, hoping he wouldn't have to face any Shellfoots or Morelys; but when he stood up to move to another area, he came eye to eye with Nuna Shellfoot. Josiah's knees trembled and his mouth shook when he tried to pass her a civil smile. Nuna's black eyes wouldn't let Josiah's go. He finally turned his head away and saw Ratliss.

"Well, look who's here," Ratliss said. "Goodman Remie is it?" Remie stepped around the Chief and kept walking. "Leaving so soon? A strong man like you?" Ratliss said to Remie's back, adding: "By the way, Mr. Remie, I believe I have your hat."

***

When Hector told Josiah about losing his hat, Josiah burned the duplicate and put the choir robes back with their ten companions in the Believers' barn. Remie further covered his tracks by spreading rumors about drunk boys staying at the hotel. He told the many gullible locals with whom he transacted liquor sales:

"These crazy kids shows up at my still in their daddy's car. One a 'em is named Tom somethin'. They was all drunk and sweaty from runnin'. They buys some whiskey and tells me all about what they done down there at Ke'was and how. I'd rat 'em out since Ratliss is sneakin' around tryin' to blame a Scaler, but I ain't no snitch. You waits and hear who Ratliss is askin' about. He don't want to bother with them Strand people, so he'll be pointin' at one a us."

Consequently when the Chief questioned the people who talked to Remie, he heard Remie's fabrication. They all said the cemetery was destroyed by "rich kids," one named Tom, staying at the Strand. It was a fact they said, but they couldn't ever tell who told them.

However they always assured Ratliss the story came from the same person: "Someone who knows."

1921

Ke'was End
"He played along with them."

Without question, the year-round residents of Corycian felt the ground under them shift while Prohibition dug its way into the island economy.

The Captain's Guest House leased basement storage space to one of Henry's bootlegger friends from the mainland. Cases of liquor were ferried to the beach and then stored below the house. The area could be reached through a tunnel from Ephraim's days that few still knew about.

It was agreed that the Captain's Guest House wasn't going to attract attention by serving alcohol; perhaps, an occasional treat of Nuna's elderberry wine in the parlor, but that was to be it.

Nonetheless, taxis from the Strand and the Westside Ferry brought alcohol to the Captains' house with clients who secreted flasks from which they imbibed, usually in private, if nervous about an upcoming reading or séance.

After Henry had ushered the second incoherently drunk man from the lobby, he began to shut down his store earlier in the day so he could give a hand at the Captain's if things got "turbulent," as Henry termed it.

The turbulence arrived the very next afternoon, minutes after Henry came in to see how the day was going. Dodie Merkel, an attractive palm reader, came screaming from her upstairs room. Dodie's 3 p.m. appointment, a drunk bootlegger, was lurching down the stairs behind her.

"What kind of scam is this," the ossified man shouted, pulling up his suspenders . "Is it a brothel or not?"

The rumor of prostitution under the guise of spiritualism at Ke'was End took on a life of its own during the blurry years of

Prohibition. What happened with Dodie Merkel made everyone edgy. So Hansen Ratliss took even more trips down to Ke'was End, telling Henry he wanted the Chief's presence there known around town.

"I don't listen to those rumors," Ratliss said to Henry. "I have a feeling they are spread deliberately. Anyway, I'll be coming by here more often. Let me know if you think anything funny's going on, all right Henry?"

Henry moved close to Ratliss and whispered: "I suspect they's someone's eyes on us right here and now." He stepped away and said, loudly: "Come on in the store, Chief, and I'll pack up them scallops you ordered. That's what you come by for, right?"

Once inside the store, Henry scooped shaved ice into a tin bucket, put butcher paper on top, and fresh Bay scallops on top of that. He talked while he fixed the bucket for the Chief:

"Just brings the bucket back when you comes by this way. These here is on the house. Say...uhh... Chief...Someone been creepin' around them woods between Nuna's place and Mr. Ezra's. You know, behind the cemetery?" Henry took off his fishing cap and ruffled his tight grey curls. "I think it's a kid. I tracked him one night , but he's a lot faster'n me, and he's quiet as a mouse."

"A kid?" Ratliss said. "Huh. Is he alone?"

"Far's I can tell," Henry said.

"How old?"

"Well, he's boney and fast - anywhere from 12 on up, I'd say, but he been nothin' but a streakin' shadow when I seen him."

"He's not 12, but Josiah Remie's small. You know him, Henry?"

"That old coot has slowed down too much to be runnin' through the woods as fast as this kid do. From what folks tells me, Remie been drinkin' his way through the Volstead and he looks the worst for it. But, now you say it, I betcha it's Remie's kid. Don't think he was around that night in the cemetery, but he's sneakin' around here other times for sure."

The most recent time Henry saw Inri Remie, the boy ran with the adrenalin of fear fueling his feet. Inri felt Henry's eyes on his back while he leapt over fallen trees and tripped over a leaf-hidden rock. He came out on Brook Road which he had to cross to get to the woods leading to Pipers' Cove. The boy was breathless when he rested in some shrubbery above the house where Hector Wesley lived with Lindy Meade and their children: Twirly, 15, and Ray-Ray, 12. Old Mrs. Wesley lived in there somewhere, too.

It was a ramshackle house, patched where it needed patching and built onto at whim wherever a right angle was left to add some kind of room. Inri had spied on the Wesley household before, but mostly he heard them fighting with each other and, well, that just got boring.

Inri startled at a familiar sound. It was a whistle his father always used in the woods. Inri crept toward the soft tune. The clouds darkened the night and there weren't many lights around the Wesley place, not even by the outhouse which Inri thought he could see.

The whistle sounded again. Inri heard a screen door slap and saw Twirly Wesley step out on to the kitchen stoop. "Is that my horny boy?" Twirly said, sipping on a drink, rubbing her hand over her ample breasts, and reaching up to give her hair a signature twirl. "I'm in heat all right, big boy, you sniffed me out," the bosomy blonde whispered, grinding her hips around. "You wettin' your whistle back there, Josie? Is that you back there?" Twirly said as she sashayed toward the outhouse.

Inri heard his father's whistle again and felt his stomach turn. Twirly was just a kid. Then he heard Twirly gasp and giggle. Inri saw Josiah jump out and grab her. Josiah was naked.

Inri felt his empty stomach roil as his father grappled with Twirly who appeared to be just as eager since Inri heard her say many times: "Josiah! Josiah! Josiah!"

Inri watched in horror. He did not feel aroused, only repulsed.

1922

Calliope Point
"You could have been playing baseball at Choate."

JB Bakker was 14 when he first noticed Blossom Stoli's beauty. They'd been in the same class since first grade, so JB had been aware of Blossom for years, but she hadn't been a continual presence in his thought stream until 1922.

Blossom had curly blonde hair and eyes like a sweet-cream cow. Taken alone, her orbs were too large and too draped in lashes, but added to Blossom's classic face, the resulting composition was alluring.

When Babs Bakker was home from Farmington, she teased her younger brother: "You don't have to be ogling Blossom Stoli in the lunch room, JB. I hear all about it from my friends. Everyone can tell you're doing it. You are mocked endlessly."

To his great relief, JB wasn't sent away to boarding school. Pammy had fought Burston tooth and nail about it. Burston said Pammy was turning JB into a "mama's boy."

"Well at least he'll know he's someone's boy," Pammy said.

The Bakker's marriage suffered more bitter moments after Babs went away to school. For the most part, Burston had his drinking under control; but when he didn't, everyone felt it.

One such night, Burston spoke in a whiskey-thick voice across the dinner table to JB. "You know you could have been playing baseball at Choate with your cousins. Nate was smart enough to join Sam where they have a *real* baseball team,"

"*We* have a real baseball team," JB said. "I've never seen these guys work so hard at anything. You know that kid Ray-Ray Wesley? Dumber than a post about some stuff, but that guy can slam a baseball. And Beanie Antolini? He runs like the wind, I swear."

235

Noticing Burston's lack of interest, JB said: "Besides, Sam and Nate wanted to go to prep school. I didn't."

Burston cut a piece of his steak and chewed it thoughtfully. He swirled the whiskey in his glass and took a slow sip. He said, while cutting another piece of meat, and not looking at his son: "First of all, you speak as poorly as you write. Who ever taught you that appropriate conversation includes the words 'stuff' and 'guys'? And second of all, a proficient team doesn't form itself because you have 14 males with all their limbs."

These were issues of Burston's constant harangue. JB's careless language skills and Corycian Island School sports. The school had trouble fielding team sports. A year might register a new class of 12-16 children, but the gender split determined what teams resulted and for how long. When the class population ran toward female dominance, the turf was converted for field hockey play. If the groupings were split down the middle, the school ran intramural sports, pick up games that came with spring and fall when Principal Stoli wanted to get everyone outside.

But in the early 1920s Stoli saw JB Bakker's class evolve into a group of 12 boys who loved baseball and two girls who loved math, with two male-dominated classes following behind. Stoli jumped right in to coach the high school team while teaching the upcoming classes America's game throughout their grammar school years.

Radios had come to the vast majority of Corycian Island homes by the 20s. It seemed as if everyone knew the major leaguers and their stats because the whole town tuned into Graham McNamee's enthusiastic, on-air commentary about Babe Ruth, Walter Johnson, Dazzy Vance, and all the greats. So, Stoli's team attracted strong local support. Sly's Marina, below Pipers' Cove, donated uniform shirts and island moms volunteered to keep them clean. The fire department held fairs to raise money for equipment. Westside Market provided buckets of cool water for the players and Marmie treated the team to ice cream cones whenever they won. Neighbors worked as referees during practices, consulting rule books over questionable plays. Early evenings every block in the center of town rang with the thump-thump pocketing of balls to mitts with boys and their dads playing catch.

In JB Bakker's freshman year, Stoli arranged a roster of competitions: Four public high schools from the mainland to compete in eight games, half to be held on each school's home field.

The class worked as one unit to prepare for their first round of play. The girls learned how to keep box scores of runs, at bats, and errors. The boys practiced how to slide, bunt, steal, and catch. Parents groomed a manicured field. The grammar school kids traded baseball facts and charted stats in their math classes.

That spring the Corycian Island Scalers went 4-0 against the other schools. JB Bakker was the stand-out pitcher. They were contenders in, what Stoli dubbed, the "Mainland vs. Island World Series," playing the Midhampton Clammers.

JB pitched a perfect game in the last of the three game series played on a field in Ridgehampton to avoid home-field advantages. A caravan of cars left Corycian Island the afternoons of the series. The bleachers, which held 300, overflowed. Another few hundred people were scattered around the perimeter of the field on blankets, with a number of boys perched in trees.

Georgie Stoli's family sat front and center in the Corycian bleachers, the best seats in the house. They all had an interest in the game: Frances Stoli to cheer on George who she knew felt ill-equipped to be the team's coach. Blossom to cheer on JB Bakker who she hoped might kiss her at Nate Lawson's 16th birthday party the next weekend. And Aster Stoli, who kept an eye on Blossom because she'd been reading her sister's secret diary and Aster wanted to watch how brazenly Blossom would flirt with JB.

Corycian Island
"The Talk of the Town."

Corycian islanders had settled into their new-found wealth from alcohol only to learn that inland property was in great demand, whereas once only seaside lots sold for inflated values.

SUZANNE MCLAIN ROSENWASSER

Newcomers described Corycian's architecture as "quaint, picturesque, and romantic." They saw old Colonial homesteads, like the Lawsons and the Morelys, that seemed rooted to the land on which they stood ("quaint"). They admired handcrafted cottages, like the Wesleys or the Stolis, that sat on sandy lanes near boat slips ("picturesque"). And they fully-appreciated the Carpenter Gothic style homes of the Victorian era that dotted the hills of Pipers' Cove and Calliope Point ("romantic").

However, the newly wealthy men of the 1920s, who bought multiple acres northeast of Union Harbor, wanted grandeur in their summer homes. So they hired world class architects to design neo-classical mansions. The imposing homes had Grecian columns, Gothic windows, and grand entrances with belvederes above them on the second and third floors, facing the Sound.

The relentless hammering of construction echoed through the island in 1922. When local builders reacted to the need for smaller homes to house the families of newly arrived workers, islanders sold one-quarter acre plots for record prices or built small cottages on their properties to rent.

It was the greatest immigration from the mainland Corycian Island had seen since just after the fish oil factories came down in the 1880s.

Town census records showed that the year-round, island population had increased to 949. Gracie Williams, the post mistress, had heard from Dottie Barnett, the town clerk, that 43 babies had been born in the year since the last census, and now with all these mansions going up - well, it was the absolute talk of the town.

Pammy Bakker hated the talk of the town. It seemed to be her life, even though she had little to do with the newspaper her husband ran. That didn't stop people from approaching her with their complaints when she was out and about, so she tried to go out as little as possible. A trip to Westside Market wasn't even safe. When Pammy ordered roasts and chops each week, old Calvin Darner, the butcher, always embarrassed her with a personal comment. His latest:

"Nice seein' you at Mass up at the convent's chapel. Us Catholics needs to stick together, don't we now, Mrs.?"

Sticking together was something Pammy had no intention of doing with Catholics. She just went to Mass to learn how to pray. The prayers in Latin sounded authentic. The incense made her feel at home. But she had no sins to confess and no apologies to make for not receiving the sacraments, and she didn't need the local butcher questioning her.

"Bet you were goin' to Mass over there on the mainland like the rest of us. Not that I ever seen you. But, now with St. Anthony's doing the Mass and all, I'll bet I sees you doin' all sorts a thing there, ain't that right, Mrs?"

Pammy looked around to see if there were others waiting behind her. She pretended not to have heard:

"I'd like a nice cut of bottom round for a pot roast, Mr. Darner. Say 5-6 pounds. And let's go with a pork roast about the same size, if you please

"Hows that daughter of yours doin'?" Darner asked, chastened enough to change the topic. "My boy Davey always had it for her. Kissed her under the sand table in first grade he told me. She ever tell you that one, Mrs.?"

Pammy could never figure out what Darner's hours were. Sometimes a few weeks went by before she saw him appear out of the cooler. He opened every greeting with a question she didn't want to answer. She thought of what she'd like to say, the truth:

"I only go to Mass because I don't know what else to do."

1923

Corycian Island
The Mail

Nathaniel McElroy Lawson
Choate Preparatory School
Wallingford, Connecticut

March 15, 1923
Dear Mom and Dad

I'm not going to write this like they teach us in English class, so don't tell me I haven't learned the proper structure of a letter because I have. I just want to sound like myself, not like someone trying to get an "A." And by the way, that's all anyone does here - try to earn "A's" - I mean it. Everyone wants to be the best at everything.

I'm not going to lie: I don't love it here as much as last year. I've talked to Sam about it and he understands. He'll be graduating come June and I'm not sure I want to be here alone. Even the Bakkers noticed I wasn't happy when I was home for Christmas.

But it got worse. Everyone came back after Christmas break with new resolutions made to their parents to be A students. It's unnerving. And the teachers (we're supposed to call them professors so they sound smarter, but they aren't any better or worse than at home) - anyway, the teachers make it sound like everyone can earn an "A," and everyone else at school goes along with it. I don't think my history teacher liked it when I raised the question of societal structure, like you talk about, Dad. Grades are like money here and everyone thinks they're rich, so they want A money. I remembered what you said. For a free enterprise system to work there has to be a firm bond of respect, regardless of wealth. Some people have "A" money, others have "D" money, and a few have "F" money, but they all need to respect that they share the earnings of the same dollar. The professor challenged me, and you would have been so proud, Dad. Just being around the Strand has taught me practical things the boys here won't learn for years.

I talked about how a dollar spent on Corycian passes from a Calliope resident to an island carpenter for a piece of hand hewn furniture and then from the carpenter to a Scaler for a few pounds of fish and from the Scaler to the town for his land taxes and from the town to the road crews for their wages and from one of them to the Red Cross volunteer fund.

Remember when we used to play that game on the beach at night, just the four of us and we'd add places on Corycian the dollar passed through? Anyway, all the kids kept saying: "What hick town do you come from?" and stuff like that. All I felt was homesick when they did it.

Maybe it's because it's rainy season and it's grayer and darker up here than it ever was at home. I miss being with the things I know. Last year it was all new. This year it's old.

I think I want to come home and finish school on Corycian. What do you think?

I love you all. I miss being with you too much for this to work. However, I don't want you to think me a quitter, and if that's the case, I'll stay.

Nate

***

Barbara Jean Bakker
Miss Porter's School
Farmington, Connecticut

From: Babs
To: Whoever feels like reading this at our house
Date: May 15, 1923

Can you believe next year is my last at Farmington? I'm aghast. Seriously. It has all gone by so quickly - and Father, you were so, so right that this is the place for me. I think about that quite often. Thank you for your guidance. I'm in my third year of enlightenment and in awe of a whole new world of knowledge.

I think you will be pleased to know that I'm applying for the Editor position at *The Salmagundy* for my Senior year. I've earned it after three years of reporting on all the boring club meetings on campus and taking photos of the "Top Three" whatevers. At least this year my scenics are making the front page, and I have a byline on a feature I wrote about how we learn in a community of women. I've enclosed it.

I never dreamed I'd connect so well with women after the contentious years we've spent together, Mommy, and I mean no offense. You know we have our squabbles. I hope you'll find I've grown leaps and bounds since last summer. I'm looking forward to having months to show you how adult I've become.

How's Blossom Stoli, JB? I hear you kissed her at Winter Frolic. Oops, did everyone just read that? Ha. Ha. No secrets, remember?

Love, the one and only - Babs
P.S.: I'm applying to Wellesley, Radcliff, and Barnard. I'm going to be a journalist!

***

At the Corycian Island School, JB Bakker, 16, leaned over to the girl next to him in English class and asked her to pass a folded note to Blossom Stoli, three rows to his right.

Blossom was bent over the paper Mr. Brennan had handed out. Her fountain pen was poised above a few lines of her precise cursive. She jumped when the boy at the desk behind her poked her shoulder. He leaned up to her neck and his creepy voice said:

"Ohhhhh, Blah-summm, another love note from Bakker."

Blossom looked around to see an absorbed Mr. Brennan helping another student. She took the note, opened it, and slid it under the paper for her essay. She checked to make sure Brennan wasn't moving along, then read the note and replied. The missives went back and forth. Each time JB's note reached the desk behind her, the boy poked Blossom harder. The round of notes said:

> **Blossom** -
>
> Can you beleive how dum this assinement is? Who knows where they see themselves in five years and what thier wishes are? Look at Ray-Ray staring out the window. How long has that kid been in the 11th grade anyway? Oh, and of course, your scribbling away. What did you put?
> *JB*

> **JB,**
>
> I just made stuff up. You need to learn how to spell before you criticize Ray-Ray.
> *Blossom*

> **Blossom** -
>
> I can spell when I want too. Why'd you're father tell the Seniors they can't have thier Last Dance outside?
> *JB*

JB,
> Ask him.
> *Blossom*

Blossom -
> I'm going to run for presdent of our Senior class and we'll have our Last Dance outside. You'll see. In the meantime. Do you want to go with me to this years?
> *JB*
> PS. English isn't my best subject. Math is and I'll bet my math grades are a whole lot better than yours.

JB,
> Well you should at least know how to conjugate a verb. You're the newspaper publisher's son, for heaven's sake (smile). Yes, I will be pleased to attend the Last Dance with you this year in the gymnasium (smile).
> *Blossom*

***

Pammy drove JB to an agreed upon corner near the Stoli's house the night of the dance. JB said Blossom and he wanted to walk over to the school together.

"You look so handsome, JB. Have fun tonight," his mother said, appraising his new double-breasted blazer which looked so smart with his summer blonde hair and powder-blue eyes. Pammy didn't say every girl at the high school had a crush on her baseball star. She didn't say he reminded her of Burston. She just said: "I can't wait to hear all about it when you get home."

JB rang the doorbell of the Stoli's house and her father answered the door. Coach Stoli, as JB knew him, said: "Come in, son. Come in."

JB threw the clunky corsage box from his right hand to his left and shook Stoli's hand while trying to maneuver the step up into the house at the same time. He felt seasick.

"Blossom will be downstairs in a minute," Stoli said. "Take a seat why don't you." JB sat in the chair Stoli indicated. "You've done a fine job this year, son. It sure has been a pleasure to work with you."

JB's face broke into a broad smile, and when he was about to speak, he followed Coach Stoli's head when it turned to the stairs. Blossom had just reached the landing at the bottom step.

She smiled at them shyly, those doe eyes looking up from a froth of blonde curls. Her lips were lacquered red. She wore an ashy-pink organdy, drop-waisted dress that came, daringly, just below her knees. The sheer fabric scooped low beneath her neck into cap sleeves. Just enough skin showed beyond the outline of the silk, form-fitting slip beneath. She wore pale textured stockings with strapped high heels.

"Frances..." George Stoli called for his wife after collecting himself from his first sight of this grown-up version of Blossom. "Frances!"

George whispered to his daughter: "Has your mother seen you?" Then louder, "Fra-annnn-ces!!!" and turning to JB he said: "There are glasses and cookies all put out...Frances!!"

"What's the matter, daddy?" Blossom was saying, at the point of tears. "Mommy picked the dress out with me, daddy. It's the style!"

Frances Stoli came into the living room from the back of the house.

"For goodness sake, George, what is it?" she said. Frances looked at Blossom.

"Oh you look so beautiful," she said. "The dress is lovely, and the shoes are perfect. " Frances put her hands to her mouth. "Oh dear, you're so grown up." Then saw JB. "Oh, hello, JB. Uh..." looking back at Blossom. "Excuse us for one moment, please."

Frances led Blossom to a mirror in an alcove. "The red lipstick draws attention to the short skirt, Sweetheart. Daddy's not ready for any of this, so it would be a good idea to take the lipstick off

246

for now. He'll think you've dulled the whole outfit down. You can put it on in the gym where it's darker. He'll never notice when he's walking around chaperoning."

Frances smiled and drew Blossom close. "You're not our little girl any more. Great for you, darling, but very scary for us."

Màthair
"They're nothing but men!"

When liquor became illegal, the Sisters of St. Anthony refused visiting priests to use actual wine during recitation of the Mass in their chapel. The Mother Superior told every priest, upon arrival, that her rules stood by the Volstead Act:

"I cannot ask the Chief of Police to monitor the Holy Mother Church's property for illegal trespassers, and then have him discover we are perpetrating illegal activities ourselves, Father."

The Mother Superior felt smug about her victory over what she assumed was a lackluster lot of drunken priests who were sent to the convent for healing. Most of them spent their first days tied to their beds:

"Sweating, puking and mudding in their persnicketty pants," Mother Superior thought while she cleaned up after a Monsignor who'd arrived with vomit all over his cassock. "Drowning in their sins without a memory of this part. They come to, after we've polished them all up, and they want to be Pope all over again. Priests! They're nothing but men."

Prohibition gave the Mother Superior an edge because the priests weren't arguing with her about stocking communion wine; however, she noticed they seemed to be getting alcohol anyway, as evidenced by the stench of it on, supposedly sober, Father Pastini's breath in the confessional booth.

Mother Augustus believed the liquor was coming in when a priest-in-residence said the Mass, usually at 6 a.m., seven days a week. Occasionally, the priest didn't appear and didn't answer persistent knocks upon his locked door. When this occurred on Sundays, a day on which it is a mortal sin for Catholics to skip Mass, Mother Augustus had to inform the gathering of congregants, a smattering of immigrant fishermen and that Bakker lady from Calliope Point, that the priest was "indisposed."

On Sundays Mother Augustus had to answer questions:

"It's not a mortal sin for us because we came to go to Mass, right Mother?"

"What do we do about holy communion? I pledged to go to communion every Sunday. Now what am I gonna do?"

"Do I need to say an act of contrition because I was glad when Mass was cancelled?"

Mother Superior Augustus, silently, cursed.

1924

Ke'was End
"I am the child of Great Spirit."

Ismy Shellfoot Morely was now seven-years-old; "almost eight," she liked to say. Ismy had seen Makieweesug when she was only three. It was one of her earliest memories. She had been scurrying in front of her grandmother on a walk along the path through the woods.

Nuna stopped when Makieweesug appeared in front of them. A long silence passed; then, the spirit seeds faded back into the woods.

Toddling Ismy, with her mouth in the 'o' of awe, looked at her grandmother. Nuna told her: "They be little spirit seeds. 'Mah-kee-ah-wee-sug' be what Runapewak say. Your great-grand daddy talk 'bout d'ese little ones. Mr. Ezra be knowin' dem, and now you, little Ismy - and me, too."

That day, the three-year-old shook her head up and down.

"Pewitty," she said, then put her thumb in her mouth.

"Lissens is all, sweet girl. Just lissens good, and you be seein' all sorts a pretty t'ings," Nuna said.

Now Ismy visited with Makiaweesug regularly at play. She told spirit her secrets: What Ismy saw and what she heard; what she thought was real and what she thought was not.

When Bay enrolled Ismy at the Corycian Island School, the child had to make sense of a whole new scenario. The people at school weren't like the people Ismy knew and loved at Ke'was End. These adults shouted their thoughts at Ismy, like her current teacher, a mainlander who took the ferry to work at the school. His name was Aidan Case. It was his first year, too.

Mr. Case wasn't familiar with the culture of the island, but he got a taste of it with each lesson. One day he talked to the class about families, showing pictures of dog, cat, chicken, pig, horse, and human families. "So let's go around the room and hear about your families, ok?" the new teacher asked. "You know, as an introduction to each other."

The teacher persisted when no one volunteered. He looked at Ismy and she heard his thought: "Well this one thinks she's got all the answers." Ismy began to wonder if his thought was a compliment when she heard Mr. Case address her out loud: "Ok, Miss. You start. Tell us about your father."

The room got really quiet. Issues of fatherhood among islanders were less clearly defined than those among people from the mainland. Everyone stared at Ismy. They knew Judah Morely had been killed in the Great War, but they also knew how Ismy loved to make up stories. The little girl didn't seem the least bit flustered. She looked at Mr. Case and said:

"I am the child of the Great Spirit."

"Excuse me?" Aidan Case asked, thinking he was being sassed.

Ismy never used more words than she had to, so she was silent. Another student tried to explain: "Ismy's from down at Ke'was End..."

"Miss Morely can answer for herself, young man. Now, what did you say, Miss Morely?" the teacher prodded.

"My father is the Great Spirit, I said, Mr. Case. I come from the seeds of spirit."

Aidan Case looked over at the other student who shrugged his shoulders and repeated: "Ismy's from Ke'was End."

To most, that statement summed everything up. Ismy's hair, naturally coiled into tight curls, framed her creamy tanned face. The blue eyes she had at birth were now as green as emeralds. Mr. Case had no idea what it meant to be from Ke'Was End, but he knew there was something different about Ismy Shellfoot. He watched her as the days progressed. He noted Ismy talked, laughed, and giggled like the other girls, but not always with anyone present.

Nuna, Bay, and Eula spoke to each other about Ismy's unique communications when they sat on the beach that October.

In front of them, Ismy danced and leapt about in her dainty way, interpreting the warmth of the day. Her sun-bleached ringlets shone in the light. She turned in free-flying circles and jumped into the air. Then her steps slowed to loping sad ones; she stopped and ran to her mother who took the child into her lap and rocked her. "What is it, Ismy?" Bay asked.

"Daddy's gone," Ismy said. "We were dancing, but he left."

The women coaxed her to get up and dance with them, but Ismy refused with a rough head shake. That night Ismy lay on her stomach drawing with a black, tailor's crayon on an old copy of *The Corycian Island Reader*. She drew without pause, clearly envisioning what she wanted to produce. When she finished, she showed her drawing to Nuna and Bay.

There was a stick man, with huge black eyes and a turned-down mouth, fishing from the side of a boat and staring at something in the distance. The fisherman had a thick chain around his neck with a circle hanging from it. The boat was oddly moored at a large mound of land next to the sea.

Nuna froze as she took in the details. "Mystifier!" she whispered to herself. "Mystifier ange."

Ismy watched Nuna pass the drawing to Bay and, even though Nuna whispered, Ismy heard her grandmother say: "Dis child see beyond de beyond."

At the Corycian Island School, Ismy's proclivities confronted a broader community. She was teased by some of her peers. One was a large girl who pushed smaller kids around.

"Hey Weirdo," the girl called out at Ismy on the playground when the lower grades were having recess. "Yes, you, weirdy weirdo!"

Ismy had no idea why this big third grader was shouting directly at her and had less of an idea what the name meant. The girl walked straight toward Ismy and shoved her down to the ground.

Ismy, who was a stranger to aggression, sat with a chafed rear end on the dusty playground field, watching the big girl lead her pack away to find other kids to push down. And for some reason, as Ismy got up and dusted off her skirt, she thought of her drawing of the mad stick fisherman.

Calliope Point

Babs Bakker returned to Connecticut following her winter break. Two weeks later her father brought a letter home from the post office which he read at the dinner table to Pammy and JB:

Barbara Jean Bakker
Miss Porter's School
Farmington, Connecticut

Mom, Dad, and JB:

I've been accepted to Wellesley. Can you believe it? I couldn't be more proud of myself. My advisor said being the Editor of *The Salmagundy* gave me an edge, but I slipped a few pages of *The Corycian Island Reader* (with those "Summer Reports" I did) into my application letter, and I think that's what clinched the deal.

Hurrah for me! I'm going to work at the *Reader* again this summer, Father, so prepare yourself for that. I need to learn everything you know about journalism.

Love,
Babs

Burston waved the letter in the air and spoke with flushed enthusiasm:

"Our little girl has made it to the big leagues." He read the letter again to himself beaming with pride.

The image of that moment was one JB held in the back of his mind.

Pipers' Cove
"I know who you are."

The Believers' Camp at Pipers' Cove remained a popular destination for faithful from all over the northeast. They visited for the day or leased one of the small cabins on the premises. Once summer came, Josiah Remie had little time for his own pleasures and that made him surlier than usual since he had to control his intake of alcohol.

More often than not, his effort was effective. Josiah muddled through the chores of being Jesus and Camp Director in a remorseful way that seemed to touch the congregants' hearts.

"Reverend Remie," Josiah's son, Inri, overheard a camper say, "is the quintessential Believer. Like Jesus, he hides nothing. The good Mr. Remie's life is an open book. When he feels pain, we feel pain. That is the way of the Lord."

Inri thought about that conversation for days. Could it be Josiah knew what he was doing? They felt Josiah's pain? Josiah was the way of the Lord? In his answers to himself, Inri found something in his father to admire. Josiah's ability to hide in plain sight was an asset his son made great efforts to emulate. Inri began to think *that* was the way of the Lord.

So when he dropped out of school, Inri donned the role of invisiblity and spent his time darting around the island to spy on people in their homes. The young man soon realized he could hide in front of people, too, consequently his father had nothing left to teach him.

Inri was sitting at his mother's kitchen table picking the calluses on his bare feet. He heard Josiah coughing and hacking a wad of sludge from his chest as he made his way toward the house. Inri continued his task without looking up when Josiah came into the room.

"What you're doin' right there is disrespectful to your dear, dead mother," Josiah said.

Inri flicked a piece of dead skin across the room and snarled: "Is that so? Disrespectful? Well you knows all about that."

"Don't you never talk to me like that again, you hear" Josiah said with a slap of his hand that somehow turned into a punch when it landed on his son's jaw and knocked the boy off the chair.

Inri looked up from the floor at Josiah's wrathful face. He saw vomit on his father's beard and smelled the foulness. Inri got up, curled his lip, and spat words at Josiah:

"I knows I own this house and can keeps you outta it. One of them Red Cross ladies told me that my momma left this house to me in her will and not to you. So get out - get outta my house. I swear I'll have Ratliss take you away. I know what you do. I know who you are."

"Why you dumb turd," Josiah said, "whatta you know about anything anyway? You think I don't know you're a little creep? Yeah I sees you hidin' out watchin' me with my girls. I see you watchin' me be Jesus and wishin' you could have yourself what I have. Don't toy with me, boy. No one toys with me."

"Get out," Inri said.

Josiah laughed, a guttural raw laugh that had no humor in it. "You ain't nothin' but a whiney mama's boy. And a dead mama's boy at that," he said and left.

Ferry Rides and Futures

On a Saturday afternoon, JB and Blossom took a ferry ride over to the mainland to see a feature film playing at the Midhampton Cinema: "The Hunchback of Notre Dame."

JB held Blossom's hand when the hunchback was lashed in the square; he put his arm around her when the beautiful girl was rescued from torture by Quasimodo; he pulled Blossom close when she sobbed at the hunchback's death.

JB kissed Blossom before the lights came up and again on the ferry back to Corycian Island after he gave her a gift. It was a silver wishbone holding a little pearl and hanging from a chain.

The note JB gave her read:

Dear Blossom,
    This wishbone stands for what my wishes are and where I see myself five years from forever.
    You are the pearl.
    JB

That same Saturday Gracie Williams handed a special delivery letter to Sissy Lawson when she arrived at the post office to retrieve her mail. The return address was familiar:

Nathaniel McElroy Lawson
Choate Preparatory School
Wallingford, Connecticut

Sissy opened the envelope with a motherly smile. She knew what Nate would write:

Dear Mom and Dad,

    I gave it more time like I promised, but I've made the decision to come home to spend my Senior year at Stoli's school. Tell JB for me, ok? And thanks for understanding, Mom and Dad. I gave great thought to this decision, and I appreciate all the support you've given me. I learned in Wallingford that I never want to leave Corycian. You know what I mean, in the sense of it being my home, the one you have given me that so many of the boys up here don't have. Can you imagine how awful it must be to have a family you don't want to see? They all think I'm crazy for doing this, especially the baseball coach. Ha-ha. I guess that proves I'm a Corycian Islander.
    See you in the spring, for good.

    Nate

1925

Corycian Island School
"The Last Dance"

Spring came to the island with a rush of youthful breath in 1925. Lily of the Valley peeked up among crocus which flashed out from the last morning frosts. Blades of grass burst into soft hues framed by pussy willow and forsythia buds, all pushing out toward the warm sun. Dogwoods stood ready to pop into flower.

The baseball field behind the school was alive with the last innings of play in a PTA vs. Seniors game arranged by George Stoli. The sun was setting, casting a golden net around a green field full of families on blankets and the packed bleachers of neighbors out for some fun.

Stoli's first team of Corycian Island "Scalers" had completed its last season. With the addition of Nate Lawson, a power-hitter if there ever was one, the Scalers had taken home the trophy for their small division now comprised of five towns. It was the biggest thing that had happened at the Corycian Island School since...well, an award for sports had never been earned. So the win was historic, as was the PTA vs. Seniors game. It was the 8th inning of the game being played in early June.

Burston Bakker was the umpire, mostly because of his booming voice. Ray Moultrie coached the Scalers and Tommy Lawson coached the PTA. Each team had the assistance of Bugsy Walton, the most avid baseball fan on Corycian Island who officiated, at great length, on the questionable plays. Tiny Antolini, father of Scaler outfielder Beanie, was at bat for the PTA. Tiny he wasn't. JB was on the mound, looking at the 300 pound trash collector warming up at home plate. The score was tied. JB called a time out and walked over to his first base man, Nate Lawson.

"I want to look afraid of this guy, Nate, so I need you to look like you're consoling me. I'm betting they told him to bunt, and he's pissed because he wants to clock another ball over my head like he did last time. I'm gonna run in for the bunt and get it over to you. I have no doubt that's his plan."

But JB was wrong. Tiny Antolini's hit cracked the bat and nearly took the skin off the ball. It sailed into right field only to be missed by Jimmy Darner, the butcher's son, and the weakest link on the Scalers' team who'd been drinking beer between innings.

JB saw the PTA crowd jump to its feet, cheering for Tiny. The school kids stayed seated, gushing out "Oh, No!" in unison. Tiny's hit drove in two runs since Stoli was at third and Tommy Lawson was on second.

Every year after that the PTA vs. Seniors game transpired with the retelling of Tiny's hit, one islander to another, giving birth to an island legend.

***

The Class of 1925 held its Last Dance two weeks later. It was outdoors, with dinner catered by Marmie's and Old Post Road cut off from thru traffic. Lanterns hung down from trees and chaperones chatted on the school's front lawn while high schoolers, sitting at tables on the walkway outside Marmie's enjoyed their meals.

After dessert, Wes Smith's Band blew out Paul Whiteman's "Charleston." Forks dropped, conversations ended, and the entire high school started dancing in the street, kicking their legs with sheer abandon and scandalizing their elders.

THE CORYCIAN ISLAND READER
Vol. 17, No. 23 June 14, 1925
Class of 1925 Holds Starlit Last Dance Outdoors

The President of the Class of 1925, JB Bakker of Calliope Point, announced early on in his candidacy that his platform included the task of bringing 1925's " Last Dance" outdoors. That campaign promise came true when the Board of Education voted unanimously to support the Class President's plan. The outdoor dance became a reality last Friday night.

Sitting under lanterns, high school students enjoyed a special dinner prepared by Marmie in her transformed, sidewalk cafe, followed by dancing on Old Post Road to the music of Island musicians "Wes Smith and his Band of Renown." The "Last Dance" was held under starlit skies. The street was alive with young people and their parents, who turned a few hours into "An Evening in Paradise," this year's theme. JB Bakker commented that the dance "was an enormous success. I saw our town work together to make something great happen and that always impresses me."

The highlight of the evening was clearly the newest dance craze, *(cont'd p. 17)*

The following Sunday, families and friends gathered on the school's front lawn. Administrators and PTA leaders processed to chairs placed on the concrete expanse at the school's tall, entry doors. Principal Stoli directed the Class of 1925 to the seats of honor, benches from the cafeteria lined up to accommodate them. Younger students perched on the roofs of cars or in the limbs of trees, with a few in the bell tower of the Presbyterian Church across the way. Parents and relatives sat on wooden chairs provided by Fogarty's Funerary.

Pammy Bakker sat with the Lawsons and Babs, who was home from Wellesley. Burston stood at the rear taking photos for the *Reader*.

The class entered, led by Blossom Stoli, the Valedictorian, and Nate Lawson, the Salutatorian. A line of 11 classmates followed them - girls in white dresses and boys in their Sunday best. They marched from the side of the school next to the Presbyterian cemetery, out to the sidewalk, and up a center aisle leading to their seats in front.

The speeches repeated the word 'future' in thematic passages delivered in stilted voices. Principal Stoli awarded 13 diplomas with a handshake, followed 13 times by loud cheers. Blossom and Nate concluded the ceremonies by reading alternate lines of Constantine Cavafy's *Ithaca*. JB listened intently from his place on the dais as Class President. He clearly heard Blossom say:

"Have Ithaca always in your mind.
Your arrival there is what you are destined for."

Then JB heard Nate, a few lines later:

"Ithaca gave you a splendid journey.
Without her you wouldn't have set out."

At that moment JB knew he had made the right choice to stay right where he was after graduation.

***

Burston Bakker was alone editing copy at his desk in the *Reader's* office following the ceremony. He had a few hours before the graduation parties began. It was best for him to stay away from JB so as not to spoil the celebration.

JB had decided to commute to college on the mainland: "It was good enough for Georgie Stoli," he said whenever Burston objected. A silence had grown between them on the matter and Burston was angry with Tommy Lawson, too. Tommy was fine with Nate working at the Strand, "an education in itself," Tommy told Burston, who said: "Well, my son is going to throw his life away at some community college because he wants to stay near Blossom Stoli. It's that simple and that ridiculous."

It was as if Burston had spoken of little else for two months, so Pammy was glad when he announced he had work to catch up on before joining them for the joint party they were hosting with the Lawsons for their sons.

Burston had to restart proofing a column about the island's aquifer three times. He couldn't concentrate, so he was glad when a tall, leather-faced man knocked at the screen door.

"What can I do for you, sir?" Burston said, standing and removing his glasses.

"I just needs to get some questions answered," the large man said. He wore denim overalls and a flannel shirt despite the summer heat. His broad brimmed hat was as weathered as his face.

"I be Menlo Abenaki from the mainland," he said. "Down east a ways. I be from the Poosepatucks."

"Well, pleased to meet you, Mr. Abenaki," Bakker said, nodding. "How may I accommodate you?"

"I hear'd about a indian mound over ta here and I comes ta see it."

"Hmmm, an indian mound," Burston said. "Not sure I know much about that being true, but I can tell you where our natives live. It's straight down Old Post Road to Ke'was End. The Shellfoots ought to have the whole story. Mind if I ride with you? I'd be curious to hear what they have to say?"

"I be walkin' on over, thank you. How far?" the man asked.

"Let's take my car," Burston said. "If you'll just let me freshen up a bit, you'll find it parked right out there. The green one. I'll only be a minute."

Soon afterwards, Burston pulled in front of Henry's store. "I'll check to see if Henry Shellfoot's here. He goes off fishing sometimes. He can answer your questions," Burston said. "Just wait here a moment."

The man watched Bakker walk toward the produce store and was startled when he heard a knock outside his window. He saw the berry-brown, summer skin of Nuna Shellfoot's face:

"What's you be needin'?" she said.

"Uh...well...I..." the man fiddled with the door handle and finally opened it with a jerk. Standing up and looking down at Nuna, he said. "I be Menlo Abenaki from over at the east end. I comes to find out if a indian mound be close ta here."

"Why you be wit' dat man?" Nuna asked.

"He brung me to you," the indian said. "I comes to see the mound I hear'd talked about."

"Oh, dat," Nuna said. "Dat be back here." She motioned for the man to follow her. "You Poosepatuck?" Nuna asked.

"Yes," the man answered.

"But from the east ways, you say?" Nuna confirmed. "De last dat comes be Poosepatucks up west ways. Dey hear'd 'bout indian mounds, too. Disn't say who dey be talkin' to."

"Hmm," the indian said. "them university peoples be de ones sayin' what's what?"

"Ha!" Nuna said. "Una-versty? No, de mound lady just be dis bazodee one called Add-laid. She de one t'inks dis be a indian mound of some sorts like dey build in de long-ago days. She don't know what she don't know, dat one. De Mon-talks be comin' by here and dey knows what what."

Nuna waved to Henry who was walking toward them with Burston Bakker. A breeze from the sea blew around them and rustled the green leaves of a huge tree.

"If dat oak tree be talkin' out loud we be hearin' all de trut'," Nuna laughed.

When the other men joined them, Nuna pointed ahead, saying: "Straight dis way. See? At dem cedars. My, dey be gettin' so tall, de graves don't look so high no more."

When Menlo Abenaki saw the mound, he tried to imagine it without so much foliage in the way. He had seen a picture of indian mounds in Georgia that another Poosepatuck showed him in a Shinnecock bar. Then Abenaki went to the public library and found more pictures of mounds in the midwest.

"This fellow at Shinnecock, the one with the book havin' the mound pictures and all, he says you indians over on Ke'was got one a these, and I comes ta see it. You sayin' that hill over ta there? That one there inside them trees?" the man asked Nuna.

"Mound be de way de Add-laid lady calls it. But I tole her my faduhs say it be graves from alla de eye-land. So many dead at one time dey all be piled in one place. All kinda peoples. All-a-wanna. Dey be sick all over de place, and rest to'geder."

"Yes, all-a-wanna. So white people, too?" the Poosepatuck man asked.

"All peoples. Runapewak peoples, don't ya know, all-a-wanna," Nuna said.

Menlo Abenaki was quiet on the trip back to the ferry in Bakker's car. Burston broke the silence: "Frankly I took you over there because I thought there was a story in it for me. You know. 'Indian Mound discovered on East End Island.' I've heard about it, of course, but never paid much attention to it. I don't know if that's because I'm not much of a newspaper man or I'm not much of a spiritualist."

"Spiritualist?" Menlo asked.

"Yes," Burston said. "People come to Ke'was End to practice spiritualism. You know - trances, mind-reading, tarot cards - like that."

"Humph! " the indian said. "That hilla graves back there look like them mounds I seen in photos, kinda. But none a them said they was white people in 'em. I only seen photos but I studied 'em good. All them trees make this one look small, but if there's whites in there, I don't knows what indians does about that."

"Well, Nuna Shellfoot is an indian. That's indian land she lives on, handed down from her ancestors," Bakker said. "The Runapewaks are indigenous to Corycian Island as I understand it, but made up of Algonquin tribes originally."

"Hmmm," Abenaki said. "That band don't sound like nothin' I never hear'd before. The Mon-talks decides that, far as I know."

Inri Remie heard the whole conversation. He had just settled himself into a pile of dead, mossy tree trunks near the mound, hoping to catch the Shellfoots at something. He didn't know what exactly.

Then that woman Nuna, had appeared with three men: Henry Shellfoot, the newspaper man, and a huge man with in-dian braids.

Inri didn't understand everything they said, but he knew the indian man was there from the mainland questioning the Shellfoots about their land and saying he never heard of a tribe called what the Shellfoots call theirs.

1926

Ke'was End
Chief Wild Elk

A curious coalition of visitors boarded the Westside Ferry August 23, 1926. They were an odd enough group to attract the attention and conversation of all the deckhands, and even the ferry's captain who had his second mate take the wheel while he stepped out to see who everyone was talking about.

The crew stared at Chief Wild Elk, the Grand Sachem of the Montaukett tribe famed among Long Island indians for taking the U.S. government to court when Brooklyn authorities condemned an indian burial ground and approved a building permit for the site.

Chief Wild Elk stood with four members of the Montauketts. They all wore modified indian dress, mixed with the modern convenience of trousers and suit coats. For instance, Chief Wild Elk wore a woven stole around the shoulders of his tailored jacket. To a collared shirt he added a breastplate of ivory and jade crafted to depict a feather. The Chief's braids flowed down the stole from under a felt fedora.

Another among them had wrapped his braids in beaver skins. He, whose skin appeared far more black than copper, wore a waistcoat under his jacket, with a lanyard at the collar of his shirt. The necklace was made of fine silver beads interwoven with colorful gems. A third man wore a simple suit and a shirt without a collar. His hair hung to his shoulders and he had a large bird's feather tucked behind his right ear.

"What in the heck are they comin' over ta here, for?" the Captain of the *Menantic* asked a deckhand.

"Don't look like they's on no war path," the ferry man chuckled.

The chief and the members of his tribal council were there to investigate claims that an indian mound existed on land bequeathed in the 1882 grants to a tribe called Runapewak, a band unknown to the council. However, this was not common knowledge and all sorts of rumors sprang from the ferry staff:

"You shoulda seen all the knives they had strung around them sashes they had on."

"I hear'd one say they was from Brooklyn. Since when they got indians in Brooklyn?

"Nuna Shellfoot ain't a indian, after all, don't ya know!"

Henry Shellfoot met the indian council at the ferry slip. They packed themselves into the Model T. Henry was very solemn as they rode across Old Post Road to the east end. "First time over this way, Chief?"

The Montaukett looked straight ahead and spoke: "I suspect our people were here to originate your people being here, Mr. Shellfoot."

Henry drove along quietly for a few minutes before he said: "That should be a good thing, right?"

"Good depends on how one views the outcome," Chief Wild Elk replied.

The group arrived at Ke'was End, Nuna greeted them, and directed them toward the path to the woods. Chief Wild Elk stopped when he saw the peak of a hillock through the cedar trees. The indian asked in his white man's way: "This is it in front of us?"

"Dat depend on what's you t'ink 'it' be," Nuna replied.

"I'm told, Miss Shellfoot, that you claim it to be an indian mound, though no such findings have ever been reported east of Georgia. I'm also told Miss Shellfoot that you claim to be a Runapewak indian, a tribe of which we have no record in our office files. What records have you?"

"First off, I say no such t'ing about dem graves and next: de Runapewaks be spirit-tellers. We tells our story to keeps it. Tells it and pass it 'round."

"Is it true you are the last Grand Sachem's daughter?"

"Gran'daughta"

"And it was he who received the Land Grant in 1882?"

"Yes," Nuna said.

The Chief walked on toward the woods and around the length of the so-called mound several times, looking for something he didn't discuss with the others who stared from fixed positions nearby with Nuna and Henry.

"I'm told there are white remains in here," Chief Wild Elk said.

"Yes," Nuna replied, adding what she knew from Eula Morely's history. "De smallpox comes and takes dem all-a-wanna. So dey here."

"Runapewak is a sacred Algonquin word, as you must know Miss Shellfoot. We are unaware of any tribe being 'runapewak,' the true people. Runapewak is an idea of the Gods, not the name of a tribe."

"Humph," Nuna replied. "What kinda spirit be tellin' you dat?"

Chief Wild Elk noted Nuna's insolence and spoke down to her: "I am also curious about this spiritual colony you run here with the Morelys. Is that a tradition of your indian heritage?" Wild Elk asked.

Nuna contained her fury. She spoke directly:

"How much dem resort peoples payin' you, Mr. Chief? How much dey payin' ta buy dis land away wit' a lie?"

Chief Wild Elk looked back and said calmly:

"If this is an indian burial ground of any type, Miss Shellfoot, I assure you I will do all I can to protect the land."

He started toward the Model T, calling over his shoulder to Nuna: "You'll hear from the council when the investigation is finished."

Another indian opened the car door. When they were all settled, Henry gave a nod to Nuna and drove off.

Indian Summer
"Amen to that..."

The autumnal equinox arrived on Corycian Island in splendor each year. A warm sun brought lush indian summer days to

September, coaxing George Stoli to offer a surprise afternoon off for school children "to enjoy the sun" on September 23, 1926, an act which drew islanders out to the water's edge. It was a magnificent day, one of the last to be enjoyed before fall's chill lulled them into sweaters.

George Stoli watched from his window as the school emptied of running, skipping kids full of the gift of freedom. He shook his head and sat back at his desk. He had a few things to finish up before he joined his family at West Neck beach.

Frances, Blossom, and Aster Stoli packed a picnic to enjoy with their father later. The trio set off with skips in their steps and walked farther down the sandy strip of West Neck than they'd ever ventured before. They could see the Westside Ferry crossing the bay in front of them, just past the long dock from the terminal .

A natural, granite seawall rose in magnificence behind them, dwarfing the merry threesome in its glory. The Strand Hotel sat atop it all, lording over the heights in the distance. The Stolis strolled along, oblivious to the time and loving the day; lifting their skirts to wade in the warm water and lazing back to take naps on dry sand in the comfort of the sun.

Frances watched her girls frolic and thought: "George will come soon to make this a perfect day."

***

Josiah Remie was in Hector Wesley's fishing boat off the coast of Sirens' Beach. Josiah was in the midst of a happy drunk, not something which occurred too often. The bright mood had prompted him to say:

"Well, take a lookie at this beautitful day, Hector. I say we make a plan to take out that heathen statue behind where them nuns live. I figure we took care a the whores at Ke'Was, by turnin' 'em over to them resort people. Truth won out there, don't ya know, with some cash for us to boot."

"Amen to that, Josiah!"

"So, I says, Hector, let's do a job on them witches' asso-she
-ettes at Sirens' Beach." Josiah laughed. It was not a joyful sound.

Later, with fishing lines dropped, the cohorts rocked on the
water off the cove. Their feet rested on the boat's rim and they
stared at the alabaster Lady of the Seas rising above them. Josiah
took a swallow of his whiskey.

"I feels pleased, Hector. We done right by them real estate people with Ke'was End and now we gonna chip away
at this place. Get these nuns to move somewheres else. Them
developers'll love to get ahold a Sirens' Beach." Josiah dwelt in
the rush of power he'd just given himself. Hector said nothing,
fearing he'd say the wrong thing and Josiah would change his
mind about going after the nuns.

"How strong's the engine you got on this boat?" Josiah asked.

"Well, it's strong enough to haul nets fulla fish," Hector said
defensively.

"Think we could rig it to pull that statue down from her
heathen heights?"

Hector laughed and slapped his thighs. He took out his hip
flask and clicked with Josiah's before they each took a long drink.

"You bet we can," Hector replied, wiping his mouth on his
sleeve.

They spent the next few hours bobbing in the sun, drinking
and planning.

***

The Shellfoots, Morelys, and Ezra Goldsmith took the sublime day to plan a systematic harvest of the vines, stalks, and
gourds that would be the construction materials of this year's
Sukkoth.

Ismy, who was 11 now, knew nothing about the destruction
of the Sukkoth when she was just a baby. She'd never understood
the passion with which they all approached the task each fall, but
she loved the tradition.

"I'd like to braid the stalks for the trim," Ismy declared as
they stripped leaves from dry corn.

"You got it, kiddo," Bay said, infused with the gorgeous day, gifted from out of the blue.

"What part do you like the best, Mama?" Ismy asked.

"Hmmmm, I guess making the bamboo frame," Bay said. "I like to see the form of things."

"And I like to see what things become," Ismy said. She stopped and looked out at the water just beyond them past the fist of granite that punched out into the sea. "Do you feel the electricity in the air today, Mama? It's like a charge or something, I don't know, can you feel it?"

"I think it's just the rush that comes with an unexpected, sunny day," Bay said.

"Yes, it is unexpected," Ismy replied, with a frown creasing her forehead.

***

Tommy Lawson and Burston Bakker sat on the grassy rise between their properties and enjoyed afternoon cocktails with Sissy and Pammy. Their older children had left for college. JB and Nate were horsing around on the beach below them.

Sissy pointed out toward the ocean and said: "How strange the sky looks over there."

They all stood and agreed that a threatening cloud was fast approaching.

Burston said: "That's a menacing look the water has taken on."

Tommy stepped over to the edge of the grass. He funneled his hands at his mouth and called out to the beach below: "Come on up, boys. Weather's coming in." Tommy waited for a response and didn't get one. "Nate. JB. Listen to me now and get up here."

Nate turned to where his father was and called for JB to follow him. They climbed up the embankment and ran into their homes as the rain started to fall. Both families watched from their picture windows as the bay grew more angry. The blue water had turned a steely gray.

***

At 2:30 p.m. when the wind picked up out of nowhere, the Stolis' picnic things blew all about. Blossom and Aster chased around after napkins, hats, and even Aster's shoes. They laughed and made a game of it.

Frances watched them with her hand to her forehead blocking the wind, as well as the sand that had begun stinging her cheeks. Frances' smile faded and a hint of worry coursed through her. The water looked very dark and rough. "Where is George?" Frances wondered, realizing the path at the landing was a good distance away.

***

Needles of rain sliced at the windows of Marmie's. A group of baymen sat on the stools, wet slickers squeaking on the plastic seats. They debated whether a sudden drop in barometric pressure warranted pulling their boats into dry-dock. Then Marmie reached over and turned up the marine report on the radio. The announcer said: "A tropical storm should blow over Long Island and Connecticut late this afternoon attended by shifting gales."

"Don't sound like much," said one Scaler and the others agreed.

But 10 minutes later, the west side of Corycian Island was lashed by winds registering 74 mph and those same fishermen were scrambling to save their families and their homes. Before the clock on Town Hall struck 3 p.m., a 35-foot storm surge off the west hit the shore with a 15-foot tidal wave pushed by gusts of wind gauged at 140 mph.

***

Frances Stoli and her girls were fighting fierce winds to get to the landing when they saw the wave coming. It sucked all the water from the shore. Sand appeared as the water dragged them into an enormous curl that smashed the Stolis against the seawall, rolled out again, and delivered them back in the second round, limp and dead, onto the rocky cliffs.

***

The two men out in a fishing boat off Sirens' Beach didn't heed the warnings of the wind and dark water. They were too drunk after celebrating their success hooking Hector's cables around Our Lady of the Sea's base, an easy task since the grass was so high and no one was out and about.

Then a blast of wind grabbed Hector's boat and pushed it back into a massive wave they saw rolling in at them. The boat swirled up into the white water and, when it came down, it pulled the statue with great force into the sea. Hector and Josiah rose from the water, gasping for air; they swam over to the overturned boat and clung to it. The water appeared calm for a moment and the wind stopped. They looked over and saw the statue was gone, but neither had a moment to rejoice, for another wave, twice the size of the one that hit them before, was about to take them with it.

***

"Feel that?" Ismy said to the group at Ke'was End who just sat down to rest after stripping vines and stalks for the Sukkoth.

"De wind?" Nuna asked. "De wind gotta a funny feel today."

Everyone noticed the sky getting darker in the west.

"We better get busy weighing down these piles before they get blown away and we have to start all over again," Ezra said. When the rain threatened to soak them, they ran into Ezra's kitchen.

"De sound looks mad for sure," Nuna said, staring out at the rising waves that crashed against the rock jetty. "Dat water get to spinnin' somet'ing awful in a storm."

"Hope the baymen gots in," Henry said.

They took turns looking out the window, watching corn stalks and grape vines sail by and head out toward the jetty with a ferocious wind.

Ezra was fiddling with his radio, trying to get news about the storm.

***

Little did any of them know a hurricane had pumped itself up out in the Atlantic Ocean where it met with an atmospheric, high-pressure system that drove it into the Long Island Sound with seismographic fury.

After two hours of crushing winds, crashing trees, and rain that balled into hail, the sun came out. People emerged from their homes slowly, fearing another storm might strike any minute.

Areas from Pipers' Cove to Calliope Point suffered rushing floods from the impact of the first wave that struck the island coast line. The Heights' was ripped apart with the winds, the Strand's windows rained broken glass, and first floors of town buildings in the center were flooded.

Ratliss moved police headquarters to his second story apartment and called Rosie Griffin at the switchboard, located on the second story of the Post Office:

"Shelter Island Emergency Operator, how may I assist you?"

"Ratliss here. How are things over there, Rosie? Everyone okay?"

"Thanks for asking, Chief. I've been up here monitoring the switchboard as an emergency system. It's pretty busy, but the lines are down on the west side, and I can't reach the mainland. That may just be clogged wires."

"Hold the fort, Rosie. We'll get through this. Connect me to 3365, will you? Màthair?

"Will do, Chief. I'm here if you need me," Rosie pulled the plugs and made the connection.

"Mother Augustus speaking. How may I help you?."

"I'm so glad your telephone is working," Ratliss said. "How are you down there?"

"We've fared quite well, thank the Lord. Though it appears the storm took down Our Lady of the Sea, a sacrifice we'll make for no loss of human life."

"I'm sorry about that, but glad to hear all's good because I'm calling to say the rest of the island hasn't fared very well." Ratliss went on to tell her of the destruction, but Mother Augustus cut him off.

"Chief Ratliss, how can we be of service?"

"We need a place to bring those who require emergency care."

"That's fine. We are well-equipped. Màthair is dry and our sisters are able nurses. We'll prepare immediately."

"And...Mother...We need a place to bring the dead."

Mother Augustus remained silent for a moment, then spoke: "Yes, I see.... Of course. Well, we have a large room off the parlor that can be suitably arranged. I will see to it. Go on and take care of your duties, Chief Ratliss. You can be assured of our commitment. How soon will people be arriving here?"

"I feel I should caution you. Several of the dead are children. They were released from school early, you see, and were playing on beaches around the island."

Again silence. Ratliss gave it due respect and went on: "Dr. Simmons will arrive soon after I call him. I will send Officer Schaeffer over with Red Cross supplies. Volunteers with larger cars will escort the first arrivals, who are families flooded out around Pipers' Cove, I think. There are people calling to donate food and clothes. I will appoint a collection spot. They'll sort it and bring to you whatever will furnish your requests. The rest will be distributed to needy folks around the island. And...uh... the deceased will arrive in the ambulance or fire truck - as they appear."

"God bless us all," Mother Augustus said.

The Sisters of St. Anthony tied their voluminous veils with string behind their shoulders and donned black, cleaning pinafores to protect their linen surplice. They hiked up their bell sleeves with rubber bands, hitched rosaries and skirts up under black cinch belts, and went to work pulling couches and chairs out of the room off the parlor and pulling in tables. They assessed their supplies, making huge pots of stew and soup in the kitchen, and praying, praying, praying for the souls of the children and others whose broken bodies would be under their care.

The first group of survivors arrived before Dr. Simmons. Tommy Lawson drove them in the able Ford truck from the Strand. They were soaking wet families huddled under thick blankets who disembarked at Màthair's portage silently, shivering with cold and fear. One refrain repeated itself: "What happened at West Neck beach?"

Tommy Lawson, who lived above the low lying beach knew the answers. When he stepped from his house after the storm passed, he saw that the buildings of the Believers' Camp had been wiped away, along with the trees, the cars, even Inri Remie's house, the front door of which sat high atop the Sermon on the Mount rocks.

In answer to the question "What happened?" Tommy answered truthfully: "God only knows."

Mother Augustus assessed each family's needs and assigned them to her corps of ready sisters which was being directed by Father Albert, a recuperating priest who was pointing to the approaching ambulance. The nuns hurried the families to their second story rooms.

Dusk fell over the calm bay and a weird sun dropped through the closed stillness of devastation. The sky was fused with brilliant colors, irony in the aftermath.

A volunteer fireman drove the ambulance and Dr. Simmons emerged from the passenger door. He walked over to Mother Augustus and Father Albert to speak quietly, gesticulating to the back of the vehicle.

The driver was around back, opening the doors and helping JB Bakker and his burden down. The young man held the limp body of nine-year-old Aster Stoli, whose face was as grey as the sand that clumped in her hair.

Aster was wrapped in a a fresh blanket and JB cradled her to his chest. Mother Augustus reached for the body, gently, but JB shook his head and went forward.

As he walked to the entry some of the nuns stroked Aster, others touched JB's shoulder or back. He just kept moving forward beyond the large, oak doors. A sister greeted him with a quiet nod. She tried to free Aster from JB's arms, but demurred upon encountering the strength of his hold. JB brought Aster to the chapel, a place he had been with his mother. He found light from the moon entering a tall stained glass window. JB slid down into the pew. The light bathed the child in his arms. He had come there to pray, to ask for a miracle - a miracle for Mrs. Stoli and Blossom.

"Here, God," he said. "Here, see, you took Aster. Now, please, God, please, give us her mother and Blossom. Please. I'm praying, God. That's what I'm supposed to do, right?"

Sister Mary Luke was sent by one of her superiors to keep an eye on JB so the others could assist with the bodies still to be removed from arriving vehicles. Sister Luke watched JB weep over the dead child in his arms and she heard his prayer for the others.

The sister yearned to comfort the young man. The desire was so great, the nun felt her knees shake, and when JB looked slowly up at her, she turned into the crevice of the door frame, sure he had seen her sin.

"Sister?" she heard JB whisper. "Sister? Could you get someone to help with Aster?" He spoke haltingly, rousing Sister Luke. "Sister? Help me, please."

The young woman came toward JB and bent slowly to help, daring not to look into his eyes. She steadied JB as he lifted the child and directed him to the designated room where he lay Aster on a table.

Sister Luke covered Aster's torso with an altar cloth. Then the nun took her handkerchief and with water from a holy font, gently washed Aster's face while JB looked on. Sister Luke could feel his breath and smell his fear.

Two nuns came into the room to take Aster where others were caring for the arriving bodies. Unbeknownst to JB, Blossom and Frances Stoli were among those brought there in the last few minutes.

Sister Luke motioned for JB to follow her back to the chapel where she indicated he kneel and pray. JB fell to his knees in the pew. His shoulders shook with bursting sobs. He couldn't get Blossom's voice from her telephone call out of his head:

"Meet us at West Neck beach when you can, ok? Father let everyone have a 'fun in the sun day' this afternoon!"

"You know what? " JB had said. "I'm going to stay around here with my cousin, if that's ok. We don't get a chance like this too often."

JB tried to wonder if Blossom was alive, but he knew she was dead. He saw the wave that hit West Neck beach from the widow's walk of his father's home. JB and Burston had leaned against the frame of the house and stared at the furious bay when the storm first stirred. Sailboats bobbed and dashed in a swelling sea. Then the waves came in faster and a dock splintered apart, its large timbers surfing curls that propelled them to the shore.

"Holy Toledo," Burston said, looking through his binoculars while JB positioned his camera: "Look at the *Menantic!*" he shouted.

The flat-bottomed ferry rose straight up with a wave that snapped its tethers. Through the binoculars Burston saw crew members holding onto the rails at the height of a wave which, with a great suck of water, rolled itself into an even bigger wave, throwing people into the sea. The ferry rushed at great speed over jagged rocks and through tangled boats toward the pilings by the landing. "Blossom's on West Neck beach," JB shouted. He broke from the hold of the horror and ran down the stairs.

"Where are you going?" Pammy called out frantically when JB and Burston passed her. Burston answered for his son: "Blossom Stoli's on West Neck beach!" Burston saw the alarm in Pammy. "Don't worry, Pammy. I won't let him do anything crazy."

Burston caught up with JB when a falling limb from one of the huge chestnut trees on their yard crashed to the ground. JB fell as well, startled by the earth shaking beneath him. Burston caught up to JB, knelt down and pulled his son into his arms. They leaned against a tree trunk while rain dashed at their faces and debris from the storm flew around them. JB was sobbing.

"Shhhh, son. Shhh," Burston said. "We don't know for sure, that Blossom was on the beach."

When the storm subsided, JB and Burston walked down Shore Road toward West Neck beach together. They found a crowd of rescuers scouring the area for the living or the dead. They helped carry four lifeless bodies to people at vehicles. The bodies were wrapped in tarps and blankets, then transported to designated areas to await identification by family members.

In order to reach the proffered barn or garage for such storage, teams of men and women shoveled sand from the necessary roads. JB found Aster face down off Sunset Road on a path to the cliffs. He walked reverently up to her, knowing her from the calico sundress and her long, yellow braids. JB brushed at the sand on the tiny frame. Dr. Simmons called to him to bring her to an ambulance and before JB knew it, he was riding with Aster and unable to look for Blossom.

Burston walked the beachfront near the ferry slip. He could see the ripped hull of the *Menantic* in the distance. On the cliffs, he saw George Stoli pulling at pieces of debris with other men, trying desperately to reach the landing at West Neck.

Burston headed forward to join the effort. Then he heard anguished cries coming from the rocks above him. It was George Stoli standing by two bodies. The man's back was arched and he was screaming at the sky.

Stoli's howls bounced and echoed from harbor to harbor and cove to cove where lifeless children and their mothers washed up amid broken boats on shores all around Corycian Island.

***

Having weathered the hurricane safely at Ke'was End in Ezra's house, the assembled group headed out to see what devastation the roaring storm had wrought.

They noticed the abundance of sunlight pouring into the backyard. Nuna looked for the highest fir which bore her osprey's nest. It was gone. In fact an entire line of huge trees missing from the familiar vista.

"Look how many trees are down!" Ezra exclaimed. They all walked as far as they could get to see the worst of it. Henry stopped them when he caught sight of the granite jetty. A broken boat and a body were clearly impaled on the sharp teeth of its rocks.

"Best thing for us be goin' up to the Captain's," Henry said, turning them all around, "Things down here looks bad and them electric lights disn't be comin' back any too soon."

"There's plenty of wood in the mudroom," Eula said. "I just had a delivery. The food should be in good supply."

"Ezra and me'll get over to the store, too, for candles and the like" Henry added. "When we get ourselfs safe, I'll make a report to Ratliss about the situation on the jetty."

When the storm subsided Hansen Ratliss rode around the flooded streets of the island in a small motor boat with two town councilmen. They assessed the damage to the town's infrastructure. First Bridge had been washed out, taking down the ivy-covered arch spanning it. The loss of the bridge made access between the Heights and the center of town impossible. So aid workers had to cross the rushing water of Deer Creek on foot. The mouth of the creek was jammed with the hulls of once sleek boats, all pointed upwards with the force of the water's rush when they hit the narrows. Now the wreckage waved back and forth with the undulations of a gentle bay. Volunteers roped off the broken road and lit torches to illuminate a sign:

"Bridge Gone"

The floodwater receded about four hours after the storm passed. Karen Moultrie found her way up to Ratliss' apartment and handled the telephone calls that Rosie Griffin allowed to be put through. When Ratliss called in from the firehouse, Moultrie told him her home telephone on the east end was out:

"And Rosie couldn't connect me to the Captain's house or Henry's store," Moultrie said. "Do you think you could send someone down there to see if they're okay, Chief?"

"Definitely. I'll go myself as soon as I can. How did you manage to get up to the center, Karen?"

"Well, I was up here at Corny Tennet's house when it hit. Old Post Road at Midway isn't too bad and that's the way we came, so I don't know about downeast ways."

"You're a wonder, Karen Moultrie," Ratliss said. "Thank you. I'll get down to Ke'was."

Knowing the other three areas of the island were well-tended, Ratliss took it upon himself to drive east when the roads cleared. He drove the new car the town had bought the department. Old Post Road was free of debris on the lower end because of the large lima bean fields on the way to the Captain's house. Shell Road, between the Morelys and the Shellfoots was a different story. The puddles and pot holes were visible from the paved street. Ratliss parked the car on the town road and walked. He noticed that he couldn't see any tree tops behind the Captain's house. It was if the skyline of an old painting had been erased, giving a stark, unfamiliar feeling to the place.

Ratliss saw Henry Shellfoot open the Captain's front door and step out with Ezra Goldsmith coming out behind him. They were clearly anxious.

"We're glad to see you, Chief," Henry called walking toward him. The car won't never make it through the flood on Shell Road so I was just about to start walking to the center."

"Is someone hurt?" Ratliss asked.

"Not us, " Henry said. "The guests were gone and so it was just the Morelys, Mr. Ezra and us Shellfoots. No we're fine, but there's a body down on the rocks."

"A body, you say?" Ratliss nodded and directed the men to lead the way. "Let's go."

Henry led them out through the meadow. The old oak in its midst had withstood the storm's wrath, but the familiar path they took to the beach was blocked by fallen trees. Henry turned to the right and found a clear path where the forest stopped, closer to the granite jetty on the beach below. When the tail of boulders came within clear view, the three men stood near a sand dune. Ratliss said:

"So. What do you think?"

Ezra pointed to the beach: "From here, it looks like three victims and a boat."

The men made their way closer. One body was splayed on the bones of the granite tail, along with the cabin of a fishing boat.

Two others appeared to be closely bound and covered in sand where the jetty met the shore.

Wading through the debris of dead fish, wood, and oil slicks on the narrow beach by the jetty, Ratliss saw a bloated body half covered with sand. The head was oddly contorted around an arm. The Chief knelt down and dug where the hand reached from the sand. He uncovered the statue from Màthair, Our Lady of the Seas. As Ratliss dug further, he found a silver chain that wound around the statue's hand, torquing the neck of a man's bulging face. A silver medallion on the chain glistened in the sun.

"Recognize anyone?" Ratliss asked the other men because he didn't really know what else to say.

"No, but I wouldn't expect to," Ezra said. "Henry?"

"Hard to tell. This one got on fishin' boots. That one on the rocks, don't look to. Should we get him from the rocks before the tide comes in?"

"We're going to have to. I think we have time. I told Karen Moultrie to send a back-up if I didn't call her in an hour. Meanwhile, we need to get this fellow disengaged from the statue. Henry, let's see that knife you got. I'm gonna cut the chain. We need a few younger and more agile than us to handle the body on the rocks."

Karen Moultrie's grown sons came over to the beach within an hour and fifteen minutes of Ratliss' conversation with their mother. They crab-crawled out on the granite tailbone like they had done many times, and swam the body back into shore.

"Any idea who it is?" Ratliss asked as they carried the pulpy body up to dry land.

"No, sir," the young men said, laying the body gently onto the soft grass.

"Lord have mercy," Ezra said, looking away.

Neither Ratliss nor Henry said anything. They took in the red hair that bushed out from the bruised face and focused on the slight frame.

"Josiah Remie?" Ratliss and Henry said together, one more incredulous than the other.

THE CORYCIAN ISLAND READER
Vol. 18, No. 38 September 23, 1926
Deadly Hurricane Strikes Without Warning; Kills 14 Islanders

A hurricane wrought widespread destruction, including the loss of fourteen Island lives, when it struck Corycian Island's West banks unexpectedly Sept. 23rd.

According to the National Coast Guard representative, Admiral William A. Hamby: "Warnings did not come into the weather service until minutes before the hurricane swept into the Long Island Sound from the Atlantic."

Local reports reveal a huge wave broke out from Corycian Island's northwest point that rolled back to form an even larger one which hit the shoreline with incredible force minutes later. This sent rippling effects around the Island's coast, causing death and mayhem.

In an unfortunate coincidence an hour before the unpredicted storm, Principal of the Corycian Island School , George Stoli released students to enjoy " a fun in the sun day." Many heeded his instructions by going to the beach. Of the fourteen killed, seven were children. These included Principal Stoli's daughters - Aster, 9, Blossom, 18 - and his wife, Frances, who drowned in the storm waters. They were not alone. Others who were spending precious time with their children perished as well. (A complete list of the deceased is included in the accompanying story below).

Houses in Pipers' Cove floated from their foundations. Structures at the Believers' Camp are in scrap heaps. The massive alabaster statue of Our Lady of the Seas was ripped from her perch and dashed through the raging waters to become an instrument of death to a local fisherman, Hector Wesley, whose fishing boat was found dashed on the rocks at Ke'was End near another Islander who lost his life, Josiah Remie. (cont'd on page 2)

The day after the bodies were removed from the beach, Nuna went out to clear the path past the cemetery. Since the storm, Nuna had watched the mother osprey circling the periphery of the beach forest endlessly. Nuna saw it was the same osprey who honored them at Judah's burial since fish hawks mate for life and return instinctively to the same nest each summer. The mother osprey was searching for the fallen tree that held her home.

Nuna wore old dungarees of Ahane's and had one of his work shirts tied at her waist. Her tiny feet (shoes still on) were inside Ahane's rubber boots. She had bright yellow fabric tied around her hair to keep it clean. Her face shone like burnt sugar in the sun. It was full of Nuna's forty years of life and made serene and beautiful from them.

She stood in the clearing staring at the horizon that once held the osprey's fir tree. She saw that the line of fallen trees pointed north and tried to calculate, by envisioning its fall, where the osprey's tree might be. She thought she saw her osprey staring at her from a standing pine way off in the distance.

Nuna was well aware that osprey protect their habitats with the same sharp beaks and claws they use to dive-bomb fish. The week before the hurricane, a visiting teenage boy taunted an osprey family on the south causeway with thrown rocks. The boy lost a good part of his scalp to the male bird's fury.

So Nuna had no intention of touching the eggs if they were in tact. She just wanted to find them because she feared, under all that rubble, the mother osprey might be unable to sense her chicks. Nuna wanted to point them out to her.

She scanned the line of trees that still stretched above the cove below. She stopped at the rise of graves, now topped by a fallen tree. She spotted what she believed to be a nest where the tip of the pine tree had stretched once it crossed the land to which it fell. Remarkably, three large eggs, cushioned by the huge nest, seemed to be in tact.

Nuna looked above her for the mother osprey. The tree had found a clear path to its landing and huge firs still stood all around the site, including the cedars that grew up the sides of the large gravesite.

Nuna made her way back out to the clearing and searched the sky for the fish hawk. She walked over to Henry's and borrowed his binoculars and looked some more. After two hours, Nuna unwrapped the bright, yellow fabric she wore around her head and lashed it to a branch of the pine tree that held the nest. She was sure the mother osprey had seen her earlier and would recognize the sign Nuna left near the incubating chicks.

***

The townspeople had many funerals to get through, most of them involving multiple members of the same family. Tolling bells rang like they had during the Great War, as mourners lined the streets once again to pay respects to the dead.

George Stoli walked bravely behind his family's cortege to the cemetery next to the Presbyterian Church. In his mask of mourning, Stoli looked so different to those who walked behind him, clustered shoulder to shoulder.

George took steps empty of the promise his walks once held. His students wept and their parents' eyes rose to the abandoned paper sack, which sat within plain sight in the window of his office across the street.

JB didn't walk in the procession. The emotions of the memorial were compounded by the reality of all the death he had lived with for a week. He waited at the open graves. His knees trembled. Pammy stood at JB's side. Babs and Burston stood behind them, with the Lawsons on either side, and neighbors spread out around the perimeter of the cemetery. All heads were bowed in grief with handkerchiefs full of tears and muscles taut in every heart. It was another beautiful fall day. A soft breeze blew through the trees which stood with leaf-stripped branches in ironic contrast to the blue sky above them.

George Stoli acknowledged his neighbors with a bow of his head after the three caskets were lowered into their graves. He walked silently up to JB who struggled with tears. Stoli shook JB's hand. He looked the stricken boy in the eye and grasped the back of his neck, pulling their foreheads together. Then he patted JB's back, two hearty pats, and walked on toward his home, just down a lane within clear sight of the cemetery.

JB stood over the graves for much longer than anyone else. His family abided when he asked to be left alone for awhile. He didn't know how to leave. Everyone who touched him, hugged him, and prayed for him said Blossom was in a better place. But JB knew there was only one place Blossom wanted to be and he had promised to always be there beside her, so now, he didn't know how to leave.

Inri Remie came to the Stolis' service and stood alone by the keeping shed for the gravedigger's tools. Inri wasn't hiding, but few saw him. He stayed there, leaning against the vine-covered shed near a pile of fresh dirt kept to fill in sinking graves.

The two people who did notice Inri were the gravediggers who had once been whiskey clients of Josiah Remie's. They dug all the graves on the island for pets and people, on private land, consecrated ground, or communal space. Now they stood away from the Stolis' graves, respectfully leaning on shovels and waiting for the last mourner to depart.

Pinky Lester was one of the gravediggers, so named because he was once lily white. However, Pinky turned a perpetual shade of pink when he spent more time than ever outside digging what with the war, old folks dying, the flu, and this catastrophe. Pinky was bald, short, and v-shaped. Digging graves builds shoulder muscles and he had plenty. Muscles bulged beneath his overalls. Pinky had white eyebrows, white eyelashes and downy white hair.

Pinky dug graves with "Tick" Terzian, a nick-name bestowed on a young boy who grew up deep in the woods with his family in a basement. His father owned the land and dug the cellar with the intention of building a house above it. When the first floor was laid, the family moved into the cement foundation of the basement.

Tick's father lost interest after that. He said he liked the closeness of living underground and never bothered with walls or a roof above it to build the house. He cut a few windows into the ceiling/floor so light came into the basement, and he liked to point out, they were dry as bones down there. Tick rarely went to school and hardly came into town as a child, but when he did he was said to be crawling with ticks.

As a grown man, Tick still lived in the basement; however he'd contracted a condition known as alapacea and didn't have a strand of hair, and therefore not one visible tick, on his body. That didn't rid Tick of his nickname which never bothered him. He had weathered several fevers through the years and was a few tick bites short of a fully functioning brain.

"Didja see that Inri Remie over by the tool shed, Tick?" Pinky asked after JB Bakker had stumbled away. They were shoveling dirt into the three-grave pit.

"Holy tornadoes, I seen him all right. Disn't comes to get his daddy but creeps around lookin' at the Stoolies," Tick said. "Didja get the message about havin' to dig a double in the paupers' grounds?

"Who?" Pinky said. "What call?"

"I pickt mine up at the post office, like I do. Gracie holds 'em for me. You got a telephone, right?"

"Yeah, but I get real tired of gettin' up when it keeps ringin' and I'm tryin' to drink a damn beer," Pinky said.

"Well, it's Remie and Wesley being put down as paupers and now we can't get whiskey from them no more. Who d'ya know, Pinky? I'm about out since that hurricane day when I dranked so much. But I damn wisht I knew old Josiah was gettin' his-self kilt. I'd a stocked up, don't ya know. We growed up in the woods, Josiah and me. Never did like him much, but I bought his whiskey and now what're we gonna do, Pinky?"

"Hector Wesley didn't get claimed?" Pinky asked.

"Nope. That house a his went down in the hurricane, too. Wesley's mama were in it and they can't find her nowheres.

Gracie Williams tole me Ratliss tried to get that Lindy woman to bury him but she said Wesley wouldn't marry her so she wouldn't bury him. Yup, it's in backa the dump with the paupers for the two of 'em."

***

After the hurricane, Mother Augustus hired locals to haul the statue of Our Lady of the Seas up off the beach at Ke'was End and back to Màthair where the pedestal to support the statue had been moved inland. The winch the haulers used had broken as they pulled the heavy relic up from the beach, so they had to leave to get another one. Hence the statue was standing in a grotto of small trees when Eula Morely came upon it.

Eula thought her eyes deceived her. She hadn't inquired about the bodies on the beach and knew nothing of the statue. Eula stared and refocused.

The lady's alabaster beauty blended so naturally with the white sand and the soft foliage of the shoreline.

Eula walked calmly up to her, free of the fence at Màthair and on the Morely's property. Eula felt no hindrance nor weakness, only awe. It was daytime and the lady had come to her. Eula touched the statue's white, veined hands, one with broken fingers. She stroked its face, touching the broken nose and feeling for wounds like a healer.

A breeze blew through the sea grasses and the stone body felt warm in the sun. Eula found herself reaching around the tall statue. She pressed her cheek into the warmth of the stone and held the broken madonna in her arms, realizing only then that each had lost a son.

***

Once Nuna saw that the osprey had removed her eggs from their resting place, she and Henry began to clear the trees from the path to the ancestral gravesite.

"How'd that get here?" Henry asked when he saw the yellow fabric tied to a tree branch. "This yours, Nuna?" he handed it to her and continued to assess the amount of work ahead of them. "Cuttin' up this big tree's gonna take some time," Henry went on. "I'll gets the Moultrie boys and Mr. Ezra to help. You and me can saws off summa the branches to start." He handed Nuna a bow saw. "We can get at them thinner ones."

Wearing Ahane's work clothes again, Nuna sawed at the branches of the toppled fir until the sap seemed to glue the bow saw to her hand. She was fiddling with it, trying to scrape away some of the syrup from the grip with a piece of bark, when she saw the color blue. Nuna put down the saw, pulled some broken branches off the grave beneath the tree, and called for Henry:

"Comes sees what dis be," Nuna said, disturbing nothing. "You sees dat?" She pointed. "Dat blue t'ing pokin' out down by de tree trunk?"

Henry put his hands up on his forehead to keep the sun from his eyes and focused where Nuna indicated. He saw what looked like a piece of pottery. He tried to brush away some dirt with a fir bough, saying: "There's something on it, Nuna. I can't make it out. Looks like drawings." He stretched his arm through the tree branches. "I can't reach it from here. We sees it good when we gets the tree up."

***

The month of October was spent cleaning up the ravages of the hurricane. Crews of island men cut fallen trees for firewood or planked them for lumber. They helped repair each other's rooftops, barns, docks, and boats. Electric power was out for the coldest months, so they took care of neighbors who needed food, shelter, candlelight, or firewood.

November brought the same work load, and the entire focus of Thanksgiving was gratitude for their community, an act of faith that filled every islander with a sense of belonging.

By December, the snow drifts were five feet high. Horses pulled sleighs, loaded with provisions from one door to the next;

as it neared Christmas the sleigh drivers carried saws to provide help cutting holiday trees and on the 24th of December, several sleigh drivers donned Santa hats and brought donated gifts and food to the needy

The Town Board agreed to continue to use the school as a shelter for those who'd lost their homes. Principal Stoli wasn't in any condition to resume his leadership and other families were in deep mourning as well. School could wait, a lesson in life was taking place.

Islanders also came to the aid of people like Inri Remie and the Wesleys who had lost their fathers and their homes. Relatives of Lindy Meade let her live in a small cottage with Ray-Ray and Twirly Wesley. Since they were all rather large themselves, it was not the most comfortable of situations.

The owners of the Westside Ferry Company offered Inri the use of an unused apartment above their offices just far enough in from the ferry slip to have avoided the catastrophe. The housing came in return for a job to help clean up the storm debris around the area while Inri lived there. It was not Inri's first choice as a solution, but it was his only one, and the ferry company gave him a uniform, a jumpsuit with *Westside Ferry* written on the back. He liked that part.

He still went out at night, now gazing in the windows of homes in Calliope Point, and occasionally, walking down to the Stolis', just north of the center. There weren't any candles lit in the Stoli house, but George was in there. Inri could see him sitting in the living room in the dark. Just sitting there. The school was still closed. Stoli couldn't work. He hadn't spoken much since the howls he screamed the day of the hurricane and he hadn't left his house since the day he buried his family.

In a closed Town Board meeting, the Supervisor said: "If Stoli isn't fit to come back yet, we'll find someone to fill in until he's ready."

As it turned out Allan Trimmer, who was mathematics teacher at the school, acted as principal until Trimmer's official appointment a year later when it became obvious that George Stoli may never work again.

1927

Calliope Point
"We'll have our Island back."

At a family dinner on New Year's Day, Nate and JB told their parents: "We've been accepted to Columbia. We'll start as freshman January15th. We've got it all figured out about living. If it's okay with all of you, this is what we'd like to do."

Pammy's eyes filled with tears and she looked to Sissy for a response because the lump in her own throat prevented her from saying what she felt. Since Blossom's death, Pammy had prayed for JB's release from grief. She watched him mope around the house, sit on the beach with a book, refuse his father's requests to shoot scenics for the *Reader*. She understood that when he went out, people mentioned Blossom. Even on a sail in the *Barnacall* when they pulled into the Westside Marina, a baseball team mate jumped aboard to tell JB how much he had always loved Blossom.

Going off to college with Nate would bring JB peace and she hoped the same for herself. Sissy said it all for her: "You have our blessings, boys. We knew you'd find a way to go forward."

And sooner than anyone realized it would, April arrived. Tommy and Sissy Lawson had worked all winter with a ready and willing staff, trying to get the hundreds of broken windows at the Strand repaired in time for a summer opening, but it didn't look good. Glass was in short supply, as were building materials because the hurricane had hit so many coastal areas before it quit somewhere above Cape Cod.

One of the quicker repairs had come from the telephone company, which had managed to restore greatly needed communication lines for island access not long after the monster storm swept through. But when April arrived, Tommy knew they couldn't open the Strand that season. He told Burston first and said he was going to make the announcement at the next Town Board meeting. Tommy broke the news in the "New Business" portion of the monthly meeting held in Town Hall at 7 p.m. that Tuesday. The board members nodded in agreement and the Supervisor spoke:

"I agree. The whole of Corycian Island isn't prepared to have a season this summer, Tommy. We just haven't made it back. The loss of the Believers' Camp alone is devastating. Not to mention the ferry company operating at half-capacity without the *Menantic*. Summer people who own houses are coming out here to take care of their repairs, not to entertain and be cheerful. This storm isn't finished toying with us yet. Now it's going to cost us an entire year."

There was head-shaking and mumbling among the board members. Tommy listened and then spoke without much forethought:

"You know it's funny in a good way. We'll have our island back again for a whole year, too. Like it was when we were kids or when our parents first came here. Just islanders working together to help each other when times are tough."

Buzz Walbridge chuckled: "Makes us realize how lucky we are that Ratliss turned a blind eye to the whiskey business. Most of us have some change in the bank and the town's coffers are fat with real estate taxes and..." he smirked, "shall we say, miscellaneous earnings."

Tommy Lawson picked up on that: "You know, you're right, Buzz. The town does have a big surplus. I saw the year-end statements. Burston you published them in the legal notices, right?"

"Sure," the newspaper man said. "It was a hefty sum. Don't recall the amount, but we all remarked on it."

Tommy said: "I move the town makes loans to worthy islanders to rebuild their lives this summer in preparation for a bigger and better island economy in 1928."

After some discussion, Tommy's motion was passed unanimously and the generous agreement struck a chord for the bustling tune that moved Corycian Island along through months of rejuvenation and reconstruction.

The first neighborhood to blossom was in Wade's Woods, inland from the coast, with housing intended for purchase by summer people, so the cottages were constructed without heating units or much insulation. They were pretty to look at, but habitable only in warm weather.

The houses were adjacent to the Stoli's area. George sat in his chair listening to the hammering for months on end, never looking out his window. Red Cross volunteers and friends made sure he ate every day and they always tried to convince him to take a walk, but in 1927, George sat in his chair and slept there, as the Corycian economy hummed along outside his door.

It was still the era of Prohibition as well, and again, Chief Ratliss gave more deference to the value of a dollar in his hometown than to the law of the land.

1928

Corycian Island
"Josiah! Josiah! Josiah!"

The summer season arrived with a shock of heat, the smell of new paint, fresh lumber, and an "Opening Gala," at the fully-booked Strand Hotel on the last weekend in May.

Once the tourists returned, they continued in a steady flow. The new activity was abuzz with people needing things - Now! A few tourists asked about how the hurricane affected a local providing a service, but fewer listened to the responses. As for the summer people who owned houses, their worlds were in place once they arrived for the 1928 season. Sleeker sailboats replaced the already sleek ones lost to the storm. New windows and shingles adorned this cottage or that one; repaired docks floated in the bay. With the flora of spring, Coyrcian Island returned to life.

Inri Remie began to walk down to the obliterated Believers' Camp at night. He wasn't sure he missed his father, but he missed following Josiah and hating him for what he saw. A new community center had been built in the footprint of the lost one and frames were up for the small cottages that housed Believer campers. The Remies' property, off in the distance, was still piled with rubble. Inri was 25 years old without a clue about how to proceed with that.

One night in mid-July he thought of visiting his father's grave behind the dump in the paupers' plots, but he knew the islanders who scavenged the trash heaps at night might see him there. So, he walked over to the huge boulders in Pipers' Cove where his father performed the "Sermon on the Mount." Inri pretended to be Josiah emerging as Jesus. Inri puffed up his chest and raised his arms, dropping them flat when he heard a voice:

"I know what you're doing over there, Inri Remie. You're being your daddy, that's right ain't it?"

Inri tried to hide in the rocks but he knew it was too late to do so physically, so he stepped out. "Who's that?" Inri heard himself say. "I don't like it when people hide themselves."

"You should know, you hid yourself around me enough."

Inri knew the voice and for some reason it made his stomach hurt, nonetheless he held onto his false bravado.

"So I liked to watch you, huh?" Inri couldn't believe his daring.

"Would you still like to watch?" Twirly Wesley stepped out from behind one of the boulders. She was naked, completely naked, except for a silver chain around her neck, the one her father had worn until his death. Twirly twisted the chain and brushed her lips with the silver dollar medallion. She twirled a curl of her hair.

"I knew you were watching when your daddy and me went at it. I seen you, Inri. Now I thought I'd give you something to see for yourself."

Inri froze in place. He thought he saw Mrs. Stoli there for a second - like she had been that time in the door frame - before... and then Twirly pressed herself against him.

"Do you miss your daddy, Inri? Do you miss him like I do?" Twirly said. "Are you lonely without him, Inri? Are you lonely like me?"

Twirly backed Inri against the rocks and fumbled with his pants, holding him in her hand as soon as she could break him free of fabric. Twirly's touch set Inri on fire. He grabbed her buttocks and pulled her up to him, pushing himself inside her and feeling full like he never had before. Then he heard Twirly say: "Josiah! Josiah! Josiah!"

Inri threw Twirly to the ground and ran blindly from the campground, trying to outrun the sound: "Josiah! Josiah! Josiah!" When he stopped to catch his breath, the words rang louder and aroused him, making his stomach wretch. So Inri tried to outrun the grunting, perverted memory of Josiah and Twirly outside the Wesley's house when she was a teenager. He ran toward the center to George Stoli's.

"Josiah! Josiah! Josiah!" Inri heard when he stopped. He grasped his thighs to catch his breath, looked up, and saw he was at the tool shed in the Presbyterian cemetery.

"Josiah! Josiah! Josiah!"

Inri didn't remember picking up the hedge clippers, but he realized his penis was gone when he ran through the schoolyard - for that was surely him howling and there was blood, oh God, so much blood.

***

Twirly took to Westside Beach with her breasts exposed the next day.

The arriving ferry was crowded with walkers coming from the mainland. When they saw Twirly, shimmying as she liked to do, applause broke out from the passengers on the deck. Of course that just encouraged Twirly who broke into an elaborate, breast-themed dance.

That was the night the first call about naked George Stoli came into the police. He was reported to be walking through the yards of the new houses that occupied Wade's Woods where he'd often strolled as the school's principal with his paper sack. But now he walked as George Stoli, free of life and mystery, wearing only an old cowboy hat and smoking a cigar.

Ke'Was End
"Dis be de Runapewak"

Ismy Shellfoot Morely was a wise, young girl by the summer of 1928. August had come. The eighth grade would start in September and worlds of things had happened already.

But Ismy didn't expect much from a new school year. The last one had been mostly about doing community service after the hurricane. Ismy missed those days because no one but family was on Ke'was End. She had never known that kind of freedom and worked with a smile doing what she could to help out. She loved the busy-ness of those days. The happiness in the midst of all that sorrow.

As a result, a return to normalcy in the current summer of 1928 seemed boring to Ismy. The excitement that followed the hurricane was long over and it was just the same spiritualists as always who leased at The Captain's House.

Ismy's one excitement, seeing Blossom Stoli in spirit sometimes, remained a secret. Telling this story would make too many people upset.

Besides, Ismy had begun to wonder if that's who she wanted to be. The weird person. She knew no one else like herself at school. They saw little other than what sat beneath their noses.

In July, Ismy had lazed around in the heat and had seen Nuna talking with a man on her porch. She heard the man tell Nuna there wasn't a tribe called Runapewak. Ismy heard these words from the lawyer:

"But Miss Shellfoot, Runapewak is not a recognized tribe; that is, the United States government doesn't list it among its bands of indigenous peoples."

The words danced around her and hummed in Ismy's head throughout the rest of July, until one day in August when she knew that the lawyer was coming back. Ismy looked for Nuna to tell her.

"Granny," scrawny Ismy called running up to Nuna who was in her garden. "Granny, that lawyer man's coming back to say we're not Runapewaks." She threw her arms around her grandmother.

"I know he be," Nuna said, patting the young girl's back. "Shh, now, I know he comin' alla de time. It be ok, Mystifier, spirit bring de trut'. Come dis way. Let me shows you some'ting."

Nuna led Ismy into her keeping room where lavender and rosemary hung from the beams to dry. Ismy took a deep, slow breath as her grandmother had taught her to do. Nuna pulled open the top drawer of a bureau and motioned for Ismy to look inside.

There, laid out on fine handwoven linen, the girl saw a shard of granite, a photo of the cemetery's obelisk, and a large piece of blue pottery, next to several clipped Editorials and Obituary Notices from *The Corycian Island Reader*.

The word "Runapewak" was underlined in the articles. The granite shard and the pottery bore the same hieroglyph of stick figures.

Ismy looked closely at each while her grandmother spoke:

"Even dat Chief Elk-man gots to know de A'gonquin picta for Runapewak." Nuna pointed to the drawings on the obelisk in the photo, taken by Burston Bakker when the stone memorial was still in tact.

"See? Dis Runapewak sign be part a dat big cem'tery stone. Runapewak carves it and dem booglie mens chops it off dat time. Den Maduh Eart' opens up de trut' more whens de hurr'cane comes. Sees how dat blue pot say dis same picta? Spirit be talkin' don't ya know."

Ismy traced the stick figures on each of the items with her fingers.

Nuna went on:

"Chief Elk-man say we be an eye-dear of de Gods. Dat be right, Ismy. We born in de Gods eyes. We be dear to dem. We de tru peoples, all-a-wanna."

THE END

Healing Properties: Coming in 2016:

1929

Corycian Island

Inri Remie

It didn't bother Inri Remie that his penis was gone, but every other year-rounder on Corycian Island was affected by it. Inri's neighbors wondered how he...well, they wondered about all sorts of things it wasn't polite to talk about in 1929.

However Inri only thought about his condition when he had to empty his bladder (sitting down) or when he saw a pair of hedge clippers (the instrument with which he deformed himself). But even in those moments, he didn't fully associate with the truth.

Islanders protected him to some degree. Ted Simmons, Corycian Island's doctor, had created a shield to direct Inri's urine, so that solved an immediate problem. Henry Shellfoot, through the Red Cross, made sure Inri had food during his convalescence. And once Inri was up and around again, Cappy Hensen avoided scheduling him to prune the hedges on the grounds of the Westside Ferry Company where Inri worked in return for scant lodging.

Nonetheless by the spring of 1929, there was one small detail that also raised new questions and talk about Inri's missing appendage:

On April 21, nine months after Inri's "incident," Twirly Wesley gave birth to a freckle-faced, large-eared, red-haired boy. The midwife said Twirly had screamed: "Josiah! Josiah! Josiah!" as she pushed the baby out into the world, but Inri's father, Josiah, had been dead too long to have conceived the child with Twirly, and anyone who counted backwards could pinpoint the date of conception to the days before red-haired, large-eared, freckle-faced Inri met up with the hedge clippers.

***

Healing Properties continues the story of the people and places of Corycian Island with grace, humor, and spirit from 1929 through the 1950s.

Author's Personal Notes:

Islands have always held a strong allure for me. In addition to visiting a few, I have lived on an island that is one hundred miles long, another that is just four miles wide, and one that hosts the greatest city in the world. Each has attracted me with "an ether sifting through the universe," just like the mythical Corycian Island. I have relied on my memories of the influences of these places to create Corycian Island and the people who tell her spirit stories. I have also referenced historical accounts to add a dimension of truth. Thusly, I have formed a piece of fiction, with a nod to the wonderful resources below:

Dunhill, Priscilla. *An Island Sheltered.*
New York: Bright Sky Press, 2002.

Durst, Kevin. *Glitter That Was Once Gold.*
Canada: Trafford Publishing. 2005.

Duvall, Ralph G. *The History of Shelter Island: 1652-1932.*
New York. 1932. Green, Louise Tuthill. *Images of America: Shelter Island.* New Hampshire: Arcadia Publishing, 1997.

Herman, Stewart W. *God's Summer Cottage.* New York, 1980.

Leita, John and Laura. *Long Island Oddities.*
South Carolina: The History Press. 2013.

Native Languages of the Americas: Algonquin.
http://www.native-languages.org/algonquin.html

Strong, John. *The Thirteen Tribes of Long Island: The History of the Myth*. The Hudson Valley Regional Review

Weigold, Marilyn E. *The Long Island Sound: A History of its People, Places, and Environment*. New York: NYU Press, 2004.

I also have to acknowledge *Wikipedia* and remind all users to donate each year. Volumes of basic facts are at our fingertips for free, but it costs money for *Wikipedia* to be there. As a writer who once stopped everything to head to a library for answers, *Wikipedia* is magic. But I still love the deep resources of a library. So, get your library card renewed today.

I grew up in an era when self-publishing was known as "vanity press," so believe me, it's difficult to tell myself that I've written something worthy enough to offer others to read. However, I've been to the "show." Even signed a contract with a major publishing company in the 70s. It's a world where little is done "all-a-wanna" and it quickly consumed my manuscript and me. Today, I prefer the support of the independent authors I met at scribd.com in 2008: Helen Winslow Black, Barbara Alfaro, Sunny Lockwood, Rolando Garcia, Steve Ullom, Carla Sarrett, and Mary Yuhas, all of whom, long after the site changed focus, remain supportive. Two of the authors I met there, Ingrid Ricks and Laura Novak, provided invaluable commentary about the *Don't Ya Know* manuscript for years. Seriously, for years. And Ted Alexander, another author, spent hours reading and re-reading pages as the novel grew, always encouraging me along the way. Support the independent spirit of these authors and read their work.

Gina Surerus and Mia Kishel helped me do life while believing in my dreams and reading along. Chris Rosenwasser always has my back and my husband, Michael, listened to me read the book aloud while he drove from Georgia to Massachusetts once and then again on another long-distance drive two years later. He read the book on the computer, on paper, on the beach, while eating and while talking to me about it.

Erin Brown edited an early manuscript, providing solid ideas for the book's framework. Janie Berry collaborated with me tirelessly on the cover, literally hanging the moon.

And finally, there is a clear answer to the nagging question, why self-publish? The answer is for Edie, our precious granddaughter, so she discovers the power of her Oonuh.

CPSIA information can be obtained at www.ICGtesting.com
Printed in the USA
BVOW05s0020100915

417368BV00001BA/8/P